COME BACK TO ME

MILA GRAY

SIMON PULSE

New York   London   Toronto   Sydney   New Delhi

ᐯᐯᐯ

SIMON PULSE

An imprint of Simon & Schuster Children's Publishing Division

1230 Avenue of the Americas, New York, New York 10020

First Simon Pulse hardcover edition December 2015

Text copyright © 2014 by Mila Gray

Originally published in 2014 in Great Britain by Pan Books,

an imprint of Pan Macmillan, a division of Macmillan Publishers Limited

Jacket photograph copyright © 2015 by Yumiko Kinoshita/Anyone/amanaimages/Corbis

All rights reserved, including the right of reproduction in whole or in part in any form.

SIMON PULSE and colophon are registered trademarks of Simon & Schuster, Inc.

For information about special discounts for bulk purchases, please contact Simon & Schuster Special Sales at 1-866-506-1949 or business@simonandschuster.com.

The Simon & Schuster Speakers Bureau can bring authors to your live event. For more information or to book an event contact the Simon & Schuster Speakers Bureau at 1-866-248-3049 or visit our website at www.simonspeakers.com.

Cover designed by Karina Granda

Interior designed by Tom Daly

The text of this book was set in Chapparal Pro.

Manufactured in the United States of America

10 9 8 7 6 5 4 3

Library of Congress Control Number 2015942693

ISBN 978-1-4814-3965-7 (hc)

ISBN 978-1-4814-3967-1 (eBook)

For Venetia & Amanda

You only live once. But if you do it right, once is all you need.
—*Mae West*

Jessa

A whorl in the glass distorts the picture, like a thumb-print smear over a lens. I'm halfway down the stairs, gathering my hair into a ponytail, thoughts a million miles away, when a blur outside the window pulls me up short.

I take another step, the view clears, and when I realize what I'm seeing, *who* I'm seeing, my stomach plummets and the air leaves my lungs like a final exhalation. My arms fall slowly to my sides. My body's instinct is to turn and run back upstairs, to tear into the bathroom and lock the door, but I'm frozen. This is the moment you have nightmares about, play over in your mind, the darkest of daydreams, furnished by movies and by real-life stories you've overheard your whole life.

You imagine over and over how you'll cope, what you'll say, how you'll act when you open the door and find them standing there. You pray to every god you can dream up that this moment won't ever happen. You make bargains, promises, desperate barters. And you live each day with the murmur of those prayers playing on a loop in the background of your mind, an endless chant. And then the moment happens and you realize it was all for nothing. The prayers went unheard. There was no bargain to make. Was it your fault? Did you fail to keep your promise?

Time seems to have slowed. Kit's father hasn't moved. He's standing at the end of the driveway staring up at the house, squinting against the early morning glare. He's wearing his Dress Blues. It's that fact which registered before all else, which told me all I needed to know. That and the fact that he's here at all. Kit's father has never once been to the house. There is only one reason why he would ever come.

He hasn't taken a step, and I will him not to. I will him to turn around and get back into the dark sedan sitting at the curb. A shadowy figure in uniform sits at the wheel. *Please. Get back in and drive away*. I start making futile bargains with some nameless god. If he gets back in the car and drives away, I'll do anything. But he doesn't. He takes a step down the driveway toward the house, and that's when I know for certain that either Riley or Kit is dead.

A scream, or maybe a sob, tries to struggle up my throat, but it's blocked by a solid wave of nausea. I grab for the banister to stay upright. Who? Which one? My brother or my boyfriend? Oh God. Oh God. My legs are shaking. I watch Kit's father walk slowly up the drive, head bowed.

Memories, images, words, flicker through my mind like scratched fragments of film: Kit's arms around my waist drawing me closer, our first kiss under the cover of darkness just by the back door, the smile on his face the first time we slept together, the blue of his eyes lit up by the sparks from a Chinese lantern, the fierceness in his voice when he told me he was going to love me forever.

Come back to me. That was the very last thing I said to him. *Come back to me.*

Always. The very last thing he said to me.

Then I see Riley as a kid throwing a toy train down the stairs, dive-bombing into the pool, holding my hand at our grandfather's funeral, grinning and high-fiving Kit after they'd enlisted. The snapshot of him in his uniform on graduation day. The circles under his eyes the last time I saw him.

The door buzzes. I jump. But I stay where I am, frozen halfway up the stairs. If I don't answer the door, maybe he'll go away. Maybe this won't be happening. But the doorbell sounds again. And then I hear footsteps on the landing above me. My mother's voice, sleepy and confused. "Jessa? Who is it? Why are you just standing there?"

Then she sees. She peers through the window, and I hear the intake of air, the ragged "no" she utters in response. She too knows that a military car parked outside the house at seven a.m. can signify only one thing.

I turn to her. Her hand is pressed to her mouth. Standing in her nightdress, her hair unbrushed, the blood rushing from her face, she looks like she's seen a ghost. No. That's wrong. She looks like she *is* a ghost.

The bell buzzes for a third time.

"Get the door, Jessa," my mother says in a strange voice I don't recognize. It startles me enough that I start to walk down the stairs. I feel calmer all of a sudden, like I'm floating outside my body. This can't be happening. It's not real. It's just a dream.

I find myself standing somehow in front of the door. I unlock it. I open it. Kit. Riley. Kit. Riley. Their names circle my mind like birds of prey in a cloudless blue sky. Kit. Riley. Which is it?

Is Kit's father here in his Dress Blues with his chaplain insignia to tell us that my brother has been killed in action or that his son—my boyfriend—has been killed in action? He would come either way. He would want to be the one to tell me. He would want to be the one to tell my mom.

Kit's father blinks at me. He's been crying. His eyes are red, his cheeks wet. He's still crying, in fact. I watch the tears slide down his face and realize that I've never seen him cry before. It automatically makes me want to comfort him, but even if I could find the words, my throat is so dry I couldn't speak them.

"Jessa," Kit's father says in a husky voice.

I hold on to the doorframe, keeping my back straight. I'm aware that my mother has followed me down the stairs and is standing right behind me. Kit's father glances at her over my shoulder. He takes a deep breath, lifts his chin, and removes his hat before his eyes flicker back to me.

"I'm sorry," he says.

"Who?" I hear myself ask. "Who is it?"

Jessa

Three months earlier . . .

O h dear God, who in the name of heaven is he?"
Didi's grip on my arm is enough to raise bruises. I
look up. And I see him. He's staring at me, grinning,
and I have to bite back my own grin. My stomach starts somer-
saulting, my insides twisting into knots.

"Kit," I say, half in answer to Didi, half just for the chance
to say his name out loud after so long. My eyes are locked with
Kit's, and when he hears me speak his name, he smiles even
wider and walks across the living room toward me.

"Hey, Jessa," he says. His eyes travel over me, taking me in,
before settling on my face. He rubs a hand over his shorn head,
a self-conscious gesture that makes the somersaults double in
speed. He's still grinning at me but more sheepishly now.

"Hi," I say, swallowing. I'm nervous all of a sudden. I haven't
seen him in nine months. I wasn't sure he was going to be here
today, and though I've run through this moment dozens—hell,
thousands—of times in my head, I find I'm completely unpre-
pared for it now it's actually happening. In all those imaginings
I never once factored in the way he'd make me feel—as though

I've just taken a running leap off a cliff edge. I'm breathless, almost shaking, finding it hard to hold his steady blue gaze.

He looks older than his twenty-one years. His shoulders are broader, and he's even more tanned than usual, both facts well emphasized by the white T-shirt he's wearing. I can feel Didi squeezing my arm with so much force it's as though she's trying to stem an arterial bleed, and I know if I turn around I'll see her drooling unashamedly. She might go to a convent school, but Didi's prayers center around asking God to deliver her not from trespassers but from her virginity.

"Happy birthday," Kit says now. He hasn't taken his eyes off me the whole time, and my skin is warming under his relentless gaze. I can feel my face getting hotter.

"Thanks," I manage to say, wishing I could come up with a better response, something flirtatious and witty. I know I had something planned for this moment, but my brain has chosen to shut down.

"Hi!"

It's Didi. She has let go of my arm and now thrusts her hand out toward Kit. "I'm Didi, Jessa's best friend. You must be Kit. I've heard a lot about you."

Plenty of emphasis on the *lot*. I make a mental note to kill her later. Kit glances over at me, clearly struggling to contain his amusement, before turning his attention fully back to Didi. He shakes her hand, introducing himself properly, and it gives me a chance to mentally pull myself together and really get a look at him. He's six foot but he seems taller, maybe because he's standing so straight. I recognize the ink marking on his arm, poking out from beneath his sleeve. It's the same tattoo that Riley has. A Marine Corps emblem. My fingers itch to trace it. Oh God. For months I've been telling myself to get over Kit, ordering myself to forget him. Didi rolls her eyes at me every time I mention his name. She's even added my name on Urban Dictionary under the word *pathetic*. But now, as I watch Kit casting his spell over her, I can see she may finally be ready to cut me a break.

She's firing questions at him like she's a Chinese matchmaker, asking all about his job and his uniform. I wouldn't be surprised if she starts asking him next how much he earns and whether he has a girlfriend. I would interrupt, but I'm still trying to gather my wits and formulate a sentence, and, truth be told, I'm kind of hoping she does ask him whether he has a girlfriend. Though another, bigger part of me doesn't want to hear the answer. Because what if he does? Taking a breath, I remind myself he's been in Sudan for the last nine months living with a bunch of guys, sleeping in a room with a dozen other men, eating in a mess hall. It's not like he's been going to parties or out clubbing every night, so it's highly unlikely he's managed to find himself a girlfriend in that time.

Kit answers Didi's questions politely, nodding and giving the standard-issue responses that they're trained to. In other words, no detail whatsoever. All I know is that he and Riley have been in Sudan along with the rest of their marine detachment, protecting the US embassy in Khartoum. That's all. They only got back yesterday.

As I listen to Didi and Kit talking, Didi telling him all about how she only moved to Oceanside six months ago and how her big ambition is to finish school and move to LA (thankfully she omits to mention her other big ambition—to lose her virginity), I realize I'm fixating on Kit's lips, imagining what it would be like to kiss him.

Nothing has ever happened between Kit and me, nothing ever could, so imagining is all I can do. He's my brother's best friend and has been since they were fourteen. We've known Kit since we moved to California when I was eleven. He and my brother have been inseparable since the day they met at baseball try-outs. It's the kind of bromance you see in the movies. Not the *Brokeback Mountain* kind, luckily for me, but something I was always a little envious of. Kit and Riley have probably not gone a day since meeting without seeing each other. They're closer than brothers. It's a friendship that persists despite the fact that my father hates Kit and has tried everything in his not inconsiderable power to pull the plug on it.

I glance through the window out into the garden where my father and Riley are firing up the grill. As though operating on some kind of sixth sense, my father's head snaps up. He was a marine sniper in his day, and he has an eerie ability to sense whenever he's being watched. He has me in his sights. Then I see him register Kit. A dark scowl passes over his face before Riley ignites the charcoal, sending flames soaring as high as the nearest palm tree, and my father turns back around to bark orders at him. Honestly, only in my house does a birthday party get turned into a military operation.

It's never been exactly clear why my father hates Kit so much, but I know it has something to do with his father, who is also a marine, and who served in the same company as my father back in the eighties. It could also be that my father blames Kit for some of Riley's more questionable life choices—namely signing up as an enlisted marine, rather than going to college and becoming an officer, which is what my father had expected him (read: preached at him from birth) to do. Then there was the time they burned down the garage while setting off fireworks. And the time they both streaked across the bleachers during a televised football game. Yeah, now I think about it, there are maybe a few reasons why my dad holds a grudge against Kit.

Kit's father is now a marine chaplain, having found God after a long battle with grief and the bottle following Kit's mother's death. My father meanwhile climbed the ranks and is now a colonel, a role that he inhabits even out of uniform, probably even in his sleep. That could be why Kit is still in the kitchen with us and not out making fire with the men. Or maybe it's for some other reason?

Kit turns back to face me and takes a deep breath. Behind him I catch sight of Didi making a "check him out" face. I try not to laugh.

Just then my mother comes bustling through from the kitchen carrying plates laden with food.

"Kit!" she exclaims delightedly. My mom doesn't hold the grudge toward Kit or his father that my dad does. In fact she's almost as fond of him as she is of me and my brother. She treats him like her second son. Whenever Riley and Kit come back on leave it's like the Second Coming. My mom throws off the depression that she's been shrouded in since they left and buzzes back to life. I know that no matter how proud she is of them she hates the fact they're marines as much as I do. I've always suspected too that she's trying to make up for my father treating Kit like he's some sort of pariah. It gets kind of embarrassing at times. Like now.

She sets a couple of bowls of salad and marinated chicken down on the table and grabs Kit into a fierce hug. She only comes up to his shoulder, but he looks like he couldn't prise himself free even if he tried. Which he doesn't because he's far too polite, and I think he secretly likes the fuss she makes of him.

Didi takes the opportunity while my mother is hugging Kit to sidle up to me. "Oh man, I didn't even recognize him from the photos. He's so much hotter. I want to see him in uniform. Just imagine. If this is how hot he looks in normal clothes."

I ram my elbow into her ribs. I've already seen Kit in uniform. And Didi's not wrong. It rendered me speechless.

"Or naked," Didi whispers. "Actually, yes, forget the uniform. Imagine him naked."

"Shhh," I murmur, not admitting to her that I have. Many times.

"He is *so* into you."

"Shut up," I mutter as my mother lets Kit go. My pulse spikes, though. Is Didi right? Or is she just saying that because she knows it's what I want to hear?

"No, I'm serious, he can't take his eyes off you," Didi says, covering her words with a cough as Kit turns to stare at me again. "See." Didi swings toward my mom. "Mrs. Kingsley, do you need a hand?" she asks in an exceedingly loud and exceedingly obvious voice.

My mom looks up, flustered. "Oh, that would be great, thanks, Bernadette."

"Didi," says Didi abruptly. She hates anyone calling her by her given name. She grabs for the chicken and heads for the doorway, where great wafts of smoke are billowing thanks to the lighter fluid my brother has just thrown on the grill. She shoots me a look over her shoulder as she goes—eyes bugging, head tilting in Kit's direction. From this I deduce she's telling me to go and talk to Kit.

The trouble is I've never had to force myself to make conversation with Kit before. It's always come naturally. Until now. For some reason my throat suddenly feels as though it is stuffed with rocks. I can barely think a coherent sentence, let alone speak one.

"So, Jessa, how you been?" I hear Kit say just behind me.

I turn around, my heart shooting like a rocket into my rib cage.

"You know . . . good. Fine. Okay." Waffling. I'm waffling. He's laughing at me. I can see the way he's trying not to smile, biting his lips together. His lips. Okay. Focus. Don't stare.

I take a deep breath. As no one but Didi knows, I've liked Kit for years, have had a crush on him since I was about fourteen and he was seventeen, but the last time he was back on leave was the first time I felt it might be reciprocated, maybe, possibly. Possibly not. It's this *maybe, possibly, possibly not* that has kept me awake most nights for the last nine months. I kept on replaying the interactions we'd had over and over until the memories were so worn I wasn't sure if I was patching them with invented events, imagining things that hadn't happened. Had his fingers lingered in mine that time he pulled me to my feet? Did he hold me extra close when he hugged me good-bye? Did he look at me with burning intensity because he was imagining kissing me or because I had food stuck in my teeth? We've e-mailed each other regularly while he's been away, and the e-mails have been lighthearted, veering sometimes into flirtatious before just as quickly scooting back onto more solid *just friends* ground.

"That's good," he says now. Is that a smirk?

Why can't I stop staring at his lips? Why do I have to lose my train of thought so completely when he stands so close? And did he always smell this good? What the heck is with me?

I manage finally to find my voice and construct a whole sentence with verbs and nouns and pronouns. Incredible. "What about you? How was it over there?"

I catch the slight flicker as his smile fades momentarily before brightening once again. He rubs a hand over his head. "Yeah, you know . . ." He shrugs as he trails off.

Stupid question, I think to myself. Damn. For a moment neither of us says anything. I start twisting the end of my ponytail, something I do when I get nervous, then, realizing what I'm doing could be construed as flirtatious as well as ditzy, I drop my hands to my sides. Kit stands there waiting, watching me, that half smile still on his face. His expression is hard to read. He seems to be enjoying my discomfort, but there's something else about the way he's looking at me. He opens his mouth as though to ask me something, but then closes it again. The air around us feels charged, but that could be because I'm hyper-aware of every gesture I'm making and also of the fact that my father is standing not fifty feet away holding something that could be interpreted as a weapon.

"How long do you have?" I finally ask, feeling my cheeks starting to burn almost as hot as the chicken that's now smoking on the grill.

"Four weeks," he answers.

I nod and stare down at my feet. Four weeks. A month. And then he's gone again. Why am I even wanting something to happen between us? It wouldn't be worth it. He'd be gone before I knew it.

"So how does it feel?" he asks me.

My head flies up. How does what feel? For an instant I freak out that he somehow knows what I'm thinking, has read my mind.

"Being free. Being eighteen," he says, seeing my confusion.

"Well, I have one more week of school," I tell him. "Then the whole summer. And then I start college."

Kit tilts his head to one side. "USC?"

"No. USD," I answer. I waved good-bye to that dream. It's University of San Diego for me.

"I thought you wanted to go to LA?" Kit says now. "I thought there was a drama course at USC there you were really into."

My gaze flies instinctively to the window, to my father who is still busy with the dancing flames. He's yelling something at Riley. "Well, you know how it is," I say, wishing I hadn't brought it up. "My dad wanted me to go to USD. It's closer. I can live at home."

Kit looks at me disbelieving, a flash of disappointment in his eyes that makes my insides curl up. Trust Kit to remember that I wanted to go to the University of Southern California. He was the first person I told about my dream to go to USC's School of Dramatic Arts. That was last time he was back on leave. I'd been fighting with my dad over my test scores, then I'd gone down to the beach and run into Kit. We'd started talking and next thing you know I was telling him everything. Kit was the first person who actually asked me what it was I wanted to do with my life. *If you had one dream, what would it be?* he'd asked.

I told him I'd go to USC to study drama. He was so interested, so enthusiastic about the idea, that I started to get excited too— to actually start contemplating it. Then I got home, still high on our conversation, ready to start researching the application process, and found my dad waiting for me with a fully drawn-up schedule of after-school tutoring and a brochure for USD. But I don't want to think about any of that today. It's my birthday. Kit's scowling now. He glances around the room. I follow his gaze to the window. My father is standing with charred tongs in one hand, glaring through the glass. His eyes are narrowed like laser sights. Suddenly, though, his view is blocked by Didi, who stands before him holding a bowl of marinated chicken like it's John the Baptist's head.

"I better go," I hear Kit say.

I spin around. "No," I say quickly, grabbing for his wrist. "Please stay."

Kit stares down at my fingers circling his arm. He doesn't say anything, but when he looks up, my pulse quickens as I see the expression in his eyes. It's unmistakable. I'm not inventing this or imagining it. I see the desire, bright as a flame. I drop his wrist in surprise, my fingers burning.

"I don't want to get court-martialed," he murmurs, jerking his head softly in the direction of the window.

"Oh, just ignore him," I say, sounding breathless and cursing myself for it. "He's just out of sorts. You know what he's like." I hate making excuses for my father, but I'm used to it. I've been doing it most of my life.

"Yeah, well," Kit says, "I don't want him sending me on a one-man mission to Somalia or Afghanistan. Or worse, making me clean the latrines at the base for the rest of my life."

Kit looks down at my hand, which rests just inches away from his own. He glances up and his gaze rests for a moment on my lips. "I best be going," he says quietly.

I swallow. *No. Don't go*, I want to say. I want to take hold of his wrist again. I want to see that look in his eye one more time.

Just to be sure, because already I'm wondering if I imagined it. But I don't. I just nod. He steps back toward the door. "Tell Riley I'll call him later."

I nod again. For some reason tears burn the backs of my eyes. I blame it on the smoke from the grill that's wafting through the open French doors. Why does my dad have to always go and ruin everything? And more annoyingly, why don't I ever stand up to him? I'm eighteen now. I shouldn't be scared any more.

"I'll see you around, Jessa," Kit says. He grabs a couple of cupcakes from the plate on the table, grins at me, and disappears. A few seconds later I hear the front door slam.

Kit

shouldn't have left. If Colonel *I'm a dickhead* Kingsley hadn't pointed those tongs at me like he was aiming a submachine gun at my head, then maybe I would have stuck around. I swear it was crossing his mind to use my face as fuel for the grill. Whatever. What was I expecting? It's not like I've ever been welcome in their house. Well, okay, that's not strictly true. I'm welcome there whenever he's not around. Riley, Jessa, and their mom have always gone out of their way to make me feel at home. I think they feel guilty for how he treats me. I know Riley thinks his dad is an asshole, but he can't say anything. Guess I wouldn't either in his shoes.

I swing my leg over my bike with a sigh and rev the engine. While I was away, the two things I missed the most and fantasized about so regularly that I earned the title of Corporal Space Cadet from my unit were this bike and Jessa Kingsley. Okay and a rib-eye steak from Fleming's, cooked medium rare. But mainly Jessa, it has to be said. And holy shit, yeah, now I remember exactly why and simultaneously realize how much my imagination shortchanged me. I didn't have a photograph of her with me—didn't want Riley to have occasion to ask me what the fuck I was doing with a picture of his sister in my wallet, for obvious reasons, namely wanting to keep possession of my balls. Next time, though, I'm taking a photograph. Balls be damned.

Jessa Kingsley has been my secret obsession for two years. Thankfully for her she takes after her mom and not her dad— pale blond hair, creamy skin, eyes so green you'd think they were contacts if you didn't know otherwise. One day she was this small, blond kid, all elbows and knees and braces, following the two of us around all the time like a lemming, and then I go away to basic training and come back to find she's all grown up, with eyes the size of dinner plates, hair hanging straight as a sniper's aim down her back, and a smile that takes my breath away every single time.

She never grew much, in fact she's still short and petite, but she's got curves in all the right places. Though it took a while to realize that, and by then it was more like a bonus rather than the main attraction. She goes to a convent school, and the uniform is kind of like a nun's habit. And I think her dad has veto over her entire wardrobe as she's never showing much skin. I only realized how killer her body was when I saw her at the beach wearing a bikini. That sight was enough to push my obsession from borderline to all-consuming.

Coming to her house was a dumb idea, though. Now I'm not going to be able to get her out of my mind for the next month. I guess half of me was hoping I'd go around to visit and find out she'd gained five hundred pounds or at the very least a boyfriend, which would lay my dreams to rest. Maybe she does have a boyfriend. The thought makes me almost skid into the curb. Shit. I didn't ask. But no. I mean, if she had a boyfriend I would have heard about it, right? Riley would have said something, I'm sure of it. Any whiff of a guy making moves on his sister and he'd know about it and put a stop to it, even from as far away as Sudan. He'd find a way. Plus there's her father. I can't see him allowing Jessa to date anytime this century. And I can't imagine any guy meeting her father and asking her out on a second date.

I can't count the times I've thought about telling Jessa how I feel, but to be honest I've never been sure if she's interested. And admitting something like that to someone is purely a one-time deal. If it's not reciprocated, then not only do you look like a prize fool but you also lose a friendship. I don't care so much about the fool part because she probably already figures me for one, but I do care about losing Jessa as a friend. The thing is, in her e-mails recently, if I'm not mistaken, she seemed to be flirting with me. And after seeing the way she looked at me just now, and the not so subtle comments her friend was making, I'm pretty sure she must have been. A buzz settles in my chest just below my sternum, a jolt of energy that spreads outward, making my heart rate speed up.

I realize that I'm doing twenty over the speed limit and grinning like a maniac on speed. I ease off the gas. There's a sign up ahead saying "No U-turns." For a second I contemplate it anyway. But then I tell myself to stay away. Riley would kill me. Hell, her father would kill me if he even suspected what I fantasize about regarding his daughter. Actually he wouldn't just kill me. He'd torture me first, then kill me. It's a bad idea. Jessa and I can't ever be together. Not long term. She's off to college in the fall and I'm leaving again in a month, need I remind myself.

I park up by the pier and lean over the railing for half an hour, listening to the waves bash against the struts, watching the kids playing on the swings at the top of the boardwalk and the fishermen casting again and again, hoping to bag a catch. When I finally turn away, the sun is starting to sink over the ocean, and I've decided what I'm going to do. I grin, even though I know it might just be the stupidest thing I've ever thought about doing. And considering all the stupid things I've done in my life, that's pretty impressive.

Jessa

lie on my bed, playing with the necklace my mom just gave me and staring up at the ceiling. It's heart shaped (the necklace, not the ceiling), and as I play with it, I can't stop thinking about Kit. Did I mistake the look in his eyes? My stomach flutters with butterflies at the thought that I didn't. But then the butterflies are blown to smithereens as I picture my father's face staring at Kit through the window and pointing that grill tong at him. I mean, there are way too many obstacles in the way, not even taking into account the number of guns and grilling implements my father owns. I bury my head in a pillow. I guess I can wave good-bye to ever knowing what it's like to kiss Kit. While I'm at it, I guess I can wave good-bye to having a boyfriend before I turn thirty or ever losing my virginity. I'll be like the nuns who teach us Religious Studies at school. In fact I may as well just measure myself right now for a wimple and be done with it.

I didn't tell Kit about the fights that went down with my dad over college. Actually "fights" would be exaggerating. No one fights with my dad. He lays down the law. We obey. My father has post-traumatic stress disorder, which is a diagnosis Riley and I have made unofficially because he refuses to see a "head doctor" or talk about his problems. We have to walk on eggshells for fear he gets over-stressed or irritated, which is pretty much an hourly occurrence. Even the sound of a kettle whistling can set him off, which is why all our phones are set to silent.

When he does have one of his episodes, it's like a tornado rampaging through the house. He's never hit us, but he's destroyed a lot of furniture. Right now I can hear him downstairs in his den, watching the game, occasionally letting out the odd expletive or victory yell. My stomach is tensed and I feel on edge, like I'm about to take a test where the punishment for failing is death by firing squad. With grim recognition, I realize that's how I always feel when he's in the house. I don't know how my mom deals with it or why she hasn't divorced him. If I were in her shoes, I would have by now. I make a solemn promise to myself that I will never ever marry anyone in the military—not after seeing the destruction it's wrought on my own family.

A knock on my door startles me. I pull my head out from under the pillow. Riley's standing in the doorway. He glances over his shoulder, walks into my room, and closes the door quietly behind him.

"Hey," he says, dropping down onto the bed beside me. "How you doing?"

"Yeah," I say, sitting up cross-legged on the bed and shrugging. "You know."

He nods. He knows. Birthdays, Christmas, Thanksgiving . . . they are without a doubt the most stressful days of the year in our house. Having Riley here helps because at least we get to share the load and both of us can tag-team my mom. When he's not here it's all on me, something I think Riley feels guilty about as when he hands me a well-wrapped present he looks kind of sheepish.

"Happy birthday," he says.

I take it curiously, glancing at him. "What is it?" I ask.

"I got it over in Sudan."

That makes me raise my eyebrows. I mean, I can't imagine what sort of shopping malls they have there.

I tear open the wrapping with difficulty. My brother and I have spent our lives being taught to square away our rooms at the end of each day, to make our beds like we were preparing for a daily inspection, which in fact we were. The present is as tightly and perfectly wrapped as a marine dorm bed. It takes me almost five minutes to get into it.

"An iPhone?" I say in amazement when I finally manage to tear off the paper.

"Yeah, don't show Dad," Riley says unnecessarily. As if. My dad is vehemently against social media, smart phones or, well, any technology that isn't designed for military use. He's just naturally suspicious of anything he can't understand and that puts social media at the top of his list, with teenage girls just below it. Not only has he banned me outright from having a Facebook account, but he's only recently agreed to let me have a cell phone (the most basic brick-sized one on the market) on the condition, he stressed, that I use it only for emergencies. The guy in the phone store looked at me with a pity normally reserved for victims of humanitarian disasters. The only good news is that he didn't qualify what he meant by emergencies, so every conversation with Didi now starts with "Didi, it's an emergency."

"You got this in Sudan?" I ask Riley, noting it's the latest version but that it has no box to go with it. Or instructions for that matter.

Riley shrugs. "I got it unlocked for you and I put on a few apps."

I scroll through. "Candy Crush? Angry Birds?"

"You know, for all those boring lectures you're going to have to sit through in college."

"Thanks," I say, smacking him on the shoulder.

"You're welcome," he says, smacking me back. We don't say anything for a while. Riley seems different these days, especially after this last tour: older, more careworn, tired. He rarely smiles anymore, and I can't remember the last time I heard him laugh or tell a joke, which is strange as Riley was always the joker—the kid who stuck waterproof stickers of his teachers' faces in all the toilet bowls in school, the kid who covered his principal's car in tinfoil and who led his entire sixth-grade class on a Ditch Day. I guess he quit with the pranks around the same time my dad starting losing it.

I don't tell Riley, but the thing that scares me most, besides him dying, is that one day he'll come back and start behaving like Dad. The day he enlisted with Kit was one of the worst days of my life. But I smiled like always and pretended I was happy for them both. I want to ask him now about Sudan, about his job, about what he's seen, but I know he can't tell me much, and I also get the feeling he doesn't want to talk about it anyway.

"Do you want to watch some TV?" I ask, hoping he says yes because it's not like I've had a chance to hang out with him much since he got back. And it's my birthday.

"I can't," he says. "I'm going out to meet Jo." He shoots me an apologetic smile and gets up.

I try to cover my disappointment. It's decided then. I'm just going to lie here and have a little pity party for myself because who spends the night of their eighteenth birthday alone in their bedroom playing Angry Birds on a phone where the settings are all in Arabic, wearing a heart-shaped locket their mom gave them? Oh yeah, that's right, someone with no life. And no prospect of ever getting one.

"How is Jo?" I ask, smiling, though on the inside I'm sighing.

"Yeah, she's good," Riley says, his face immediately lighting up. He and Jo have been dating for three years already. They met just before he and Kit enlisted. Jo was waitressing at his favorite steakhouse. He spent most of his savings on steak and tips, trying to convince her to date him, and eventually she caved in. My brother is what some might call persistent. My mom says he just doesn't know how to take no for an answer. They seem to make it work, even though they only see each other every nine months or so. I ponder on that as Riley walks out the door. No doubt to spend the night having sex. It's not even his birthday, I think to myself grudgingly.

Not even a minute after he goes, the sound of something rapping against my window makes my head snap up. I get up from the bed and cross to the window. Riley. He always used to throw stones up at my window on the nights he'd snuck out as a signal to come down and unlock the back door to let him in. I open the window and peer out. Maybe he forgot his keys. It's totally dark out, the moon just a sliver, and the lights in the backyard aren't on so I can't see anything.

"Jessa?"

My heart leaps into my mouth when I recognize Kit's voice.

"What are you doing?" I hiss into the darkness. My excitement is marred by the fact that my dad has supersonic hearing, and if he finds Kit loitering in his bushes, he won't need an excuse to reach for his gun.

"Come down," Kit says.

I hesitate. My stomach feels like a washing machine on spin cycle. Why does he want me to come down? What if my dad hears? But my body is responding of its own accord—I'm already walking to the mirror. I drag a brush through my hair and stare at my eyes, which look slightly feverish and glassy.

I tiptoe out onto the landing, trying to think up an excuse as to why I'm heading downstairs in case I get caught. Then I remind myself it's just after nine o'clock. I don't need to have a reason for going downstairs. What I need is to get it together. I walk into the kitchen, straight over to the door and then ease back the lock and creep out, the whole time murmuring a silent prayer that I don't get caught because I might be good at acting, but when it comes to my father, I'm only winning Razzies. He can see through me like I'm a window with no glass.

I'm barefoot; the grass tickles my feet. I move swiftly across the lawn toward the bushes at the side of the garden. When I get there, though, there's no sign of Kit. I look around. Where is he? Am I losing it? Did I imagine it?

Then, though, a hand covers my eyes and an arm wraps around my waist from behind. "Boo," Kit whispers into my ear.

Shivers ride down my spine in waves. His left hand lingers on my stomach, but he removes his other hand from my eyes. I turn around slowly, shakily, suddenly self-conscious. I'm only wearing pajama shorts and a cotton camisole top, no bra.

Maybe I should have thought to put on a sweater. But it's too late. I watch Kit's gaze fall to my legs and slowly sweep upward. Goose bumps rise across the surface of my skin as though he's tracing my body with his fingers, not just his eyes. When he reaches my face, I see his smile and the way his eyes are glittering.

My breathing hitches as I stare at him. "What are you doing here?" I whisper.

"I forgot to give you this," he answers, pulling an envelope from his back pocket.

I stare at it. "What is it?"

"Open it," he says, pushing it into my hands. "It's your birthday present."

I take it and open it, the whole time aware that he's watching me. Inside are two tickets to *The Merchant of Venice* in Balboa Park in two weeks time. I look up at him wide-eyed. "Are you serious?"

He nods, smiling as he sees my grin. "I remember when you were in it," he says. "You want to go and see it? I wasn't sure . . ."

"Yes, yes," I say quickly. "Thank you! I can't wait. You're coming with me, right?" I ask, holding up the second ticket.

He shrugs. "Sure. I mean, I didn't want to presume or anything. You know, in case maybe you wanted to take Didi. Or . . ." he has been staring down at his feet, but now he looks up at me, and I realize he's fishing to see if I have a boyfriend.

"No. I want to go with you," I say, the words stumbling over themselves in their haste to get out. Should I have played that cooler? I wonder. But too late. And anyway, he's now grinning.

"Cool," he says, toeing the ground.

We both take a breath in. My eyes dart toward the house. I

guess I should head in before the game ends or my dad hears us. Without saying a word, Kit suddenly takes my hand and pulls me deeper into the shadow of the bushes. I make no attempt to protest.

"You know," he murmurs, not letting go of my hand, "I've been thinking about you. While I was away." He looks straight into my eyes, the smile gone, a look of studied seriousness on his face, and maybe, just possibly, a hint of nerves. "I've been thinking about you a lot."

"Oh," I say. Kit's presence seems to directly affect my literacy levels.

"Yeah," he says, looking down at our hands. His thumb starts almost absently to stroke my pulse point, and I draw in a sharp breath. It's as if he's stoking a fire, making my blood course through my veins like molten lava. I can feel the heat flooding my face, rushing to other parts of my body too.

"How long have you been here?" I ask, trying to keep my voice steady, though I'm losing the ability to concentrate as his thumb keeps stroking.

"About thirty minutes. I waited until I saw Riley go out."

"You've been waiting in the bushes for half an hour just to speak to me?"

Kit shrugs. "I've done sniper training. I can sit for hours in the dark, waiting and watching."

"That's comforting," I say. "And not creepy in the slightest."

He laughs quietly, and the sound makes me want to lean in closer, to press my body against his.

"I figured your dad wouldn't want me coming around and knocking on the door."

I glance over my shoulder automatically, half expecting to see my dad taking aim from the back porch. "You know if he finds you out here he's going to kill you."

"I'll take the chance," Kit says, shifting ever so slightly and drawing me closer so only a sliver of space remains between us. I barely come up to his chin, so I'm having to tilt my head all the way back. This close I can smell his scent—laundry powder and something else, something citrus, aftershave maybe.

"I just had to see you again," he murmurs, his voice as soft as a caress.

I pull back an inch, my heart galloping. I'm scared. Not of Kit, but of what's about to happen between us. It feels like I'm about to take a step off a cliff and into a void, and I have no idea whether I'll land safely or end up smashed to pieces on some jagged rocks I can't yet see. This could be reckless, stupid, dangerous. Or it could be the best thing I ever do. "I'm serious," I mumble. "If my dad finds you out here, he'll go ballistic."

Kit smiles. He lifts his hand and strokes a strand of hair back behind my ear. "It would be worth it," he says, his hand lingering, moving to rest against my cheek.

"What would?" I ask, my senses obliterated, all my focus on his hand and on his lips, so close to mine.

"This," he says, and he kisses me.

I've imagined kissing Kit a million times, but never in all my imaginings was it like this. The instant his lips touch mine I feel like I'm rocketing through space. His arms tighten around my waist, pulling me closer, the heat of his hands and his lips lighting signal fires all the way through my body. He's tender, gentle, almost careful with me, until, utterly consumed by him, I push myself up on tiptoe and wrap my arms around his neck and draw him closer.

He groans a little as my breasts press against him, and his hand falls to my hip, gripping it tightly and pulling me more firmly against him. The kiss deepens, his tongue pushing into my mouth, meeting mine. I can feel his desire, taste it, and it's feeding my own. And now I'm truly breathless, stars dancing on the backs of my eyelids, blood roaring in my head so loud that I don't at first hear Kit say my name, his lips still pressed to mine.

"Jessa," he murmurs.

It takes me a few seconds to come to. Kit has stopped kissing me. He pulls away, though his hands are still gripping my hips. I open my eyes, my breath ragged and my face burning. Kit is staring over my shoulder.

"Your dad," he whispers.

Kit

Shit. Jessa's dad is illuminated in the kitchen doorway like the captain on the bridge of a ship. He's silent, unmoving as a statue, but I can feel his eyes burning through the darkness. He's staring straight at us—or rather straight at the bushes as though he has X-ray vision and can see us hidden behind them, his daughter in my arms.

Against me, Jessa has gone rigid, frozen with fear. Her fingers bite into the tops of my shoulders. I hold her tight, making sure she doesn't move so much as an eyelash. He might be an old dude, but Jessa's dad is still a trained sniper, famous back in his day and with a shelf full of trophies to show for it. I don't want my head to join them.

We're pretty well hidden behind a thicket of leaves and branches and the moon has thankfully chosen to slip behind some clouds, so I don't think he can make us out, but any movement or noise and we're done for. His eyes might not be as razor-sharp as they used to be, but the guy has ears like an elephant. The joke on the base is that Colonel Kingsley can hear a marine fart in Afghanistan without moving from his desk at Pendleton.

The roar of blood in my ears is so loud I'm betting that's what got his attention in the first place.

Slowly I raise my hand and place a finger against Jessa's lips. They're warm and so soft that straightaway I get a tingling in my gut and an overwhelming urge to start kissing her once more, never mind her father watching . . . he can have a front-row seat. Then I get a grip. I lock eyes with Jessa. She's staring up at me, her expression so fearful that anger instantly wells up in me, taking the place of desire. Who the hell is this guy to make her—his own daughter—this scared? I force my anger down and give Jessa a smile, and then when that doesn't work, I wink at her, trying to get her to relax. She does. Her breathing settles and her grip on my arms loosens.

Keeping as still as I can, I swivel my eyes so I can watch her dad. He's still there, in the doorway, glaring out into the blank void of the garden, and it feels as if he's staring right at me, drilling through me with his eyes, spitting hatred across the darkness. If he decides to come and investigate, we're fucked. I don't care so much about myself, but I do care about what he might do to Jessa. I don't think he'd hurt her, but man, it won't be pretty. He'll probably ground her for a century. And there goes any chance I might have of seeing her again before I head out on my next deployment.

Just then, Colonel Kingsley *Sir* takes a step onto the veranda, holding the kitchen door open with one hand. Shit. There's only one thing for it. I need to go out there, bite the bullet, and hope it's just a metaphorical one. I'll act like I was hanging around waiting for Riley, not wanting to disturb them all by ringing the doorbell. He might buy it. Though how I'm going to explain the fact that I've been sitting in the bushes in their backyard I'm not yet sure. Telling him I was relieving myself on his prize begonias isn't going to go down well. Oh well, it's not like it will be the first time I've been on the receiving end of one of Kingsley's rages. One time Riley and I burned down the garage playing around with some fireworks, and Kingsley did the best impression I've seen of an angry person since Robert de Niro in *Taxi Driver*.

I prize Jessa's fingers silently free from my arms. Her eyes grow even bigger, the whites so visible they gleam. She shakes her head at me, trying to grab for my hands to stop me, but I just smile reassuringly at her and then point to the tree and nod at her to stay out of sight. She glares at me in response.

But then, just as I'm about to step out of the bushes, my hands raised as though I'm surrendering to the enemy, Jessa's dad turns abruptly around and marches back into the house. Loud cheering is issuing from a television somewhere inside. The game! I close my eyes and say a grateful prayer to the gods of baseball for saving my ass.

I turn around, grinning, and find Jessa staring over my shoulder, her face pale and stricken. "What?" I whisper, whipping around smartly. Maybe I was mistaken and he was actually going for his gun.

I turn in time to see her dad locking and dead-bolting the back door. Uh-oh.

The sound of the bolt ramming home makes me wince. Jessa's mouth falls open. "What am I going to do?" she whispers, panic lacing her voice. "I can't get back in!"

I look back at the door, checking the windows on either side in case any have been left open. Nope. There's a drainpipe that runs down the side of the house right by Jessa's bedroom window, and if it was me I'd probably try it, but I'm not sure Jessa's going to be open to that particular idea. Though I would quite like to see her try it in those shorts.

She's staring up at me half expectantly, half fearfully, and it looks like she could be on the verge of tears. Damn. This is my fault. I pause to run through the options in my head, which only takes about two seconds because there aren't any, besides knocking on the front door and making up some lame excuse about sleepwalking, that is.

Jessa hugs herself around the waist and starts shivering lightly. I pull her instinctively toward me, wrapping my arms around her as though it's the most natural thing in the world to hold her like this, which is exactly how it does feel. My chin rests on top of her head and I get a hit of her shampoo—rosemary and mint—and have to stop myself from burying my face in it and inhaling another lungful. An idea crystallizes in my head at that point, one that makes me grin in the darkness and say another prayer of thanks to the gods of baseball. It's reckless and probably crazy as ideas go, and I'm not sure Jessa is going to buy it, but here's hoping.

"Does your dad ever check on you when he goes to bed?" I ask her.

Jessa shakes her head at me, looking confused.

"Your mom?"

"She's already asleep," Jessa whispers, still looking confused.

The grin widens on my face. "Okay," I say, trying to rein it in. "I got a plan."

Jessa waits.

"Come with me. Let's spend the night together."

Jessa's mouth instantly falls open. She takes a step backward, slipping out of my arms.

"No, I don't mean like that," I whisper, suddenly flustered. Crap. She took that entirely the wrong way. "I mean, let's go for a drive, *hang out, talk.*" Man. I blew it. She's looking at me now with both eyebrows raised, arms crossed defensively against her chest.

"Look," I add, hoping my charming smile will win her around as it has other girls in the past, and then simultaneously hating myself for even trying to win her around, because Jessa isn't like other girls and this isn't a game. For the first time in my life this feels real. Not something I'm playing at. I'm nervous, something I don't usually feel when it comes to girls. I don't want to screw it up. Again, not something I usually worry about.

"You can't get back inside," I say, reaching for Jessa's hand. A frown passes across her face as swift as lightning, but lingering. "Come on," I say, hoping I don't sound too desperate but finding my throat dry as sand, praying silently that she'll say yes because suddenly a whole lot more than just a night seems to rest on her answer. "It'll be fun. I promise."

She doesn't pull her hand from mine, which I take as a good sign. She just stands there, studying me, biting her lip. She looks at the house. When she turns back to me, the frown has vanished, replaced by a small, shy smile which plays at the edge of her mouth. Those lips, man . . . I tug her toward me, take her face in my hands, and because I can't stop myself, I kiss her, just gently, savoring every single second. She kisses me back, her body swaying against mine, pressing closer. God, this girl . . .

"Okay," she whispers against my lips just before I lose my train of thought completely.

Jessa

K it pulls back, his arms still around my waist.

"Really?" he asks.

I swallow, my heart slamming fast against my ribs, then nod.

Even though it's dark, I can see his smile lighting up his face. Then he takes my hand and links his fingers tightly through mine, and just this simple action makes my heart expand in my chest like a balloon about to burst, because it feels so natural, so normal, and so right. It feels like Kit could lead me anywhere right now, and I'd simply follow, which, given I'm not one for spontaneity or risk taking, freaks me out.

Kit tugs me through the bushes toward the gate at the side of the house. He's stealthy and silent, while even barefoot I seem to be making enough noise to alert the whole of Oceanside, including the people buried in the cemetery. My ears are pricked, and I keep my eyes locked on the back door, anxious that my dad might come back to investigate, this time with his gun, but I'm even more nervous about what's about to come next with Kit. Where's he going to take me? What are we going to do? The butterflies in my stomach swarm in a giant eddy, rising up my throat and almost making me burst into hysterical laughter.

Kit draws back the bolt on the gate, easing it as quietly as he can, but it still squeaks loudly enough that we both pause, cringing. Next door's dog starts barking, and Kit grabs my hand and starts jogging toward the sidewalk and a white van parked about sixty-six feet away. When I see what's behind the van, I come to a sudden halt, digging my heels in.

Kit looks back at me over his shoulder. "What's up?" he asks.

I stare at the bike parked behind the van, mentally slapping myself. Of course he came on his bike. He goes everywhere on that thing. But he can't actually be expecting me to ride on it too, can he?

"You don't want to ride the bike?" he asks, reading my mind. "Is that it?"

I shrug at him. "Um, it's just . . ." All I can think of is my dad lecturing me about never riding a motorcycle and warning me that if he caught me doing so he would ground me for the rest of eternity and use my college fund to buy me road-safety classes.

"I promise I'll go slowly." Kit takes both my hands and pulls me toward him, and my heels, despite being glued to the sidewalk, somehow come unstuck. "I'll look after you," he says softly. "Don't worry."

The thing with Kit is that he has these eyes that are so blue and so clear they're basically hypnotic. When he stares right at you, it's like you're a butterfly pinned to a board. There's no escape. All you can do is submit, which Didi would probably claim is all about my deep-seated compulsion to please and to avoid conflict, brought about by years of having to accommodate my dad's moods. Didi's father is a psychologist, so she has a deep-seated compulsion to analyze everyone she comes into contact with. But secretly I think she's onto something. I just don't have the courage to actually confront this truth and deal with it. One day. Just not today.

Kit unlocks the seat of the bike and hands me something. I shake it out. It's an old leather jacket, soft as butter and lined with worn suede. I slide my arms through the sleeves, shivering not with cold but because it feels like being enveloped by warm arms—Kit's warm arms, to be precise. The jacket smells of him—and of motorbike—and I want to burrow down deep inside of it like an animal going into hibernation.

Kit comes and stands in front of me to zip it up. He pauses when he's done, puts his hands on the collar, and draws it up under my chin. I hold my breath, expecting him to kiss me again, because it looks like that's what he's thinking about as his eyes dance around my lips, but at the last minute he decides not to. He reaches instead for something else from inside the bike and passes it to me.

It's a helmet. Holding it in my hands, I stare at it like a strange and magical relic I can't guess the use of.

"You going to put it on or not?" Kit asks.

"What about you?" I ask, noticing he doesn't have another one.

"I've got a hard head," he says, rapping his hand against his skull.

"That explains a few things," I mutter, undoing the strap of the helmet.

"You need a hand?" Kit asks as he watches me wrestle the helmet on. My cheeks are going red because I know I must look like a total idiot standing in my bare feet, wearing skimpy cotton shorts, a leather jacket five sizes too big for me, and an oversized motorcycle helmet. As if on cue, Kit grins at me. "Looking hot," he says, his gaze sweeping all the way up my body.

I narrow my eyes at him, but the visor is down and I don't think he can see my scowl. He hops forward and helps me do up the strap, his fingers pausing to linger against my throat. Instantly I forget about the stupid helmet and about the fact that I'm standing on my street looking like I'm dressed for some bizarre kind of costume party. It's that hypnotism thing again, except it's not just his eyes this time, it's his touch.

"You could wear a sack and you'd still look beautiful," he says, dropping a kiss on top of the helmet. He says something else, but I don't hear it because all I can focus on is how he just called me beautiful. My heart does a bungee jump. Kit just told me I'm beautiful and I'm wearing what feels like a concrete turban on my head. I know Didi will laugh her ass off when I tell her.

Kit has already swung his leg over the bike and is sitting waiting for me. I wobble a bit, unused to the extra weight on top of my shoulders and the weird deafness that comes from the padded parts by my ears, then swing my leg over the seat and climb on behind him. He takes my hands and pulls me closer, wrapping my arms around his waist, then kicks up the stand and revs the engine. We take off down the street. I have to suppress a scream— of surprise and excitement both. My thigh muscles squeeze the outside edge of Kit's legs, and I knot my hands over the rock-hard slab of his stomach. I press myself even closer against his back and feel a rush like nothing I've experienced before.

It's like a roller-coaster ride. And as Kit takes the corner with total ease and confidence, I know one thing with sudden and absolute certainty: I don't ever want to get off.

Kit

When I take the corner and Jessa's body leans with mine into the curve, I almost shoot straight through the intersection. It's hard to stay focused with the feel of her pressing against my back, and I'm just glad she can't see my face because I know I must be grinning like an idiot.

I pull up at a stoplight and feel Jessa shift behind me. Without thinking, I drop a hand and rest it on her knee. She burrows even closer against my back in response, and I have to fight an urge to stroke my hand all the way up her thigh. Instead I place it firmly back on the handlebar and scan the street in all directions for cop cars. Driving without a helmet will get me a ticket, but I'm hoping we'll get lucky. We're not going far, after all—just back to my place.

As I'm glancing around, on the lookout for flashing red and blue lights, I see something far worse than a cop car and swear under my breath. Straight ahead of us, in the oncoming traffic lane, waiting at the stoplight, is Riley's car.

Has he seen me? It's dark and I can't make out his face. I look back at the light. It's still red. Come on, change, I urge it silently.

As soon as the light snaps to green, I give the bike full throttle and throw a right turn. Jessa's arms tighten around my waist and too late I remember I promised her I'd go slowly.

Mitigating circumstances. Checking in the mirror, I see Riley's car crawl across the intersection behind us. Did he see? For the last mile of the journey I find myself struggling with guilt and shooting looks in my mirror. Riley's my best friend, but more than that, he's effectively a brother to me. What kind of a guy goes behind their best friend's back to hook up with his sister? I try to imagine what Riley would say if he found out, but I don't even like to contemplate it. He'd be mad, that much I do know. The president's secret service team has nothing on Riley when it comes to overprotectiveness.

One time we were all out for pizza and some guy made the dumb but entirely understandable mistake of looking at Jessa twice. Riley got out of the booth and went over to him, demanding to know what he was looking at. The guy almost shat his pants right there in the middle of the restaurant. He's probably never looked at another girl since.

Another time, when Jessa came to the base for our send-off, one of the guys in B Company asked who the hot piece of ass was and Riley saw red. He smacked him with a right hook before the guy had even finished his sentence. He got an official reprimand for that. If Riley hadn't done it, though, I might have. Even back then I had a thing for Jessa, though I hadn't fully admitted it to myself, let alone anyone else. If I had to analyze what it is that brings out the overprotective warrior in me, I'd say it's her vulnerability—what my sister calls her sweetness. My life is basically spent surrounded by guys in uniform waging war and watching porn in their downtime. Jessa's the counterpoint.

Or maybe it's because her father's a controlling bully and I want to protect her from him. My guess is that's why Riley's so protective of her too. Not that either of them really opens up about what goes on behind closed doors. I've only managed to pick up a few clues here and there. I sigh. Could also be that my sister's right and I have a hero complex.

A car is coming up on my inside and I glance sideways in panic. It's not Riley, but it briefly crosses my mind that I could simply try to explain—tell him that I'm not just playing around. The problem with that, though, is that Riley knows me better than anyone. He knows my history and will therefore assume Jessa's just the next in a relatively long line of girls I've had meaningless flings with. It's not like I've ever had a proper girlfriend, so how would I convince him that this is different? I don't want a meaningless fling with Jessa. That much I do know. But the fact is I'm leaving soon and I'll be gone for a year. How can it be more than just a fling?

As I pull into my driveway, thoughts still stampeding around my head, I notice the lights are on downstairs. Damn. My dad's still awake. I pull the bike into the garage beside my dad's pickup and quickly kill the engine. Jessa surprises me by hopping off the bike before I can help her. I ready myself for her laying into me about driving too fast, but when she pulls off the helmet, I see her cheeks are flushed and she's smiling like she just won the lotto.

"That was amazing. Can we do it again?" she says, the words flying out of her breathlessly.

"That was nothing," I say, grinning back at her. "One day we'll take a road trip. A long one. Just you, me, and the bike." As soon as I say it I start imagining it, and for a moment I can smell the ocean breeze, feel Jessa's arms around my waist as we lean into every bend. I can picture the two of us riding into the sunset, stopping at cozy, out-of-the-way hotels, having wild adventures involving hot springs and deserted beaches. The fantasy vanishes as quickly as it appears. Why am I saying things like this to her? Getting her hopes up? I'm contracted to the military. They own my ass.

Jessa's biting her lip, a cute habit I'd forgotten about. She does it a lot, especially when she's contemplating doing something she thinks is against the rules . . . so basically everything other than breathing. But seeing the glow in her eyes as she stares at my bike, I get a buzz in my sternum. Rule breaking is something I used to be a pro at, and the thought of breaking some with Jessa, if it makes her smile the way she is now, is a total turn-on.

"What are we doing here?" Jessa asks now, looking around the garage, which doubles as my dad's workshop. "Is your dad home?" The worried look is back. I'm guessing she's afraid that if my dad finds out she's here somehow it'll get back to her dad, despite the fact that my dad and her dad don't speak and I'd absolutely trust my dad never to say anything.

"We're not staying," I tell her, hoping to allay her fears. "I just wanted to pick up a few things."

"Where are we going?" Jessa asks gleefully, the worry erased, and I have a sudden urge to pick her up and swing her around, her enthusiasm is that infectious.

"It's a surprise—quit asking."

She purses her lips at me, but I ignore it and head toward the door that leads into the utility room. "Wait here. I'll only be a moment."

I forget to wipe the grin off my face before I walk into the kitchen, where my dad happens to be making tea.

"What you grinning for?" he asks me, arching an eyebrow as he pours milk into his mug. My dad might be almost fifty but not much passes him by.

"Nothing," I answer, heading straight for the stairs.

"Last time I saw a grin like that, nine months later your sister arrived on the scene," my dad calls after me. "You watch yourself."

Man, my dad. He's always handing out pearls of wisdom, mostly ending with the moral *always wear a condom*. I shake my head. As if I'm going to sleep with Jessa. In all honesty, the fantasy was never fully fleshed out. It was usually just me kissing her, holding her, waking up with her in my arms, nothing beyond that. Totally PG compared to some of the fantasies the other guys in my unit would happily share. But with Jessa it felt wrong to imagine something so intimate, as if doing so would be taking advantage of her. Having said that, now I've actually kissed her I think I'm going to have trouble not letting my imagination make up for lost time.

I push open the door to my old bedroom. I have a room on the base where I keep most of my stuff, but when we're on leave I stay here. There's a single bed sitting against the wall—the same bed I lost my virginity in at age fourteen (to the babysitter). There are faded baseball posters on the wall and a row of trophies sitting on a shelf above the desk. My nieces and nephews sleep here when they're staying over, so there's also a heap of stuffed animals on the end of the bed and a pile of diapers and baby stuff on top of the dresser. My sister failed to heed the "always use protection" advice my father likes to dole out. Though at least she waited until she was married, my dad likes to point out.

I head straight for the wardrobe, grab my backpack and stuff a couple of sweaters into it, then throw in two blankets from the laundry cupboard before heading back downstairs again. My dad's watching the end of the game, so as quietly as I can I dig through the kitchen cabinets for a thermos and a flashlight. I fill up the thermos with tea, grab some containers from the refrigerator, and finally make for the door.

"I'm heading out, Dad," I shout over my shoulder.

My sister has left a pair of old flip-flops by the back door, so I swipe them as well as the keys to the truck that are hanging on a hook.

Jessa's standing by my dad's workbench waiting for me, and when I see her, I let out the breath I didn't even know I'd been holding. The sight of her standing there in my old leather jacket, her legs bare, is the same as a punch to the solar plexus. "Okay," I say, tossing the bag onto the flatbed of the truck. "Good to go?"

I unlock the passenger side for her, but just as she starts to move toward me, the door to the utility room flies open, blocking her way, and my dad appears.

"Where you say you were going?" he asks.

I can see Jessa's feet poking out from under the door, but thankfully the rest of her is hidden. "Out," I answer, feeling just like I did the time I was fifteen and got caught stealing his car to go on a date. Back then I had no licence. I have to remind myself I'm twenty-one now and not doing anything wrong, legally speaking at least.

"Seeing Riley?" my dad asks.

"No. He's with Jo. I'm just going to go for a drive. . . ." I clear my throat. I'm not a good liar. "Mind if I take the truck?" I add.

"Sure," my dad says, "though last time I checked, the steering wheel was on the other side."

44

I blink, then realize that I'm holding the passenger door open. I close it slowly, glancing nervously in Jessa's direction.

"How was the party?" my dad asks.

"Okay," I mumble, walking around to the driver's side.

"You see him?" my dad asks, his face set in a glower. There's only one person on the planet makes him glower that way, and that's Jessa's dad.

"Yeah."

"Still being a stubborn asshole?"

"Um," I say. *Yes, but his daughter's right behind you, so I can't admit that because I'm hoping to make out with her some more tonight, and can you please go back inside already?*

"How was Jessa? She have a good birthday?" my dad asks, thankfully changing tack.

"Yeah, I think so," I say, making a move to get into the truck and hoping he'll take that as a hint and go away. Where are the gods of baseball when you need them?

"You tell her yet?"

I stop with one foot in and the other out and stare at my dad over the roof of the truck.

"Tell her what?" I ask, feeling like I have fire ants marching up my back.

My dad throws back his head and laughs. "Tell her what?" he says as though I've just cracked the funniest joke he's ever heard. "You *know* what."

Don't say it. The ants march up my neck and swarm across my head into my ears so all I can hear is buzzing.

"That you like her," my dad says. And then he adds, seeing my mouth fall open, "Oh, come on, you think I don't have eyes? I might be an old bachelor and a man of God, but I still know a pretty girl when I see one and Jessa Kingsley is about the prettiest girl I've seen in a long while. I've seen the way you look at her. You should just tell her how you feel."

Thanks for that, Dad. I owe you one. I can feel my face heating up, but then I decide to just shrug it off and smile, because hell, Jessa already knows I like her. It's not like my dad gave away a big secret or anything. It's actually kind of funny.

"Yeah, maybe," I mumble, looking at my feet. "I'm thinking about it. Don't want to mess things up."

"Life's too short, Kit," he says, with a touch of melancholy in his voice that makes my head snap up, as it's not something I've heard in a long time. "When you get a chance for happiness, you have to seize it before it's snatched away."

"Okay," I say. "I'll take that on board. Carpe diem. Got it." I salute him good-bye, but still he makes no move. He just stares at me and nods a few times, his lips pressed together as though on the verge of delivering a sermon. *Please, no*, I think. We're going to be stuck here all night at this rate, with Jessa hiding behind a door and me listening to my dad telling me to seize the day, while he's the one standing in the way of me doing just that very thing.

"See you later," I say.

"Drive safe," my dad says, finally turning toward the door.

"Roger that," I say, metaphorically wiping my brow as I watch his departing back.

My dad pauses and looks over his shoulder. "Bring her home safely," he says.

"Bring who home safely?" I say, my stomach dropping to my feet with the weight of a bomb.

"The truck—who did you think I was talking about?" my dad answers innocently, winking at me before closing the door.

Jessa

"W"here are we going?" I ask again when we hit the free-way.

"If you keep asking, I'm going to have to turn around and take you home," Kit says, ramming the stick shift up a gear. His hand brushes my knee and my leg gives a little jump. He notices, because I see the smile he tries to fight down. He takes his hand off the stick and rests it on my leg for a moment, his thumb stroking my knee softly, before he puts it back on the wheel to change lanes. I shiver and Kit glances over.

"You cold?" he asks.

I shake my head. No. Most definitely not. I'm wearing one of his sweaters. But even so I'm not sure my body is ever going to feel cold again. Every time Kit looks at me, my inner thermostat ratchets up another degree. I'm starting to understand what my mom feels like when she complains about her hot flashes.

In the dark gloom of the car, I try to study him surreptitiously. I like the way the muscles of his forearms work beneath his skin as he moves through the gears. I trace the line of his arms and the broad sweep of his shoulders and then let my gaze linger on his face, which is illuminated every now and then by the strobe lighting of oncoming traffic. Kit's mom was Portuguese, and he has her smooth olive skin and long dark eyelashes. He looks over at me, feeling me watching him, and smiles—he's always so ready to smile, it's one of the things I love about him. Love? Okay, scratch that. Rewind. It's one of the things I *like* so much about him. He has an infectious smile. I catch a glimpse of his father in him just then, and it reminds me of something.

"I saw the photograph over by your dad's workbench," I say.

Kit frowns. "What picture?"

"The old one."

It was framed and hanging on a nail over the lathe. At first I thought I had to be seeing things, but closer inspection revealed that it was my dad in the photograph, standing beside Kit's dad. They were both in uniform and they both looked so young, as young as Kit and Riley. They were smiling at the camera, my dad half-turned toward Kit's dad as though laughing at a joke he'd just made, and Kit's father grinning much the same way Kit does. Kit's father was film-star good-looking when he was younger. Even today some of the people who knew him back then call him by his nickname McQueen, after the actor Steve McQueen, because of his mesmerically blue eyes. Like Kit's.

"I thought your dad and my dad hated each other," I say.

Kit smirks. "No. Your dad hates my dad. You forget my dad is a man of the cloth. He doesn't hate anyone. Or so he says."

I frown. "So what happened between them then? Do you know? Has he ever told you? My dad won't talk about it."

Kit shoots a quick glance my way. "No. I'm not totally sure of the story. Have you tried asking your mom?"

"She won't tell me. She said it's too sad and there's no point dredging up old memories."

"Well, there you go, then," Kit says. "Maybe we should leave it alone. Let them figure it out by themselves."

"It's been twenty years—I'm not sure they're ever going to figure it out."

Kit looks at me curiously. "Why are you worrying about it? Some things you just have to let go of."

I sigh and look out the window.

"What's the matter?" Kit says, putting his hand back on my knee.

I turn toward him. "Just . . . um . . . It doesn't matter." Kit looks at me, his eyebrows raised. I take a deep breath. "Just . . . I wish my dad didn't . . ." I trail off.

"Hate me so much?" he finishes for me.

"Yeah," I admit.

Kit shrugs. "I can live with it."

"But it sucks, you know?" I say, my voice rising. "It isn't fair. You didn't do anything."

Kit's voice is quiet and soft when he answers. "Life's not about fair, Jessa." When I huff again, he adds, "It's cool."

"But it makes things harder," I murmur.

"What things?" Kit asks.

"This—us—" I say, gesturing at his hand on my knee, then I stop. "Why are you grinning?"

"Because you said *us*."

My cheeks flare and my insides squirm like live bait. Have I been way too presumptuous? Is he teasing me, or did he like the sound of it?

"Let's not worry about it now," Kit says quietly.

I press my lips together. Easy for him to say—he doesn't live with my dad. If he finds out I'm dating Kit . . . hang on, I'm not dating Kit. Jump ahead much, Jessa? Well, if my dad finds out I've skipped out in the middle of the night to spend time with Kit, just the two of us, then I don't want to imagine what he'll do. Or Riley. Crap. I grip the edge of the seat so hard my knuckles turn white. I'd been so worried thinking about what my dad would do if he found out that I didn't think about Riley. But that's almost as bad to contemplate. Riley's been protective of me since we were kids. He's had to stand between me and my dad's rage on more than one occasion, and I guess the role of protector has stuck.

I've never had a boyfriend, so I wouldn't know how Riley would react, but one time he thought a guy looked funny at me and almost hit him. Riley's hotheaded, and more than once my parents were called to the principal's office because he'd got into a playground fight, but since he joined the military he seems to have mellowed. Ironic, I know. He controls his temper a lot better, that's for sure. I think the fear of becoming like our dad has something to do with it. Though I think discovering Kit and I have hooked up might test that theory.

"Hey, put some music on," Kit says, interrupting my thoughts. He tosses me his phone.

I connect it to the radio speakers and start to flick through his iTunes. There's a lot of hip hop, but also, surprisingly, a lot of blues and jazz.

"There's a playlist called 'road trip,'" he says.

I find it and press play, and Joni Mitchell starts blasting through the speakers. I raise my eyebrows.

"Joni Mitchell?" I say.

Kit smiles and shrugs. "What's wrong with Joni?"

"Just not what I expected from you."

"I have a soft and sweet side. You just haven't discovered it yet."

I smile at him. "Yes I have. You might think you're a badass soldier, but I've known you since you were fourteen, Kit. You can't fool me. I know who you are."

He looks across at me, his mouth pulling up at one side, a curious look on his face.

One of the reasons I fell for Kit in the first place is because he's not like normal guys. For a start, not many twenty-one-year-olds are as physically fit as him or Riley. The Marine Corps training is the toughest in the military, and by the time they finished their sixteen-week basic training, they were both unrecognizable. They'd both been fit before, but when they came home, my jaw hit the ground. They were pure, solid muscle, leaner, sharper-angled somehow, their eyes quicker, their posture more rigid, their bearing more confident.

But it's not Kit's physique that I'm talking about. It's the way he is, the confidence he has that's beyond his years. He speaks softly—I've never seen him lose his temper or shout—and when he walks into a room, it's like he's a magnet and everything, including the air, is drawn toward him. Although I know he can strip an automatic weapon in under ten seconds and is trained to lead men into battle, I've also seen him singing lullabies to his baby nieces while he cradles them in his arms, and jump off a pier to save a drowning dog.

"You remember the time you and Riley took me to the movies?" I ask.

Kit frowns, trying to recall it. I guess the memory isn't as deeply embedded in his brain as it is in mine. It was a night my dad was throwing a fit—about dinner being late or something equally trivial—and Riley and Kit bundled me out of the house and took me for a burger and a movie. In my head I pretended I was on a date (handily ignoring Riley's presence).

"You guys wanted to see *Iron Man Two* but it was sold out, so you took me to see *Eclipse* instead," I remind him.

Kit grimaces instantly. "Oh yeah, how could I forget the sparkly vampires."

"Don't give me that. You totally cried at the end. I saw you."

Kit opens his mouth to protest but then shuts it. "Well, you know, I'm a little partial to stories about forbidden love," he says. "Give a guy a break."

We drive for another hour, except it doesn't feel like an hour because we spend the whole time laughing and talking, and it's only when I glance at the watch on Kit's wrist and see that it's nearly midnight that I bother to look out at the dark stretch of road we're on and ask, "Are we driving all the way across the country?"

"No ma'am," Kit answers. "Five more miles and we're there."

I look out at the empty dark desert on either side of the car. It's impossible to see anything beyond the twenty or so feet that are lit up by the truck headlights. A buzz of excitement hits me. I settle back in my seat, cocooning myself inside his sweater, and he looks across at me. "That's better," he says, taking my hand and squeezing it.

"What's better?"

"You didn't ask where we were going."

I frown at him but he just keeps smiling.

"You're starting to trust me," he says.

Kit

I guide the truck slowly over the rutted ground and kill the engine. The sudden silence that fills the cab is louder than television static. I glance across at Jessa, who's staring out the window expectantly, a little line furrowing her brow. I know she really wants to ask where we are and is desperately trying not to. I put her out of her misery by killing the headlights. Immediately blackness envelops us, rushing in like a wave, swallowing the car whole. Jessa gasps. The sky above us is lit up like a chandelier.

I crack open the door and get out of the truck. "Wait there," I tell her, but she doesn't answer; she's staring at the sky with a look of total wonder on her face.

I hop up onto the flatbed of the truck and lay out the blankets I brought, regretting not bringing pillows. Not for me—I've slept on far harder ground than this—but for Jessa. I hope it's not too cold. The desert's freezing at night, even at this time of year.

Once I'm done, I hop down and head around to the passenger side to open the door. I take Jessa's hand and she slips down from the truck. She doesn't say a word. Her head is cricked backward staring up at the night sky. Putting my hands on her waist, I lift her up so she can scramble onto the flatbed of the truck, then climb up after her. Jessa's kneeling down on the blanket, and I lie down on my side beside her.

"This is amazing," she says, still not taking her eyes off the sky.

"It's one of the best places in California for stargazing," I say, though I have yet to look at the stars. Next to Jessa they kind of pale.

"I can't believe I've never been here before," she says, resting back on her elbows and stretching her legs out. I take a deep breath, trying to tear my eyes off the smooth, tempting length of them. I snatch the spare blanket and throw it over us, then lie down beside her. After a moment she rolls gently against me. I lift my arm and she scoots even closer, resting her head on my shoulder. For a long while neither of us moves, and I'm not sure about Jessa, but I know that I'm not thinking about stars. All I can concentrate on is the feel of Jessa's body relaxing against mine, the warmth of her bare legs pressed against my thigh, the feel of her breasts against my side and the cool silk of her hair tickling my neck.

The tension in her body gradually seeps away as my hand gently strokes her shoulder and arm beneath the blanket. Goose bumps prickle her skin and my gut tightens in answer. I want nothing more than to kiss her, but I don't. I don't want her to think I brought her all this way just so I could make out with her. I mean, I do want to make out with her, but I also want to take things slowly, make sure she knows I'm not putting any pressure on her. If all we did was lie here and look up at the stars, that would be enough.

"That's the Big Dipper," I say, pointing out the plow shape of stars in the sky. "And this little one here, that's the Little Dipper, Ursa Minor. See the brightest star in it? At the end of the handle? That's the North Star."

Jessa follows my hand with her eyes.

"It's always there, all night. Doesn't rise, doesn't set. All the other stars revolve around it. It's the one you look for if you're lost. It'll take you home."

Jessa is quiet for a moment. "How do you know all this?" she finally asks.

"They taught us in basic training. We have to be able to navigate without a compass at night."

Jessa tenses a little, and then her hand moves beneath the blanket and comes to rest on my stomach. Oh man. I hope to God it stays there and doesn't wander any lower, because I'm barely managing to stay cool as it is.

"What else did they teach you?" she asks, her fingertips gently and slowly smoothing their way across my T-shirt, tracing the bottom line of my ribs and then my stomach muscles. Blood pounds in my ears like a hammer against an anvil.

"To iron. I have mad ironing skills," I practically stammer. "And I also know which spoon to use for soup and which to use for dessert."

"Useful in the heat of battle," she laughs. "Why do you need to know about place settings?"

"We work in an embassy. We're guarding diplomats. They give us etiquette lessons before they send us into the field so we don't go embarrassing ourselves at all the fancy functions and act like grunts who've never seen a knife and fork before."

Jessa leans up on one shoulder and looks at me strangely, as though she's checking if I'm kidding or not. I'm not. "You get to go to parties?" she asks.

I shrug, pulling her back down so her head rests on my shoulder. I like feeling the weight of it there. "Yeah, sometimes. I mean, embassy functions, socials, that kind of thing."

"And there I was imagining you living in a dorm with a dozen guys, standing sentry all night, and living on rat packs."

She's talking about the foil pouches containing what some guy with no taste buds who works in supply believes constitutes food—the packs marines are forced to eat in combat zones. "Nah," I tell her. "No rat packs for us. We have our own chef."

She tries to sit up again but I tickle her under the arm and she collapses back down, this time almost right on top of me.

"You get your own chef?" she asks, incredulous. "No wonder you and Riley both wanted to become embassy guards."

It's true. Both Riley and I trained hard and took numerous tests so we could be selected for embassy duty. They're pretty choosy, but we both made the rank of corporal and then made the grade. But right now, it must be said, I couldn't pass a simple English proficiency test. Jessa's thigh is flung across my legs, her stomach resting on my hip, and I can feel my body responding automatically. I try to think of my old drill sergeant screaming in my face, to picture myself in the pit doing push-ups until my body cramps, but when Jessa leans her weight on her arms and looks down at me, her hair trailing down on either side of my face, her lips just an inch from my own, all those images vanish, replaced with just one—her naked beneath me.

It's been almost a year since I've been with a girl. Usually marine security guards have the easiest time when it comes to getting girls. We're based in cities, guarding embassies, we're not infantry on deployment, so we go to parties, find ways to sneak girls into our dorms, flirt with embassy staff, and have affairs, even though we're not supposed to. I've had several casual flings over the years while based overseas, and a few here in between deployments, but in Sudan there wasn't much in the way of nightlife, and all the embassy staff were male. Even if they hadn't been, though, I know I wouldn't have been looking, not with Jessa so much on my mind.

She presses her lips to mine and I have to suppress a groan. I hold her hips lightly and then stroke a hand up her back between her shoulder blades. My tongue explores her mouth, and even though I'm longing to explore more than that, to run my hands over every curve of her body, kiss every bare inch of her, I don't. I'm happy to go at whatever pace she wants to set. Besides, kissing her is plenty. I bite her bottom lip, and she lets out a gasp and digs her fingers into my waist. I'm so hard that the pressure of her weight is making things painful.

Eventually, unable to take it much more, I roll her off my chest and onto her side, turning to face her. My pulse is so elevated you'd think I'd just run a three-minute mile, and I have to take a long, deep breath to try to steady it. Jessa's cheeks are flushed and she's breathing fast. She places a hand on my face, grazing her palm across my jaw, then traces the shape of my lips. I kiss her fingertips and watch her as she takes in a sharp breath. Her eyelids become heavy, her lips part. My mind fills with the image of her lying naked in my arms, her head thrown back with abandon. My imagination is most definitely making up for lost time.

"So," she whispers. "Are you going to tell me then?"

"Tell you what?" I ask.

She smiles slyly, her fingers delicately tapping my collar bone. "Your dad asked if you were going to tell me how you feel."

I stare at her. Put me on the spot much? "Still thinking about it," I tell her, enjoying the disappointment that flares across her face. I wink at her. "Don't want to mess things up."

Jessa's disappointment gives way to a smile. I kiss her once more, then draw away, rolling onto my back and pulling her under my arm. She sighs contentedly and rests her head on my chest, just below my chin.

I think about what she said earlier, about how she sees through me, how she knows me. Her words struck me hard as a kick to the ribs, jolting something free inside of me—a truth I'd been avoiding. Ever since I became a marine, I've felt like I belong to a different tribe, always on the outside looking back in at the rest of the world, playing a role that I put on the first time I wore my uniform.

But with Jessa, I don't ever feel that way. Lying with her right now, under this endless sky, it feels like we're the only two people in the world, and for once I'm not on the outside, I'm right on the inside, exactly where I belong. When I'm in uniform, I feel like I'm pretending to be someone—someone I'm not sure I really am. When Jessa looks at me, my body lets go of all the tension it's been holding, all the pretence, and just relaxes, and it feels good. It feels better than good. It feels like freedom.

I like the way she sees me, I think to myself as I stare up at the million dead and dying stars above us. It's someone worth striving to be.

Jessa

All he does is hold me, his hand gently stroking my waist, occasionally pressing his lips to my forehead, but I have never felt so connected to anyone before in my life. My lips still burn, my cheeks are stinging from where they scraped his stubble, and my heart is beating supernaturally fast.

I was nervous—stupidly nervous—when he lay down beside me, that, being way more experienced than me, he'd have expectations, but now I smile to myself. I should have known Kit would never push. I smile wider when I remember how he felt when I lay down on top of him. He was definitely turned on. And the fact he hasn't tried to go faster than I want to ironically makes me want him even more. Last summer I had a fling with a guy that ended because he kept trying to convince me to do stuff I wasn't ready to do. If he'd just played it cool and not put any pressure on me, then maybe I wouldn't still be a virgin. Half of me wishes I wasn't because Kit's so obviously not, but half of me is also glad, because if I had to choose anyone in the world to lose my virginity to, other than say Ryan Gosling, it would be Kit.

Kit suddenly sits up. "Man, I forgot. Are you hungry?" He turns around and grabs his backpack, emptying out some containers from inside.

I pull the blanket around my shoulders and sit up. "What you got?" I ask.

"Pasteis de nata," he says, handing me a little pastry with yellow cream inside.

"Where did you get these?" I ask.

"I made them," Kit says, smiling.

I pause with the cake halfway to my lips. "You made this?" I say.

"Uh-huh," he says, waiting for me to bite into it.

"Did they teach you how to cook, too, at etiquette school? Because I've never seen Riley so much as boil an egg."

Kit shakes his head. "My mom taught me."

I close my mouth. Kit's mom died when he was nine. I never met her and I've never heard him speak about her much. I'm not sure he wants to talk about her now, so I take a bite of the cake and—whoa . . . oh my God . . . this is *really* good. I finish it off in seconds and Kit's already handing me another. "This is so good," I say with a mouth full of pastry.

"I know," he answers smugly.

"I didn't know you could cook."

"I have many, many skills. As you will soon discover."

He catches my eye, and I totally do not misread the look he's giving me. My stomach flip-flops and heat rises up my neck. If he's that good a kisser, I can only imagine how good he might be at the other stuff.

After I've eaten at least six of the cakes, Kit stands up and shakes out the blanket to get rid of all the crumbs, then lays it down on top of me again. "You okay?" he asks. "Not cold? Tired?"

"You're such a gentleman," I say as he sits back down and puts his arm around me.

"I have four aunts and fifteen female cousins. I had manners beaten into me."

"Not by your dad?" I ask, twisting to face him. My dad still yells at us if we put our elbows on the table or start eating before he's done saying grace.

"No," says Kit, smiling. "He was browbeaten by all the women in the house. My mom and all her sisters. He gave up trying to win against an ocean of estrogen."

I like the image of Kit's dad being overwhelmed by his mom and her sisters. It's easy enough to picture. Whenever I've met Kit's family, I've never been able to get a word in edgewise.

"What else did they teach you?" I ask.

"To put the toilet seat down."

"Always a good habit. Could they teach Riley, do you think?"

"I'll ask." He twists a strand of my hair around his finger. "I can braid hair too."

I narrow my eyes at him. "You can braid hair?"

"Oh yeah. French braids, normal braids, you name it. Just don't tell anyone in my unit because my reputation is on the line here. If they ever found out, that would be it for me."

"Okay, I promise," I say. "Though you might have to make it worth my while."

"What? Buy your silence?" he asks, sliding his eyes in my direction. "With money?"

"No," I whisper. "Maybe some other way."

"Some other way?" he asks, his lips now against my ear. "I can think of a few ways that might work. Except . . ." He pauses, his voice so low it gives me chills. "I'm not sure you'd be able to stay silent."

My whole body arches toward him, my skin contracted in a shiver so tight it's painful. Just his words make my breathing speed up in aching anticipation. Is he going to follow through? But he doesn't. He just links his fingers through mine and turns to face me so we're nose to nose.

"I meant it when I said I was thinking about you a lot when we were away," he says. "I couldn't get you out of my head."

Cold desert air fills my lungs as I draw in a huge breath. "Me neither," I whisper. "I mean, *you*. Out of *my* head."

"Truth?"

I nod.

Kit lifts his hand and traces a finger along my cheekbone and then my lips. "Since when?" he asks.

"Last time you were back. You remember? That time at the beach . . ."

He stares at me for a moment in disbelief before his face cracks into a grin. "Oh, I remember all right. You were wearing a yellow bikini. It's burned on my retina." He rolls his eyes to the sky and rubs his hand across the bridge of his nose. "Man, what I would have done to kiss you back then."

He liked me back then? "You should have," I say. If only he had. We've wasted so much time, that's all I can think.

"And I wouldn't be alive today if I had. Your brother would have had a piece of me."

It's the first time either of us has mentioned Riley, though I'm certain Kit must have been thinking about him too.

"You okay with this?" he asks when I don't say anything. The grin has gone and his expression has turned deadly serious. "I realize I'm putting you in a difficult situation. I mean, neither your dad nor Riley are going to be happy if they find out about us."

"Well, we'll just have to keep it a secret, won't we?" I say, leaning closer so my lips are barely an inch from his.

"Are you sure? That's what you want?" Kit murmurs. "Because if you're not sure . . . if you don't want to get in trouble, I'll understand. If you want it to be just this one night and nothing more."

I kiss him before he can say anything else.

After a few minutes, Kit prizes me off him. "I better take you home," he sighs.

I groan inwardly. I wish we could stay here forever. But Kit's right. We need to get going before I get totally busted, because then this really will be the only night we ever get to spend together. My dad would ground me in a way that makes a life sentence at Guantánamo seem like a day at Disneyland.

Kit jumps down off the back of the truck and holds his arms out for me. He catches me and holds me for a few seconds, touching his lips to mine.

"There's going to be more, right?" I murmur against his lips.

"Oh, you better believe it," he answers, smiling as he kisses me again, his hands winding through my hair, tugging me closer. "We're just getting started."

Kit

In the silvery light of the predawn, I park a block from Jessa's house. Jumping out of the truck, I jog around to her side and open the door. She pulls off the sweater she's wearing—my sweater—and the flip-flops, and I try not to stare, even though the top she's wearing isn't leaving much to the imagination.

"You sure this is going to work?" she asks me as we walk hand in hand toward her house.

"I thought you were starting to trust me?" I say.

In answer she bumps her head against my shoulder.

Just before we round the corner onto her street, I pull her against a tree and run the flat of my hands up her arms. She sighs, a sound I could really get used to. I take her face in my hands and kiss her, a lingering kiss that makes me feel light-headed. The sun's rising by the time I let her go, smoky gold-and-red light making Jessa's skin glow golden. Her hair's all messed up so I smooth it down. There's not much I can do about the inky smudges beneath her eyes or the swollen chapped lips. Girl looks like she's had a wild night in someone's bed. One day, I remind myself. If I get lucky.

"Okay. Good to go?" I ask. She shakes her head but lets me pull her toward her house.

The lights are all off at Jessa's house. It's a few minutes before six, but just to be sure no one is awake, we crouch down behind her dad's car, and I spend a couple of minutes surveilling the front of the house. Confident we're in the clear, I nod at Jessa. She takes a deep breath and then leans forward, giving me an unrivalled view of her cleavage, and kisses me one last time before she scoots toward the side gate.

Next door's dog starts up howling when she draws the bolt, and I wince as a light snaps on in her parents' room. I spring to my feet and bound up to the front door, feeling like I could run a marathon, which is pretty impressive considering I've not slept in twenty-four hours. I'm pretty proud of my foresight too in packing my jogging gear last night. I managed to swap clothes before the drive back, ditching my jeans for a pair of shorts and some running shoes.

Halfway up the garden path I see the curtain in Jessa's parents' room twitch. I press my finger to the buzzer just as Jessa slips through the side gate.

A door slams inside. This is followed by Jessa's dad shouting, and about a minute and a half later a very sleepy-looking Riley comes to the door wearing just a pair of boxers. He squints at me painfully through the morning glare.

"Dude, it's like not even six. What the hell are you doing here?"

"You said you wanted to go for a run," I say, trying to smooth my face into something resembling innocence.

"I meant this afternoon," Riley groans.

"We've got a physical fitness test in a couple of weeks," I remind him, starting to stretch out.

Both Riley and I will pass the test easily and he looks like he's about to tell me that, so I lean quickly on his competitive streak. "I'm going to beat your ass this time," I tell him.

Last time I got a 289 and Riley got a 293 out of a possible 300. Just like I knew it would, my threat works. Riley can't stand the thought of losing. "Fine," he huffs. "Let me get some clothes on." He goes to close the door on me, but I wedge my foot in the gap and push past him.

"Can I get a glass of water?" I say.

Riley grimaces and glances toward the stairs.

"I'll be quiet," I say. "I'll tiptoe like a mouse."

I pirouette past him, and Riley stops trying to argue and jogs upstairs to get dressed. Jessa's waiting by the back door, and as soon as I unlock it she comes darting inside. She's skittery and nervous, and she looks anxiously over my shoulder. I put a hand on her waist and pull her behind the kitchen door. She looks up at me with those eyes as wide as the ocean and gives me a smile— the smile of someone who just got away with a bank heist; or the smile of a girl who just spent the night making out under the stars.

I kiss her and she loops her arms around my neck. Somehow, maybe because we're in her kitchen, maybe because we know we could be walked in on at any moment, or maybe just because we're both still buzzing on the memory of the night and the relief of having got away with it, this kiss is the hottest yet. For the first time I let my hands rove from her waist, stroking up her sides, my thumb tracing the curve of her breast. She inhales loudly, pushing her hips against my now very obvious erection. Crap. I take a step back, holding her at arm's length, and take a deep breath. Down boy. I don't want to try explaining that one to Riley.

Jessa grins at me, a dangerous look in her eye. Oh, she knows. I shake my head at her. This girl is going to get me into all sorts of trouble. *Bring it,* is my brain's shamelessly immediate response.

"Can I see you later?" I ask, cursing myself for how eager I sound.

She nods.

"Okay, I'll call you," I tell her, then remember I don't have her number. "Wait," I say, pulling out my phone, "what's your number?"

Jessa takes the phone out of my hand and quickly taps in her number. I watch her, feeling a buzz in the pit of my stomach at the possibility that this girl might become mine. When she's done, she hands me back my phone with a shy smile. For a moment I forget where I am and can think only about pulling her into my arms again and feeling her body against mine. I take a deep breath. Riley will be back any second.

"You should go, get some sleep," I say. Go, before I really am put in a compromising position, is what I'm thinking.

Jessa smiles at me, biting her bottom lip (imagining something that's against the rules, I hope), then reaches up on tiptoe to kiss me good-bye. Just as she does, the door swings open, and we both jump back as Riley walks into the kitchen. He stops mid-step as he takes a look at Jessa and me, and I can see his instincts flare.

"What are you doing up?" he asks Jessa, eyes narrowed.

"I heard the doorbell," Jessa answers smoothly before looking at me and crossing her arms over her chest. "Thanks for that," she snarks. "You know, some of us like to sleep in on a Sunday morning."

"Sorry," I tell her, shrugging, and take the opportunity to position myself behind the counter before her brother can connect the dots: Miss Scarlet slaying Colonel Mustard in the kitchen with a candlestick.

"You want water?" Jessa asks me now, turning and reaching up into a cabinet for a glass.

My eyes dip straightaway to her ass. I mean, she's wearing the shortest pair of shorts imaginable and she's stretched on tip-toe right in front of me. The girl is taunting me. Jessa Kingsley, innocent, sweet Jessa Kingsley is sexually taunting me. And I am sexually slain. I'm just glad I had the foresight to stand behind the counter.

Jessa fills up the glass and then hands it to me. She holds my gaze, trying hard not to smirk. I think of all the ways I'd like to transform that smirk into something else.

"What were you doing last night?"

I look over at Riley, who's looking at me the same way I've seen him look at people he's interrogating. Did he just see me staring at his sister's ass? I look back at Jessa, who's leaning against the countertop with her head cocked, arms crossed against her chest, and an amused expression on her face.

"Oh, you know," I mumble. I'm not half as good as Jessa at this whole acting business, and I'm not used to lying to Riley. "Not much. You?" I deflect.

"I hung out with Jo," he answers, the suspicion immediately transforming into a sly smile. He must have got some. "So, good to go?" he asks, heading for the front door.

"See you later," Jessa says, sauntering past us and up the stairs.

I stare after her behind Riley's back like a starving man in front of a feast, having to consciously stop my feet from following her up the stairs.

"Yeah," I call back, "laters."

Jessa

ell me everything!" Didi demands the moment I sit down beside her. "Every little thing! I want all the sordid details." Her eyes bulge like satellite dishes. "Did you . . . ?"

"No!" I say. "And I've told you everything already." She was the first person I called when I woke up this afternoon.

"Does he have a big—"

"Didi!" I yell. "I wouldn't know!"

Didi pulls her sunglasses down her nose, which is wrinkling in disappointment. "So you didn't . . ."

"Oh my God, Didi! How many times do I have to tell you? We just kissed. That's all. There was no sex."

Didi collapses back down on her towel with a sigh, pressing a hand to her heart. "It's just so romantic."

I cover my smile by pulling off my T-shirt and adjusting the straps on my bikini self-consciously. Didi always chooses the busiest section of the beach to lay out her towel, and today is no exception. If the beach were a stadium concert, we'd be in the middle of the mosh pit. I'd rather be somewhere away from the pier, somewhere quieter, but I know Didi won't move. Her eyes are glued to the group of guys beside us who are playing a sweaty, boisterous game of volleyball. That would be why Didi chose this spot—so she could have front row seats.

Didi seems convinced that life is a conspiracy, a game that the rest of us get to play while she's trapped on the sidelines watching, waiting for someone to come along and invite her to join in—preferably someone riding a white stallion and carrying a bouquet of red roses. This is why she always places herself in the center of any action, to increase the chances of being in the right place at the right time when he does arrive. Didi never wavers in her belief that one day he will, and for that I admire her. Though I also worry she's reading too many historical romance novels with bare-chested, chisel-jawed men on the front covers.

I'm sure it won't be too long a wait, though, considering the attention she's attracting in her polka-dot two-piece. It makes her look like a 1950s pin-up, giving an upward thrust to her boobs that Madonna would be jealous of. Didi would never go anywhere or be seen by anyone without her makeup and hair in perfect order. Even at the beach she exudes glamour. Next to her, I blend into the sand like a chameleon.

Didi suddenly props herself up on her elbows. "Show me the text message he sent."

I dig in my bag for my phone and hand it to her. "How am I supposed to use this?" she asks after staring at it for several seconds. "It's in Arabic."

I take it from her. I've not yet managed to fix the language setting. But I have at least figured out how to open messages, so while I still can't send any, I can read incoming ones. When I woke up, I might have thought everything with Kit had been a dream if it weren't for my chapped lips and his text.

"Oh my God," Didi sighs dramatically, reading out loud. "*I had a great night. Sweet dreams.*" She holds the phone to her chest and looks at me. "He is *so* into you."

My heart does a little bounce at the words. Is he? Every time I remember the way he kissed me, I get a flutter in my stomach, but is he into me in the way that Didi's suggesting? A tiny voice of doubt nags at me. This is Kit, who has never dated anyone for longer than a week. Kit, who really knows how to kiss (and must have learned that somewhere). And then there's my inclination toward suspicion. If anything good ever happens to me, it usually has a price tag attached. Like the time I was fifteen and won an open-call audition for the part of Lyra in a theater production of *His Dark Materials* and my dad refused to let me do it. Or the time a boy I liked—Matt Trenton—asked me to his junior prom. I was so excited, bought a new dress, spent weeks fantasizing about finally getting my first kiss, and then my dad went and ruined it all. When Matt came by to pick me up, my dad dragged him into his study for *a few words*. I'm not sure exactly what those words were, but when Matt came back out, he could barely look me in the eye, and for the whole evening he kept at least three feet of space between us. I cried myself to sleep that night.

Anyway, it's why I'm cautious now about Kit. He's like a shiny gold coin that I want to keep in my pocket and hold on to. I'm scared to take it out and look at it in case it gets tarnished, or in case someone catches a glimpse of it and tries to snatch it from me.

"Is he coming here?" Didi asks, tossing back my phone.

I shake my head. "No, he's going to his cousin's. They always have a family lunch on Sundays." I try not to sound disappointed.

The truth is I can't wait to see him again, and not knowing when that will be is making me feel jittery.

"What's he like? Is he a good kisser?" Didi asks, rolling onto her stomach.

"The best," I say, closing my eyes and getting an instant flashback to that moment in the bushes when Kit put his arms around my waist and drew me toward him. I don't have huge amounts of experience, having only kissed two other people before him, but now I can't even remember the others. "Just"—I sigh, remembering Kit's lips grazing up my throat and suppressing a shiver—"amazing."

"Who's amazing?"

Didi and I both jump. I spin around onto my back. It's Jo, my brother's girlfriend. Which means Riley can't be far behind. Jo drops her bag into the sand and stands there squinting down at us. She puts her hands on her hips, and a sly smile stretches her lips. "Are you two talking about boys?"

"No," I say immediately, feeling my cheeks starting to get hot.

"Yes," says Didi at exactly the same time.

Jo cocks her head, her brown eyes narrowed. I kick Didi with my foot, managing to spray sand all over the towels. It's not that I don't trust Jo, but at the end of the day she's Riley's girlfriend, and I can't take a chance on him finding out about Kit and me.

Didi flares her eyes at me, warning me to just go along with whatever she's about to say next. "We were just discussing a guy I'm really into," she says, grinning up at Jo.

"Who?" Jo asks, collapsing down beside us, her eyes bright with the lure of gossip.

"Um, I met him at a party," Didi says.

I have to stop myself from pulling a face or kicking her

again. Didi is the worst at lying. Where is she going with this?

"What's his name?" Jo asks.

Didi freezes. Her eyes dart briefly toward mine and I can see she's starting to panic. "Peter," she suddenly blurts.

Peter? Where did she get that from? I jump to my feet. I need to cut this conversation short before Didi digs a huge hole for us.

"I'm going for a swim. Coming?" I say, glaring down at her.

Didi bounces to her feet. "Sure," she says, looking thoroughly relieved at the out I just threw her.

"Thanks for that," I mumble as we jog to the water. "That was a totally awesome save."

"Any time," Didi answers, flashing me a smile.

I do a double take, not sure if she's being serious.

Kit

The sand is burning hot, but I don't even notice—I'm too busy scanning the bodies on the beach trying to find Jessa. I feel like I do just before we head out on maneuvers: wired. Nerves and excitement and anticipation fighting it out to see who'll win, my stomach balling into a tight knot.

I spot Riley first, then Jo. They're making out on a towel. I make a beeline for them, scanning the beach in all directions for a flash of blond hair.

"Would you two get a room?" I say, dropping to the sand beside Riley.

Riley opens one eye and gives me a look that tells me he's going to get me back for this interruption later. I wink at him. Jo pushes Riley off her and straightens her bikini top.

"Hey, Kit," she says.

I lean over and kiss her on the cheek. "Hey, Jo, how's things?"

She gives a little shrug as if to say *you know*. There's always a tinge of sadness behind Jo's eyes, as though being in love with Riley brings just as much pain as it does pleasure. I know it can't be easy only getting a month with each other every nine months or so, and I also know that she's tried to break it off with Riley a couple of times saying she can't hack the long distance, but each time she's relented, much to Riley's relief.

I watch her stroke a hand idly up Riley's arm. He puts his arm around her, pulls her close, and kisses the top of her head. I get a flashback to last night when I did the same to Jessa, and automatically turn my head to start looking for her. She said that she'd be here, but I don't want to be obvious and ask Riley where she is. Then I see the two empty towels lying beside Jo's and spot a bag with a copy of *The Hunger Games* poking out of it. Jessa's? Maybe. She's a big reader.

"So did you have fun last night?" Jo asks.

"Huh?" I turn back to Jo, my heart leaping like a live animal in my chest. How does she know about last night?

She gives me a cheeky smile. "You've only got four weeks of leave. Three weeks and five days, to be precise." She glances at Riley, and I see that flash of melancholy in her eyes again and realize it's not a flash at all, it's permanent, like a crack in a rock. Plastering on a smile, she turns back to me. "And knowing you, Kit, you're not going to waste any time. So what did you get up to last night? Any gossip we should know about?"

"Hey," I say, trying to deflect the question and wondering at the same time if maybe they know. Maybe they saw Jessa and me at the stoplight after all. "What are you implying?"

"Last time you were back on leave you made the most of it, that's all," says Jo, tossing her dark hair over her shoulder. I shoot a look in Riley's direction, but he's still smirking. I'm just being paranoid, I tell myself. They can't know anything.

"That's not true," I say, grateful that Jessa isn't around to hear this conversation and eager to change the topic before she turns up.

Riley smirks at me. "Bro, it is totally true. You had more women than Hugh Hefner."

"I did not," I mumble.

Riley gives me a skeptical look in answer.

"Just try not to break too many hearts this time around," Jo says with a pointed look in my direction.

I turn away and scan the waves, glad that I'm wearing my mirrored shades. Jo's referring to a friend of hers who she set me up on a date with last time I was back. I took her to dinner and we shared a good-night kiss, but I never called her to ask her on a second date because I just wasn't feeling it. Jo's exaggerating to say I broke her friend's heart. To my knowledge I've never broken any hearts. I've never dated anyone long enough for hearts to get involved. And Riley's way off the mark likening me to Hugh Hefner. Last time I was back after nine months without female company I had some fun, for sure, but he's making out it was dozens of women, and it was more like three. And then Jessa appeared on my radar, and for the last two weeks of leave I didn't so much as make eyes at another girl. This is exactly why Riley can't find out about Jessa and me, though. He thinks I'm a total player. And nothing I say will ever make him think differently.

My thoughts divert at that instant as though someone's flipped the switch and killed all the power to my brain. The only thing that registers is the sight of Jessa walking toward me. She's wearing the same yellow bikini she was wearing the first time I properly noticed her curves. My mouth drops open as though it's on a loose hinge. My memory didn't do her justice.

A tidal wave could hit the beach and I don't think I'd be able to react. My focus is totally locked on Jessa as she walks up the beach, lifting her arms to shake out her hair, which is plastered to her back. Water drips crystals down her stomach and legs. She looks like a Bond girl. No. Better than a Bond girl because there's no effort to it, she isn't even aware of how hot she is. She hasn't yet noticed me, she's too busy talking to her friend—what's her name again? Didi, that's it—but then she turns her head, sees me and freezes mid-step. A smile instantly lights up her face.

I'm on my feet walking toward her before I remember I'm supposed to be playing it cool in front of Riley, but it's too late to drop back down to the sand and act nonchalant, so I just stop and wait for her to get closer.

"Hey," I say when Jessa draws near. Whoa. I check myself. I sound way too eager. I clear my throat and try again. "How you doing?"

Eyes front, I tell myself, fighting the urge to let my gaze wander south. In the background I see her friend Didi grinning like a lunatic and poking Jessa in the ribs. So subtle. I wonder how much Jessa told her about last night. Judging by the size of the grin, everything.

"What are you doing here?" Jessa asks, barely disguising her happiness. "I thought you had a family lunch to go to?"

I pull off my sunglasses. I can't say the words in front of Riley, but I hope she can read the answer in my eyes. *Because I wanted to see you.*

She bites back a smile.

"I skipped out before dessert," I whisper.

Riley clears his throat, and Jessa glances nervously over my shoulder. Her back immediately straightens. She moves quickly past me, and I turn around to see Riley staring up at me with eyes narrowed to slits.

I put my sunglasses back on, feeling as transparent as a pane of glass. Crap. There's no way we're going to get away with this. The thing is I can't stop staring at her. Invisible strings are yanking on my eyeballs, forcing them to turn in her direction. She's bending over her bag rummaging for something—how the hell am I supposed to tear my eyes away? Only a blind man could legitimately claim not to have noticed her body. I almost feel like turning to Riley and just admitting I have the hots for his sister. It might be easier than trying to pretend I'm blind.

"Didi," Jessa says. "Can you put some sunscreen on my back?" She tosses the sunscreen into Didi's lap.

Didi is sitting on her towel reapplying her lipstick. For the first time I notice that Didi looks like she's dressed for a photo shoot rather than the beach, in contrast to Jessa, who isn't wearing a scratch of makeup. I'm totally digging the natural look. It suits Jessa just fine.

Didi glances at Jessa, then at me, and with a sly smile she wipes her hands on her wet bikini top and then buries them in the sand. She holds her palms up and shrugs. "Can't. Sorry. Sandy hands." She picks up the sunscreen between thumb and forefinger and tosses it in my direction. "Maybe Kit can help."

I catch the sunscreen, and Didi gives me a *you can thank me later* smile. I doubt Jessa will be thanking her later, judging by the evil look she's throwing Didi's way. She looks over at Riley, anxiety written across her face, but luckily Riley is distracted by something that Jo is saying and doesn't seem to have heard.

I stare at the bottle of sunscreen in my hand then figure what the hell, like I'm going to pass up this opportunity. I walk over to Jessa. Our eyes catch and something passes between us, a jolt of electricity that makes me feel alive and buzzing despite the fact I haven't slept in close to thirty-six hours. I walk behind her and gently pull her backward a few steps so we're out of Riley's sight line.

Brushing her wet hair over one shoulder, I stroke the nape of her neck. Jessa shivers, which only makes me want to do it again. She takes her hair and twists it up high, holding it on top of her head. She's got a light tan and a constellation of freckles on her shoulder that I want to trace with my fingertips. I could happily stand here all day just studying her, trying to imprint the sight of her onto my memory. I know that when I'm back on deployment this image, this snapshot of Jessa holding her hair up, sweat and salt water beading on her hairline, sun-kissed skin glowing, is one I'm going to reach for often.

She looks at me over her shoulder with a quizzical expression, and I realize that I'm standing there like a dork still holding the unopened sunscreen as she waits. Crap. Get it together. I squeeze out a generous handful and start applying, stroking my palms up her back and across her shoulder blades, conscious that this is the first time I'm actually touching her body, her bare skin.

My fingers slide beneath the string of her bikini top and her back stiffens. She shudders, she actually shudders, drawing in a shallow breath, and I stroke my hands softly down the sides of her arms, feeling the pinprick of goose bumps that rises up in their wake.

I finish by running my hands down either side of her waist and resting them on her hips, lingering there for a moment, imagining pulling her back against me. God, what I would give to be somewhere private with her right now.

"Anywhere else?" I whisper in her ear.

She inhales loudly, turning her head to me, her eyelids half-closed. My lips are inches from her ear. Making sure Riley and Jo aren't watching, I dip my head and drop a kiss on her neck, just above her collarbone. She tastes of salt and coconut sunscreen. I close my eyes and inhale her, my fingers tightening on her hips, brushing her stomach.

Her body tenses and she lets out a small moan—more like a sigh—but then in the next instant she pulls out of my grip and is gone. My eyes flash open. Jessa has dropped down onto her towel and grabbed one of Didi's magazines and is rifling through it. Riley is frowning at her. He looks up and catches my eye, still frowning, and I wonder if he saw. No. He can't have. If he had I wouldn't be standing. He'd have knocked me to the sand already, and my jaw would be buzzing from his fist.

I walk over to him and sit down, my pulse hammering, deciding it's a wise idea to put as much distance between me and Jessa as possible for the moment. I can still taste her on my lips, and I wonder if I should have gone for a swim to cool off. Instead I rip off my T-shirt and lie back, resting on my elbows, acting as casual as is possible, though my heart is thumping loud enough to drown out the sound of the surf.

"So," Jo says, sitting up and looking at Didi and Jessa. "One more week of school, huh?"

"I know!" exclaims Didi. "I can't wait. The last eleven years of my life have been torture. My last school was godawful, but this one is worse. I'm so over physical education, detention, and wearing a uniform. Five more days and my life is finally going to begin."

Jo gives a small half smile and looks away, and I watch Riley squeeze her arm. Jo works as a waitress in the day and goes to night school. She wanted to go to college and get a degree, but her mom has MS, no husband, and no health insurance. Being the eldest of three, Jo had to get a job the day she left school. She's the sole breadwinner for her family. Riley sends her money from his paycheck each month and would send her more, but she won't accept it. I don't know how she does it. I never really wanted to go to college. I had a dream to join the marines and I followed it. I can't imagine what it would be like to have a dream and not be able to pursue it.

"Well, I plan on having a wild summer and then an even more wild and crazy four years in college," Didi announces.

"Where are you going?" I ask her.

"USC," she answers with a smile before glancing toward Jessa and biting her lip in a grimace.

Jessa gives a tight, bright smile which I don't buy for a second. That's gotta suck, knowing your best friend is going to the college you want to go to.

"What are you girls doing for prom?" Jo asks.

"When's prom?" I ask, sitting up.

"Next Saturday," Jessa mumbles.

"Who are you going with?" Jo asks. "You got dates?"

"No," Jessa says quickly. Was that for my benefit?

"What about Peter?" Jo asks.

"Who?" Didi says.

"The guy you said you liked," Jo answers, giving her a knowing smile. She then glances my way and I frown at them both, confused. Who's Peter?

"You can't go to prom on your own," Jo says. "No one goes to prom alone. Not even the dorks and the dweebs go on their own."

Jessa shrugs.

"Are you putting us lower down on the social ladder than dorks and dweebs?" Didi asks.

Jo laughs. "No, but come on, you girls telling me you can't find dates? I find that hard to believe."

"We go to an all-girls school," Jessa says. I can see she's squirming a little at the interrogation, her cheeks going red. I know it's not just the fact she goes to an all-girls school. I bet her father wouldn't even let her go with a date. I remember her telling me about her junior prom disaster.

"Well I think that's tragic and we can't let it happen. Riley?"

"Huh?" Riley says, turning to Jo. He hasn't been listening. He's been watching the volleyball game going on next to us.

"Your sister and her best friend don't have dates for prom."

Riley looks at her blankly, not knowing where she's going with this but instinctively aware it's going somewhere he's not going to like. Meanwhile I'm totally ahead of him. I've figured out exactly what Jo's going to say next, and I'm totally down with it. Especially if it means getting this guy Peter out of the picture.

"You guys need to take them." Jo looks at me as she says it, nodding encouragingly.

Riley pulls a face. "What?" he asks.

"Why not?" Jo says. "Girls, what do you think? How about Riley and Kit take you? They could be your dates."

"Seriously?" asks Didi, glancing at us both. "That would be awesome." She elbows Jessa in the ribs. "Wouldn't it?"

Jessa frowns. She looks down at the sand, digging into it with her heel. "Um, I'm not sure my dad will allow it."

"Why not?" Jo asks. "He can't object to Riley taking you to prom."

"Riley?" she asks, her head flying up.

"Yeah," Jo says. "And Kit can take Didi." She turns and winks at me, and in that same second I realize with horror that Jo's gotten the wrong idea. She thinks I have a thing for Didi. I'm not sure how she got the idea, and I almost blurt something to set her straight, but before I can, Jessa speaks up.

"Okay, that could work," she says. She looks at me. "I mean, if Kit's okay with that."

She gives me a small smile and instantly I see what she's doing. This might be the best way of us getting to prom together.

"Sure," I say, acting noncommittal. "I guess."

Jo claps her hands together in delight, figuring her little matchmaking effort has worked perfectly.

The girls all start chatting about dresses and whatever and I zone out. Somehow I'm taking Jessa to her high school prom. Sweet.

"Dude."

I turn my head. Riley's leaning over, trying to catch my attention. "Didi?" he asks, pulling a surprised expression. "Isn't she a little young for you?"

I raise my eyebrows at him. If he thinks Didi is too young for me, what about his sister? "She's eighteen," I whisper. "How's that too young?"

"Bro," Riley says, his expression darkening. "She's my sister's best friend. You are not allowed to go there."

"Cut me some slack, okay?" I answer, riled. I have no intention of going there, but I can't admit that to Riley or I'll blow our cover. But at the same time I'm thinking if this is how he reacts to the thought of me making a move on Didi, what the hell would he do if he knew I'd already made a move on his sister?

"I mean it," Riley says, getting to his feet. He stares down at me, a hard stare, and he looks like he's about to say something else before he thinks twice and stomps off.

I watch him go. Shit. I dig my fingers into the sand. Maybe I should just back away now, tell Jessa we can't see each other anymore. But then I glance in her direction. She's laughing at something Didi's saying and then she looks my way and my breath catches in my chest like a fishing hook just snagged in my lungs. Walking away has always been so easy—I've never had to think twice before. But with Jessa walking away feels impossible.

Jessa

The warning signs are all there. When I get home from the beach, a heavy silence shrouds the house. The atmosphere is so thick with tension that even opening the front door is like pushing against wet sand. All the happiness buzzing through me drains the instant I set foot inside the house. Riley is driving Jo home, and I look at the clock in the hall, praying that he makes it back on time for dinner.

As I tiptoe toward the stairs, I realize I'm holding my breath. I glance at the door to my dad's study. I don't know how I know he's in there, I just do. If he wasn't at home, then the house wouldn't feel this way.

The smell of roast chicken wafts from the kitchen, but the radio is off, another sure sign. My mom always likes to listen to the radio while she's cooking, except on the days when my dad is in one of his moods. It's the signal flare I've come to watch for. Since Riley has been gone, things have been calmer and there have been fewer episodes. My mom and I are both naturally quieter, more used to reading my dad's moods and tailoring our own to his. Riley, being louder and less aware, seems to trigger my dad more often. One time it was for playing his music too loud, another time for bouncing a ball against the side of the house, stupid things, little things, things that any normal human being would not freak out about.

My mom comes out of the kitchen when I'm halfway up the stairs. I see her before she notices me, noticing at once how pale she looks and how on edge. Her movements are fluttery as she tidies her hair and straightens her apron, her eyes flickering the whole time to the study door. She catches sight of me and jumps, her hand flying to her mouth.

"Oh, Jessa," she whispers, "you scared me."

"Sorry," I whisper back.

She glances at the study door again and then at me, her gaze dropping to my sandy shorts and wet hair, a frown creasing her forehead.

"Go and get changed. Hurry. Dinner's on the table at five."

I nod and run up the stairs, my heart beating so loudly I worry he can hear it. God, why does it always have to be this way? I ease open my bedroom door and take care to close it silently, but obviously not quietly enough because my dad immediately starts shouting.

I head into the bathroom and turn the shower on fully, hoping to drown him out along with the somehow more stressful sound of my mom's murmured attempts to placate him.

Under the waterfall of water I close my eyes and summon up the memory of Kit's hands running over my back, his fingers gripping me by the waist as though fighting the desire to pull me backward into his arms. A tingling, warm sensation moves through my body, a surge of heat that travels like lightning from my core and settles as an ache between my legs. My eyes flash open. Breathing hard, I rest my head against the shower tiles as I imagine Kit in the shower with me, standing behind me, pulling me back against him, his rock-hard abs, the strength of his arms.

The front door slamming jolts me out of my fantasy. It's Riley. As usual a little slow to read the situation, he's burst right into a flammable environment waving a lit match. My dad starts shouting at him. Through the thunder of the shower I hear Riley reply and I wince, anticipating the full-blown shouting match that's about to kick off. Riley's tone, however, is quiet and respectful—the tone we've both learned to adopt in order to defuse the situation—and after a beat I hear my dad's study door shut. It worked. There's no more shouting. I step out of the shower and grab a towel. My hands are shaking. I can't work out whether it's from nerves or from thinking about Kit.

"Pass the potatoes, please."

My father is the only person who's so far said a word all dinner. We eat in silence, the three of us anticipating the fall of the knife and praying none of us are beneath it when it happens. I can barely eat. Riley keeps his head down, shoveling his food up in silence, though at one point he looks up and winks at me. We just have to get through this hour and then we're free, is the message he's giving me. No, I think to myself, *you're* free, you get to go to Jo's. I have to stay home. I wish I could just leave too, drive around to Kit's house or to Didi's. It's so unfair. I don't even have my license yet. My dad refused to pay for lessons and wouldn't let my mom buy me a car for my birthday. Just another way he sees fit to control my life. I spear a carrot and try not to think about how I have to live this way for another four years, but it's too late—tears burn my eyes and I have to blink them away. Crying is another surefire way to send my dad over the edge.

"So, Jessa." I look up. My mom gives me a nervous smile, which flutters at the edges of her mouth. "Are you excited about prom?"

I stare at her, confused. Why is she bringing this up now? "Um, I guess," I say, glancing at my dad, who thankfully doesn't seem to be listening.

"Are you and Didi going together?"

"Yes," I answer, my throat getting tighter and drier.

"Kit and I are taking them," Riley says.

I shoot him a look. What is he doing? Automatically I brace myself, hands flat on the table as though readying myself for a blast. I glance at my dad again.

He's looking at me, his fork half-raised to his mouth. I swallow. He puts his fork back down. Bad sign.

"Kit?" he says, his voice a bullet.

Riley shrugs and keeps eating. "Don't worry," he says. "He's taking Didi. I'm Jessa's date."

"Oh, isn't that lovely," my mom bursts out in a fake, breezy voice that fails to hide the note of fear. She looks at me. "We'll have to go shopping for a new dress."

"Does Didi know what kind of trouble her date is?" my dad asks.

Heat rises up my throat, floods across my face as my blood boils beneath my skin. Before I can stop myself I'm on my feet. "What have you got against Kit?" I yell.

As soon as the words have left my mouth, my legs start to shake and I collapse back down into my seat. My dad blinks at me in shock. I'm even more shocked than he is. I can't believe I just did that. I've never, ever had an outburst before, let alone at the dining table. A mortuary-like silence swirls around us, so thick and solid you could cut it with a blunt knife.

Out of the corner of my eye I see my brother staring at me open-mouthed.

"You're always so mean about him," I say in a quieter voice, trying not to let it shake. "And I don't understand why. What's Kit ever done to you?"

A muscle twitches at the side of my dad's eye. His mouth forms a ruler line. My insides turn liquid. Where are these words coming from? Usually I just think them. I'm never stupid enough to voice them.

"Go to your room," my dad orders in a voice made of steel.

I stare at him, trying to muster some defiance, my jaw clenching and unclenching as words form and then dissolve on my tongue. I want to stand up to him, to demand he give me an answer, explain why he hates Kit so much, but Riley gives a small but firm shake of his head warning me not to push my luck. I look at my mother, who's staring down at her hands clasped in her lap, and feel an overwhelming sense of rage at her as much as at my father.

Not letting it show, I stand up and put my napkin down on the table before leaving the room, my legs still shaking.

Half an hour later Riley finds me sitting on the edge of my bed. I haven't moved in all that time. I've only just stopped shaking, and my ears are still pricked, waiting for the fallout. The rage I was feeling vanished before I was even halfway up the stairs, replaced by anxiety.

Maybe my mom was able to calm my dad down, because it's

been silent ever since—I've heard only the sounds of the table being cleared, followed by my dad's study door opening then closing and the blurry noise of the game coming on the TV.

"You okay?" Riley asks.

I nod at him as he comes to sit beside me.

"What got into you?" he asks. I lift my head at his tone. There's a flare of admiration in his eyes that I've never seen before, as though he never expected I had it in me.

"I don't know." I shrug, looking away. Is he going to wonder why I flew to Kit's defense?

"You know what Dad's like," Riley says. "There's no point in trying to argue anything with him."

I nod. "I know."

I feel Riley's eyes on me. "How's he been while I've been away?" he asks.

"Better," I admit. "This is the first time in ages he's . . ." I stop, as usual unsure what words to use to describe my dad's episodes.

"Must be 'cos I'm around," Riley says, trying for a humorous tone that comes out as bitter.

"No," I say quickly, not wanting him to feel responsible, though there is some truth in what he says. "Who knows what triggers it," I say, keeping my voice light.

"I wish he'd get some help," Riley says, sighing. He gets up and crosses to my window, where my bookshelf is, and starts running his hand absently over the books. After a moment he glances up at me. "He's never"—he breaks off, frowning, and clears his throat before continuing—"hit you or Mom, has he?"

I shake my head. "No. Of course not. He wouldn't. I don't think he would ever hit us," I say.

Riley raises an eyebrow at me as if to say we both know

that's not a certainty. I frown some more. I don't want what he's implying to be true. I want to believe there's a line my father wouldn't cross.

"If he did ever lay a finger on you or Mom, you'd tell me, right?" Riley asks.

I nod.

"Promise me. Because if he ever did . . ."

I struggle to find my voice. "I promise," I say finally, though it's a lie. I couldn't tell him, not given how I know he'd react. Riley's over six foot two. He's taller than my dad now. Stronger too. I don't want to see the two of them get into any kind of confrontation.

Riley comes and sits down beside me again. "He's such a bastard."

I flinch at the word. "He wasn't always this way, Riley."

He used to be the kind of dad you see in sitcoms. Or maybe that's just how my memory has chosen to re-create the past. "He used to laugh all the time. Don't you remember?"

Riley doesn't say anything.

"He used to play sharks with us on the bed, and tell us pirate stories and do magic tricks." I remember all my friends being jealous of me because my dad was the dad who could make chocolate eggs appear from behind their ears. Now they all just pity me. Those who know, that is, which is only Didi and a handful of others. "He used to be like other dads," I say quietly.

Riley's jaw tightens. "Yeah," he mumbles. "I remember." He exhales loudly. "So why'd he have to change? Why'd he have to become such an asshole?"

I glance sideways at him. We both know what made him this way: Iraq.

Riley catches my look. "No, I mean, what exactly happened to him over there. He led tours in Serbia, Afghanistan, and Sierra Leone before Iraq, and they didn't turn him into this. Iraq did."

We sit for a moment in silence. I'm trying to picture the kinds of atrocities he might have witnessed, things I've only read about in the paper. Riley's got much more of an idea, but I don't want to ask him.

I try to avoid reading war reports because I always superimpose Kit or Riley into the story. I wish I could turn to Riley right now and beg him to quit. I wish I could tell him how much I miss him when he's gone, how scared I am that he'll die or witness something so bad he becomes like Dad. I wish I could tell him how hard Mom takes it whenever he leaves and how she has to swallow pills to get through the day. But I can't, because what good would it do to tell him all these things? He has to go. Just like Kit, he's contracted to the marines. He couldn't get out even if he wanted to. So instead I just rest my head on his shoulder and wish there were a way to make him understand without having to find the words for it.

Riley rests his head on top of mine, and for a moment I feel like maybe he does get it, that he does understand, and is trying to let me know he'll be okay, that he won't become like Dad.

Just then my phone rings on my desk. Without even looking, I know it's Kit. I spring to my feet and dart to the desk, grabbing it in case Riley sees his name flashing on the screen.

Riley gets up. "Who is it?" he asks as the phone continues to ring in my hand.

"Um, Didi," I say.

"Okay," Riley says, making for the door. "I'll see you later. I'm going to Jo's."

For the first time ever I don't feel a wave of sadness at watching him go. Instead I happily wave him off and kick the door shut.

"Hey," I say breathlessly into the phone.

"Hi," Kit answers in that husky drawl of his that makes something inside me unfurl like a sail.

I drop down onto my bed and curl onto my side, wishing he were lying behind me, whispering into my ear.

"What are you doing?"

"Lying on my bed."

"Want me to come over?" he asks.

My eyes fly open. "No," I say, thinking of my dad and the precarious ledge we're balanced on. There's still time for him to flip. "I mean, yes, I'd love to see you." He has no idea how much. "But no. You can't come over."

"We could rendezvous at twenty-two hundred hours outside the back door."

My stomach flips. The thought of letting Kit kiss away all the stress of the last hour, of feeling his arms around my waist holding me up, is almost enough to make me say yes, but then I remember my dad. "I can't. Not tonight."

There's a loud silence on the end of the phone. "Is it your dad?" Kit asks.

"Yeah," I admit, blood rushing to my cheeks. "It's not a good time," I explain, hoping he doesn't press for details.

Another heavily weighted silence. "Okay," he says. "But tomorrow. Can I see you then? That is, unless you're seeing Peter."

I smile. I've already explained to Kit that Peter was a figment of Didi's imagination. Then I groan, remembering what tomorrow is. "I have school."

"It's your last week," Kit says, "Take a day off."

"I can't."

"Why not?"

"Because . . . ," I say, then stop. I don't feel like telling Kit that I've never ditched school. I have a near perfect attendance record, with only one sick day to mar it since middle school.

"Wait," Kit says, his voice low in my ear. "Have you *ever* ditched school before?"

I hesitate long enough for him to pounce. "Oh my God. You haven't, have you?"

"No," I admit. He's going to think I'm so square.

"Right," he says, "you have five days of school left. You are skipping one of those days. You choose which. I'm going to take you on an adventure that would make Ferris Bueller jealous."

"I can't," I say. "If my dad finds out . . ."

"He'll what?" Kit asks.

Go mad. Ground me. Take away my phone. Any or all of the above.

"Come on," Kit taunts. "Live a little, Jessa."

Maybe it's those last four words or maybe it's the way he lingers on my name, but suddenly I feel a little light of rebellion switch on inside me. Riley gets to live. Most of the girls at my school get to live—they're always taking days off, going to parties, passing around their fake IDs, boasting about what club they got into and how many guys they've slept with. Until last night, I've never so much as stayed out past my curfew. I don't even own a fake ID. Why shouldn't I rebel just this once?

"Okay," I say and am hit immediately by a wave of butterflies and second thoughts.

"When?" Kit asks. "Tomorrow?"

"I don't know. No, not tomorrow, I have choir practice."

"Choir practice?"

"Thursday," I say.

"I'm not sure I can wait that long to see you."

I bite my lip. I don't want to wait that long either. I'm conscious of the clock ticking by, of the days slipping past toward when he has to leave.

"I might have to pick you up from school tomorrow."

"I ride with Didi," I say.

"I'm sure she won't mind."

"Okay," I say. "But not on your bike."

"Deal," Kit says with a smile in his voice.

"And you have to bring me straight home." I feel like an idiot for insisting on all these things. I'm pretty sure the girls he's been with before didn't give him lists of rules and regulations. Will he figure I'm not worth the trouble?

"Fine," he says, then, after a pause: "Listen, are you okay with the whole prom thing?"

I sit up. "What do you mean?"

"You sure you want to go with me?"

It takes me a moment to realize that he's worried I don't want him to be my date, and I almost laugh out loud. "Yes," I say. Then I pause. "Are you okay being Didi's date?"

"Yeah, so long as she is."

"She's fine with it," I say, then add, "Are you sure you want to come? I mean, it's a high school prom. It's probably going to suck."

"Are you kidding me?" he asks. "Yes. I want to come." He breaks off. "To the prom that is."

I burst into a grin. "I knew what you meant." But now I can't get the image out of my head of the other thing. I scrunch my eyes shut. No. Still won't go anywhere.

"On that note, I'm going to say good night," Kit says, laughing to himself.

"Good night," I whisper, not wanting him to go, wishing he could stay on the line all night.

"Sweet dreams," he murmurs in my ear.

Kit

'm not sure of the protocol for waiting outside a Catholic high school. I'm scared I'm about to be arrested for loitering or trying to solicit. It looks more like a prison than a school—red brick walls block the view, and the only thing visible beyond is the steeple. I can't believe Jessa's been going to school here for five years. No wonder she's never skipped out for a day. I'd imagine they'd come looking for you. They probably stick spiked heads on the walls to warn students off even trying.

I went to public school with over three thousand kids, so no one really gave a damn on the days I didn't show up. And the days I did play truant tended to coincide with the days my dad was on a bender, so he didn't care much either. Leaning back against the hood of the truck and staring up at the wrought-iron gates in front of me, inscribed with some words that I'm guessing are Latin, I can't help but feel like I'm breaking Jessa out of jail.

At five to four the gates open as though visiting time is over, and a gaggle of girls comes racing out. My eyes go blurry staring at the maroon plaid that fills my vision. How am I supposed to recognize her in this blaze of color? But then I spot her. How could I have doubted for a moment that I wouldn't recognize her? Even dressed identically to three hundred other girls, she stands out from the crowd.

She hesitates at the gate, letting a stream of cars pass before she walks toward me, a small, shy smile on her lips. She's holding a pile of books in her arms and her bag slung over one shoulder. Oh man. I'm down with the school uniform. Does that make me a dirty old man?

She stops just in front of me and brushes her hair out of her face. She's biting the bottom edge of her lip. Again she's not wearing any makeup, but she doesn't need to—her skin glows and her lips look good enough to eat. Before she can get a word in, I take her face between my hands and kiss her, completely forgetting where we are.

Jessa opens her mouth almost immediately, inviting me in. I pull on her bottom lip with my teeth, and she moans softly before jerking suddenly back out of my arms as though surprised at her own behavior. A couple of girls walk past, staring at us over their shoulders, eyes round. I grin at them and they scurry on.

"Sorry," I say, "I got carried away. It's the uniform."

"Yeah," she says, giving me a sardonic little smile that wrinkles her nose. "Don't tell me, you have a thing for Catholic school girls."

"I do now," I murmur, opening the door for her.

She climbs in and I jog around to the driver's side.

"Where to?" I ask.

She shoots me a sideways look. "Home. I told you, I can't be late."

I pull out into traffic and take her hand across the seat. It feels illicit, dangerous, as though we're Bonnie and Clyde on the run. For a moment neither of us says anything. We're still getting used to the newness of the situation. Jessa Kingsley is in my truck, wearing her school uniform, and all I can think about is tearing it off her.

I ask her about her day, and she starts filling me in on all the ridiculous rules, doing hilarious impressions of her teachers. This is the side of Jessa that I like the most, when she's buzzing and happy and laughing freely. I never see her like this on her home turf, where she's usually on edge, eyes downcast, rarely smiling. And even out of the house, if she's in a group, she has a habit of staying in the background and not making herself the center of attention—it's why it took me so long to notice her, I think. But when she's like this, she lights up a room. It's like the sun coming out from behind a cloud.

"Why are you grinning?" she asks.

"I'm just happy to see you," I say.

"Me too," she answers, leaning across and kissing me on the cheek.

"I wish I could take you somewhere now," I say, shooting her a sideways look. "Other than home, that is."

"Somewhere like where?" she asks, a glint of mischief making her eyes shine.

"Like somewhere for dinner. Or to the beach. Or the park."

"Well," Jessa says, stretching and giving me a flash of skin as her shirt rides up, "I'd rather go somewhere private."

I look across at her. Her skirt has hiked up too, and I can see the tops of her thighs, tanned and seemingly endless. I put my hand on her knee and stroke the soft skin on the inside of her leg. She shifts ever so slightly toward me letting my thumb stroke higher, and I almost swerve into oncoming traffic.

Whoa, hands on the wheel. I'm going to crash if this continues. Out of the corner of my eye I see Jessa pulling off her tie and then . . . unbuttoning the top buttons of her shirt. What the . . . She starts fanning herself. "Don't you have AC?" she asks.

"This truck's older than me. Wind down the window."

She does and the wind blows in, ruffling her hair. I put my foot to the floor, overtake a slow driver, and then take the next right.

"Where are you going?" Jessa asks, sitting up straight.

"A back way," I answer, ignoring her quizzical look.

About eight blocks from her house I pull down a dead-end street that I know winds up at an empty lot. I pull the truck into the weed-covered driveway and kill the engine.

"What are we doing here?" Jessa asks before turning back to face me with raised eyebrows.

I look at her sheepishly. Am I being presumptive? I don't want her to think I've lured her here to have my wicked way, though there is definitely some truth in that hypothesis. "You want to go?" I ask, suddenly worried.

Her face transforms into a grin, and I notice the freckles dancing across the bridge of her nose. "No," she says, looking at her watch. "We have fifteen minutes."

And before I can say a word, she leans over and kisses me.

I wrap my arm around her shoulder and kiss her back, letting my tongue explore her mouth, running my hand down her throat and through her hair, loosening it with my fingers and tugging out the elastic.

Jessa starts tentatively, just like the other night, and I match my touch to hers, not wanting to rush her or make her feel pressured. She rests her hands on my shoulders, but as the kiss deepens and we both start to get lost in it, her fingernails bite into my skin, and she curls her hand around my neck to pull me closer. Unable to stand it a second longer, I lift her across the seat and into my lap.

She opens her eyes to look at me, and I see the sheen of sweat across her brow, running down her neck, making the skin glisten across the top of her breasts. I kiss the edge of her collarbone, and she throws back her head with a sigh. I keep kissing all the way up her neck until I reach her jaw, and then I kiss a trail of heat all the way along to her ear, finding a particularly sensitive spot that makes her gasp loudly.

"I've been thinking about this all day," I whisper in her ear.

"Me too," she answers back.

I move back to her lips, sure I won't ever be able to get enough of them. She grips me by the shoulders and lifts up so she's straddling me, and suddenly I'm conscious of my erection. She is too, because she looks at me, flushing, before quickly looking away. I wonder how intimate she's been with a guy before.

I take her face in my hands again, brushing her hair out of the way, and kiss her gently now, softly, so she knows that I'm not getting carried away. Her hands stroke my hair and then my face, before moving down my chest. At my waist they linger before she slowly slides her fingertips beneath my T-shirt and starts to trace the lines across my stomach. My muscles contract in a shiver. She presses closer so my head is filled with the scent of her and kisses me deeper, her fingers meanwhile keeping up their steady exploration of my chest.

I let her, keeping my own hands on her hips, just gently

resting them there, not pulling her against me, though I'm aching to, and not letting them do any exploring of their own, though I'm aching to do that, too.

Her shirt rises up and my fingertips skim the soft skin at the edge of her waistband. I let them trace a few patterns but force myself not to go any farther, just savoring the feel of her on my lap, the warmth and softness of her skin and lips. I totally lose track of time until I hear a car pulling down the road behind us.

"Crap," I say. "I think we're going to be late."

Jessa instantly disentangles herself from my arms, jumping out of my lap.

"What time is it?" she asks before remembering she's wearing a watch. "Oh God, it's four thirty. I need to get home."

I'm already starting the engine, though my foot is shaking on the gas, and I need to rearrange my pants before I can drive anywhere. Jessa is too busy doing up her shirt buttons and smoothing down her hair to notice.

I drop her a block from her house. She hops down from the truck and I lean across and kiss her good-bye. "Same time tomorrow?"

"Same time *and* place," she answers, before slamming the door and running off.

Jessa

Who are you? What have you done with Jessa?" Didi is looking at me suspiciously, one eye half-closed as she applies mascara.

"What are you talking about?" I ask as I yank off my tie and start undoing my shirt.

"You . . . you just . . . you seem so . . ." Didi pauses with the wand halfway to her eye. "Different," she pronounces.

"Different how?" I ask, glancing in the rearview mirror to check no one is around before I pull off my shirt.

"Well, you're ditching school for one. The Jessa I know would never do that. I think Kit is a very bad influence of the very best kind."

"What?" I ask, laughing and pulling a T-shirt on over my bra.

"I like this new Jessa," Didi declares, tossing the mascara into her colossal makeup bag.

"You didn't like the old Jessa?"

"Oh I did, I just think the new Jessa is happier." She turns to me, grabs my face between her hands and starts to apply lipstick to my lips. "She glows."

I pull a face, but Didi ignores me and keeps applying. I think about what she just said. She's right. I am happier. And I do feel different. I feel fearless, or if not quite fearless, at least braver. And isn't that a good thing? I'm tired of living my life always holding my breath, cowering as I wait for the bomb to blow. Being with Kit makes me feel alive, wired, excited. It's like Didi said the other day at the beach—it feels like life is finally beginning after being stuck on pause for the last eighteen years.

"Okay, do this," Didi says, puckering her lips and blotting them together. I copy her. "There, perfect," she says, letting me go.

I wriggle out of my school skirt, keeping my eyes on the side mirror to check no one is walking past. I made Didi park two blocks from school. Kit's due to meet me here in five minutes.

"So do you think he's going to take you somewhere and ravish you?" Didi asks, her eyes bright with excitement. "Maybe he's booked a motel room! Maybe by the time I pick you up this afternoon you won't be a virgin!"

I roll my eyes at Didi as I pull on a pair of shorts, but a shot of adrenaline races through me at the same time. Is that what he has planned?

"What?" Didi asks in mock offense. "You totally need to get on that. He's leaving soon."

"Don't remind me," I say.

"Have you talked about it?"

I shake my head. "No. Not yet." He's met me every day after school, and we've driven to the same spot and made out, each time cutting it closer and closer with the time, and each time I've felt like I'm about to explode out of my skin if we don't do more than just kiss. "It hasn't even been a week, Didi. I mean, I don't even know how I feel about him or how he feels about me."

"Why don't you ask him?"

"And be *that* girl?"

Didi shrugs.

I sigh and slump back in my seat. "What's the point? He's leaving in three weeks." And what am I expecting, I feel like asking her, a declaration of love? I don't want to find out I'm just another girl to him, so why bother asking? If I can only have these three weeks, then I want them to be magical and perfect, and I don't want to ruin them by asking him on day five where he sees things going. If I ask him that, I doubt things will be going anywhere.

I'm just buttoning up my shorts when there's a thump on the window. I jump, my heart rocketing against my ribs, half expecting to find my father or one of my teachers at the window demanding to know what I'm doing out of uniform, but it isn't. It's Kit.

He gives me a sexy half smile that turns my insides liquid and jerks his head, inviting me to get out of the car.

I turn to Didi. "Okay, bye," I say in a rush.

"Damn, he's so hot he'd make an Abercrombie model weep," Didi whispers, looking over my shoulder at Kit. "You have to sleep with him." She hugs me. "That's your mission for the day," she whispers in my ear.

I roll my eyes at her again and, grabbing my bag, hop out. Kit picks me up and swings me around, his lips finding mine before I even have time to say hi. I only vaguely hear Didi honking her horn as she drives off.

After a minute Kit lets me go, though his arms stay around

my waist. We stare at each other for a few seconds, both smiling as though lost for words, and I'm struck anew, as I always am, by the color of his eyes, how much they remind me of a summer sky. I know that whenever I think of Kit in the future I'll think first of a summer day, because he makes me feel like I'm basking in sunshine, warmed through. He spins me around, takes my hand, and marches us toward his truck.

"Where are we going?" I ask as soon as Kit starts the engine.

"It's a surprise," he answers.

I grin and slide across the seat so I can wrap my hands around his arm. He's wearing a gray T-shirt, and I run my hand over his bicep and down his forearm. I still can't quite believe I get to do this after fantasizing about it so often.

About three blocks from where we started, Kit takes a left turn into a quiet residential street and parks. I turn to him. "What are we doing here?"

Kit doesn't answer, he just pings his seatbelt and then opens his door.

"What?" I ask. "Where are you going?"

"Swap," he says. "You're driving."

"What?" I say again, panic gripping my insides. "I don't know how."

"I know," he says. "I'm teaching you."

I stare at him, my mouth falling open, but he's already heading around the front of the truck to my side, and I've got no choice but to scoot over to the driver's side.

He gets in. "You've got your learner's permit, right?"

I nod.

"So we're all good," he says, climbing into the passenger seat.

I grip hold of the steering wheel. "I'm not sure this is such a good idea," I say, looking across at Kit nervously. "Are you insured?"

"Yes, don't worry," he says, grinning and resting his arm on the back of my seat. He runs me through the pedals, pointing out the clutch and the brake.

"A stick shift?" I say, pulling a face.

"You gotta learn on a stick," he says. "No other way."

I swallow and stare at the dashboard. "Okay, I can do this."

"You can do this—it's easy, like riding a bike."

"Except I can only kill *myself* riding a bike."

Kit rests his hand on my shoulder. "You're going to do fine. You need to learn how to drive."

He's right about that, and if I wait for my father to buy me a car or agree to lessons, I'll be waiting until I'm old enough to retire. I turn to face the road and take a deep breath. "Okay," I say.

Kit shows me how to start the engine and put the truck into gear. He puts his hand on my leg to show me which one to use for the clutch, and my leg jerks up on reflex, making me stall. We start again, and this time he doesn't touch me; he just points. I ease away from the curb and before I know it, I'm driving at eight miles an hour.

"Okay, a little more gas," Kit suggests, and as I push my foot to the floor we start bunny-hopping down the street. "Second gear," Kit says.

I ram the gear stick down into second and then into third, Kit helping me out by putting his hand over mine.

After half an hour of driving up and down residential streets, Kit shows me how to park, then he gets me to swap sides with him.

My pulse is racing and my legs trembling. "I just drove a car!" I say as he moves off.

"You did. And you were pretty good at it," he says. "You're going to take your test before I leave."

The sudden reminder of his leaving date makes my shoulders slump.

"What?" he asks.

I shrug and give him a weak smile. "Nothing."

He doesn't buy it and leans over, brushing a strand of hair out of my face. "What's up?"

I don't want to bring it up, to talk about his leaving and what it might mean for us, because we've only been seeing each other for five days. We're not even officially dating. I'm not going to ruin the day by worrying about tomorrow.

"Tell me where we're going now," I say brightly, hoping to distract him.

He refuses to tell me, so I settle back and enjoy the ride, letting the wind blow through the truck and whip away all my anxieties. I look across at Kit while he drives, one arm resting on the windowsill, and take a mental snapshot. Then I remember I have my new iPhone and pull it out to take a real photo. He glances across at me when I point the phone in his direction and smiles. I scroll to the photo on my phone and see myself in some not too distant future doing the same thing, staring at the image of Kit driving, smiling at me, and I know I'll strive to recall the detail of this day so that I can relive it, struggling to remember the feel of his lips on mine. A dull ache expands in my chest and a solid lump rises up my throat and I look out the window, trying to straighten my face out.

We're heading into the city, I notice. I get a little flutter in

COME BACK TO ME

my stomach thinking about what Didi said about Kit taking me to a motel. Is that the plan? No. Even as I think it, I dismiss the idea. Given how slow he's taking things, I don't think that's in the cards. A part of me slumps in quiet disappointment. The thought of having sex with Kit makes my heart beat faster. I can't stop thinking about it. I want to sleep with him, but I'm also scared, because I don't think I'll be able to sleep with him and then act like it was nothing. If I have sex with Kit, it will involve more than giving him my body, it will mean giving him my heart. And he's leaving.

He's leaving and I don't want him to leave me heartbroken.

He's going to leave you like that anyway, a voice in my head pipes up.

He turns to look at me then, smiling, and I realize it's true. Whether I sleep with him or not, I'm going to be heartbroken when he goes. *So you may as well sleep with him,* the same voice says.

"What are you thinking about?" Kit asks.

I feel my cheeks starting to blaze red. "Nothing," I mumble.

He raises an eyebrow at me. "I recognize that look," he says. "You were thinking about kissing me."

"I was not," I argue. I was actually thinking about having sex with you, I want to say, but I don't.

"Whatever you say," he smirks.

Kit

For an actress, she can be lousy at pretending. I like that, though. I like that she doesn't hide her feelings around me. Around her family she wears a mask, but I can always tell how she's feeling just from the tone of her voice or the look in her eye. Maybe I'm just getting better at reading her. Or maybe around me she just doesn't feel the need to pretend and can let her barriers down.

Right now I can tell she's thinking about me leaving. It's playing on my mind too—the more time I spend with Jessa, the harder it gets to contemplate going anywhere. I've never felt that way before. I've always counted down the days, excited to be on the move again, anxious to get back to my unit, to feel the adrenaline rush of doing my job and doing it well. But now I'm willing the days to slow down, to stop rushing by so fast. I find myself staring at the calendar, mentally checking off the weeks left, even figuring out how many dates that might allow me with Jessa—if that's what these secret meet-ups even are. Are we dating?

I feel like it would be wrong to make things more formal

between us because how is that fair on her if I'm leaving? It's not like we could date while I'm away. I'm not even sure how long I'll be gone for. Or what the comms will be like wherever we're going.

Riley manages it with Jo, my inner voice argues. Yeah, but look at Jo. Look how unhappy she is. I don't want that for Jessa. I want her to be happy. I want her to go to college and have fun. She deserves that after all the misery her father lays on her. And if she meets another guy while she's there? I muse broodily. I hate the idea of that. Can't stand even to imagine it. But what right have I to expect her to wait for me?

I pull the truck into a parking space right beside the beach and push all these thoughts aside. I want today to be perfect. "Did you bring your bikini?" I ask.

She nods, staring out the window. "I love La Jolla," she answers, jumping out of the truck.

"We're not staying," I say.

She frowns at me, her bag halfway to her shoulder. "We're not?" she asks.

"Nope," I say, pointing at the row of red kayaks on the beach. "We're going kayaking to the sea caves."

Her face lights up and I get a rush, that feeling I always get around her when she smiles at something I do or say. It's addictive. It just makes me want to keep doing more and more, finding new ways to make her smile. I have a few ideas about things I want to do to her to make her more than just smile. I have fantasies that involve hearing her scream my name, but every time I go there I have to cut myself off. The slowness is killing me, but it's the only way. I don't just want Jessa for her body. I want all of her. And besides, there's a novelty factor in taking it slowly. I'm enjoying the intoxicating tension that's building up.

Turns out that kayaking is a lot of fun, but it's even more fun when you get to stare at Jessa in a bikini while you paddle. I hardly notice the sea lions, I'm so busy ogling. It's a good thing the water is freezing cold and she has her back to me. This time I got to slather her with sunscreen without anyone watching and so I made the most of it, insisting on covering her whole body, including her legs and arms.

I watch her pointing out a pod of dolphins and grin.

"Better than school, huh?" I ask.

"So much better," she says, grinning back at me. "I could be stuck in algebra right now."

"I've a math problem for you," I say. "We have five more hours left before I have to drop you back home. How many of those hours can we spend kissing?"

Jessa flicks water at me. "Maybe four and a half, depending how fast you can paddle us back to the beach."

I make it in record time, leaving the rest of the group in the dust. Heaving the kayak up onto the beach, I help Jessa hop out and then pick her up and carry her up the beach while she fake protests. I head to a spot out of the way of prying eyes and lay her down on the sand, hovering over her. She lets out a yelp as water drips onto her stomach, but her arms are already pulling me down, her lips already parting, her eyes already closed.

I rest my weight on my arms and lower myself down until I'm lying on top of her, one leg thrown over hers, pinning her in place. Her breasts press against my chest. She runs a hand down my back. I shiver as she pulls on my neck as though she wants all of my weight on her, and I relax my arms a little and press down on her even more. She draws in a breath.

We're skin to skin for the first time, and her lips, when I finally taste them, are coated in salt and tantalizingly warm against the cool of her skin. Instantly I get hard. Painfully so. I try to shift my weight so she isn't fully aware of the fact, but she grabs my waist and holds me in place, lifting her hips up so she's pressing herself against me. Shit. I let out a groan at the feel of her, of her fingers digging into my sides, of her body rocking against mine. I let my hands travel the length of her body, brushing the edges of her breasts before trailing them up her thigh.

She throws her head back and I kiss the base of her throat, licking the salt from her skin. Fuck. She keeps pushing against me, and it's taking every ounce of control I possess not to lose control. It's been so long since I've been with a girl, and the heat from Jessa's mouth, the press of her fingers, and the sound of her sighing when I run my fingers along her thighs is pushing me to the limit.

With a huge amount of self-possession I break away and heave myself off her, then flip over onto my front. I rest up on my elbows and stare at Jessa, who's lying with one knee bent up and her arms sprawled by her head. She looks like a half-ravished siren—her hair is spread across the sand, her cheeks are bruised red, her chest is rising and falling fast. I place my hand on her stomach and feel the muscles tremble as she takes a sharp breath in. "You're going to get me arrested," I murmur, leaning over and kissing her belly.

She holds my head on her stomach, and I roll so I'm lying perpendicular to her, my head resting just by her hip. Her fingers stroke my hair, and I close my eyes and listen to the sound of the surf and the call of gulls. I'm so fucking happy right now I wish I could freeze-frame this moment and stay in it for the rest of my life.

"You know," Jessa murmurs after a few minutes.

I'm drowsy, my heart only just slowing to a normal rhythm. I turn my head a little to let her know I'm listening.

"I used to dream about this," she says.

That captures my attention. I lift my head and see she's thrown one arm over her eyes to shield them from the sun. I move so I'm on my side facing her, my hand resting on her hip.

"I used to imagine that one day you'd notice me," she continues, her eyes still hidden from me. "And we'd hang out like this in public." She raises her arm a little and squints at me with one eye open.

"You did?" I ask, surprised. I had no idea.

"Yeah," she says, smiling softly. "When I was about fifteen. Remember that summer? Just before you and Riley joined up?"

I nod, stroking my hand from her hip to her waist. I think it's the part of her body I love the most . . . so far. I haven't explored all of her yet. I'm sure there are other parts I'm going to like just as much, if not more. "You liked me back then? I was a punk."

"You still are," she laughs.

I catch her hand in mine and pull her arm away from her face, pressing it into the sand and then kissing her. "I was an idiot for never noticing."

"I was fifteen. I had braces and no boobs. I'm not surprised you didn't notice me. And besides, you were busy with some other girl. Mercedes I think her name was. It broke my heart watching you two together."

I rack my brains. Mercedes? Oh my God. She's talking about

my cousin's friend. Some girl from Baltimore who was visiting for the summer. Yeah, I think I had a fling with her. I don't even remember if I slept with her or not. Jeez, Jessa has a scarily good memory.

I try to remember what Jessa looked like at fifteen, but the only memory I can dredge up is a time we went bowling together. She didn't smile once all night or say a word. She hid behind her hair, and I remember thinking she looked a little like Cousin Itt from *The Addams Family*.

The truth is I hardly noticed Jessa at all until Riley dragged me to see some play she was in. I guess she was about sixteen. The first five minutes she was on stage I didn't even realize it was her. It was only when Riley whacked me in the stomach and asked me whether I understood a word Jessa was saying that I figured out that the golden girl on stage who had me mesmerized was actually my best friend's sister.

She owned that stage, and when I got to my feet to applaud at the end and saw her smiling as she took her bow, I remember wondering what it would be like to kiss her. But the day after the play ended she was back to being the quiet, introverted Jessa of old, as if the character was a costume she'd been wearing and had now set aside.

Now I know that that's the real her and the quiet Jessa who hovers in the background and hides herself from the world is the costume, the armor she wears in order to protect herself from her bully of a father.

"Sorry," I say again, tracing figure eights around her belly button, enjoying the way her stomach muscles flutter in response. "If I'd have known . . .

"No, don't apologize," Jessa says, smiling at me. "I hid it

pretty well. I didn't want Riley to guess. Or you, for that matter. I knew you wouldn't be interested."

I shake my head at her. This is exactly what I'm talking about. "You're good at that, aren't you?" I say.

"At what?" she asks.

"At hiding the way you feel."

She cocks her head at me and a hurt look crosses her face. I get to my knees and pull her up so she's facing me. I take both her hands in mine. "Never hide the way you feel from me, okay? I want to know everything you're thinking and feeling. If you're scared. If you're unhappy. If you disagree or don't like something I say or do. You don't need to hide it from me. I want to know. I don't want there ever to be any kind of untruth between us." I'm not your father, is what I want to add. You don't have to hide who you are when you're around me.

She looks startled, and I'm not even sure where I'm going with this, so I kiss her hard on the lips, snatching her words and her breath.

Jessa

Kit tells me to stay where I am and runs back to the truck to get something. When he's gone, I muse on what he's just said to me about always telling him everything. And what did he mean about me being good at hiding how I feel?

I guess there's some truth in that. I've learned to mute myself around my father, to hide my anger at him, my hurt at my mom for putting up with it and not standing up for herself or us, my feelings of betrayal toward Riley for enlisting and leaving me to deal with Mom and Dad all by myself. Maybe I hide my feelings because I don't feel that they're justified. Didi would claim that no feelings are unjustified, that they are what they are and that I need to unpack the thought processes behind them in order to deal with them, but I'm scared of what might come out if I do that. It might be like opening Pandora's box.

The only time I feel I can truly be myself is when I'm on stage. Or, I'm realizing, when I'm with Kit. At school I'm the good Catholic straight-A student who never messes up. At home I'm the good, quiet, studious, and respectful daughter who doesn't cause trouble. On stage or with Kit, though, I get to throw off all these identities and inhabit another person. I can be angry, passionate, funny, tragic, playful, seductive, powerful. I guess it's ironic that the only time I'm ever myself is when I'm not myself. My usual self, anyway.

Kit's walking back toward me across the beach smiling at me, and as I watch him, I feel a warmth spreading through me that isn't just from the sun. It's that unfurling feeling I felt before, like a flower is blooming inside my chest.

"Okay," says Kit, sitting beside me and unpacking a picnic basket. He lays out several containers on top of a blanket. "You hungry?" he asks, taking the lid off one of the containers. Inside are the same type of pastries he brought when we went stargazing. In another are some bread rolls. He hands me one.

"Try it," he says.

I take a bite. "Wow," I say, brushing crumbs from my lips. "This is amazing. Did you make it?"

He nods, grinning.

"It tastes like a cloud. Like a sugary cloud."

"Try this," he says, handing me a thick wedge of Spanish potato pie.

He holds it while I take a bite. It's so good I snatch the rest from his hand.

"Kit," I say, licking my fingers. "You're going to make someone a great husband one day."

He smiles and rolls me onto my back, holding me by the wrists.

"How about boyfriend?" he asks.

I freeze, uncertain what he's implying. He stays hovering over me, staring down at me.

"Yeah," I venture, "you'd make a good boyfriend, I guess."

"You guess?" He tickles me under the ribs and I buck against him, trying to get free. He holds me tighter.

"Okay, okay, yes, you'd make an amazing boyfriend."

He kisses me, and once again my body responds instantly, melting against him, a magnetic pull from deep inside me drawing me toward him.

"Want to find out just how amazing?" he murmurs in my ear, before kissing my neck just below my jaw, an area of skin that seems especially sensitive, and, given how often he kisses me there, something he seems to have figured out. My breathing stalls. All I can do is nod.

Kit pulls back to look at me, his eyes sparkling. He kisses me, keeping his eyes open. I do the same, struck dumb by the fact that we seem to have segued into being boyfriend and girlfriend without any awkwardness, without tiptoeing around the issue. It's just a fact. Bold and obvious. And every doubt and anxiety about what I mean to him and whether I'm just another girl who means nothing to him gets swept away.

When we stop kissing and draw breath, I'm humming with happiness. I can't stop smiling. I can't wait to tell Didi. I feel like I want to shout it from the rooftops, brand his name on my skin. I want everyone to know. *I'm Kit's girlfriend.* I always used to scoff in private about girls who defined themselves in association with a boy, but now I get it. Then I remember I can't tell anyone about us.

"Guess we have to keep it quiet," Kit says as though he's read my mind.

We're lying on our backs, holding hands, staring up at the sky.

"I guess," I say, wishing we didn't have to.

Kit rolls onto his side to face me. "For now, at least," he says.

He props himself up on one elbow. "I know I'm leaving in three weeks."

I put my finger against his lips. "Shhhhh," I say. I don't want to think about that or talk about it.

"So I know it's only going to be a short-term thing."

I frown at him. "Shhhhh," I say again.

He closes his mouth and nods before rolling onto his back again. He brings our clasped hands up to his lips and kisses the back of my hand.

"I'm going to be the best boyfriend you ever had," Kit says.

"You're the only boyfriend I've ever had," I answer dryly. And if my dad finds out about him, he'll be the only boyfriend I ever do have.

Kit turns his head. "Really?" he asks.

I nod. "Yep."

"But where'd you learn to kiss like that?" he asks.

"I have kissed boys before," I say. "Last summer in England when I went to stay with my cousin. I was seeing a guy there."

"An English guy?" Kit asks, his nose wrinkling.

"Yeah," I say. "But don't worry, he had nothing on you."

"Good," Kit says.

"Anyway, like you can talk," I say. "You've been with hundreds of women."

Kit pulls me into his arms so I'm lying on his chest, my hair hanging over us like a curtain. "I don't remember any of them anymore," he says, kissing me. "Only you."

Kit

can't believe I just did that, asked her to be my girlfriend. It kind of came out of nowhere, but once it was out of my mouth I realized it was what I've wanted all along. And I meant what I said, too—I'm going to be the best boyfriend ever. Not that I have any experience of being one. But I'm a fast learner.

"I'm going to cook you dinner one night next week," I say.

I can feel her smiling even without looking at her.

"I like it that you can cook," she says. "It's sexy."

"You should see what I can do with a whisk," I murmur against her ear. "And a palette knife."

Suddenly the image of Jessa covered in whipped cream flashes into my mind.

"I'm really turned on by that," she answers drolly.

I reach for a pastry with my spare hand and press it into her mouth.

She giggles and spits it out but then starts licking her fingers. "These are so good," she says. "Will you teach me how to make them one day?"

"Sure," I say. "How about now?"

Jessa turns her head to me. "Now?"

"Yeah," I say. We've been at the beach over an hour and a half and it's getting hot.

"Where?" Jessa asks.

"At my place."

She props herself up on one elbow, giving me a distractingly great view of her breasts. "Yours?" she asks.

"My dad's out," I say with a grin, hoping she can't read my mind.

She narrows her eyes at me. "Sure, let's go," she says after a beat.

I drive like there's a demon on our tail, but halfway home I glance across at Jessa sitting with her bare feet propped on the dash, legs coated in sand, and wonder if I'm running ahead of myself. What happened to taking it slowly and enjoying the anticipation? By the time we get back to my place I'm back in control and planning on just giving her a baking demonstration. That's all. No making out.

I open the back door and lead her into the kitchen. Jessa's been to my house before but not for a while, and I feel nervous, self-conscious, as she stands there looking around. All I can think about is how it looks like I've brought her back here so I can sleep with her, which isn't true, but which automatically makes me think about sleeping with her, which in turn makes me picture her naked, which makes me then picture us making love on the kitchen floor. Fuck. Think about something else instead. I try to banish the thoughts but still they flood in thick and fast, taunting me. Focus on the baking, I tell myself tersely. That's what you brought her here for. Baking. Not sex.

"Let me check I have all the ingredients," I say, moving quickly to the cabinets and starting to pull down the flour, eggs, sugar, and baking powder.

"Kit?" Jessa says.

I stop, holding the kitchen scale in one hand and a baking tray in the other, and look at her. She's standing in the middle of the kitchen, still barefoot, her hair hanging down her back and her T-shirt sticking to her with sand and salt water.

"I don't want to bake," she says.

"You don't?" I ask, trying to stay cool.

She shakes her head, a small and mischievous smile playing on her lips.

Oh, fuck it. I toss the things I'm holding on to the side, not even caring when I hear something clatter to the floor. I stride toward Jessa and pull her into my arms. "Works for me," I say, kissing her.

She presses herself against me and I lift her up. She wraps her legs around my waist, and I run my hand down the smooth, warm skin of her thighs. I kiss her harder, loving the feel of her opening up to me. With one arm I swipe the objects from the counter top and place her down on it. She keeps her legs wrapped around my waist and I grip her thighs, loving the feel of it, of her wanting me, not knowing how the hell I got so lucky but not daring to question it either.

I taste the salt on her skin as I trace my tongue up her neck. She breathes fire in my ear, whispers my name, as though urging me on. Her hands drop to my waist and ride up inside my T-shirt, smoothing over my stomach all the way up my chest. I bury my lips in the curve of her neck and shoulder and hear her breath catch in her throat.

I let my hands finally trace the shape of her breasts, though over her T-shirt, and relish the sound of her sighing when my thumbs rub over her nipples. She clutches me harder, clinging on to me when I let my lips wander over her collarbone.

She pulls back out of my arms and tugs on the bottom of my T-shirt. There's a wildness in her eyes, they're slightly unfocused, and I hold my arms above my head and let her peel it off. She tosses it to the floor and then takes a deep breath, her eyes wandering over me. I swallow, my heart beating hollowly. She runs her hands over my stomach, slowly, tentatively letting her fingers trace a path to my waistband. I'm holding my breath, fully aware that we're on the edge of something here and not wanting to push her.

She leans forward and kisses me, biting my bottom lip, tugging it between her teeth, and all I can hear is my blood roaring in my ears, my gut tightening in response. I've never wanted any girl the way I want Jessa. I grip her by the hips, pulling her against me, and she lets out a gasp.

Then my phone rings.

It takes a second for the sound to permeate through the lust fog in my brain, to realize that it's my phone ringing and it's coming from my back pocket. I take an unsteady step backward and Jessa's legs drop from my waist, leaving me feeling unanchored and at sea; the room tilts violently. I pull my phone out of my pocket, glancing at Jessa, who's sitting on the countertop breathing hard, her cheeks flushed.

Damn. It's Riley. Great timing. I hit okay, noticing as I do the mess all over the floor. The bags of sugar and flour have exploded, and the kitchen is a winter wonderland. The scale lies on the counter beside six broken eggs, one of which is sliding down the side of a cabinet to meet the flour on the floor.

"Kit?"

I close my eyes. "Uh, yeah?" I say, wondering why I answered the phone. I could be kissing Jessa right now. What a fool.

"Where are you?"

Shit. I could say I'm home, but what if he comes over? I glance at Jessa still sitting on the countertop, her eyes fixed on me, her hair in disarray.

"Just chillin'," I say, hoping he can't hear how out of breath I sound. "It's Riley," I mouth to Jessa. Her eyes widen in panic.

"You wanna hang out? Go to the gym maybe?" he asks.

"Um, nah," I say. "I'm kinda busy."

"Doing what?" Riley asks, then he pauses and I hear the chuckle in his throat. "Oh, I get it. Are you with a girl? Are you getting some?"

I don't answer. Shit. Am I that obvious?

"Who? Wait," he says, his tone switching to anger. "It's not Didi, is it?"

"No."

"Oh yeah, she's at school. Who then?" Riley asks, back to his normal teasing tone. "Where'd you meet her?"

"Just around," I say, not able to look in Jessa's direction.

"Is she hot?" Riley asks. "Man, how'd you do it?"

I cringe, rubbing a hand over my eyes. "She's beautiful, yeah," I say quietly, though I'm sure Jessa hears.

"Well, I'll leave you to it. Tell me all about it later. I want details, bro."

"Yeah, sure," I say, swallowing dryly.

He hangs up, still laughing. I picture how quickly the laughter would die if he knew I was with his sister. I close the phone and put it back in my pocket. Jessa hops down from the counter, pushing her hair behind her ears and straightening her T-shirt. The mood has been well and truly killed.

"Maybe we should clean up," she says, looking around at the mess.

I follow her gaze and then look back at her, noticing how flushed her cheeks are still. "Yeah. Maybe."

Jessa looks at me. She doesn't make a move to start cleaning up. The energy starts to ripple again—I can feel it—making us move toward each other as though we're magnetized.

"When's your dad back?" she asks, her gaze falling to my lips.

I look at the clock on the wall. It's almost three. "Not till later. Six maybe."

Jessa does a silent calculation in her head, then glances at me shyly. "Show me your room?" she says.

Jessa

really do just want to see his room—I'm not suggesting anything. Though when Kit takes my hand I realize that's a lie. I'm
totally suggesting something. He leads me in silence up the
narrow stairs. It's a small house and clearly the home of a bachelor. It hasn't been decorated in years. On the walls are photographs of Kit in uniform, of Kit's cousins at various weddings,
and Kit's mom with Kit and his sister when they were babies.

There are four rooms off the landing. Kit opens the first on
the right, and I smile straightaway because it looks like it belongs
to a nine-year-old. There are soccer and baseball trophies on the
shelf, and a narrow single bed pushed under the window. There's
even a baseball pennant on the wall. The room is neat and tidy. I
notice the dresser is piled with diaper bags and toys.

"Is there something you need to tell me?" I ask.

He grins at me. "Yeah, I'm incontinent." He laughs. "Nah,
it's for my niece and all my cousins. At last count I'm a second
cousin about thirty times over."

"Wow," I say. I only have one cousin in England. I'd love a big
family.

I pick up a photograph in a heavy silver frame that's sitting in pride of place on the bedside table. "That's my mom," Kit says.

He didn't need to tell me. It's so obvious. He looks just like her. She's dark-haired, with almond-shaped brown eyes and beautiful high cheekbones.

"She looks like a film star," I say, taking in the red-painted lips and the glamorous white dress she's wearing.

"That was her on her wedding day," Kit says.

I set the photograph down and turn to Kit. His focus is still on the photograph, but after a moment he turns and looks at me. I see a shadow of sadness in his eyes that I want to chase away, so I rise up on tiptoe and kiss him gently on the mouth. Slowly he puts his arms around my waist and draws me nearer. Unlike in the kitchen, this time we kiss each other slowly, gently, our hands staying chastely at waist height. Things heat up fast, though, as they always seem to when we start kissing. I wonder if this is how he felt with all the other girls he's been with, because I've never felt this way with a boy before, like I want to crawl beneath his skin, melt into him, lose myself in him completely.

A sudden burst of confidence makes me take a step back from Kit and pull off my T-shirt, glancing up only briefly to check his expression. He looks surprised, but then this gaze drops to my bikini top, and he closes his mouth, tugs me by the arm, and leads me toward the bed. He lays me down gently on top of the covers and then lies down beside me, resting on his side. The bed is so narrow the two of us couldn't both lie flat anyway. I look up at him as he rests his hand on my stomach and watch his face, which is completely transparent. It's awe—that's the only way to describe the way he's looking at me, as though I'm made of gold, or sunlight.

"Fuck, you're so beautiful," he says, stroking his hand across the flat of my stomach. He runs his fingers along my hip bone as though he's playing an instrument, learning the keys, and then he traces the outline of my ribs all the way up until he meets my bikini, and goose bumps chase themselves across my skin, which is drawn as tight as a drum. Then, without warning, Kit dips his head and kisses the top of my breast. I suck in a breath and hold it as his tongue starts to trace circles across my skin. His other hand comes up and cups my other breast, making it swell against his tongue.

Holy shit. My eyes fly open as he presses his mouth over the thin material of my bikini and sucks on my nipple, drawing it hard into his mouth.

He hasn't even made a move to take off my bikini top, but I can feel a pulsing between my legs, a strong pull that turns into a sweetly painful ache when Kit brushes his thumb over my nipple and squeezes it.

I stop wondering where we're going with this, stop caring about anything. My mind disconnects as the sensations pulsing through my body take over, obliterating everything else. All I can think is all I can feel, every single touch magnified until it seems like my cells are exploding in a chain reaction. Kit's hand slips beneath my back, curves up my spine, finds the knotted string of my bikini. He's just about to release it when we both hear someone calling his name.

Kit's off me in a flash and I sit bolt upright. My head is spinning, my body still burning from his touch, but now adrenaline scores through my bloodstream too. I scramble frantically for my shirt, which is lying on the floor, as Kit crosses to the door. Who is it?

"Kit?"

Oh my God. It's his dad. I grab the T-shirt to my chest and start hyperventilating in panic. Kit is standing by the door, holding on to the handle, his head bent. He takes a deep breath. "Yep?" he shouts. He's trying to keep his voice casual, but there's a note to it that shrieks his guilt.

"What's the mess down in the kitchen?" his dad asks. He's just outside the bedroom door. Kit glances at me over his shoulder. I dart behind the door not needing to be told. Kit pulls the door open, blocking it with his body, so his dad can't see inside. I try to press as close to the door as possible so he can't see me through the crack.

"What's going on?" his dad asks.

"Nothing," Kit answers quickly. Too quickly. "I was baking. Dropped something."

"Looks like a hydrogen bomb went off in there." He pauses. "You often bake shirtless?"

"I . . . uh . . . I spilled something on my T-shirt. Had to put it in the wash."

"In the wash?" his dad asks. "I found it on the floor in the kitchen in the middle of all that mess that you're about to go downstairs and clean up."

Kit doesn't say anything for a moment, and I wonder for a heart-stopping few seconds if he's about to come clean, but he doesn't, he just nods and says, "Yep, I'll be down in a minute."

His dad hovers for a few more seconds, and I imagine him narrowing his eyes at Kit and trying to peer over his shoulder into the bedroom. Kit finally shuts the door. He leans back against it, wincing. "Shit. That was close."

"I thought you said he wasn't back until six?" I say.

"Must have got it wrong." Kit shrugs at me, that dangerous grin tugging at his mouth.

I shake my head at him as I pull on my T-shirt. My heart is still pounding. It's not funny. I look at my watch. "I need to get home," I say.

Kit frowns. "I'm not sure how we're going to get you past my dad."

I stare at him. He'd better find a way. My dad will kill me if I'm not home by dinner.

"Okay," Kit says, pacing the room, "let me think." I cross my arms over my chest and watch him. "Okay. I'll go down and clean up the kitchen and act like nothing's up. You wait up here, and when the coast is clear I'll come and get you."

I raise my eyebrows.

"Or we could just come out and tell him."

My arms drop to my sides. "Tell him?"

"Why not?" Kit asks.

"Because . . . he'll wonder what we were doing up here . . . and in the kitchen."

Kit shrugs. "He won't mind."

"*I* mind."

Kit nods. "Okay. Well, wait here then and I'll come get you." He crosses to the door and is about to open it before he stops and walks toward me. He puts his arm around my waist and hooks me to him, then cups my face and kisses me.

"You're so goddamn sexy, you know that?"

I don't get a chance to answer before he lets me go and disappears out the door.

Kit

start sweeping up the mess, thinking of Jessa upstairs. Man, my dad's timing sucks. If he hadn't come home would we be having sex right now? No. I can tell that Jessa's not ready. And besides, I think it would be her first time, and if it is her first time it needs to be special, not some quick *wham bam, thank you, ma'am* with one eye on the clock. I would want to spend all night making her ready, making sure she remembered it for the rest of her life.

I glance at the clock. I need to figure a way to get her out of here. My dad's in the front room listening to Miles Davis, which means he must be working on his Sunday sermon. If I'm lucky, he'll stay put and I can try to sneak Jessa down the stairs.

I sweep up the remains of the flour and sugar and then sprint up the stairs. We have fifteen minutes. Jessa's sitting on the edge of my bed, her foot tapping silently. She jumps up the moment I open the door and I beckon her over, taking her hand.

We jog down the stairs and straight through into the kitchen, my ears pricked for any sound from the front room. We make it into the truck, and I gun it out the driveway at breakneck speed.

We make it halfway before the front door flies open and my dad comes out. I consider for a moment keeping on going, but then I see he's holding something in his hand. It's a bag. Jessa's bag.

I pull the hand brake on.

Jessa doesn't say a word. She's just staring out the window. We watch as my dad strolls over. I wind down the window.

"Hey," I say, feeling like I just got caught fleeing the scene of a crime.

My dad's eyebrow is twitching in amusement. So is his mouth. I give him a shrug as if to say, *Cut me some slack, have you looked at this girl?*

And he gives me a look as if to say, *Yeah, I don't blame you, but son, we're going to talk about this when you get back.*

He holds up the bag. "I think you forgot this," he says.

Jessa reaches for it. "Thanks," she mumbles, her gaze stuck to the floor.

"We gotta go," I say. "I'm running Jessa home."

My dad nods. "See you later. Bye, Jessa," he says and ambles back into the house.

Jessa doesn't speak the whole way back. She does switch clothes, though, back into her school uniform, which gives me an unrivalled view of both her body and her litheness as she contorts to wriggle out of her shorts and pull on her skirt. I almost crash catching a glimpse of her in her underwear when she changes out of her bikini bottoms and have to force my eyes back to the road.

"Don't worry," I say as I see the anxiety pulling at the edges of her mouth as she checks herself in the mirror.

"Do you think he'll say anything?" she asks, tucking in her school shirt.

"To your dad?" I laugh. "No."

"To Riley I mean," she says.

I shake my head. "No. I'll talk to him. Listen, my dad's a chaplain. Keeping secrets is part of his job."

She looks a little more reassured. "Okay," she says as I pull over. "How do I look?" She smooths down her hair and looks at me, and I notice that the free-spirited, relaxed Jessa has vanished. She's back to her anxious old self.

"Like you had a really, really good day at school," I say.

Finally she smiles.

"I had the best day at school ever," she says, leaning over and kissing me. "Thank you."

I pull the truck into the driveway and let a slow breath out, readying myself. Just as I guessed, my dad is waiting in the kitchen for me.

"You want some?" he asks, spooning coffee into the coffeepot.

I nod and reach for another mug.

"Does Riley know?" he asks as he pours out the water.

Cut straight to the chase much?

"No," I answer.

"You going to tell him?" my dad asks, giving me a look.

"Wasn't planning on it," I say.

My dad nods to himself, taking his sweet time to screw the lid on the coffee and put it away. "You sure?" he asks. "Secrets like that between friends have a habit of coming out. You don't want to ruin things between you."

"Him finding out about me and Jessa, that will ruin things between us," I say with a bitterness to my voice that surprises me.

"And sneaking around behind closed doors—you think

you'll get away with that?" my dad asks in a perfectly reasonable tone of voice. "Think it's fair to her?"

I frown as I take the coffee he hands to me. It's as bitter and black as tar. Ever since my dad gave up drink, he subsists on eight cups of this a day, refusing to do anything so namby-pamby as add milk. I swear it runs through his veins like diesel oil.

"What if her father finds out?" he asks.

"He won't," I say, shooting him a warning look.

My dad raises his eyebrows at me. "He won't hear it from me. Doesn't listen to a word I say anyway," he says, laughing under his breath. "But you've got to think about what happens when he does find out."

"I don't care."

"I know you don't. But what about Jessa? You're thinking with the wrong head."

"I am not," I say indignantly. But is he right? Am I so absorbed in her, in wanting her, that I'm not thinking straight?

"She mean something to you?" my dad asks.

"Yes," I say, wishing he'd just drop it.

"Really something?" my dad presses.

I look at him. "Yes."

He nods at me as though pleased about something. "Then do the right thing."

"What is the right thing?" I ask him. I feel like I'm thirteen, asking for his advice about girls. Except when I was thirteen, my dad was only a year into his recovery and I hadn't yet forgiven him, so chats like this one never happened.

My dad puts a hand on my shoulder and squeezes. "Always the honest thing," he says, before grimacing and adding, "which isn't always the easiest thing."

"You think I should tell Riley?" I ask.

My dad gives a noncommittal shrug, telling me it's up to me. "If you tell him, you should probably tell her father, too. Don't make the same mistake I did."

My head flies up. "What do you mean? What mistake?"

My dad walks to the sink and empties the remains of his coffee. He keeps his back to me.

"Is this why you and her dad fell out?" I ask. "Over a girl?"

My dad sighs heavily and turns back around. "I can't tell you," he says.

"Why not?" I ask. This is the first time he's ever come close to telling me what happened between him and Jessa's dad. I figured a while back that maybe it had to do with something that went on overseas when they were both in the same marine unit, but it makes much more sense that a woman was involved. I can't believe I didn't figure it out before. "Why not?" I ask again when he doesn't answer.

"Not my story to tell," my dad says.

"Whose story is it to tell?" I ask.

"Your mother's."

I blink at him. "She's dead," I say.

My dad walks toward the doorway. He's not yet fifty and still physically an impressive man—stocky, broad-shouldered—but the fight with the bottle added a good ten years to him and he looks closer to sixty, his skin tanned to leather and his hair completely gray. The mention of my mother seems to have aged him another five.

"And maybe it's best we don't go disturbing old ghosts," he says over his shoulder to me before he closes the door.

Jessa

You look like Lana Turner."

"Who?"

"Blond bombshell film star from the forties. Oh my God, Jessa, don't you know anything?"

"My film knowledge only goes back to the eighties. Sorry."

Didi does something to my hair, framing it around my face. It still smells slightly singed from the curling iron, and I'm starting to feel like a Barbie doll. Maybe Didi was denied one as a child and is making up for lost time.

"You just need some lipstick," Didi says, reaching for her makeup bag. "Not that it's going to stay on for long," she adds as she starts to dab it on my lips.

"Like I'm going to get a chance to kiss Kit with my brother there."

"I'll deal with your brother. Don't worry about that," Didi says, spinning me toward the mirror.

I do a double take. Didi's right. I do look like I just stepped out of a 1940s movie. My dress is floor-length dark blue satin, pulling in slightly at the waist. Didi's done my hair so it's side-parted and hanging loose and wavy down my back. My lips are bright red, and because I don't normally wear makeup I feel ridiculous, like a clown. I think about wiping it off but I don't want to offend Didi, and then I realize that maybe it's less clown than I think, and it might be fun to pretend for a night to be a blond bombshell seductress.

I walk down the stairs, feeling Kit's eyes on me without even having to look up. I can't look up. I'm too nervous. Halfway down, though, I can't help myself. I raise my head, see him staring at me, and almost lose my footing. As it is my stomach kangaroo-hops at the sight of him. He and Riley are both wearing 1940s-style black tie. I don't know where they managed to find suits like that, but it makes me want to build a time machine and head back to that decade permanently. Then I remember the Second World War and decide that's maybe not such a good idea. Kit's eyes have widened, his lips are parted. His gaze travels down my body in a way that makes me feel unsteady on my feet. When he raises his eyes to mine, I see the desire in them, and it gives me a thrill like nothing I've ever known.

"You look nice," Riley says, though he's frowning as he says it.

"You look beautiful," Kit mouths behind his back.

This year's prom committee decided on the US Grant Hotel in San Diego, renowned for its five-star splendor, as the venue, and when we walk into the ballroom, I'm rendered speechless by how beautiful it is, with glistening golden lights reflecting off the polished floors and the lights of downtown reflecting in the windows. There's a DJ set up in one corner, a table bowing under the weight of canapés along one wall, and bowls of punch, which I suspect from the levels of rowdiness and screaming have been laced with something stronger than orange juice.

One couple are practically eating each other's faces off in the doorway, and we have to squeeze past them. Kit winks at me, and when we walk into the ballroom, I feel his hand slide gently down my back in a caress. It's just the lightest pressure but it electrifies my skin. I start to imagine his hands sliding under the dress and over my body and then that becomes all I can think about. When Riley asks what I want to drink, I just stare at him blankly.

"You want a drink?" he asks for the third time.

"Yes," I say.

He gives me a weird look before gazing around the room with a faintly furrowed brow. He doesn't look that impressed with the decor or the venue, and I bet he's thinking of the lost hours he could be spending with Jo. I wish he'd at least try to pretend to be happy to be here. I hardly ever get to see him anymore. After Dad's little drama the other night, Riley's been home even less.

He and Kit make a beeline for the bar, and Didi runs off to touch up her makeup in the bathroom, leaving me to stand there watching all the couples in various stage of making out, wondering how I'll be able to keep my hands off Kit for the whole night.

"Jessa?"

I spin around. A guy I don't recognize is standing behind me, smiling at me uncertainly. "Jessa Kingsley?" he asks.

"Yes," I say.

His smile widens. "It's me, Todd. Todd Hansler."

My mouth falls open as I suddenly place him.

"Oh my God. Todd. What are you doing here?" I shake my

head in amazement. The last time I saw Todd was back in sixth grade. We went to school together on the base at Panzer.

"We just got back from Germany," he starts explaining. "My dad took a desk job. He's working with your father now on the base at Pendleton."

I'm still trying to reconcile the memory I have of the short, overweight boy with buck teeth who used to read comics in the school cafeteria with the tall, athletic, and self-assured guy with perfect teeth who's standing in front of me now.

"Wow," I say, finding it hard to hide my surprise. "Oh my God. You're . . . I wouldn't have recognized you. How long has it been?"

He laughs. "I don't know. At least five years. You haven't changed a bit. I would recognize you anywhere." He takes a step back and his gaze sweeps up my body.

I shuffle awkwardly. "I'm not sure that's a compliment," I say. At twelve I wasn't exactly winning any beauty pageants.

"Oh, it is," he says. "Rest assured. You look great." I don't think I'm mistaking the look on his face when he says it, and it makes me blush.

"Who are you here with?" I ask, looking around and hoping to take the focus off me.

"Oh, some girl," he says dismissively.

"Who?" I ask.

"Stephanie Murphy. She's having a hair-and-makeup crisis in the bathroom."

"Oh," I say, wondering how he knows her and why he's come with her.

"So congratulations," he says, gesturing at the room. "Where are you going to college?"

"USD," I say with a forced smile, feeling that familiar pang of regret as I say it. "What about you?"

He grins at me. "USD too. Guess we'll be freshmen together." He pauses. "I'm going through Officer Candidate School at the same time."

"You're enlisting?" I ask, though I'm not surprised. Todd's family is a military family like mine.

"I'm hoping to get a commission once I finish college," he says.

"An officer, huh?" I say, trying to look impressed.

"Yeah," he says. "I heard Riley already enlisted."

"Yeah. He's a marine security guard now. He's back for a few weeks." I twist my head around to see if I can see him. "He's here somewhere. You should talk to him."

There's no sign of Riley, but I spot Kit walking toward me holding two drinks, his focus fixed firmly on Todd. When he reaches us, he hands me one of the drinks and stays standing right by my side, his arm brushing mine.

"Um," I say to Todd. "This is Kit, my . . ."

"Boyfriend," Kit finishes for me, holding out his hand for Todd to shake. His expression is pleasant and relaxed, but there's a bright hardness to his eyes that makes me duck my head to hide my smile. He's jealous. Todd looks surprised and throws a questioning look in my direction before turning back to Kit and taking his hand.

"Hi, good to meet you."

I see the tendons in Kit's arm grow taut and the tan skin of his hand pale as he squeezes Todd's hand in a Vulcan death grip of a handshake.

"This is Todd," I explain quickly, hoping I can get them to

release each other and make nice. "We knew each other when we were kids. We were on the base together in Germany."

"Right," says Kit, finally letting go of Todd's hand. Todd grimaces, flexes his hand, and lets it drop to his side.

"He just got back," I hear myself telling Kit. "He's going to OCS."

"Congratulations," says Kit, still holding Todd's gaze.

"You in the Corps?" asks Todd, though I can tell it's just a polite question, not an interested one.

"Yes. MSG," replies Kit.

"Impressive," Todd says with the smile of a politician. He nods at me. "I'll leave you to it. Better go find my date. It was good to see you again, Jessa. Let's catch up soon."

He kisses my cheek before walking away.

I turn to Kit, resting one hand on my hip.

"What?" he asks, shrugging at me.

"What was that?" I ask.

"What was what?"

"You just scared him off."

Kit takes a sip of his drink. "I didn't like the way he was looking at you."

"The way he was looking at me? He wasn't looking at me any way."

Kit almost spits his drink across the room. "He was looking at you like he was mentally undressing you."

I press my lips together. He might have a point.

"I'm sorry," he says, turning to face me, his voice soft and a small smile of apology forming on his lips. "I just don't like the idea of another guy looking at you like that. The only person I want to mentally undress you is me."

My heart gives a little leap. "Just mentally?" I whisper.

Kit steps even closer to me, and I get a waft of his aftershave. Why does he have to smell so damn good all the time? How am I supposed to keep my distance?

"Have I told you how beautiful you look tonight?" Kit says.

I smile at him. His focus is on my lips.

"If I don't get to kiss you soon there's no telling what might happen."

I glance over his shoulder. "Where's Riley?" I ask.

"Over at the bar, talking to the bartender."

I spot him. He has his back turned, thankfully. "Come on," I say to Kit.

"Where are we going?" Kit shouts over the music as he starts to follow me.

I weave my way through the dance floor, which is already crowded, making a beeline for the balcony. Outside a few couples are taking selfies against the skyline. I draw Kit to the far end, into the shadows behind a potted plant. We set our glasses down on a table and next thing I know Kit is pushing me backward against the wall. His hands slide up my sides and his lips find mine in the dark. There's a desperate hunger in our kiss, as though it's been years and not just a day since we last saw each other.

He grips me to him and I wrap my arms around his neck. His hand trails all the way down to my thigh and I hoist it up onto his hip and he holds me like that, pinned to the wall.

For a second he peels backward and looks at me, his face dark with desire. I'm glad I'm hanging on to him or I wouldn't trust my legs to keep me up. Behind him my classmates are setting off Chinese lanterns from the balcony. As they drift upward into the sky, they illuminate Kit's face, making his eyes glimmer with flecks of gold. He leans forward and kisses me again just as I make a wish that it will always be like this, that we will always want each other the way we do now.

"Shit, there you are!"

We burst apart like free divers coming up for air.

Didi's standing panting in front of us. "Riley's looking for you." She looks over her shoulder. "Shit, he's coming!"

She turns back around and lunges at Kit, using her thumb to wipe off the telltale signs of red lipstick smeared all over his face.

"Go hide," she orders me, waving her hands at me in a shooing gesture.

Not needing any more encouragement, I dart past her to the other end of the balcony, sliding into a group of girls who are all talking about college. It feels like I have two hearts in my chest, each trying to beat faster than the other. Out of the corner of my eye I see Riley appear in the doorway, carrying two drinks and frowning as he looks around. He spies Kit and Didi and marches toward them.

Kit

Riley appears in the French doors, scanning the balcony.

"Just go with this," Didi says.

I'm not sure what she means, but next thing I know she's throwing herself on me, laying a kiss on my cheek and putting her arm around my waist. I'm too stunned to do anything and when I look up, I see Riley has seen. He's walking toward us, shooting me a sniper death stare. Shit. Didi's hanging off me like a decoration on a Christmas tree. Maybe she's overdoing it. I wonder if Jessa is watching.

"Where's Jessa?" Riley asks, his expression stony. "I got her a drink."

"I think she's in the bathroom," Didi says. "I'll take that if it's up for grabs, though," she says, snatching the drink from Riley's hand.

Riley is still glaring at me. Catching the tension between us, Didi backs away. "I'm going to go find her," she says. She cuts me a panicked, apologetic look over Riley's shoulder before she disappears back inside.

"Dude," Riley says the moment she's gone. "Aren't you fucking some other girl?"

"I'm not fucking anyone," I spit back at him, furious for reasons I can't even decipher.

"Well, don't screw around with Didi. She's too good for you."

His words hit me like a punch to the gut and I take a half step backward. Did he really just say that? "What's that mean?" I ask, aware that my voice sounds calm, though inside my anger's brewing dangerously.

"Nothing," says Riley, seeming to realize what he just said. He shoots me an apologetic shrug, but I'm not about to let it go.

"No. I'm serious," I press. "What do you mean? You don't think I'm good enough for her?"

Riley slaps me on the shoulder trying to be all buddy-buddy. "She's eighteen. And she's probably never had a boyfriend before. She doesn't need some major player fucking with her and then dropping her when the next piece of ass comes along."

"Nice," I say. "You think that's what I'd do?"

Riley looks at me like he doesn't get why I'm so mad at him. "That's what you always do. You've never had a girlfriend before, Kit. I'm just telling it like it is."

"A guy can change," I say, grinding my teeth. "What if I told you I'm dating someone and that I really like her?"

Riley laughs at me like I just cracked a hilarious joke. "If you really liked her you wouldn't be here tonight making out with Didi. That's exactly what I'm talking about, bro."

"It wasn't my idea to be Didi's date. It was your girlfriend's. I was doing her and Jessa a favor. I'm not into Didi. And we weren't making out." I don't care if I'm blowing our cover—I'm so mad I can hardly see straight.

"Yeah? Not what it looked like," Riley smirks. "And she definitely looks like she's into you."

"It's not what you think." For a moment I almost come clean and tell him the truth, but his words are still smarting. Fuck him. Riley's my best friend, but right now I don't want to be anywhere near him.

"I'm going to check out the DJ," I tell him. "Maybe you could find Jessa. I think she'd like to spend some time with her brother while he's back. She misses you." With that parting shot I leave. He claims I wouldn't make a good boyfriend, but he's not exactly winning any prizes in the brother stakes.

I head back inside, my fists clenched with anger, my jaw tight. I told Riley to look for Jessa because I'm too mad to speak to anyone right now. I don't want to ruin her prom. I already acted like a possessive jerk. Problem was I just couldn't help it when I saw that guy looking at her like he wanted to dip her in hot sauce and eat her. I've never felt such a wave of possessiveness like that before about anyone. I probably shouldn't have introduced myself as her boyfriend, but what the hell else was I going to do? Let him flirt with her in front of me? Fuck. I hate this. I hate this pretending. And I hate Riley for making me question whether I'm good enough for his sister. I think about what my dad said, about telling him and her father. It's easy for him to say.

I head through the press on the dance floor, my feet carrying me toward the double doors that lead to the stairs and down to the lobby. I just want some quiet. There are couples making out like we're in some seedy lap-dancing club and a pile of sticky vomit on the stairs, so I head the other way toward the emergency exit.

This stairwell is blissfully free of both vomit and people. I figure I'll just head to the ground floor and take a quick walk to get my shit together before I head back inside, but halfway down the stairs I run slap bang into another couple making out with the kind of abandon that suggests they've forgotten they're in a public place. Was my prom like this? I don't remember. I was too busy getting laid in the back of my truck. With my head down I creep past them as silently as possible, but just as I pass them I hear the girl whimper. I whip back around.

The guy has her pressed against the wall, her dress is bunched up, and I can see her underwear. The guy is holding her around the waist with one arm and tackling his belt with the other.

"Get off," the girl mumbles.

"Oh, come on," the guy slurs. "Why else did you invite me?"

"I said stop," the girl says again, her voice infused with fear.

That does it for me. I grab the guy by the back of the collar and haul him off her, hurling him against the handrail. I grab a handful of his shirt and hold him in place, half hanging over the stairwell.

"She told you to stop," I growl.

The guy holds up both hands. "I wasn't doing anything," he says.

Out of the corner of my eye I see his hand form a fist and come flying toward me. I duck his punch, still keeping hold of him, and throw him against the wall, my fist slamming into his gut.

He folds over instantly. The guy looks like a football player, but his instincts are dulled by liquor. He stumbles forward then tries to rush me. I stick my leg out and trip him, then follow through with a right hook to his jaw. He crumples to the ground and starts moaning. This is just one of the reasons I don't drink, I think to myself wryly. I've never touched a drop of alcohol in my life, other than a beer when I was fourteen. I made a vow to myself after seeing my dad almost drink himself to death that I wouldn't ever follow in his footsteps, and in situations like this I'm doubly grateful.

I turn to the girl, take her hand, and pull her up a few steps, out of his way.

"Thank you," she says.

I turn to her for the first time. She's pulling the sleeve of her dress back up and wiping away tears, her mascara smudged down her face.

"You're welcome," I say, running my eyes down her dress to see if it was torn or if she's bleeding. She looks okay, just a little drunk and a little shaken up. "You want me to show you back upstairs?" I ask.

She smiles at me and nods, and we start heading back upstairs. I shoot one last look at the guy to make sure he isn't planning on a sneak attack, but he's now rolled onto his side and is clutching his stomach, looking like he's about to vomit.

"I'm Serena, by the way," the girl says to me as I open the door for her.

"Kit," I say.

"Thanks, Kit," she says, pausing, then kissing me on the cheek.

"Yeah," I say, wondering at how quickly she's moved from crying to flirting. "No problem."

"There you are!"

I look up. It's Jessa. She's walking toward me, and I can tell by the puzzled look on her face that she just saw Serena kissing me. Crap.

"Hey, Serena," she says with a frosty smile.

"Hi, Jessa," Serena says, looking from me to Jessa and figuring it out. "Oh, is this your date?"

"Yes," Jessa says firmly, coming to stand by me.

Serena smiles at her a little ruefully. "You got a good one, Jessa, hold on to him," she says.

Jessa's mouth does this cute little pout, and her brow furrows with confusion as she watches Serena walk away.

"What was that about?" I ask her.

"What was what about?" she asks, turning to face me.

"Were you jealous?" I ask, trying not to laugh.

Jessa's cheeks flush. "I just saw you walk out of a stairwell with Serena Riddell, the girl voted most likely to become a porn star, and watched her kiss you on the cheek."

"You *are* jealous," I say, laughing. "It's very hot, by the way. Keep it up."

"What were you doing?" she asks, still pouting.

"I was going for some air and I ran into your friend Serena—"

"She's not my friend," Jessa mumbles.

"—being mauled by some guy in the stairwell."

"Oh my God." Jessa's hand flies to her mouth. "What did you do?"

"I punched him."

"You punched him?"

"Would you rather I let him rape her?"

Jessa stares at me, her expression morphing into righteous indignation. "I hope you punched him in the balls."

I smile at her. "He won't be walking for a while," I say.

Jessa smiles at me—a smile that makes all my anger about Riley evaporate in an instant. Her eyes are strikingly green, made more so by the blue of the dress, and right now she's looking at me in a way that makes me feel like I'm more than good enough.

Jessa

It's around midnight when Didi bounces up to me and announces there's an after-party at Serena's house. Riley, who, to give him credit, has made an effort in the last four hours to at least look like he's having fun, shakes his head.

"I have to go. Jo's waiting."

"Well," Didi says, sliding her arm through his. "Thank you so much for being my date."

Riley looks down at her with a bemused expression on his face. "*Your* date?" he asks.

Didi hiccups. How much punch did she have? "I mean, Jessa's date. Obviously Jessa's date."

I press my heel into her foot to shut her up.

"Are you going to go to this party?" Riley asks Kit in a pointed way.

Kit looks at me. "Um, I don't know. I could drive them there. At least I'm sober."

"That would be awesome," I say, grinning at him, though I have no intention of going to a party at Serena's house.

Riley glares at Kit but then kisses me good-bye and heads off.

"Are you two really coming?" Didi asks. "You don't have to, you know. I can get a ride with Stephanie. She's leaving now."

"I'm supposed to be staying at your house tonight," I remind her.

"I'm sure you'll figure something out," Didi says, grinning at me.

Kit takes my hand without a word and leads me down the stairs to the lobby. I think maybe we're going to head outside and grab a taxi, head somewhere like the beach, but instead he walks brazenly up to the reception desk. In his suit, with his dark hair and perfectly sculpted body, he looks like a model in a Dior aftershave advertisement, and I let him pull me along, getting a brief thrill from the looks and the murmurs we're attracting from my school friends waiting for taxis in the lobby as they see us pass.

"Can I help you?" the perfectly made-up girl behind the desk asks.

"Your best suite, please," Kit says.

"What?" I almost shriek. I pull on his arm. "What are you doing?" I hiss.

He turns away from the receptionist. "I'm getting us a room."

"What?"

Before I can stop him, he's pulling out his wallet and slapping a card down on the counter. I grab it before the girl can. "That's ridiculous. It's like a thousand dollars a night here."

"It's three thousand five hundred dollars a night for the Presidential Suite," the girl says with a tight, smug smile.

I make an *I told you so* face.

"You're worth it," he responds, grabbing for his card.

I hold it behind my back and pull him away from the desk. "Kit," I whisper, "I'm not letting you spend that on a hotel room."

"Why not?" he asks.

"Because." I take a breath. "If you spend that much on a room, I feel like you'll expect something. . . ." I look away. I don't know how to explain it. It's not that I don't want to have sex with him. I do. It's just that I hadn't planned on it being tonight.

"Whoa, Jessa." Kit takes my face in his hands and tips my head up so he can look me in the eyes. The expression on his face is deadly serious. "That's not what I intended. If all we do is spend the night watching comedy-channel reruns, I'll be happy. I just want to hang out with you. We have a whole night, for once."

I look back at him, trying to read if that's the full truth.

"I promise you." He kisses me on the tip of my nose. "I'm fine with just mentally undressing you," he whispers.

I smack him on the arm. "Who says it has to be mental?" I say, pulling him back to the counter.

I convince Kit not to get the Presidential Suite—we don't need a living room and salon, after all—but the woman behind the desk upgrades us to a Deluxe Suite with a sly wink, and when we open the door to the room, we both turn to stare at each other before Kit sweeps me up into his arms, kicks the door shut with his foot, and carries me over to the enormous bed.

He lays me down gently before standing up to pull off his tie and jacket. He folds them over the back of the chair and then walks to the end of the bed and slides off my shoes, putting them down on the floor. I watch him, my chest rising and falling fast as my heart starts to race. He looks up and gives me a small smile, and something tugs at me. I'm suddenly nervous as hell, even though I know we're not going to have sex.

Kit comes and lies beside me. He places his hand on my waist, and for half a minute we just watch each other, lying on our sides, face to face. My breathing speeds up and butterflies cluster in my stomach. The look he's fixing me with is pure desire, but it's laced with something more, something deeper and more intense that makes my heart expand as though it's trying to squeeze past the bars of my ribs. He wants me, but he's also letting me know that he's happy with just this, that this is enough for him.

I place my hand on his cheek and trace his cheekbone and his jaw. He presses his lips to my palm and takes my hand, kissing my wrist and then slowly dropping kisses all the way up to my elbow. Little shivers shoot up my arm and neck. I close my eyes and draw in a breath as his lips brush my shoulder and he eases down the strap of my dress before tracing a line along my collarbone and neck.

Finally he reaches my lips and kisses me, slowly, tenderly. There's a fire in my belly and it spreads out, flames licking down my legs. A gentle throbbing echoes out from my core as his hands start slowly exploring their way down my body, following the curve of my hip and running down to my thigh. I roll against him, pushing my body against his, wanting to feel the hardness of his chest, the weight of him on top of me, but Kit takes my wrist and pins me flat to the bed, not with any force but enough to let me know he's taking control.

"Tonight," he says, looking down at me, "is all about you. I just want you to lie here and let me take care of you."

I can't speak—my heart is beating too fast and my lungs won't fill with air.

"I want you to know what you mean to me, okay?"

I try to protest but he cuts me off. "And if I'm going too fast, or you want me to stop, at any point for whatever reason, just say. Okay?"

I nod, not trusting myself to speak.

He leans over me once more and starts kissing me gently, his tongue twining with mine, teasing and sure, and after a while I relax, sighing as I sink into the bed. He nudges my head to one side and moves his attention to the spot just beneath my ear that he knows makes me squirm. His hands begin to wander down my dress. The satin feels like cool water flowing against my body, but Kit's hands sear heat through it, making me feverish, my skin so sensitive to the touch, it hurts. He sweeps his hand over my breast, surprising me, and I arch up with a cry, my nipple hardening.

He pulls the strap of my dress down and takes it in his mouth, and I have to clutch the sheets to hold myself down. His tongue traces patterns across my skin, and I let go of the sheets and run my fingers through his hair, gripping him by the shoulders as he sucks harder, making my stomach muscles contract tight and a low throb start up between my legs.

Kit sits up and pulls me up with him so we're both kneeling on the bed. I start undoing his shirt and he watches me the whole time, a strange look on his face, like he's having to fight every instinct in his body not to pick me up in his arms and toss me back onto the bed.

When I strip his shirt off and place my palms on his chest, he doesn't make any move, but his arms are locked tight by his sides and the muscles in his neck are taut as a bow. I lean forward and kiss him, breathing in deep, tasting his skin, but after a few moments he pulls back.

"Can I undress you?" he asks.

I nod, nerves making me gulp in breaths, which makes my head spin.

Kit reaches toward my knees and takes hold of the hem of my dress. Slowly he starts lifting it, running his palms along my thighs as he does. I lift my arms in the air and he slides my dress up and over my head. I keep my eyes closed, embarrassed and a little self-conscious. I'm kneeling in front of him, almost naked, and I can feel his eyes on me, as warm as his hands.

"Open your eyes," I hear him say.

I do. He's looking right at me. He takes my face in his hand and kneels closer. "You are so goddamn sexy, I could just look at you all night." He brushes my lips with his and then lowers me to the bed.

I'm so taut with expectation, so painfully, deliciously on edge, that when Kit starts stroking his hands across my stomach and breasts I think I'm going to burst into flames. Every time I try to reach for him he brushes my hand away. "It's just about you, remember," he murmurs, a smile in his voice.

He spends an age just stroking my stomach, caressing my breasts, dropping kisses on every inch of me . . . except for the one place I'm desperate for him to touch. I'm still wearing my underwear and I'm aching for him, so turned on that I wrap my arms around his neck and pull him down, desperate to feel his weight on top of me, to feel him next to me skin to skin. He groans and tries to pull away, but I hold on tight.

"I want you," I say.

"No," he answers. "Not tonight."

"Please," I hear myself say, and I can't believe I'm begging. My skin is burning; my eyes are burning; thoughts evaporate in my head faster than they arrive. I can't think straight; I just know that there's nothing I want more right now than Kit. I need him.

Kit kisses me, harder this time, and I feel his arousal, can feel how hard he is. He wants me too. I try to reach for him, but he scoots out of my arms and backs away with a playful smile on his lips.

I watch him through heavy lids. Stubble is darkening his jaw, and there are thin red lines across his chest where I've scratched him. I don't have time to process this before his hands are on my hips. I lift up without him even having to ask me and, keeping his eyes on me the whole time, he pulls off my underwear.

I bite my lip as I watch him, the muscles in his arms contracting as he lifts me, the wave of barely restrained desire that crosses his face. My hips lift of their own accord. Kit kneels between my thighs, parting them gently, and then he kisses me, right between my legs, and I let out a gasp of surprise and pleasure, pleasure that instantly ratchets up another notch as his tongue starts to circle and tease.

Holy . . .

I bite my lip even harder to stop myself from screaming out, my fingernails digging into his back. Within seconds Kit brings me to the brink of orgasm, my first with any guy, but as though he senses it he pulls back, stopping. I flop down onto the bed, letting out a moan, and after a moment, during which my heart batters against my ribs in frustration, his fingers start exploring where his tongue left off. When he pushes inside me for the first time, my eyes fly open and I rise up off the bed. He rubs me with his thumb, and again in seconds I'm on the brink, calling out his name. He stops abruptly once more, and I want to cry at the pleasure mixed with pain he's causing me. I'm blinded by how much I want to feel him inside me, but before I can reach for him, he bends again and, using his tongue, brings me to the most insane, body-melting, bone-crushing orgasm I've ever experienced.

I don't know how long it lasts, but I lie there feeling wave after wave of pleasure pulling me down into a hazy dreamland. I'm vaguely aware of Kit lying beside me, stroking my belly and dropping the occasional kiss on my shoulder as I shudder, my muscles still spasming. Slowly the world starts to press in again, and I become aware that I'm still lying naked, splayed on the bed. I curl onto my side, pressing against Kit, and he pulls me into his arms and kisses the top of my head.

It's only now that I start to become embarrassed. I just lay there. I didn't do anything. He must be so frustrated. Oh God. I reach for him.

"What are you doing?" he murmurs, his lips against my ear.

"I want to return the favor," I say, looking up at him.

He shifts out of my reach. "You don't need to," he says, taking my hand and kissing the palm. "That wasn't a favor. I loved it every much as you seemed to."

"Really?" I ask skeptically. The guy I hooked up with in London expected everything to be quid pro quo (definitely more quid than pro).

"Yes, that was just about the hottest thing I've ever experienced," Kit says, laughing under his breath. "I'm just lying here wondering when we get to go for round two."

"What?" I ask, propping myself up on one elbow.

"I want to make you come like that all night."

I feel myself flush. "No," I say, shaking my head. "It's your turn."

"That can wait."

"Why? Why are you doing this?" I ask, half in wonder and half petulantly.

Kit's jaw tenses and he frowns. "Because," he says, looking away, "I want to prove to you that I'm not what your brother thinks I am."

My breath catches. Is that what this is about? "I know you're not, Kit," I say softly, trying to pull his head back around so he's facing me.

His eyes flash at me. "Do you?" he asks, and I see the hurt in his eyes—put there by my brother—and the fear. He thinks I might believe it.

I nod. "I know exactly who you are, remember?"

There's a nakedness in his expression, a vulnerability I've never seen in Kit before. He's normally so confident and self-possessed.

"I've never felt this way before, Jessa," he says. "I don't want to fuck it up."

Kit

Jessa stares at me, her eyes welling with tears. She looks so beautiful and vulnerable, and I can't believe she gifted me her body the way she just did. I'm not going to screw it up, no matter how she looks at me, no matter what she says.

I get up from the bed.

"Where are you going?" she asks me.

"To run a bath," I say, grinning at her.

In the bathroom I switch on the hot tap, empty in all the bubble bath containers, and take a deep, deep breath. When that doesn't work I hold my head under the cold tap. I need to cool down. I can still smell her on me, taste her on my tongue, and it's driving me crazy.

When the bath's ready and I think I finally have a grip, I head into the bedroom. Jessa is still lying naked on the bed, and I have to pause in the doorway, all my resolve coming undone in an instant. I don't think I'll ever tire of seeing Jessa with no clothes on. She has no idea how beautiful she is. I like it that she seems to have abandoned her inhibitions, too. She seems to enjoy the way I look at her when she's naked, and there's a knowing smile playing on her face when she stands up and sashays toward me. I have to turn around. She's taunting me so badly. I know what she's trying to do. She's trying to make me relent.

I make her get in the bath first. Then I shrug off my pants and boxers. I'm not shy about my body. I work out a lot, and from the reactions I've had from the girls I've been with I know it doesn't disappoint, but seeing Jessa's face when I turn to face her, I wish I had a camera with me. She gulps and draws a huge breath before a dangerous smile spreads across her face.

She scoots forward in the bath and I climb in behind her, drawing her back against my chest, my thighs on either side of hers. Soapy, slippery Jessa is even more sexy than naked, sashaying Jessa, and I wonder why I thought I could keep the upper hand in this situation. She turns around to face me, her body half-obliterated with soap bubbles, and reaches beneath the water for me.

I jolt at her touch, half the bathwater splashing over the sides and onto the floor. I try to protest, but then she starts moving her hand and I sink down in the bath and give up trying to argue.

It isn't the end of things. After the bath, I get out wobbly-legged and wrap Jessa in a towel before leading her back to the bed. I dry her, taking my own deliciously sweet time, before starting all over again, enjoying how wet I can make her, how her body responds to my touch, arching and moving against me, how with each caress she grows bolder and less inhibited.

We fall asleep at dawn, wrapped in each other's arms, and the last thing I think to myself before sleep pulls me under is that there's nothing I wouldn't do for this girl. She owns me completely.

Jessa

Y ou were better than her. Way better."

I turn my head away from the stage and toward Kit. He's lying back on the picnic blanket, resting on his elbows, grinning at me with that Cheshire Cat grin. A look that makes me want to be the cream.

"I'm serious," he says, seeing my raised eyebrows. "You were. It was the first time I ever got Shakespeare. This was good, but the version you were in? Way better."

Around us most people have packed up their picnic baskets and blankets and are making their way to the exits, but Kit and I haven't made a move yet. I don't want this night to end. It's been the best birthday present ever.

"You even remember it?" I ask, lying down beside him. I can't believe Kit remembers a play I was in two years ago. "Riley fell asleep."

"Yeah, of course I remember it," Kit says. He leans over and brushes my hair behind my ear, something he does frequently, and one of the reasons I'm wearing my hair down more often. "You're good, Jessa, really good."

"And you're biased," I say, feeling my pulse speed up at his touch.

"But I'm right about this," he answers. "You love it, don't you? Acting, I mean."

I shrug and turn once more to the stage. "Yeah," I admit. "I love being up on stage." I think about how when the actors came on stage tonight I held my breath, how I got that tight-tummy sensation when the lights dimmed, how I was reciting Portia's speeches in my own head, wishing it were me up there instead. "I love the high I get from it," I say, turning back to Kit. "There's nothing like it."

He's watching me with that look he gets sometimes when I talk, his face lit up, and I get that tight-tummy sensation all over again, but for different reasons. "Well, actually that's not true," I say, shifting toward him, suddenly forgetting all about acting and thinking all about Kit naked. "There is something better."

Kit grabs my wrist and pulls me down on top of him. "Don't tempt me, woman," he growls into my ear. He kisses me on my forehead and we lie there, me with my head nestled on his shoulder, relaxing into each other's arms. It's been five days since our night together after my prom. With school out we're managing to spend most days together, though Kit has been training for his physical fitness test with Riley most mornings, and I've been doing some volunteering with Didi at the veterans hospital where her dad works. Our schedule goes something like lunch, driving lesson, making out. We've had a few full-on sessions on his single bed, mapping each other's bodies, getting more intimate than I thought was possible, but though we've come very close, we've still not had sex yet. Kit keeps on saying that there's no rush, though he's leaving in sixteen days so I beg to differ.

I think he might be planning something, though—he's king of the romantic gesture, after all. He turned up tonight with a bouquet of flowers and a picnic hamper stuffed full of goodies he'd made himself, and I have a collection of texts on my phone that would probably make any woman in the world swoon. He even managed to fix the Arabic setting on my iPhone, which makes it a whole lot easier to send him messages back.

"You should be an actress, Jessa," Kit says now, his hand stroking my arm.

I shake my head. "Who actually makes it as an actress? Everyone wants to be one. If you gave me a cent for every girl in California who dreams of becoming one, I'd be able to pay my own way through college. What are the odds of making it?"

Kit leans away so he can look at me. "So that's it? You're going to quit because there's a little competition?"

"I'm just being realistic. In this economy I need to get a degree in something that will guarantee me a job. Something like law or business."

"Wow." Kit's eyes bug.

I frown at him. "What?"

"Did your father make you rehearse that speech?" he asks.

I can feel myself scowling. "Kit, I'm just being practical," I say. I sit up and start packing up the picnic hamper. It's getting late, we need to go. I start shoving the container lids on, snapping them into place.

"Screw that," Kit says, sitting up. "You need to do what you're passionate about, what you love. Life's short, Jessa. You only get one shot. Make it count."

I glare at him. "And who's going to pay for it? I can't afford college unless my parents pay my tuition. And they won't pay for me to go to USC. And they certainly won't pay for me to do an acting class. I couldn't even take it as a minor. I can't take a loan either. How will I ever pay it back on waitress tips? Because that's what I'll end up doing—waitressing."

Kit watches me zip up the picnic bag. He waits until I finally look his way.

"If you knew you couldn't fail, would you do it then? If you knew for sure that it would pay off?"

"Yeah, of course," I say, standing up. "But that's a stupid question."

He springs to his feet and snatches the bag out of my hand. "Then you can't let money stop you. You're basically saying you don't believe in yourself enough to try."

"I don't, I guess." I start walking, tears blurring my eyes. Why are we even having this conversation? It feels like he's trying to pick a fight with me. And I don't want to fight. Kit steps in front of me, walking backward, blocking my path.

"I believe in you," he says.

I roll my eyes so he can't see I'm close to tears. "Can we change the subject?" I ask.

"Okay," he says, taking my hand and leading us back to his truck. "For now."

As we drive back to Oceanside, I think over what he's just said. Anger pumps through me. How can he expect me to pursue acting just because it's something I enjoy? It would be crazy and stupid. He has no idea what he's talking about. I like it that he believes in me, but he's blinded by bias.

I glance at him as he drives, the lights of oncoming traffic strobing across his face. "What about you? Are you doing what you love?"

He looks across at me before turning back to the road. "I was," he says.

"And now?" I ask in a whisper, because that's all I can manage.

"Now, I have to leave you."

He says it so matter-of-factly that it takes a while for the full meaning of what he's saying to sink in, and when it does, I feel as light as helium. "It's always been easy before," he says with a small shrug, his eyes back on the road. "I've never had anyone waiting for me back home."

"Who says I'm going to be waiting for you?"

He looks at me and I catch the trace of anxiety in his face.

"Just joking," I say quickly. "Of course I'm going to wait for you."

He shakes his head. "No. I don't want you to."

"What?" I ask, feeling as if I've just had lead injected into my veins.

"I mean . . . Fuck, Jessa. If you ask me do I want you to be waiting for me the day I get off the plane? Yes. Do I want to talk to you every night on the phone and know that you're my girl and that I'm coming home to you? Yes. Am I going to be thinking of you every single moment while I'm gone—yes. But it's not fair to you asking you to wait."

His hands are tight on the steering wheel, his knuckles white.

"You shouldn't have asked me to be your girlfriend then," I say, trying to sound calm, though on the inside I'm anything but. "Because I'm not going to stop caring about you or thinking about you or wanting you just because you're getting on a plane and we're not going to see each other for a while."

Kit gives a soft, sad smile. "It's a year, Jessa. You're going to college."

"So?" I ask, anger now making my voice shake. What's he suggesting? That I'm incapable of staying faithful? "Jo and Riley do it."

"Yeah," Kit answers. "And look how hard it is on her. On them both."

"But they love each other," I say, hearing the pleading note that's crept into my voice. I look away as soon as I say the words. Oh God. That came out wrong. I'm not saying I'm in love with him. That's not what I want him to think. Or is it?

Kit lapses into silence. I cringe against the door. After a moment he takes my hand across the seat and squeezes it, and I feel myself coming back to him. I know what he's doing. It's not that he doesn't want me. He's trying to protect me from hurt. He doesn't see that not being with him is going to hurt so much more.

"I want to do this," I say, twisting in my seat so I'm facing him. "It's not like I'm going to date anyone else. Who could ever come close?"

"You say that now," he says with a mocking half smile.

"Yeah," I say, determined to get through to him somehow. "And I'll say it in a year. You don't get it, Kit. You're all I thought about for nine months when you were gone, you're all I'm going to think about for the next twelve until you get back. I don't want anyone else. I just want you. That's not going to change."

He doesn't speak for a minute, he just frowns at the road, but gradually the frown fades and he shakes his head, a smile breaking on his lips. He looks across at me. "I don't deserve you," he says.

I lean over and kiss him on the cheek. "Yes, yes you do."

"I want to make you dinner tomorrow night," Kit suddenly

says. "Can you come?" He glances quickly at me, and I see the nervous way he swallows. My pulse quickens instantly.

"To your house?" I ask.

"Yes. My dad's going to my sister's to babysit. He's going to be gone all night."

"All night?" I ask, feeling the fizz of excitement in my stomach.

He nods. And I realize that maybe Kit was waiting to see whether we really had a future beyond these four weeks before he would allow himself to sleep with me. Maybe he never planned to if we were going to break up. As soon as the thought occurs to me, I know it's true. It would be just like him. All I can think is thank God I managed to convince him that we're staying together.

"Can you say you're staying over at Didi's?" he asks as he pulls over a block from my house. "I want you for the whole night."

I slide over toward him, slipping into his arms and letting him kiss me. I think that's answer enough.

Kit

I open the door to Jessa already feeling nervous, but when I see her standing there wearing a yellow sundress, it feels like there's a tornado ripping through my insides. I've never been nervous before with a girl, and even though we've had a few very X-rated sessions, tonight feels different. I want it to be perfect.

She gives me a shy smile, looking up at me through her lashes.

"Come on in," I say, stepping aside to let her in. My arms are shaking. Why are my arms shaking?

As soon as I shut the door, I pull her against me and kiss her, standing with my back against the door to steady myself. For a moment, when she twines her fingers in my hair and flattens her body against mine, I contemplate just forgetting dinner altogether and carrying her straight upstairs, but then I force myself to stop. One step at a time.

I link my fingers through hers and pull her into the kitchen, where pots are bubbling on the stove. She offers to help, but I sit her on a stool in the middle of the room and open the refrigerator, pulling out a bottle of champagne.

"What are we celebrating?" she asks when I hand her a glass.

"Us," I say, clinking my glass of water with hers.

"You aren't having any?" she asks.

"I don't drink," I say.

She nods thoughtfully and doesn't ask anything further. She knows the reason why, and I love it that she doesn't need to ask questions. She takes just a sip from her own glass and then sets it down on the side.

I start prepping the salmon I'm cooking and check on the vegetables that are roasting in the oven. My mind's struggling to remember the recipes, though, with Jessa sitting there watching me.

"Have you seen much of Riley?" I ask, trying to distract myself from the very graphic thoughts of what I plan to do to her later.

"No," she says, "not much. He's pretty much living with Jo. He comes back for dinner." She shrugs. "I think you see more of him. How's training going?"

"Good," I say, thinking of the workouts I've been doing all week, partly as a way to let off steam in the buildup to tonight, and partly so I get to kick Riley's ass in the physical fitness test we have to take soon. "Test is in two weeks. Same day as yours."

"What?" Jessa asks.

"Your driving test. I've booked you in."

Jessa stares at me. "What? I'm not ready."

"Yeah, you are. And it was the only slot they had before I leave." I shrug and turn back to the stove.

"But . . ."

"If you pass, you pass," I say over my shoulder. "If you fail, you fail. No biggie. You can take it again."

Jessa presses her lips together, and I can see she's trying to think up excuses, but then she nods and says, "Okay."

I smile to myself as I start pan-frying the salmon. "You know, Riley keeps asking about the girl I'm seeing."

I hear Jessa slide off the stool. She sidles up behind me and slips her arms around my waist. "He does, huh?"

"That thing with Didi—taking her to prom—didn't help. He can't believe I'm serious."

"What did you tell him?" Jessa asks.

"That it's going great. That I'm digging this chick. That she's amazing."

She laughs against my back.

"He wants to meet you," I say.

Jessa releases me and leans up against the counter. "My mom asked me the other day if there was anything I wanted to tell her."

"What do you mean?"

"She said I was glowing and if she didn't know better she'd think I was in"—she stops abruptly, her cheeks flushing—"um . . . a relationship."

I turn my attention back to the pan, but my heart is beating faster all of a sudden. "What did you tell her?" I ask.

"That I was just happy school was out."

A weight settles on my shoulders, dampening the happiness I'd been feeling. I set the fork down on the side and turn to face her. "I want to tell everyone, Jessa. I'm sick of this."

She stares up at me with those big green eyes and rests her hand against my cheek. "Me too," she says softly. "But we only have two weeks. I don't want them ruined."

I look at her long and hard for moment before turning back to the food.

* * *

The table's set with candles and flowers and my mom's best china. My dad gave me license to use it. He knows exactly what I have planned—I couldn't exactly keep it a secret. I think he contrived the excuse of going to my sister's, because when he told me he was spending the night there he winked at me and told me not to burn any pans or get anyone pregnant while he was gone. He hasn't mentioned anything more about telling Riley, which is a relief, though it nags at me. It's why I brought it up with Jessa. But if she doesn't want to tell him, I can't exactly come out with it. It's just hard sneaking around all the time. I want to walk down the street with her; I want to be able to take her out to dinner and go to the beach without being paranoid someone's going to see us.

"That was so amazing. You could be a chef," Jessa says, pushing away her finished plate and patting her stomach.

"That was always my fallback," I say, clearing the plates to make way for dessert.

"Your what?" she asks, getting up to help.

"For when I get out of the corps."

"To become a chef?" she asks.

I set the plates down in the kitchen. "To open my own restaurant, maybe just a small café to start with, something cool, great coffee, awesome vibes, great music."

Jessa leans against the countertop. "I can picture it now," she says, grinning at me.

I forget about the dessert. I can't stop my eyes wandering over her body, barely constrained by her dress, from starting to imagine what it will be like to undress her later, to finally get to make love to her. I take a step toward her and pull her to me, holding her hands. Now's the time to tell her.

"Jessa," I say, stroking her hair behind her ear. "I think this one will be my last tour. My four years are up after this."

Her smile fades. "You're going to leave?" she asks.

"Well, they have you on nonactive duty for four years and they can call you back up at any time, but I'd be out, yeah."

"Really?" she asks, and I see the start of a smile pulling at the edge of her mouth.

"Yeah," I say.

"Why?" she asks. "I thought you loved it."

I shrug. "Things change. My dad's not getting any younger. I've got other dreams I want to pursue." I pause. Does she realize she's one of them? "I guess I got into the marines because I was following my old man, and because I wanted to be the best of the best, to know that I could beat the best. And I've done that. I've served my country, I've done my part. But some of the shit I've seen . . . I'm tired of it. I want to start a new chapter. I want to try staying in one place as well as one piece, and being master of my own destiny. I guess I'm just done with following orders and I want something new."

"Kit?" she interrupts.

"Yeah?" I ask, realizing I haven't taken a breath.

Jessa stares up at me solemnly. "Take me to bed."

Jessa

Kit stares at me for half a second processing what I've said, then without a word he takes my hand and leads me out of the kitchen and up the stairs. My legs start shaking, half with nerves and half in anticipation of what's to come. I can't believe he's going to quit. For me. No, not just for me, I remind myself, but I know I'm part of the reason why, and the knowledge makes me lightheaded and light-blooded, too. Is that even a thing? It feels like it should be. My blood feels as if it's infused with light particles.

A life. We could actually have a life together. A normal life. Seeing each other every day, dating like a normal couple, maybe not even in secrecy, because I feel with Kit beside me every day I would be brave enough to face anything, even my father's wrath.

At the door to his room, Kit pauses and turns to me. "Close your eyes," he says.

I look at him suspiciously. "Why?"

"Because I've got a surprise to show you."

"I've seen it already." I smirk.

"Not that. Man, you're filthy," he laughs, covering my eyes

with his hand. I hear him open the door and then he ushers me inside his room. Finally he moves his hand.

"Oh my God," I say, staring at the brand-new double bed that's replaced his old single one. "You bought a double bed?" I spin to face him.

"Yeah," Kit answers with a smug grin. "A single bed wouldn't be big enough for all I have planned for you."

I walk toward it. He didn't just buy a double bed—it would seem he also bought a thousand pillows and a feather comforter.

"New sheets and everything. One hundred percent Egyptian cotton. That's supposed to be the best," he says proudly. "I even redecorated."

I tear my eyes off the bed and stare around the room in amazement. He's not lying. He's painted the entire room a beautiful warm shade of white, removed the shelf with all the trophies and replaced it with a bookshelf, and exchanged the dresser with an antique chest of drawers. A vase filled with wildflowers sits on the top. Candles litter the bedside table. Tears spring to my eyes, and I know it would be pathetic and girly of me to cry over this, but I think it might just be the most romantic gesture anyone has ever made in the history of romantic gestures.

"I don't know what to say," I stammer as Kit continues to grin at me. Then I realize something. "What did your father think?" I ask.

"He's cool with it. I explained everything."

"Everything?" I ask in alarm.

"No, I don't mean about tonight." He takes a step toward me. "I told him I wanted this to be your room too. When I'm away. I want you to feel like you have somewhere to come to. I want to be able to picture you here, in my room. When I'm pulling an all-night shift I want to be able to imagine you naked in my bed back home, waiting for me."

My mouth drops open. "And he's cool with that?" I ask.

"Oh yeah," says Kit, still grinning so wide I can see his dimple. "I didn't tell him about the naked part, though."

I poke him in the ribs.

"He even wanted me to give you this." He rummages in his pocket and pulls something out.

"What is it?" I ask, seeing full well that it's a key ring with two keys on it.

"A key," he says.

"To your house?" I ask, staring at him in amazement.

"Yeah. I want you to be able to come and go as you please. And so does my dad." He takes my hands in his, pressing the keys into my palm. "So if things ever get out of hand at home or you need to just escape, you can come here."

I'm trying really hard not to cry. I swallow the lump that's wedged in my throat. "What's this other key for?" I ask in a hoarse voice.

"That's for my truck."

I look at him in disbelief. "Your truck?"

"Yeah, I put you on the insurance. And I also installed AC, seeing how you don't like your hair getting all messed up when the windows are down."

I stare at him, speechless. I have no idea what to say. Finally I just reach up on tiptoe and kiss him. "I don't know what I did to deserve you," I whisper.

Kit pulls away so he can see my face. "I know it's not what you signed up for. Dating a marine. Not seeing me for twelve months."

I kiss him to shut him up.

"So you like it?" he asks, gesturing around at the room.

"I love it," I say.

Kit steps forward and takes my face in his hands. "I love you," he says.

My heart, which is already beating like crazy, bursts in my chest like a rocket. I don't get to answer him before he kisses me, tipping my chin up with his hand.

I melt into him, instantly undone, and loop my arms around his neck. When he picks me up and lays me down on the bed, I'm aware of nothing except for the cool softness of the sheets against my back, the warm solid feel of Kit pressing me down into the mattress, and the electric caress of his hands against my body. God, I'm so ready for this, for him.

It becomes a struggle for air, for touch, for closeness. An urgency takes hold of us as we tear at each other's clothes. I rip off Kit's T-shirt, desperate to feel his skin against mine, and he tugs me to my knees and pulls my sundress off over my head in one swift move. I'm not wearing a bra and he lets out a groan and pulls me toward him, his hand in the small of my back, his other hand cupping my breast. His lips find my nipple and suck, making me cry out and grip his shoulders.

We tumble back onto the bed and I scrabble to undo his belt. He kicks off his jeans and underwear before easing mine off. I look up at him, breathing hard as he stands at the end of the bed looking down at me. I'm already ready and I reach for him, but Kit gives me a sly smile and shakes his head. Oh God. My stomach contracts in anticipation as I watch him lower his head and start to kiss his way up my legs. My bones dissolve, every cell in my body igniting in a chain reaction. My nerve endings are frayed electrical wires. Every touch of his lips sends up a spray of sparks that travels all the way to the tips of my fingers and toes. I grab hold of the brand-new covers on the bed and hear myself moaning as Kit parts my legs and keeps kissing me until my head spins.

He has me in the palm of his hand, and the ache in my core is a tight, sweet pull that quickly becomes a throb. He trails another wave of kisses across my belly, and by the time he reaches my neck and starts kissing the spot just beneath my ear, I'm almost in tears I'm so frustrated, aching for him to be inside me. My body is arched painfully, taut as a bow, my breathing ragged.

"Kit," I say.

He kisses my lips, silencing me, and then I hear him reaching for something on the nightstand. I keep my eyes closed as he rolls on a condom, and only when he settles over me, resting his weight on his arms, do I open my eyes. He's watching me, waiting for me to give permission. I nod, and he presses slowly against me, guiding himself in, the whole time watching me carefully. I inhale sharply at the sudden pain and then again at the wave of pleasure that follows quickly in its wake. He stops, and I can tell he's scared of hurting me. He knows I'm a virgin. I wrap my legs around his waist and hold on to his shoulders, urging him on. He pushes harder, easing fully into me with a groan, and I let out a gasp as he fills me completely. I rake my hands down his back, not wanting him to stop. "You feel amazing," he whispers in my ear as he slowly, gently builds up a rhythm that makes me gasp for breath.

He kisses my neck, my lips, my breasts, and I run my hands over his rock-solid stomach and chest, and though it stings for a moment, soon I forget everything except the feel of him, his weight on top of me, the pure strength of his body.

I feel like he owns me, like I own him, like I never want to let him go. Within seconds, I start to feel a fire spreading through my limbs, a crazy, intense spiraling of pleasure that he stokes with every stroke, until I feel like I'm going to burst. Kit moves faster and I raise my hips and move against him, wanting more of him, all of him.

His eyes are half closed, and a trail of sweat snakes down his chest.

"I love you," I tell him, the words falling past my lips just as everything builds to an exquisite point and I come. I collapse backward onto the bed, crying out, and Kit collapses down on top of me, breathing hard.

Little sparks travel down my legs. I stroke my hands through Kit's hair and trail a hand down his spine, feeling deliciously languid and loose-limbed, loving the feel of his body sinking into mine. I trace the muscles across his shoulders and back and shiver as another wave of pleasure rocks through me.

After a few moments he starts to roll off me, but I hold him in place. I don't want him to go anywhere. Instead he wraps his arms around me and rolls with me in his arms so I'm lying on top of him, my head on his shoulder, our limbs entwined. For several minutes we stay like that, neither of us speaking, our hearts slamming into each other.

"Fuck," Kit says, a laugh in his voice, "that was amazing." He kisses my forehead. "Are you okay? Did I hurt you?"

I open my eyes, though it feels as though they're made of lead. "Are you kidding?" I ask. "Now I know what all the fuss is about. When can we go again?"

Kit

We make love once more, this time slower—I'm aware she must be sore, though she claims not to be—and then once again in the small hours of the morning, both of us drowsily breaking out of sleep and reaching for each other. Each time is better than the last, even though each time I'm pretty sure it couldn't possibly get any better. I get her to tell me exactly what she likes, how she wants to be touched, and she does the same with me until it feels like we know each other in ways no one else will ever or could ever come close to knowing.

I wake in the morning when a slat of sunlight breaks through a crack in the curtain. The first thing I become aware of is the warmth of Jessa's naked body pressed against mine, and instantly I'm aroused. Oh man. At this rate I'm going to be walking like John Wayne.

Jessa mumbles in her sleep and pushes back against me. I take a deep breath, trying to imagine what it would be like to wake up to her in my arms naked like this every morning. I can't believe we've only got two weeks left. The chances of us getting to spend another night together like this one are slim to none—Didi's going on vacation with her parents, so Jessa won't be able to use the excuse of staying over at her house—so I close my eyes and revel in the moment. This night is going to be what gets me through the next year.

I press a kiss to Jessa's shoulder and she rolls over so she's facing me, her eyes still closed. "Is it morning?" she asks with a smile on her lips.

I kiss her, all the while thinking *this girl loves me*. She loves *me*. "Yes," I tell her.

She sighs and opens her eyes. Even though they're shadowed from lack of sleep, they're sparkling bright, and I'm struck by the look in them. It's as if she's transformed overnight—at my hands, I remind myself a little smugly—into a total seductress without a trace of innocence left about her. Her hair is in total disarray, her cheeks flushed. She looks well and truly ravished. "I wish we could stay in bed for the next two weeks," she says, pouting, "until you have to go."

"I think if we did that, neither of us might ever walk again," I say, laughing. "Are you hurting at all?"

She shakes her head and then makes a face, biting her bottom lip. "Maybe a little." Her hand, however, still reaches under the covers for me. I push my head back into the pillow. Oh man.

Later on, as we lie there, willing the clock to slow down, Jessa rolls onto her side to face me, resting on her elbow.

"You wouldn't have slept with me, would you," she asks, "if I'd said I didn't want to date you beyond these four weeks?"

I shake my head at her. So she figured it out. "No," I say. "Why?"

"Because it wouldn't have been fair to you," I say. "And then, selfishly, I knew that if I slept with you, then for the whole of the next year on post I would never have been able to get you out of my mind. I'd have just relived it over and over every second of every day. Which is what I'm going to be doing now anyway." I laugh ruefully at how much I'm going to replay this night. "But I would have been picturing some other lucky guy getting to have you, getting to come back to you every night. I didn't want that. It would have been torture. To know you, to make love to you, and then lose you. I couldn't do it."

Jessa watches me for a few moments and I stare back at her. Then she leans down, her hair tickling my face. "You're never going to lose me," she murmurs against my lips.

Jessa

Over the next few days, Kit and I steal every chance we get to make love. I can't get enough of him and it seems he feels the same way, because we pretty much work through every position known to man. When I'm not with him, I can still feel him, the lingering echo of his weight pushing into me, the imprint of him on my skin. Butterflies skirmish in my stomach just thinking about him. My mom makes more comments about how happy I look, and I think she's fishing for info. Didi begs for details, but I just grin and tell her it's even better than they make it look in the movies.

I even manage to ignore my dad's moods. They bounce off me as though I'm wearing a suit of armor. The only thing that ever threatens to derail my happiness is when I think about how little time we have left. We're on the downhill slope. There are just twelve days to go before he ships out.

I'm counting them off on my calendar when Riley sticks his head around my bedroom door.

"Hey," he says, "Kit just called. It's his dad's birthday today and they're having a party for him at his cousin's. He wants to know if we want to go."

For a moment I stare at Riley blankly. I knew it was Kit's dad's birthday, but I didn't know they were having a party.

"If you don't feel like it, I can tell him you're busy or something. He said his dad wanted to invite you, though."

His dad wanted to or Kit wanted to? I have to hide my smile from Riley.

"So, you want to go or not?" Riley asks, his fingers drumming the door. "It'll be fun. We can tell Mom we're going to the beach or something." He pauses. "You know, we haven't had much chance to hang out together since I got back."

He noticed? Or did Kit have a word with him and suggest he spend more time with me? He gives me a hopeful smile crossed with an apologetic shrug, and so I say, "Sure. Yeah, sounds good," trying to keep my voice and my face neutral.

Riley looks pleased. "Okay. Ready to go in thirty minutes?"

I nod. I'd planned to sneak out of the house and see Kit later this afternoon—but now I get to spend the whole day with him, and the fact that it's not in private is made up for by the fact that I also get to hang out with Riley. And any extra time I get to spend with both of them is a bonus, given how quickly the days are tripping past.

I grab my phone to check the time. There's a message flashing. It's from Kit. "Coming?" is all it asks.

I don't answer. I'm going to keep him hanging.

Forty-five minutes later Jo, Riley, and I rock up to Kit's cousin's house on the other side of town. There are streamers and balloons outside and music floating through the open windows along with the delectable smell of grilling meat.

The door's wide open and inside it's jumping. At first I'm overwhelmed by the noise: music, chatter, shrieking children, laughter. If you were to create an atmosphere that was the polar opposite of my own birthday party, then this would be it.

Kit's family is boisterous and loud—and, it strikes me as I look around the room, happy. This is what a family should be like, I think to myself sadly. Riley catches my eye as we walk through the room, and I know from the smile he gives me that the same thought is passing through his mind. He puts his hand on my shoulder and squeezes, and I wonder if I should just tell him about Kit and me. If he could see how happy Kit's making me, how being with him gives me a chance to be part of a family like this, then surely he'd be okay with it?

Next thing I know, though, I'm swept up by Kit's sister, Tessa, who I haven't seen for over a year, since the last send-off for Kit and Riley. She's a smaller, prettier version of Kit, with the same deep dimples that suggest mischief, and piercing blue eyes that light up the moment she sees me. She links her arm through mine and drags me toward the kitchen.

"So, a little bird tells me that you and Kit are a thing," she whispers in a stage voice that could match Didi's for subtlety.

Alarmed, I glance over my shoulder, scared that the whole room just heard her announcement, but Riley and Jo are busy chatting with some of Kit's cousins, and thankfully the music is so loud it seems to have drowned her out.

"It's okay," she says, seeing my anxiety, "your secret is safe with me." She winks at me and points through the kitchen window at Kit, who's busy manning the grill. "I've never seen him so happy," she says, and indeed he does look happy, laughing with his cousins as he flips burgers. "Whatever you're doing," she says, patting me on the shoulder, "keep doing it."

My cheeks instantly flare red, because the very first thought that leaps into my head is of Kit and me having sex, and I want to reassure her she doesn't need to worry about us ever stopping that.

Tessa turns then to pick up her toddler daughter, who's making a beeline for the back door waving a plastic cooking utensil in her ketchup-stained hand. When I turn back to the window, I notice Kit is looking my way. He shoots me a grin and I make a face at him.

"There you are! So glad you made it!"

I spin around to find Kit's dad standing with arms spread wide and a grin on his face to match Kit's. I step into his arms and hug him, feeling a momentary pang of sadness that I find it easier to hug Kit's dad than I do my own.

"Happy birthday!" I say, pulling out a card from my bag.

He takes it and kisses my cheek. "You are a sweet girl, Jessa Kingsley. My son hit the jackpot with you."

I can't help but smile, because I feel exactly the same way about Kit.

"Who hit the jackpot?" Riley asks, appearing with perfect timing at my side.

"No one," I say quickly.

"Did you get something to eat?" Mr. Ryan adds, helpfully distracting Riley with the one thing that's always guaranteed to distract him: food. He starts ushering us out into the garden, giving me a pointed look as he does. I know he wants Kit and me to come clean with Riley, and I start to wonder if inviting us all here wasn't just a big ruse. Now I think about it, in fact, it seems like the most likely scenario. And it's only confirmed when he steers us straight toward Kit and then stands there beaming at all of us as though he's brokering peace talks between warring countries.

Kit chooses to ignore him and starts serving us food, deliberately avoiding eye contact with me as he does. I hang back until the others have moved on with their plates and are looking for somewhere to sit.

"Hot dog?" Kit asks me, holding one up with his tongs and trying his hardest to keep an innocent expression on his face.

"Maybe later," I answer with a smile, unable to stop myself from staring at his lips. "I'll take a burger, though."

He drops one on my plate, and I move on quickly before he can offer to cover it in ketchup and before Riley or Jo pick up on the sparks that are flying not just from the grill.

Kit

I watch Jessa walk across the garden toward Riley and Jo. She glances over her shoulder as she sits and throws me a sly smile, and I get a tightening in my gut in response. A big part of me is totally turned on by the fact that she's right in front of me and I can't touch her, can't run my hands over her body, can't kiss her. And I know that Jessa's getting off on it too. Even now she's turning side on to me and deliberately flicking her hair over her shoulder so I can see the spot on her neck where I like to kiss her.

She's giving me an unparalleled view of her legs as well, and I wonder if she chose to wear that particular sundress for a reason. It's the same one she wore the night we first slept together, and all I can picture when I see her in it is how I slid it off her that night and how she wasn't wearing a bra underneath. She's trying to torment me. Damn. It's probably punishment for my not warning her about today. Though that wasn't my fault. I had no idea Sunday lunch was going to be co-opted into a birthday party and that my dad would then insist on inviting both Jessa and Riley to it.

Despite how much fun it is to be forced to admire the goods from afar and not touch them, I'm also dying to walk right over to her, pull her to her feet, and kiss her into next century. Maybe, I reflect, the time to come clean is now. It's why my dad set this whole thing up in the first place, after all.

I hand the grill tong to my cousin Matt and head over to join Jessa.

I'm not sure what I plan to do, but I don't get to find out, because before I'm even three stops from them, Jo's on me. "So who's this girl, then?" she asks.

"What girl?" I ask, aware of Jessa turning to look at me.

"Riley says you're seeing someone," Jo says, smiling at me.

"Boning someone," Riley snickers, taking a bite out of his burger.

"Dude. I'm not—" I break off because I don't want to say the word *boning* in front of Jessa and also because I'd be lying anyway.

Riley's eyebrows leap up his forehead. "Oh, come on . . . it's us. You're not usually so shy about sharing all the details."

Out of the corner of my eye I see Jessa tip her head so her hair falls in front of her face, hiding her expression. Oh man.

"I'm dating her," I say, glaring at Riley. "It's not like that. It's . . . different."

"So you're not boning her?" Riley asks, burger juices trickling down his chin he's laughing so hard.

"Oh my God! He's blushing!"

I glower at Jo, who only laughs more, which makes my face get even hotter.

"So when do we get to meet her?" Jo asks teasingly.

"I'm not sure," I stutter, having to fight the urge to look at Jessa.

"Is she pretty?"

"Can't be," interjects Riley, "otherwise he'd be showing her off."

"She's beautiful," I say. "Totally stunning."

"So why can't we meet her then?" Jo asks, eyes narrowed. "What's the deal?"

"She's busy. Couldn't make it today."

"Dude," smirks Riley, "you're being as coy as a Disney princess. What's going on?"

"Nothing. I told you, she's busy that's all."

"Oh, let's leave him alone," Jo laughs. "Maybe he doesn't want to introduce you, Riley, because he's scared she'll run for the hills when she realizes what kind of company he keeps." She turns to Jessa. "What about you, Jessa? Were there any cute boys at prom?"

Jessa pushes her hair behind her ear. "Nope," she answers, taking a sip of her drink. "Not a one." I make a note to self that Jessa is a really good liar, though there's a telltale flush to her cheeks that gives her away if you're looking for it.

"What about that guy Todd?" Riley asks, and I find myself turning to stare at Jessa, waiting for her response.

She throws back her head and laughs. "No way," she says. "Not my type."

"Well, you just make sure your type knows your brother is a marine with a big gun."

Jessa rolls her eyes. But she's still smiling. I don't think she minds Riley's overprotectiveness, despite her protestations. If anything, she enjoys it. Jo, though, is looking curiously between Jessa and me, and I'm wondering if she's starting to put it together. Surely everyone can see the crazy chemistry between us.

I stand up before I do or say something that gives us away.

"The burgers are calling," I say walking back toward the grill. "Don't forget your hot dog later," I add, shooting a glance in Jessa's direction.

Satisfyingly, her cheeks flush even redder.

Jessa

As arranged, Kit picks me up after lunch from the hospital where I'm volunteering, and I take the wheel. I'm getting good thanks to our daily lessons. Today Kit makes me drive all the way to San Diego. It's only when he starts giving me directions that I realize we're not randomly driving around, we're heading somewhere.

"Where are we going?" I ask.

"Surprise," he answers.

"I know your kind of surprises," I say.

"You won't guess this one," he replies, indicating at me to pull over.

I look out the window. We're parked on Congress right beside the park. Kit jumps out of the truck and I follow suit, immediately intrigued.

"Where are we going?" I ask again as he leads me into the park.

"Promise you're not going to kill me and I'll tell you."

My heels dig into the ground. "What?" I ask. I have visions of Riley and Jo waiting for us.

"We're going to the theater."

"We are?" I say. "Cool. Why would I kill you?"

"For an audition."

I yank my hand from his and come to a halt. "What?"

"They're holding open auditions for an Oscar Wilde play." Kit looks at me, his expression a mixture of nervous and excited.

"Kit," I say, shaking my head, "I can't do it. I haven't prepared anything."

"You told me you remembered all the lines from the play you were in."

I stare at him. Is he insane? My heart is beating as fast as a hummingbird's wings. "But I haven't had a chance to practice," I argue.

Kit takes my hands. "Nothing like being thrown into the lion's den. Look, what have you got to lose?"

"My dignity?"

He laughs. "Come on, just do it. Even if you don't get a part, at least you'll know you tried." I pull my hand from his and cross my arms over my chest. "And if you do it," he says, giving me a look I know full well. "I will take you home and give you a multiple orgasm."

I draw in a breath, my body reacting to his words even though my mind is still adamant that I'm definitely not going to do this. "That's so unfair," I hiss.

He steps nearer and takes my hands again. "I'll kiss you all over," he murmurs, kissing my neck, "just the way you like, paying extra-special attention to . . ."

"Okay! Okay! I'll do it."

He pulls away, grinning at me. "Sexual bribery," he says. "What else can I get you to do?"

* * *

Backstage is so crowded with people doing vocal exercises and reciting monologues that I immediately freak out and try to walk away, but Kit is standing right behind me, and he catches me by the shoulders, spins me around, and marches me over to the sign-in desk.

He gives them my name and then leads me to an out-of-the-way corner, where I sit down and start hyperventilating. "I'm going to kill you later," I say.

He puts his arm around me. "Before or after I give you that multiple orgasm?"

"You're so . . ." I glare at him, but I can't stop the smile. Even though I'm as nervous as hell, I've also got butterflies raging inside me, the good kind of butterflies, the kind that let you know you're alive. It's the same buzz I always get before I step on stage, a feeling that's addictive, but which I'd tried to pretend I could live without. And only now do I realize I don't want to. Kit's right.

I start running through the only monologue I can remember, from *The Merchant of Venice*, praying it's enough. When they call me, Kit squeezes my hand and kisses me on the cheek. "Knock 'em dead," he says.

I figure that the worst that can happen is that I make a fool of myself. When I walk out onto the stage and stare out over the auditorium, my heart leapfrogs into my mouth. How am I here? Doing this?

Four shadowy figures in the middle of the front row point me to a cross marked out on the stage and order me in bored voices to begin. It feels like I'm on *The X Factor*. I swallow dryly and take a deep breath, trying to sink into the role of Portia. Then I start.

When I finish, a silence saturates the room. No one says anything, and immediately a sinking feeling weighs me down. Oh crap. Blood rushes to my face, my heart beats hollowly in my throat, and I spin on my heel and stumble toward the wings, but I'm not even halfway there before a voice calls me back.

"Could you read from this?" the person asks in a clipped voice. I see whoever it is holding something out, and I walk over and take it. It's the script for *The Importance of Being Earnest*. I glance down at the highlighted pages, feeling a flicker of excitement that I try to tamp down, and walk back to the X.

After fifteen minutes they dismiss me, telling me that they'll call.

"How'd it go?" asks Kit the minute I step backstage.

I shrug. "I have no idea," I answer. "They said they'll call. I think they say that to everyone, though."

"How do you feel?" he asks as we step outside into the sun.

I stop and turn to him, throwing my arms around his neck. "I feel amazing. I don't even care if I don't get a callback. It was fun. Thank you. Thanks for making me do that."

"You can thank me after," he says.

In the truck on the way home I think of where I'd be and what I'd be doing without Kit in my life. I would never have gone to that audition. I would never have learned to drive. I would never have discovered this bold, brave, fearless side of me. I'd never have come close to feeling this happy. I'd never be on my way to a multiple orgasm.

Kit

Two days after Jessa auditions, the doorbell rings just as I'm finishing up a weight session in the basement. I jog up the stairs and find Jessa flinging open the door. I love it that she has a key and is starting to use it. It feels like we're living together when I see her coming in the door like this.

She's bursting with excitement. Behind her I see her bike thrown haphazardly on the lawn, the wheels still spinning. She biked over? She throws herself on top of me. "I got it! I got the part!" she screams.

I pick her up and spin her around. "I told you!" I say triumphantly. "Didn't I tell you?"

She squeezes me around the neck like a boa constrictor. "Kit, I can't believe it. Thank you. Thank you." She starts covering my face in kisses. "It's not the main part or anything, but it's a professional production! And I'm in it!"

I pull her toward me and kiss her on the mouth. Her excitement transmutes into desire almost instantly, her legs tighten around my waist, and she seems only then to become aware I'm not wearing a shirt. Her hands hungrily start to explore and she lets out a series of moans as I kiss her throat and slide my hands beneath her T-shirt.

"Let's go upstairs," she whispers hoarsely.

I don't need any encouraging. Hoisting her around my hips, I carry her up the stairs. Before we make it to the bed, Jessa's already half naked, her clothes littering the floor. I toss her down on the bed, but she gets to her knees and pulls me down, then flips me onto my back and straddles me with a seductive little smile before shimmying down my body.

And then she returns the favor.

Afterward, I lie cradling her head on my chest. My heart is still hammering like crazy. I can't stop marveling at just how unin-hibited and confident Jessa's getting in all areas of her life, not just the bedroom. I'm not sure I've ever seen anything sexier than her straddling me, taking control like she just did. I love seeing her coming out of her shell, not just for obvious reasons (like getting to benefit exponentially) but because of the happi-ness flooding out of her like sunlight.

She starts telling me all about the role and how she'll need to rehearse three days a week for the next eight weeks.

"What about your dad?" I ask. "Are you going to tell your parents?"

Jessa shakes her head. "No way. He'll probably tell me I can't do it. The performance dates coincide with the first few weeks of college. I think I can manage, but if he finds out, I know he'll say it'll interfere with my studies."

"What about all the rehearsals?" I ask warily. The lying is getting too easy. All the deceit is starting to leave a bad taste in my mouth, as though we're constructing a house of cards that one day is going to collapse on us.

Jessa shrugs. "I figure I can lie and tell him I'm volunteering at the hospital, taking more shifts."

"I can't believe I'm going to miss it," I say, running my hand up her back.

She lifts her head and looks at me.

"I won't miss the next one. I promise," I say.

She kisses me, and I get a kick from the fact that she hasn't said there won't be a next time. I'm confident that now she's back in the game she's not going to quit acting again. I'm not going to let her, anyway. This is what she was made to do. I can totally see her one day gracing billboards and walking red carpets.

Jessa rolls out of my arms and gets up. She stretches languidly, and I prop myself up on my elbow to watch her, scoring her onto my memory. This girl is the only girl I'll ever need, is what I'm thinking. She walks naked over to the dresser, and I grin to myself as I get a double view of her perfect ass and her front reflected in the mirror.

She opens the drawer filled with her clothes and pulls out some clean underwear. I watch her get dressed, wishing that she lived with me full time and I could watch her get dressed every day. In her white lace bra and panties she walks over to me. She sashays, in fact, no doubt driven to tease me by the naked desire she sees in my eyes.

"Stop," I say. "Let me look at you."

"Take a photo. It will last longer," she smirks.

"Okay," I say, reaching for my phone in jest.

She doesn't stop me, and I realize with surprise, and not a little bit of excitement, that she isn't joking. She tosses her hair

COME BACK TO ME

over her shoulder and turns, giving me a view of her perfect ass, the flat of her stomach, and the curve of her breast swelling over the white lace of her bra. Holy shit. I take a photograph. And then she turns toward me, biting on her bottom lip, and I take another.

"I want you to have something to remember me by," she whispers as she turns her back and pulls her panties down offering me a perfect view of her ass.

I nod dumbly. That works for me.

"Don't you dare show anyone, though," she growls.

"As if," I say. "You're for my eyes only." I reach for her, but she dances out of my way.

"I have to go," she laughs, hopping over to grab her jeans off the floor. She does her hair in front of the mirror as I flip through the photos on my phone. I wish I could use them for my screen saver, but yeah, probably not a good idea. I'll have to password-protect my phone, or someone in my unit is bound to scroll through and find them, and I'm not having anyone jerking off to these except me.

"What's this?" Jessa suddenly asks.

Her tone makes my head snap up. Shit. She's holding a piece of paper in her hand. Fuck. She's found the letter from my commanding officer. It arrived today, and it contains the details of my next deployment.

She turns toward me, her expression stony. "Why didn't you tell me?" she asks.

I jump off the bed and walk toward her, but she steps backward out of reach.

"Jessa," I say, "of course I was going to tell you. I just got it today."

She waves the piece of paper in my face. "Kabul? They're sending you to Afghanistan?"

I nod.

She stares at me, and I see her eyes are bright with tears. "And Riley too?" she asks.

I nod.

"Why? Why Afghanistan?" she asks. "You were just in Sudan. I thought they couldn't give you a second dangerous posting? I thought that was how it worked? One easy, one hard."

"We don't get to choose. We go where they send us."

She shakes her head at me. "I'll talk to my dad. There must be something he can do."

I step toward her, ease the letter from her grip, and toss it to the floor. I take her hands, which are fisted, and close my palms around them. She won't look at me. Her jaw is pulsing, and she's fighting to stop herself crying.

"Baby, this is my job. It's what I signed up for. I knew the risks. Your father can't do anything, and even if he could, I wouldn't want him to."

"But . . . ," she starts to say, her bottom lip wobbling.

"No buts. Nothing is going to happen to me. I swear it."

"You can't swear it," she says. "Afghanistan is one of the most dangerous postings in the world."

"It's safer now," I argue.

"According to who?" she asks. "Not according to the State Department. It's top in the danger rankings."

She's been doing her research. Damn.

"Jessa," I say. "I'm going to be fine. I promise. I'm good at my job."

She's turned her back on me, and her body is as tense as a

trip wire. I wrap my arms around her waist and nuzzle her neck. Finally, her shoulders slump and she turns around to face me.

"Come back to me. Promise you'll come back to me," she whispers, her lips against mine, tears pouring down her cheeks.

I stroke that stubborn strand of hair behind her ear. "Always," I say.

Barely two minutes after she leaves and just as I'm about to step in the shower, the doorbell rings. I figure it's Jessa, that maybe she's forgotten her keys, but when I open the door, I find Riley on the doorstep and he's not smiling.

I stagger backward, blood draining to my feet, my hands coming up to block the blow I'm anticipating. Does he know? Did he see Jessa leave?

"Yo," he says, walking past me into the hallway. "Did you get the letter?"

"Yeah," I say, gradually pulling my shit together and breathing out slowly with relief. He doesn't know. But thank hell he didn't time his visit five minutes earlier.

"Afghanistan?" He shakes his head. "We got screwed, man. May as well have just stayed with our old unit."

"Yeah," I say.

"You just work out?" he asks me, frowning at the towel slung around my waist.

"Yeah," I say. "I was just about to take a shower."

"Wanna go hit some balls?" Riley asks.

"Yeah, sure," I say, aware that apart from our morning runs I haven't had much chance to hang out with Riley, and since our confrontation at the prom we haven't really talked. A tension hangs over every conversation, probably compounded on my part by the fact I'm having sex with his sister. But there's also something about his expression, the furrowed brow and distracted air, that tells me something's playing on his mind and he needs someone to talk to. "I'll just throw some clothes on."

I'm hoping he's going to wait for me downstairs, but he follows me up to my bedroom. I open the door, already cringing.

"Whoa, dude, did you just get some?" Riley asks, taking in the bed with the sheets all rumpled and my clothes strewn across the floor.

He crosses straight to the foot of the dresser and picks something up, holding it between thumb and forefinger. It's one of Jessa's bras. Fuck. He waves it in my face, grinning. "Holy shit. You did!"

I fall mute. What can I say? I've been busted. He looks admiringly at the bra before putting it down and turning toward the bed. "Check out this room!" he says. "When did you do all this? Wait . . ." He stares at me open-mouthed. "You did this for a girl? Holy shit, bro—who the hell is she?" He's grinning at me like a maniac, reminding me of when we were both fifteen and first experimenting with girls. "What's she like in bed?"

Oh man. "Quit it," I say, turning to my closet and grabbing a pair of sweats.

"What?" Riley laughs. "Come on, give me the details. What's her name? When can I finally meet her?"

"I'm not sure," I say. "It's complicated." I reach for a T-shirt and pull it on over my head, smelling Jessa on it. It was the one she wore the other day while I made her breakfast.

"What the fuck?"

I whip around. Riley's staring at me and his face is turning purple. My gaze drops to the phone in his hand. *My* phone. The phone with the pictures of Jessa half naked on it. I snatch for it but I'm too late. Riley steps backward away from the bedside table, holding it out of my reach. My arms drop to my sides in defeat. It's not like there's anything I can say to get me out of this one.

He stares at the screen. "You're screwing my sister?" he asks, his voice a serrated blade.

I wince. "It's not like that."

"Then how the fuck is it?" he shouts, thrusting the phone in my face. I catch a glimpse of Jessa biting her bottom lip as she poses for me in her underwear. Grabbing for the phone, I wrestle it out of Riley's hand. "We're dating," I say.

He shakes his head at me. "What about that other girl? The one you said you were into?"

"That was her. It was Jessa all along. It's only been her this whole time." I want to say more, tell him that I love her, that she loves me too, that the last three weeks have been the best of my life, but the way Riley's looking at me, as if I just betrayed our friendship and knifed him in the gut, makes me ram my mouth shut.

"You're my best friend. She's my sister," he growls.

"And?" I shout. "What's that got to do with anything?" Riley looks like he wants to punch me, and all I can think is *bring it*. Anger blazes through me, lit by the unfairness of Riley's reaction. "Or is it that you still don't think I'm good enough?" I yell. He glares at me, not saying anything. "You know," I say, shaking my head, "you're starting to act and sound just like your father."

"Screw you," Riley says, a flare of anger mixed with pain stretching across his face. I instantly regret the words, but I'm too angry to back down.

We scowl at each other for a long second, both of us clenching our fists, both of us breathing hard.

"Fuck," Riley finally says before sinking down onto the edge of the bed and burying his head in his hands.

For a few moments I just watch him uncertainly. That was not the reaction I was expecting. What's going on? A second ago he looked like he wanted to punch my lights out, and now he looks like he's about to burst into tears. I'm totally confused.

Riley looks up at me. "Jo's pregnant," he says.

Coming straight out of left field like that in the middle of a fight about his sister, it takes a second for the news to sink in. When it does, I slump down beside him on the bed. "Whoa," I say. "That's . . ." I don't finish the sentence because I've no idea what he's thinking about it—whether he's pleased or not. I'm guessing not from the expression on his face, but don't want to say the wrong thing just in case.

"I don't know what the fuck to do," Riley says, looking straight into my eyes, more terrified than I've ever seen him, and seeing as I've watched him approaching possible suicide bombers while on patrol, that's saying something.

"What do you mean?" I ask.

"We're leaving," he says. "In case you hadn't noticed. We're going to be gone for a year. To Afghanistan, of all places. I won't be here for the birth."

"So she's keeping it?" I ask.

He swallows, a scowl crossing his face. "I don't know. We haven't really talked about it. She only just found out. It must have been the day I got back. Or around then. Can you believe it?"

I nod to myself, simultaneously thanking God Jessa and I

have always used protection and making a note to myself to never, ever throw caution to the wind. "How's Jo doing?" I ask.

Riley shrugs. "Not good. It wasn't exactly planned, you know?"

I nod some more. Poor Jo, like she doesn't have enough to deal with. Riley buries his head in his hands once more, and I put my arm around his shoulder. "Bro, I'm here for you," I say. "I'm here for both of you. Whatever you need."

After a moment Riley looks at me. "You ever wish you'd never enlisted?" he asks.

I nod. "Yeah, I'm thinking of getting out after this."

His eyebrows shoot up. "Serious?"

I nod.

"I always thought you were in it for life."

"Nah, things change."

"Does this have anything to do with my sister?" he asks, giving me an incredulous look.

"Maybe," I say.

He studies me for a second, his expression turning from confused to amazed to serious. Finally he shakes his head. "I'm sorry I lost my shit before. About you . . . and her." He looks slightly uncomfortable still, as though he's just eaten something disgusting at a dinner party and is having to smile his way through it so as not to offend the host.

"It's cool," I say. "I'm sorry I kept it a secret. Jessa didn't want you to know."

Riley grimaces and looks at me sideways. "You really like her?" he asks, still with that skeptical tone in his voice.

I laugh. "Yeah. I really like her. A lot." I'm not going to come out with the love word at this stage, not until I'm totally sure he isn't going to punch me.

Riley shakes his head wearily as though he's had enough surprises for one day and can't process any more. "Fine," he says. "Just don't screw her around." He fixes me with a drill-sergeant stare. "Or I'll hunt you down and rip you into so many pieces they won't be able to tell your asshole from your earhole."

"I won't," I say solemnly.

"I mean it, Kit," he says with a touch of menace. "Treat her right."

"I will."

His face wrinkles in disgust. "And man, do you have to have her bras and underwear lying around everywhere and pictures of her naked on your phone? I don't want to know what you two are doing."

"You were the one that was asking for details, dude," I say, laughing.

"Before I knew it was my sister."

We both lapse into silence, our thoughts shifting in unison away from Jessa and returning to the far more life-altering news about the pregnancy. Holy shit. I'm still struggling to get my head around it. I can't imagine how Riley is doing. He exhales loudly, running his hands over his head. "Fuck," he says again. "This was not part of the plan."

"Guess life likes to throw us some curveballs," I say quietly.

"You call a baby a curveball?" he asks, looking at me in disbelief. "Can you even imagine how I'm going to sit my parents down and explain this one?"

I wince. I remember the time we had to sit them down and explain we'd been suspended for streaking naked across the bleachers. That was bad enough. And I remember the time Riley had to explain he'd enlisted as a grunt not an officer. His dad went postal. Riley had to sleep on my sofa for three nights until he calmed down.

"Do you think you could tell him just before I tell him I'm dating Jessa?" I joke. "That way he might be too pissed at you to care about us."

Riley punches me in the arm and we both start laughing.

Jessa

Riley knocks on my bedroom door as I'm getting ready to go out. As soon as I turn around and see him standing there with both eyebrows raised and his arms crossed over his chest, I know I'm busted. I don't say anything, though.

"So," he says. "When were you going to tell me?"

My heart has started beating double time. "About what?" I ask, aiming for innocence, because I want to be certain he's talking about what I think he's talking about and not something else.

"You and Kit," he says.

Oh. Damn. "How did you find out?" I ask, shooting a glance over his shoulder. Are my parents around? Riley seems to pick up on my nervousness, because he steps inside my room and shuts the door.

"You know, if you're going to record your sexcapades Paris Hilton style, then don't go leaving phones lying around."

My jaw drops open. He saw the photos on Kit's phone? Oh my God. I want to die. My cheeks catch fire. I stare at him in horror, but Riley just grins at me.

"I . . . We . . . They were just . . . ," I stammer.

He holds up a hand. "Stop. I don't want to know. I told Kit the same."

"So . . ." What? What is he saying? Is he mad? "Are you okay with it?"

"Not with the photos part or with the idea of you guys, um, you know . . ." He wrinkles his nose in consternation. "But yeah . . . I'm cool with it, I guess." He looks at me. "How long's it been going on?"

I shrug, not really wanting to admit it. "Since you got back."

Riley shakes his head. "Man. You know, Jo says she knew all along, that it was obvious at the beach. I thought he was into Didi."

"Yeah, that's what we wanted you to think."

He shakes his head at me some more. "What about Mom and Dad? You going to tell them?"

"No!" I say. "Are you kidding?"

"Yeah, I figured you'd say that." He stands there for a few more seconds, chewing on his lip, nodding to himself.

I wonder if he's going to tell me to tell Dad or warn me off Kit, but he does neither. He just walks to the door, pausing to look over his shoulder just before he opens it. "And . . . if you're gonna . . . you know . . ." He wrinkles his nose, looking pained.

My eyebrows lift. Is he talking about sex?

"Make sure you use protection."

I pick up the nearest object—a book—and throw it at his head. He ducks, laughing, and darts out the door, closing it behind him, and I stand there for a full minute staring at it, speechless, trying desperately to erase that last comment from my brain.

Didi stands beside me as I wait outside her house for Kit. He's late.

"And remember to stop at the stop signs, don't just pause," she says.

"Got it," I answer distractedly as I stare down the street. Where is he?

"And if you get a guy examiner, totally flirt. It worked for me. And pray you don't get a woman. They're way meaner."

I glance in Didi's direction. "Stop making me panic."

She grins brightly at me. "There's nothing to worry about. Everyone except complete morons pass first time. And besides, you have Kit."

"What do you mean?" I ask.

"Well, you got that part, didn't you, in the play? And no one found out that you ditched school . . . and even Riley was cool when he found out about you guys. Kit's like your good-luck charm."

Yeah, I suppose she's right, I muse. Kit is something of a good-luck charm.

"I'm telling you," she continues. "Kit's like one of those leprechauns from the Lucky Charms commercial."

"Well, he's a late leprechaun who won't be getting lucky for the foreseeable future if he doesn't show soon."

"Where is he?" Didi asks.

"He and Riley had their fitness test this morning." I look again at my watch. "But he said he'd be here by now."

"He's probably picking up five dozen roses or scattering petals down the freeway to spell out your name." She smirks at me. "Or maybe he ran home to bake you special good-luck cookies."

"Shut up!" I say, just as Kit's truck appears around the corner.

"Oh, finally," I say, throwing up my arms. He tears down the street and screeches to a halt right in front of Didi's house. He jumps out of the truck and races around to me.

"Sorry, sorry!" he pants.

He's wearing his shorts and running shoes and a sweat-stained, dirt-streaked T-shirt. His face looks pretty much the same as his T-shirt. He kisses me on the cheek, and I smell his sweat and soap and deodorant—is it weird that that turns me on and makes me think instantly of sex?

"You're late," I say.

"You're gorgeous," he answers, taking my hand. "Come on, we gotta go." He starts tugging me toward the truck, waving at Didi. "Hi, Didi. Bye, Didi."

Didi waves, her eyes slightly glazed as she admires his sweaty form.

"Aren't I driving?" I ask as Kit opens the passenger door for me.

"No. I'll drive. You can't get pulled over for speeding on your way to your test. Wouldn't look good." He slams the door shut behind me and sprints around to his side.

"So how'd it go?" I ask as he pulls out of Didi's street.

"I crushed it. It was a piece of cake," he answers with a lop-sided grin. "Must be all the workouts I'm having."

"I hope you don't slack off on the workouts now that the test is behind you," I tell him.

"As if," he answers.

We both fall silent after that. He's leaving the day after tomorrow—that's what I'm thinking. And I'm fairly sure he is too. There isn't going to be much time for workouts. Kit reaches over and squeezes my hand.

"How'd Riley do?" I ask, trying not to focus on the negative.

"Yeah, fine," Kit says, his eyes on the road.

"Did you beat him?" I ask, figuring the answer is no. If he'd beaten Riley, he would have been bragging about it already.

"Yeah," Kit says.

"You did?" I say, turning to him in surprise.

"I got a two hundred and ninety-eight and he got a two hundred and seventy-three."

"Wow. He must have had a late night or something."

"Yeah, maybe," Kit mumbles shiftily.

I narrow my eyes at him, wondering what he knows that I don't. I am, of course, totally ecstatic that my brother didn't kill Kit when he found out about us, if a little less thrilled that he saw semi-naked pictures of me on Kit's phone, but ever since he found out about us, it feels like there's something going on between the two of them that they're keeping from me. Riley's been acting weird ever since, and I don't get the impression it's just about Kit and me, though I might be wrong.

Kit drops me at the test center, gives me a sweaty kiss, and tells me he'll wait. I feel like I'm being waved off to war, but luckily I'm back in half an hour, waving my paperwork in his face and jumping up and down.

"I did it! I passed!" I scream.

Kit picks me up and swings me around. "I knew you would."

I kiss him. "Didi told me you were my lucky charm. She was right."

Kit frowns. "Oh, she did, did she? I hope you told her I was a lot more than that. I hope you told her that I'm a total stud in the bedroom too."

"Are you ever going to drop it?" I ask, rolling my eyes.

"Come on . . . I gave you a multiple orgasm. That's got to buy me some kudos for a while."

He's never going to let that drop, and at just the mention of it the memory bursts pinprick-sharp into my mind and I get a shudder down my spine. That was quite possibly the best two hours of my life.

"It'll buy you an invite to my place tomorrow," I tell him.

Kit winces. "The party?"

I nod, making my eyes all big and round. I desperately want him to come. It's the party my mom throws every time Riley leaves. Unofficially it's always been Kit's going-away party too. He always comes, standing as far from my father as possible. "Please?" I say.

"Really?" he asks.

"Yeah. I want you to be there."

"With your dad. In the same room?"

"You've done it before," I say.

"Before, I wasn't sleeping with his daughter," he says with a wry smile.

"He doesn't know that," I say, running my hands over his chest.

He lets out a sigh. "I'll make it worth your while," I say, trailing my fingers up his chest.

He arches an eyebrow at me. "Oh yeah?" he asks. "Sexual bribery?"

I nod.

"Okay. I'm there. But you better pay up now."

Kit

Riley calls me the morning of the party asking if I want to shoot some hoops. I can tell from the relief in his voice that he and Jo must have come to a decision, and when I meet him down at the courts, he lopes over to me.

"How'd you feel about being a godfather?" he asks, grinning.

I slap him on the back and pull him into a hug. "Bro, that's awesome. Congratulations."

"Yeah," he says, nodding hard. He looks shit scared but also buzzing. "It's the right thing. I love her. And we'll manage . . . somehow."

I nod. What else can I do?

"I'm going to marry her," he says next. "When I get back. That way she'll be on my insurance and get all the benefits. If we had time, I'd do it now."

"You'll have to leave the MSG," I say. It's one of the rules; you can't be married if you're a marine security guard.

He tosses me the ball. "Yeah, I know. I'll see if I can transfer back into our old unit."

I start dribbling down the court. "That's . . . Man, that's big news. You tell your folks yet?"

"Nope. Going to tell them later," Riley says as I take a shot.

"You prepared a bombproof shelter?" I ask, catching the ball after it drops through the hoop.

"I'm going to tell Jessa first. Figure she'll be the only one that's happy for us."

"I'm happy for you too," I say.

Riley grabs the ball from my hands and jumps, slam-dunking the ball through the hoop and letting out a whoop.

Three hours later I'm standing on the doorstep, straightening my Dress Blues and checking the shine on my shoes. A trickle of sweat runs down my back, and I pull on my collar. There are at least two dozen cars parked along the street, and the sound of the party is traveling over the garden fence. I've been less nervous taking point in patrols through hostile territory in Iraq. I'm hoping that I can blend in—there'll be at least a dozen of us in uniform—and that Jessa's dad doesn't notice me. Not for the first time and no doubt not for the last, either, I wonder what the hell I ever did to deserve his hatred, other than burn down his garage, that is.

Okay, there were a few other times I got Riley into trouble—but he made the decision to tag along with me. I didn't pressure him to ditch school or stay out all night clubbing in our senior year. It was his idea to streak across the bleachers, and if his Spider-Man mask hadn't come off just as the TV cameras zoomed in, then no one would ever have known it was us. I didn't encourage him to try weed that time in tenth grade either, and the garage was a joint effort—Riley lit the fuse. But his dad always blamed me for everything as though I were the corrupting influence on his perfect son. The straw that broke the camel's back was my convincing Riley not to go to college and take the officer route into the corps. Not that Riley needed much convincing—he wanted to get out of the house at the earliest opportunity and away from his father. But rather than admit any of the blame might lie with him for that one, his dad placed it squarely at my door.

I remind myself that it isn't all about me. That his loathing for me goes further back, has something to do with my mom. I keep wondering if maybe Jessa's dad had the hots for her or something, but the thought makes my blood curdle. If that's the case, I don't want to know.

Jessa opens the door before I have a chance to ring the doorbell. She's wearing a short blue sundress that shows off her legs and her tan, her hair is down, and she's wearing some kind of lip gloss that makes her lips look edible. Without thinking, I reach for her. For a brief moment she presses her soft body against mine, and I get a tantalizing whiff of her shampoo and her vanilla body lotion before she dances out of my arms.

"I'm going to be an aunt!" she whispers, her face split with glee.

"I'm going to be a godfather!" I say back.

We high-five.

"I'm so glad you're here," she says, pulling me inside the house and shutting the door. "I'm worried Riley's going to choose now to make the announcement. You know—safety in numbers."

Shit. I hadn't thought of that. But she might be right. It's what I'd do. Though if I ever get Jessa pregnant I'm going to inform her father from a separate state, maybe even from a separate continent. And I'll still be sure to wear a bulletproof vest because that man has connections.

I walk into the kitchen, glancing back over my shoulder and catching Jessa checking me out. I square my shoulders and feel my chin lifting. It happens every time I wear my Dress Blues: that feeling of pride that swells through me making me feel invincible. It's probably the feeling I'll miss most when I leave the corps. But it doesn't come close to the feeling I get waking up with Jessa in my arms, I remind myself.

I follow Jessa into the back garden, where there are tables spread out and about thirty or so people drinking beer and wine, chatting in small groups as waiters hover with trays laden with more drinks and canapés. Classical music plays from speakers hidden in the bushes—the same bushes where I first kissed Jessa. I wish I could drag her behind them for a replay, but she's already running back to answer the door again.

I hover on the outskirts, like a diver hesitating on top of the highest diving platform. It's a semiformal affair, and I recognize a lot of the people, though none that I know well enough to make conversation with. Most are high-ranking officers from the base. There are whole galaxies of stars visible on all the lapels. I spy at least one general and a couple of colonels before I quit counting. Their wives flutter like butterflies at their sides. I spot Riley in one corner with Jo beside him. She's holding his hand and he's giving her a reassuring smile, though she looks as uneasy as I feel.

Jessa's father is holding court, and I recognize one of the people in the group that's circling him like beggars around a king; it's that guy Todd—the guy who was trying to flirt with Jessa at prom. What's he doing here? Then I remember Jessa telling me his dad just transferred to the base at Pendleton. Todd's wearing a suit and tie. He looks more like a pen-pushing accountant than a soon-to-be officer, and I can feel my jaw tensing just looking at him. I'd like to see him survive a single day at grunt camp.

It bugs me to see him here, especially looking so comfortable within the inner sanctum, and I realize with a jolt that I'm jealous and that thought makes me even more pissed. Todd looks up just then and catches me glaring at him. He nods his head politely in my direction, and I give him a curt nod in reply, praying like hell he doesn't say anything to Jessa's dad about me being her boyfriend. That would be just perfect.

My eyes skip across the group and light on Jessa's mom, who looks harried, laying out food on one of the tables, fussing at the tablecloth. I walk over.

"Need some help?" I ask.

She looks up, and I notice the relief on her face when she sees it's me, and also the faint fog in her eyes—a look I recognize from the old days with my dad. Is she on something?

"Oh, Kit," she says in a wispy voice. "That would be lovely."

I help her pull the plastic wrap off some of the dishes.

"Don't you look handsome," she says when we're done. She strokes a hand down my arm. Her lip trembles, reminding me for a moment of Jessa when she's trying not to cry.

"Are you okay?" I ask, lowering my voice.

"Yes," she says, forcing a smile. "I'm just having quite a day." She gestures around her. "It feels like you only just got back. And you're both going again." Her eyes skitter over to Riley, and I see her lip tremble again.

"Look after him, won't you, Kit?"

My attention snaps back to her.

"Riley," she qualifies. "He looks up to you. Promise me you'll take care of each other over there."

I nod, feeling a stab of guilt and more than a little awkward. It's always hard saying good-bye to relatives before we deploy overseas. Suddenly I get a painful prelude of what it's going to be like tomorrow to say good-bye to Jessa.

Her mom pats me on the arm, and then her smile fades as she glances over my shoulder. She hurries off, and I follow her gaze to find Jessa's dad glaring at me.

He looks away, a slight sneer curling his lip, and my stomach clenches as I see him rest his hand for a brief moment on Todd's shoulder. It's as if he's making a point, letting me know that I'm not worth his time because I'm not an officer in training.

For a second I think about turning around and leaving, but just then Jessa sneaks up behind me. "Hey," she says quietly. I turn to her and instantly feel my muscles unknotting. She's like Valium in human form.

Seeing my expression, she frowns. "You okay?" she asks.

I nod. "Yeah. What's he doing here?" I ask, jerking my head in Todd's direction.

"Oh," she says. "His dad and my dad are friends."

"Looks like Todd and your dad are having a little bromance." I can't help the bitter tone in my voice, and Jessa hears it and gives me a curious look. I kick myself, reminding myself that I'm here to support her, not to act like a little kid. I'm about to apologize when there's a chink-chink sound and we all look up. Riley's walked into the center of the lawn and is banging a knife against the side of his glass. Jo trails after him, smiling self-consciously. Shit.

"Oh my God," Jessa whispers as Riley sets his glass down on a nearby table. "Kit, he's really going to do it."

"Everyone, can I have your attention?" Riley asks.

The chatter dies down instantly, curiosity fully piqued. Someone kills the music. I glance quickly at Jessa's dad. He's frowning at the interruption. I can't wait to see how he reacts to the next bit of news. I've got a bad feeling about this. I think about diverting Riley somehow, but there's no way of stopping him now. He's smiling at Jo and everyone's waiting. The only thing I can do is stand here and show my support.

Riley clears his throat and looks around at the expectant crowd. "I . . . we . . . have some news to share," he announces.

There's a ripple of noise, a wave of chatter that skips right over his dad, who continues to glare at the two of them.

"Jo and I are getting married."

There's a moment's pause. Everyone seems to be waiting on Jessa's dad's response before they react. Riley plows on into the silence. "And we're having a baby."

The silence stretches a moment too long, and so I let out a whoop and start clapping loudly. Thankfully, everyone follows suit. The women rush forward to surround them, but I look over at Jessa's dad, no longer the king surrounded by sycophants but a lone statue standing on the periphery. He's staring at Riley with a look of total disgust. I watch him set his glass down on a table and march toward the house. Jessa, frozen at my side, watches him too.

Well, at least he's not causing a scene, I think to myself. It could be worse. But then Riley looks up, scans the crowd, and seeing his father walking away, he strides after him. Fuck. What is he doing?

"You got nothing to say?" Riley asks, grabbing his father's arm and stopping him mid-stride. "Nothing at all? Like maybe 'Congratulations, son, that's wonderful news'?"

I feel like walking over there and dragging Riley away. It's like watching a kid at a zoo poking a lion through the bars, but for some reason I can't move.

His father turns to him, the look of disappointment so clear on his face that it makes me want to run in front of him so I can shield Riley from it. "What is there to say?" he snaps. "You seem determined to screw up your life at every opportunity."

The crowd has fallen silent. This is what they want: drama. The beady-eyed wives turn to watch, biting their lips with glee. This is going to give them weeks of gossip fodder. Riley stands face-to-face with his father, his jaw pulsing, his nostrils flaring. He looks ready to throw a punch, and I finally take a step toward him to pull him back, but Jo's already there. She walks up to him and slips her hand into his, drawing him away with more dignity than I know I could muster in the same situation. Riley gives his father one last look so filled with hatred that I flinch and take a step backward, and then he turns around and starts following Jo.

"Come on," I whisper to Jessa, jerking my head toward them. I want them to know that we're on their side. I want to shield them from all the stares and gossip, and I know Riley's going to need someone to rant at. But Jessa stalks right past me in the opposite direction. I turn and see her stopping right in front of her father.

"Why are you such an asshole?" she asks him in a voice that cuts through the crowd. Everyone turns around, anxious for round two.

Oh shit, I groan inwardly. Jessa, what are you doing?

"What did you just say?" her father asks in a voice that rumbles like thunder.

"I asked why you have to be such an asshole," Jessa repeats.

There's a communal inhalation of air. I'm stunned into silence along with everyone else.

"Get inside," her father spits, his face turning red.

Jessa shakes her head at him, her own eyes flashing dangerously.

"Get inside NOW!" her father roars.

Someone gasps. Someone else drops a glass. The waiters are standing frozen, trays hovering in midair. Jessa's mom makes a sound that's something between a whimper and a sob. Shit. I need to do something. I step forward and put my hand on the small of Jessa's back.

"Let's go," I whisper under my breath, trying to steer her away. But Jessa's body goes rigid at my touch. She's breathing fast, fury setting her mouth into a line.

"Get your hands off her," her dad hisses at me under his breath. There are two bright spots of fire on his cheeks. He's struggling to keep his temper. I know that if there weren't three dozen witnesses right now he'd probably go for my throat.

"Get inside," he orders Jessa again. "Go to your room."

Jessa just glares at him, her body vibrating like a tuning fork. She seems stuck. She can't speak but can't move either. Her dad lifts his head, sees everyone staring at him, and takes hold of Jessa by the arm. She lets out a muted cry. Straightaway I'm between them. Without even thinking, I pull his arm off her and step in front of Jessa, my blood pounding like a drum in my ears.

"Calm down," I hiss at him.

"Get your hands off me," he spits back, the color rising in his cheeks.

I look down and realize my hand is locked around his arm.

"Not until you calm down," I answer.

He throws off my grip with a violent shrug of his shoulder. "Get out of my house," he says. "Who even invited you?"

I stand there, my feet glued to the ground. My anger's a living thing, coursing through me like electricity. Suddenly it's just me and Kingsley facing off against each other, and everyone else fades into the background. It's the zone I drop into when I'm on sniper duty. I feel eerily calm.

"Kit."

It takes me several seconds to realize Jessa is calling my name. She's behind me, her hands on my arms, pulling me backward. "Kit," she says again in a low, urgent voice. "I think you'd better leave."

Her words sting me, shaking me out of my calm. She's ordering me to go? While I'm doing my damnedest to protect her? I turn, confused, to face her and am struck by how terrified she looks. Over her shoulder I catch sight of her mom, a handkerchief pressed to her mouth, her eyes watery and vacant, staring around like a lost kid at a carnival, while a ring of other faces stares at me in utter shock. Shit. Jessa's right. I need to go.

"Sure," I say, my voice catching in my throat. "Wouldn't want to cause a scene."

I shrug off Jessa's hands. I'm angry. Not just at her father, but also at her, for treating me like I'm the one who's in the wrong here. Holding my head up, I make for the door.

"And don't ever step foot in this house again or let me see

you talking to my daughter," her father mutters to me as I pass. "You're no good, just like your father."

He could have said anything about me and I could have taken it on the chin, but insulting my father pushes me over the edge. I spin around: "My father's worth a hundred of you," I growl.

With relish I see the look of surprise that splashes over Kingsley's face. I step right in front of him, realizing that I'm the same height as him and that even if he has ten ranks on me, I no longer care. "At least my father owned his demons. At least he fought them. At least he doesn't claim to be a better man than anyone else when clearly he's not."

Kingsley's face turns from red to white as the blood sluices from it. I know I'm acting recklessly, I know I've stepped into the danger zone, but I don't stop, can't stop. I'm on a roll, and seven years of taking his shit and watching him terrorize his children while I stand by in silence has finally taken its toll.

"He doesn't make his wife and daughter terrified to be around him," I shout. "He doesn't look down on his son and make him feel like he's never good enough. He doesn't control his daughter and make her feel like she has to walk on eggshells around him. He lives his life trying to make amends for all the wrongs he committed, trying to honor the memory of my mother, trying to be the best parent and grandfather and man he can."

I take a breath. Faces—aghast, open-mouthed—blur at the edges of my vision, but I blink them away. Kingsley's my only focus.

"And here you are," I say, gesturing at him. "You have this amazing, perfect family. You have a son you should be fucking proud of because he's the best man and the best soldier I've ever had the honor to know, and a daughter who's so beautiful and so incredible she takes my breath away every time I look at her and who I'd walk over hot coals to see smile. And you don't even notice her. You don't do anything to make her smile. You don't even know *what* makes her smile."

With satisfaction I see Kingsley's mouth dropping open and then closing as each of my words slams into him with the force of a bullet.

"Do you see how scared they are of you?" I say. I shake my head, disgust edging out my anger. "You don't deserve them."

Finally Kingsley gathers himself. "Get out!" he roars.

"Kit, just leave. Please."

I glance around. Jessa is standing there, eyes downcast, tears rolling down her cheeks. She can't look at me, and it's only then I realize that instead of being her champion, her knight to the rescue, I've just done the worst thing possible. I've humiliated her in front of an audience. Shit. Shit. Shit. I scan the faces surrounding me—see the delight, the wonder, the shock, the utter train wreck I've made of the party. And there—there's Jessa's mom, a quivering mess in the middle of it all.

I open my mouth to say something to Jessa—to apologize, to beg her forgiveness—but my brain blanks. What the hell have I just done? I thought I was making things better and I've made them a thousand times worse.

"Just go."

It's Riley this time. He's glaring at me, though under the glare I sense both an apology and a warning. "I got it, Kit," he says tersely. "You can leave." He nods toward the door and then lowers his voice to me. "You're only making it worse."

I look back at Jessa, my heart tumbling to a standstill, aware the whole time of Kingsley breathing heavily right in front of me, the anger beating off him in waves. But there's Jessa, still staring at her feet, her shoulders shaking. I can't just leave her like this. "Come with me," I say, the words spilling over my lips before I can stop them.

She shakes her head at me. "I can't," she says. Her eyes are red-rimmed, almost glassy with confusion, as though she can't believe I would ask that of her.

I stare at her, willing her to understand I was only trying to help, that I love her, but she drops her gaze, and it feels like a judge's gavel slamming against a block. With my heart dive-bombing in my chest, I swivel on my heel and march toward the door.

Jessa

There's a silence as thick as snowfall, obliterating everything. My ears sing with static until a waiter rests his tray down and the glasses clink, and as though it's the signal everyone's been waiting for, the whispers start back up. I can tell everyone thinks this is just the interval between acts. There's a humid anticipation in the air. Everyone's eyes stay locked on my father, waiting for the thunderclap that will announce the next act.

I can't move. My breathing is coming in small, broken gasps, and my focus is fixed on my father. If there were no witnesses, I know he'd explode right now. Furniture would fly, curses would rain down, and my mom and I would duck for cover. But with so many eyes on him he's having to keep a lid on it. It's like watching a bubbling pan. His face has gone all shades of red, and sweat beads around the edges of his hairline.

He gives a grimacing sort of smile and holds his hands up to the crowd. "Well, I guess the show's over, folks," he says with a forced laugh. "He was a gate-crasher anyway. Who invited him?" He looks jokingly around at the crowd, and there are a few guffaws that sicken me. That's his response? To turn it into a joke at Kit's expense?

Suddenly all that Kit just said hits me with the force of a clanging bell, vibrating through me, making me unsteady on my feet. He just stood up to my father. No one has ever done that before. And he put his job and his life on the line to do it—to stand up for me and my brother and my mom. And I just told him to leave. What the hell did I do?

I start running toward the back door.

A hand grabs me around the wrist and yanks me to an abrupt stop. "Where do you think you're going?"

It's my father. The forced smile still on his face makes him look deranged.

"I'm going to find Kit," I say through gritted teeth, trying to tug myself free.

My father frowns briefly at me, his grip tightening. "You walk out that door now, don't bother coming back," he says.

I stare at him. His words take a moment to sink in. He can't be serious? The smile fades, and for the briefest of moments the shades pull back and I see a glimmer in his eyes that I can only describe as despair, and a splinter of terror, too. It's as if he's staring down over a precipice into a black abyss, and it startles me to see my father look so vulnerable and so scared. For a moment I waver, but then I remember the way he just spoke to Kit and something inside me comes undone. All the invisible chains I've been wearing slip from my shoulders and crash to the ground at my feet.

"It's not just his father who's worth a hundred of you," I say.

I wrench my arm from my father's grip and run inside the house. I slam the back door behind me and race into the hallway, expecting at any moment to hear footsteps stampeding after me. As I head for the front door, through blurry vision my eyes snag on the sight of my dad's car keys hanging from their hook.

I snatch them and run outside. Kit's truck is nowhere to be seen. Shaking now, adrenaline finally catching up with me, I stagger to my dad's car parked in the driveway and race around to the driver's side. It takes me a frustrating thirty seconds to figure out how to move the seat forward and how to drive with only two pedals, and by the time I ease off the hand brake, the front door has flown open. I stamp on the gas, but someone steps in front of the car and I have to emergency brake, my head almost smashing into the wheel.

"What the hell are you doing?"

It's Riley. He gestures at me to wind down the window.

"I'm going to find Kit," I tell him.

"Since when do you have your license?" he asks me.

"Since yesterday," I answer.

Riley looks stunned. But then he steps aside. "Okay, fine. Are you okay?" he asks.

I nod vigorously. I'm suddenly more than okay. I'm free. "Are you?" I ask Riley.

He gives me a weak smile and rests his hand on the roof of the car. "When you find Kit, tell him"—he pauses, frowning—"thanks from me."

Kit

I slip my key into my front door, the voice in my head yelling at me so loudly about what a dick I am that I barely hear the engine roar of a car, and it's only when I hear the screech of brakes that I turn around.

Jessa's dad's car slides to a halt at an angle, the front wheels mounting the sidewalk. Crap. He's followed me. My heart rate spikes as adrenaline floods my system, but then Jessa throws open the door and starts running toward me. She throws herself into my arms, crying and out of breath.

"I'm sorry," she mumbles against my neck.

"I'm sorry," I say at the same time, pressing her close, unable to believe that she's here, that she followed me. Thirty seconds ago I was sunk in a dark pit of misery and despair, and now I'm standing in the sunlight again.

"I was a dick," I say, the words flooding out of me. "I should have kept my mouth shut."

"No. You stood up to him. For the first time, someone stood up to him."

"You stood up to him first. You called him an asshole."

Jessa wipes her tears away with the back of her arm. "Well, he was. And he just kicked me out. Which makes him twice the asshole."

"He kicked you out?"

"He said if I followed you, then I shouldn't bother coming home." Her eyes brim with tears again.

Fuck. I stare at her. She followed me anyway? I pull her against me again. "It's okay," I reassure her. "You can stay here. Everything's going to be okay."

Her fingers dig into my shoulders, her body trembles.

"You want to come inside?" I ask her, turning toward the door, my mind spinning with everything.

Jessa shakes her head at me. "Can we go somewhere? Anywhere. I don't care where. I just want to get away from here."

I nod and take her hand, pulling her toward the truck.

We drive mostly in silence, Jessa leaning against my arm, and there's a comfort in the silence, in the knowledge that words are unnecessary, that we know exactly what the other is thinking and feeling without needing to speak. With just twelve hours left before I have to report to the base, every second is weighted, shot through with longing and sadness.

When I park, in almost exactly the same spot I brought Jessa to on that first date, the sun is sinking heavily beneath the ridge and the sky's going up in flames. I grab the blankets I have stashed in the back and lay them out on the flatbed of the truck, taking Jessa's hand to pull her up alongside me.

We lie down in each other's arms and watch as the sky fades to black and the stars switch on one by one.

"It's so beautiful," Jessa whispers. "The first night we were here I didn't really notice them so much. I was too nervous."

I grin at her. I didn't notice them much either.

"Come here," I say, pulling her toward me. While the stars are beautiful, I've only got twelve more hours to drink in this girl. I tip her chin up and kiss her slowly, loving the way her body relaxes instantly against mine and her hands run through my hair.

In silence we start to undress. I watch in silence as she rises up on her knees and undoes the buttons on her sundress, slipping it down over her shoulders and shimmying out of it. In the starlight she gleams like something otherworldly, or like the phosphorescence I saw once on the ocean. She helps me off with my shirt and pants and then, naked, we burrow beneath the blankets.

Pressed together, our legs entwined, our lips find each other and we kiss. I'm desperate to memorize every taste and every sensation, and it seems like she is too. Her fingers skim my shoulders, my chest, my arms, and with every sigh she makes, with every moan, as my hands and lips trace their own path along her limbs and over her hips and waist, the blood pumps faster in my veins.

I throw off the blanket, wanting to see her, and she obliges by sitting up and straddling me. Holy shit. That's an incredible view. I slide my hands over the contours of her body, and she smiles down on me, her hair like liquid silver flowing over her shoulders. This is how I plan on remembering her.

"I love you, Kit," she says as she lowers herself slowly onto me.

I exhale loudly, more stars bursting on the back of my eyelids than there are in the sky above us. Jessa rocks gently back and forth, but soon we're both breathing fast and she starts driving me deeper, grinding against me as though she can't get enough. And I grip her hips and pull her down because I can't get enough of her, either, and when I open my eyes, I see her head is thrown back, her back arched, and she's shivering.

I sit up, clasping her around her waist and then lift her in one swift move, flipping her over and lying her down on the blanket and pushing into her. She cries out and her legs wrap around my waist, drawing me deeper. I want to take her, inhale her, own her. I want to press myself into her flesh like a thumbprint into wet clay, leaving a maker's mark. I want to take a piece of her with me and leave a piece of me with her. How do I get enough of her to last me a year?

With every thrust I feel her muscles clench around me, the tendons on her neck growing tauter. She's biting her lip, but when I kiss her neck, she lets out a cry that's loud and uncensored and brings me straight to the brink.

I know from the way she's moving, from the way she whispers my name in my ear, that she's close, and within seconds we both come and collapse, panting, onto the blankets.

"Holy shit," I say, trying to catch my breath.

Jessa laughs, sighing happily. "Well, I'll definitely remember that for a year."

I roll onto my side and kiss her shoulder. "I'll remember that for the rest of my life."

Jessa

W e pull up outside Kit's house just as the sun is rising. For the whole way back I've been too scared to talk, scared that the lump in my throat will burst and I'll cry. I can't believe it's been four weeks. It feels like a lifetime, and yet it doesn't feel nearly long enough.

"It's just twelve months," Kit says, reading my mind.

I turn to him.

"Three hundred and sixty-five days," he says, running his thumb over my cheekbone. "It's nothing. Not compared to what we'll have."

I nod, tears stinging the backs of my eyes.

We climb out of the car, and Kit takes my hand and leads me into the house. His dad is in the kitchen. He makes no comment about Kit and me having stayed out all night, he just asks if we want coffee.

Kit goes upstairs to shower and pack the last of his things, and I stay downstairs with his dad. I'm so tired all of a sudden. The reality of where I'm at, of Kit leaving, of Riley leaving, of having no home to go back to, hits me with the blunt force of a sledgehammer. I sink down onto one of the kitchen stools and bury my head in my hands.

Kit's father places his hand on my shoulder. "It's okay," he says. "It's going to be okay."

Kit said those exact words. I look up at his father. He gives me a warm, reassuring smile before crossing to the stove to turn off the kettle.

"Your brother came around last night to get your dad's car," he says as he busies himself pouring the water into the coffee-pot. "Told me what happened." He fusses with the coffee for a moment longer before he hands me a steaming mug. "You know you're welcome to stay here, Jessa, as long as you like. I'll be glad to have you around. Gets lonely without Kit." He offers me the milk. "I want you to treat this place like your own. Okay?"

"Yes. Thank you," I stammer. "I appreciate it, Mr. Ryan."

"Ben. Call me Ben."

"Okay." I take a sip of coffee, not able to look him in the eye. I'm feeling too tired, too overwhelmed, too sad.

Kit walks back in a moment later—his hair wet, wearing his uniform—and my heart swells big enough to burst and my vision starts to blur. I don't think I can do this. I stagger off the stool and look around desperately for the exit. I head for the back door, but Kit intercepts me. He prizes the scalding coffee from my hands and sets it on the side before pulling me into his arms. I collapse there, and he just holds me with-out saying a word. I don't know how long we stand like that, in the center of the kitchen, but my coffee grows cold on the side, and it's only when the doorbell sounds that he finally lets me go.

Riley walks into the kitchen a few seconds later, wearing his uniform. He hugs Kit first, slapping him on the back, and I know it's an apology of sorts for what happened with my dad. They have their guy moment and then Riley walks over to me.

"You okay?" he asks, noticing my tearstained face.

"Yeah," I say.

"What are you going to do?" he asks.

"Stay here," I answer.

Riley nods as though he suspected as much.

"How was he?" I ask nervously.

He shrugs, and I notice for the first time the dark circles beneath his eyes. "I don't know. I stayed at Jo's last night."

"And Mom?" I feel a twinge of guilt at the mention of her name, but it's quickly stamped out by a burst of anger. She could have stood up for both of us and she didn't. She's never stood up for us.

"I spoke to her just now," Riley says. "Said good-bye." A pause. "She sounded spaced."

I look at him, frowning. I wonder if that means she's hit the not-so-secret stash of Valium she keeps in the bathroom cabinet. I can tell that's what Riley's implying.

"I'm sorry," Riley suddenly says.

I look up at him, confused, and see the anguish in his eyes and the guilt splashed across his face. "For leaving you to deal with it alone," he adds.

It's the first time Riley's ever talked to me about his decision to enlist, and the buried grudge I was holding vanishes instantly when I see just how torn up he is by it and how guilty he feels.

"It's okay," I say, and I mean it. I don't want him to feel guilty.

He gives me a sad, unconvinced smile.

"I mean it," I say. "Don't worry about me. I'll be fine."

"I'm always going to worry about you. You're my little sis," he mumbles.

"We need to go."

I look up. Kit's standing in the doorway, his bag at his feet. Riley checks the time and nods. "Okay," he says before wrapping his arms around me and hugging me hard. I hug him back harder.

"Take care," he whispers in my ear. "And look out for Jo for me. And the baby."

I nod. "Take care of Kit for me," I whisper back, my throat closing up.

I feel him nod against me. He kisses me on the top of my head before he pulls away and glances over at Kit. "I'll leave you two to it," he says, and walks out of the kitchen, throwing me a smile backward as he goes.

Kit steps forward and, taking my face in his hands, tips my head back so I'm forced to look up at him through a veil of tears.

"I love you," he says, his voice so fierce it makes something catch in my chest. "I'm going to love you forever."

I hold on to his hands. Why does he have to leave? It feels like we've only just begun. "I love you too."

He bumps his forehead to mine.

"Please, take care of Riley," I say. "Be his good-luck charm, like you were mine."

He strokes my hair behind one ear. "I promise," he says.

My lips are against his and I'm crying. "Come back to me," I whisper.

"Always," he answers, kissing me for the last time.

From: Kit Ryan <kit.ryan@vmail.com>
To: Jessa Kingsley <jessajkingsley@rocketmail.com>
Date: July 7
Subject: 361 days

Hey baby,

Thanks for all your e-mails. We've finally arrived in country. It took me a while to get an Internet connection in the room but now we're all set up. I miss you like crazy too. As soon as I figure out how to get a calling card I'll call. Internet is crap so I can't Skype.

You wouldn't believe this place. Kabul is pretty much still a war zone—the US embassy compound is huge—over a thousand people working here and we're on permanent high alert. Our detachment commander isn't too much of an asshole, though he's put Riley and me on night shift for the next three months.

Thanks for the photos by the way J . . . is that an early Christmas present? When did you steal my phone and take those? Next time please feel free to pose while I take them. I'm sharing a room with Riley so I had to lock myself in the bathroom to enjoy them. And yes, I did put a lock on my phone.

Did you speak to your mom yet? How's it going with my dad? How are rehearsals?

Love you,
K.

From: Jessa Kingsley <jessajkingsley@rocketmail.com>
To: Kit Ryan <kit.ryan@vmail.com>
Date: July 25
Subject: 343 days

Your dad insisted on making dinner last night. I'm not sure the last time he cooked anything more than a boiled egg but it was super sweet of him. I'm glad you inherited your cooking skills from your mom, though. He misses you—make sure you e-mail him. I tried to get him to talk about your mom and my dad by the way, but he changed the subject. It's so weird. I'm going to get it out of him eventually.

So . . . you asked if I'd figured out what I was doing and I have. I've decided I'm going to take a year off and try to save some money. I got a job waitressing part time at the diner where Jo works. Photo attached of me in my uniform. Don't laugh. I felt bad not contributing to the bills here and I need to buy gas for your truck too. It eats it. Don't even try to suggest sending me money again, Kit. It's so sweet of you but I'm fine. I have my first waitressing shift this afternoon. Wish me luck.

Rehearsals are going well. I've learned all my lines (all twelve of them)! We get our costumes soon. You are going to love it. Mine's basically a French maid costume.

Gotta run. I'm late.

Love you
Jessa xxx
P.S. Tell Riley to e-mail me.

From: Kit Ryan <kit.ryan@vmail.com>
To: Jessa Kingsley <jessajkingsley@rocketmail.com>
Date: August 27
Subject: 310 days

Thanks for the package, baby. I ate all the Reese's Pieces already—saving the Skittles. Was I meant to give any to Riley? Because if I was it's too late for that.

He was so psyched by the scan photo Jo sent him. He's stuck it to the wall by his bed and keeps showing it to everyone.

I think you should give your mom a chance. Just hear her out. I wish I could be there with you. You've no idea how much I miss you, how often I dream about you. My phone battery keeps running low I spend so much time looking at those photos of you.

Good luck with the dress rehearsal tomorrow. I know you'll do great. You should wear your costume to the diner—I think it would triple your tips. Do you get to keep it? ;)

Kx

From: Jessa Kingsley <jessajkingsley@rocketmail.com>
To: Kit Ryan <kit.ryan@vmail.com>
Date: August 28
Subject: 309 days

Thank you for the flowers! They're so beautiful. Even from the other side of the world you manage to keep your most romantic boyfriend title. Dress rehearsal starts in two hours. Sooooo nervous. Did I tell you your dad bought a front row seat for opening night? He even asked if he could record it so he could send you a copy. Did you ask him to do that?

So, the big news is that I spoke to my mom. She came by the other day. I think your dad had something to do with it because when I got home from work they were both there, waiting for me in the living room. It was like an intervention. The long and short of it is that I'm moving back home. I'm not sure how you're going to feel about this. I'm not sure how I feel about it. Part of me really doesn't want to go—I'm so happy here—but another part feels guilty and like it's the right thing to do.

My dad has apparently admitted he might have a problem and my mom says he's getting help and doing much better. I figured it's only going to be for ten months until you get HOME so I should just bite the bullet. I'm going to pay my way, though.

I increased my shifts at the diner and Didi's dad offered me some part-time work while his assistant is on maternity leave so I'm managing to save quite a lot, and I'm going to need every cent . . .

. . . Because I looked into the courses at USC like you suggested and I'm going to apply for their BFA in acting for next year. Didi's having so much fun there, and I keep imagining you and me living there together in some cool apartment in Santa Monica. Some place right on the beach—can you picture it? You opening up your café and me taking classes. It's just ten months, Kit. Just over three hundred days. I can't wait to see you again.

Love you and miss you so much,
Jessa x

P.S. Yes I get to keep the costume. I'm already fantasizing about the night I wear it and all the things I'm going to do to you.

Kit

We've been pulling the night shift for eight weeks, and I'm getting used to being nocturnal. It works well, as Jessa's twelve hours behind, so as I stand on guard duty I get to imagine her waking up, going about her day, and when my shift ends I know there'll be e-mails from her waiting for me, and if I'm lucky, some photos, too.

I pause halfway to Post One, remembering that this morning she won't be waking up in our bed but back in her old one. I wonder how that's going, how her dad is, whether her mom was right about him getting treatment. It's frustrating being stuck here so far away from Jessa, and I have a niggling anxiety that worries like an itch beneath a plaster cast, something I can't seem to scratch, that her living back home will change things between us—that her dad's anger at me might rub off on her, or that Jessa will lose some of the confidence she's gained and start kowtowing to his demands again. But she seems pretty set on going to USC next year from what she says, and I draw some comfort from the fantasy she painted of us living there.

I roll my hands over my phone in my pocket. The keys

are getting worn from all the scrolling I'm doing over the photographs and texts she's sending. Fuck, I miss her, I think as I crunch across the gravel toward the guard post, more than I even thought possible. It's a crescent moon tonight, thin as a rind of cheese, and the stars are blazing, reminding me of our last night in the desert. As always, I fix on the North Star—our star, as I've started thinking of it—and think about Jessa.

"I'll take sentry," Riley says to me, interrupting my thoughts.

"Okay," I say, nodding at the two guys we're replacing. I shrug my gun farther up my shoulder and head inside the guard post.

"This is alpha one to bravo two, in position," I say into my radio and listen as all the other posts around the compound radio in.

On automatic, I scan the console, checking all the alarm systems, before tracking my way through the cameras, making sure the feeds to all fifty are working.

Through the blast-proof glass I can see Riley standing sentry at the gate, silhouetted against the floodlights. The embassy is ringed with twenty-foot-high walls and razor wire. It's like a prison. Post one is the main guard post at the entrance to the embassy compound.

At midnight I swap posts with Riley. He grins and slaps me on the back. "Yo, dude, no staring up at the stars and jonesing after my sister."

"Shut the fuck up," I laugh, unshouldering my weapon as I walk out the door.

About fifteen feet out I stop in front of the barrier. I don't mind standing at the gate. It's quiet out here at night, only a few cars passing by occasionally. The night passes slowly, but then, at four, after four hours' standing, I suddenly remember I haven't called Jessa to wish her luck for the performance. Shit.

I turn around and make a hand gesture through the glass at Riley. He comes to the door.

"What's up?" he shouts.

"Can you cover for me for five? I need to call Jessa."

He raises an eyebrow and shakes his head at me.

"It's opening night tonight," I plead. "I said I'd call and wish her luck. I totally forgot."

"Okay, fine. Just hurry it up," he says, striding toward me.

He raps his knuckles against my helmet as I walk past him into the guard post. "And no phone sex," he yells over his shoulder as he takes up position where I've been standing.

Once inside the post I put my gun down and pull out my phone. It's totally against protocol to make a call while on duty, but it's four a.m., no one's around, and Riley's done it before when he forgot Jo's birthday, so he owes me one. And as for the phone sex, I save that for when Riley's in the shower and I have the room to myself.

Quickly I dial Jessa's number. It rings and rings with no answer so I hang up and try again. This time I let it ring through to voice mail, but before I get to leave a message I catch sight of something out of the corner of my eye.

My head flies up. I hang up and put the phone down on the side, grabbing instinctively for my weapon. Riley's walking forward, holding up his arm and waving.

Out of the shadows I see the shape of a man, bundled up, head bent, walking purposefully toward the gate. When he steps into the light, I see he's wearing a long brown chapan—a traditional Afghan coat. Through the glass I hear Riley yelling at him, ordering him to stop.

"Come in post one."

I jump and hit the comms button on my radio.

"This is post one," I say, watching the altercation outside the window, my thumb easing the safety off my weapon.

"This is post four. Be advised. A minivan has just pulled up against the compound wall."

"Roger that," I say, glancing at the camera feed. "Be advised we have a single foot mobile approaching post one."

"Roger that." I recognize the voice of the gunny sergeant, my direct commanding officer. "Interrogative," he asks. "Do you have a visual on any weapons?"

I scan the man. He's stopped walking toward the gate and is now placing his hands on top of his head as per Riley's barked orders. I can hear Riley now yelling at him to lie facedown on the ground with his arms and legs spread. The man doesn't appear to be listening, or maybe he just doesn't understand English. He takes his eyes off Riley for a moment and his gaze drifts toward me. For an instant that seems to stretch into infinity, we lock eyes. A smile appears on his face and then his eyes lift to the sky. Just then his coat flaps open, and I catch a glimpse of the blocks of explosives strapped to his chest and the spaghetti tangle of wires before the coat falls closed again.

Fuck. Riley doesn't seem to have noticed. He's squinting against the glare of floodlights.

Radio static bursts in my ears. "Interrogative. Do they have weapons?"

I don't answer. I'm running to the door, my gun already at my shoulder, my finger halfway depressed on the trigger.

"Riley!" I yell.

I'm running straight toward him now. He turns. Just a

heartbeat. That's how long the pause is between Riley turning at the sound of his name and the blast that comes, but it's long enough for me to see the realization flare across his face, long enough for me to read the terror and disbelief that chases it, long enough for the image to imprint itself on my retina like a branding iron on skin.

"Bomb!" I shout, but the word is sucked away in the roar of the explosion. I'm picked up, thrown backward, blinded by a flash of white light. I'm hurled against the side of the gatepost. A wave of heat surges overhead and everything fades to black.

Jessa

missed two calls from Kit before the performance, and I've heard nothing from him since. As soon as I wake, I reach for my phone to see if he's replied to any of my messages or left a voice mail or e-mail, but there's nothing, just a blank screen, reminding me unnervingly of that moment at the end of a movie just before the credits roll. There's nothing from Riley either, though maybe that's not so surprising as Riley's always been useless at staying in touch. I sit up and dial Kit's number. It rings straight through to his voice mail, and at the sound of his voice telling me to leave a message, I close my eyes, feeling a stab of pain spear me between my ribs.

"Hey," I say. "It's me. Call me back. I love you."

I hang up and put the phone down, staring at it. Something doesn't feel right, something's niggling at me, but I push the thought away with a shake of the head and get out of bed. It's just before seven, and I'm due at the hospital to help out Didi's father in less than an hour.

I fumble for my clothes, my legs a little shaky. I blame it on the adrenaline from last night that's still pumping through my body.

It was such a rush being on stage again, seeing my name in the program, hearing the applause at the end—I can't wait to tell Kit all about it. But more than that I can't wait to tell him about the shock of looking up and seeing not only Kit's dad and sister in the front row but, seated two rows behind them, my parents too.

For one heart-stopping moment as I took my bow I'd thought my dad was going to storm the stage and drag me off it. I waited backstage too nervous to show my face until Kit's dad came and got me and convinced me it was safe. And there they were, my mom and dad, waiting for me outside the back door of the theater with a bunch of flowers, all smiles, telling me how proud they were of me. My dad even hugged me.

We haven't spoken much since I moved back home, but my mom was right, my dad is definitely calmer. If I didn't know better, I'd think the doctors had prescribed Zoloft or something, he's that mellow, but my dad has always been anti-drugs—any kind of drugs, not just the illegal kind. I guess therapy with Didi's dad must be working. I'm glad. I am. But there's a long way to go before I forgive him for everything. A very long way. One day soon I'm going to have to talk to him about Kit and also tell him that I've decided not to go to USD—but I'm waiting until I know for sure he's not going to go postal. I don't want to cause a relapse or anything.

Once I'm dressed, I pick up my phone and slip it into my back pocket. Why hasn't Kit called? The nagging feeling is back, more insistent now; it feels as though someone is behind me, tapping me angrily on the shoulder trying to force me to turn around. Once again I shrug it off. I'm being stupid and paranoid, that's all. He's fine. Of course he's fine.

I'm halfway down the stairs, gathering my hair into a ponytail, thoughts a million miles away, when a blur outside the window pulls me up short.

I take another step, the view clears, and when I realize what I'm seeing, *who* I'm seeing, my stomach plummets and the air leaves my lungs like a final exhalation. My arms fall slowly to my sides. My body's instinct is to turn and run back upstairs, to tear into the bathroom and lock the door, but I'm frozen.

Time seems to have slowed. Kit's father hasn't moved. He's standing at the end of the driveway staring up at the house, squinting against the early morning glare. He takes a step down the driveway toward the house, and that's when I know for certain that either Kit or Riley is dead.

I grab for the banister to stay upright. Memories, images, words, flicker through my mind like scratched fragments of film: Kit's arms around my waist drawing me closer, our first kiss under the cover of darkness just by the back door, the smile on his face the first time we slept together, the blue of his eyes lit up by the sparks from a Chinese lantern, the fierceness in his voice when he told me he was going to love me forever.

Come back to me. That was the very last thing I said to him. *Come back to me.*

Always. The very last thing he said to me.

Then I see Riley as a kid throwing a toy train down the stairs, dive-bombing into the pool, holding my hand at our grandfather's funeral, grinning and high-fiving Kit after they'd enlisted. The snapshot of him in his uniform on graduation day. The circles under his eyes the last time I saw him. The grin on his face when he told me he was going to be a dad.

The door buzzes. I jump. But I stay where I am, frozen halfway up the stairs. If I don't answer the door, maybe he'll go away. Maybe this won't be happening. But the doorbell sounds again. And then I hear footsteps on the landing above me. My mother's voice, sleepy and confused. "Jessa? Who is it? Why are you just standing there?"

I turn to her. Her hand is pressed to her mouth. Standing in her nightdress, her hair unbrushed, the blood rushing from her face, she looks like she's seen a ghost. No. That's wrong. She looks like she is a ghost.

The bell buzzes for a third time.

"Get the door, Jessa," my mother says in a strange voice I don't recognize. It startles me enough that I start to walk down the stairs. I feel calmer all of a sudden, like I'm floating outside my body. This can't be happening. It's not real. It's just a dream.

I find myself standing somehow in front of the door. I unlock it. I open it. Kit. Riley. Kit. Riley. Which is it?

Kit's father blinks at me. He's been crying. His eyes are red, his cheeks wet. He's still crying in fact.

"Jessa," Kit's father says in a husky voice, "I'm sorry."

"Who?" I hear myself ask. "Who is it?"

"Can I come in?" he asks, his attention now fixed on my mom.

"Who? Who is it?" I repeat.

My mom's hands are on my shoulders. She's trying to pull me away from the doorway, but I refuse to budge. I'm distantly aware that I've started crying, and a voice in my head is snapping at me to pull it together, but I can't. "Who?" I yell.

He closes his eyes as though praying, and when he opens them, it's disorientating because I see Kit—the same cobalt-blue eyes rimmed at the edges with black.

The blood is pounding in my ears is so loudly I barely hear the name.

I fall away from the door, reeling backward as though he's slapped me, my brain whirring, struggling to process what he's just said. The room spins like a carnival ride and I find myself on my knees. In the background someone is crying. A rough, keening sound as though they're being hollowed out with some medieval torture device.

Kit

When I come to, it takes me a few seconds to piece together where I am. I stagger blindly to my feet, confused and lurching like a drunk, aware only distantly of a stinging sharp pain drilling through my side and that my brain feels like a ten-ton weight rattling loose inside my skull. An explosion. The pieces start to come together, fragments of memory jarring loose. A bomb. Oh shit. Riley!

My ears are ringing, the roar of the blast still echoing through me. I cough my way through a cloud of dust and debris toward the door. Riley. Fuck. Where is he? I stumble frantically toward the gate but nothing remains of it, only rubble and thick black smoke eerily lit from behind by the floodlights. For several seconds I just stand there, coughing, my eyes streaming, trying to understand. Where's the gate gone? Where's Riley gone?

I turn in a circle on the spot. Where the hell is he?

"Riley?" I yell.

Flames lick at the sky, and an orange haze mushrooms over the compound. Suddenly the alarm cuts through the ringing in my ears, a siren blare that sounds as if it's coming from someplace deep inside me. And then I hear the sound of boots stampeding, people yelling over me. I hear my name, but it sounds as if someone is calling to me from down a long, dark tunnel.

I'm dragged to my feet, and someone tries to pull me away from the gatepost, but I wrench myself free and start running—a limping half jog, the pain in my side slowing me down.

"Riley," I yell again, spinning in a circle. Swallowed by the dust and dirt that have blanketed out the floodlights and the stars, it feels as though I'm standing in a choking-hot cave. "Riley!" I shout until my throat is hoarse.

But he doesn't answer.

Jessa

Riley. No. No.

A sharp hook snags behind my rib cage, ripping upward, tearing a path through my heart, puncturing my lungs, rasping up my throat. The room spins even more violently. Faces lunge past me—my mother, Kit's father.

Kit! What about Kit?

With both hands on the floor, I steady myself and take a deep breath in. My lungs are on fire. "Kit. What about Kit?" I manage to gasp.

"He's okay. A slight injury, but okay."

He's okay. An intense burst of relief douses the pain momentarily, like water being thrown on a fire. I can breathe again. But it lasts for only a moment before the blackness rushes back in, threatening to suffocate me, and the pain returns—a razor-sharp blade slicing again and again between my ribs. Riley. How can he be dead?

Somehow I'm in the living room, sitting on the sofa, with no knowledge of how I got there. My mother is sitting beside me. She's not speaking. She's staring straight ahead at the wall, at the photograph of Riley in his uniform on graduation day. I shake my head, looking at Kit's father Ben standing in the middle of the room. This can't be happening. This isn't real. Riley can't be dead. They must have made a mistake.

"I don't believe you," I say, hearing the note of defiance in my voice. I pull out my phone. "I'm going to call him."

Kit's father kneels down in front of me. His hands—calloused and warm—close over mine. "Jessa," he says softly, "it's not a mistake. We've had confirmation."

I jump to my feet. I have no idea where I'm going. I only know one thing; that I need to get away. I need air. I need to find someone who'll tell me this is all a joke. I need to outrun this.

I make it to the door and slam straight into my dad. He catches me by the shoulders. I try to push past him. I shove with all my might, but he doesn't budge. I look up at him angrily and suddenly stop shoving as it dawns on me that he doesn't know—he doesn't yet know that his son is dead, that Riley is gone. And I feel a sharp stab of envy. I envy him the fact that he still exists in the before, in the place where Riley is still alive. And I hate him for it, while also pitying him for the blow that's about to fall that he has no clue is coming.

He's looking at me confused and blurry eyed, still wearing his pajamas. I note the gray hair peeking out the top of his shirt and the fact that he hasn't shaved yet. I see for the first time the thick, raised veins snaking over his hands. I take in all of these details with furious concentration, as if my brain has decided that if it focuses on the minutia it won't have to contemplate the bigger picture. My dad looks over my shoulder, and his face drains of blood as he sees Kit's dad and my mom in the living room.

"What is it?" he asks, his fingers digging into my arms hard.

"Riley's dead," I tell him in a voice so calm that it rattles me. Why am I so calm? How can I sound so matter-of-fact when inside it feels as if a storm is raging? How can I announce something so momentous as though I'm talking about the weather?

My father's face turns ashen. He releases me and walks unsteadily toward my mother. I watch him pull her into his arms. I see her knuckles bleach white as she grips him around the waist, her mouth pulled down into a silent scream of agony. My dad turns toward Kit's dad and a half-formed thought careers through my mind: *He needs to leave. Kit's dad can't be here. They hate each other.* But then I see that they're talking. My father is asking questions; Kit's father is answering calmly, quietly.

It sounds as if they're underwater, but I make out the words *suicide bomber* then *car bomb* then *body home for burial* before I cover my ears and collapse once more to the floor, the screams inside my head growing so loud that eventually they drown out everything.

Kit

f I concentrate with all my might on the little things—on straightening my cuffs, on polishing my boots until I can see my face in them, on picking every piece of lint off the sleeves of my uniform—I've found it helps keep the dark thoughts and the images at bay. I can still sense them there, lurking in the darkness like a pack of hyenas scrapping for my attention, but at least they're not right there in my face.

I had thought it might be better once I was back on US soil, that putting a distance between myself and what happened would make it somehow easier to deal with, but it hasn't. Sleep is the worst—one nonstop nightmare in which I'm paralyzed, watching the man in the coat approach Riley, who's standing sentry at the gate, trying to scream at Riley to run but not able to make a sound. But even during the day, if I let my concentration slip for even a millisecond, then the memories rush in like a tidal wave dragging me under. And each time it's getting harder and harder to fight my way back to the surface. They're sharp-edged, 3-D—images that burst with gory, technicolor detail. Sounds too—the blast still echoes in my head five days later, the back of my throat is still raw from yelling Riley's name, and the acrid smell of smoke still lingers on my skin despite the number of times I've tried to scrub it off. My muscles won't quit trembling either, and my hands shake even now as I try to do up the buttons on my shirt.

I glance at the bottle of painkillers on the side and think about taking one, or maybe even two or three to kill the pain. But I'm not sure even a whole bottle would be enough to numb this, and besides, I'm not even sure I want to numb it. The constant burning ache in my side just beneath my ribs where some shrapnel from the bomb blast struck me gives me something to focus on other than the voice in my head that's striving to be heard over the ringing in my ears—the voice that hasn't let up for a single second since it happened; the voice telling me *it should have been you.*

I pull open the dresser drawer to look for my cuff links, and the room tips sideways with a lurch. Jessa's clothes fill the drawer, neatly folded as if just put there. My chest constricts at the sight. I stare at the pile of underwear—delicate lace, pastel colors—fighting the urge to sink my hands into it, lift it to my face, and inhale deeply. I draw a sharp breath and manage to get a hit of her perfume, the first thing other than smoke I've managed to smell in five days. It sends my head spinning. Shit. I ram the drawer shut, making the whole dresser shake, then, resting my palms on the top to stop my arms from trembling, I squeeze my eyes shut.

Instantly I'm overcome by a fast-flowing stream of images: Riley turning toward me, the flash of comprehension on his face in the split second before the blast, the white sheet lightning that swallowed him whole, the whooshing roar of the flame that knocked me backward. The smoking darkness, the voidlike sense of something being fundamentally wrong with the world that rippled through me straight afterward as though someone had switched off gravity.

It should have been me.

My phone buzzes, and my heart explodes like a bomb in my chest. I spin around, disorientated. *Breathe, breathe,* I order myself as the room starts to spin. The slightest noise keeps setting me off, throwing me right back to the moment the bomb went off. The phone is still buzzing. Dizzily, I cross to the bedside table, where it sits vibrating, and grab for it.

It's Jessa. I stare at her name, my heart now trying to hammer its way clean out of my chest. Fuck. I jab at the cancel button. And then for good measure I turn the damn thing off. In a fit of desperation I try to find somewhere I can hide it.

I don't hear my dad knock, and when he comes into the room, I'm still pacing anxiously back and forth, looking for somewhere to hide my phone. I'm aware I probably look like someone trying to hide a bloody murder weapon.

"Have you spoken to her yet?" my dad asks, nodding at the phone in my hand.

I turn my back and, pulling out the top drawer of the bedside table, drop my phone into it before slamming it shut.

"You need to speak to her. She needs you."

He drops his hand on my shoulder, and I stiffen automatically.

"Kit. You need to talk to someone. You need to take them up on that offer of counseling."

I brush off his hand and walk to the bed, getting down on my knees to roll up the camping mat I've been sleeping on for the last three nights. I've seen the counselor once already—it was mandatory. They told me I might start to display signs of post-traumatic stress disorder and that I was to notify them if I did. Jesus, I thought at the time, I'm never going to turn into Jessa's dad. But now here I am, going crazy just like him, the slight-est noise setting me off, acting like a jerk. The realization would make me laugh if the truth of it wasn't so fucked up.

"Kit."

I startle and look up. The sadness in my dad's eyes makes me wish I hadn't. I look away, focusing on the camping mat that's half rolled in my hands. I can't deal with this.

"It's not your fault," my dad says.

I stop what I'm doing and get to my feet. "Yes. Yes, it is," I say. It's the first time I've spoken to him, to anyone, since I got back yesterday. He's the first person who's guessed what's going on in my head. My dad walks to me and puts his hand out as though to rest it on my shoulder, but I back away. "It's my fucking fault. It was meant to be me! I was on duty. I asked him to swap with me. You don't get it. It should have been me. I'm the one that should be dead!"

I stare at him, breathing heavily. My dad holds my gaze, his expression calm. He nods. I want him to understand. I need him to understand and to start yelling at me. I need him to tell me he blames me too.

"Kit, there's nothing you could have done," he says quietly. "God works in mysterious ways."

I stare at him, my eyes bugging, my breathing uneven, my head starting to spin. "God? You're talking to me about God?" I yell. "Fuck God! There is no fucking God."

Pain passes across my dad's face. I can't bear to see it. I can't fucking handle it a moment longer. I cross to the dresser and grab the bottle of painkillers, pouring out three and downing them with one dry swallow. I'm too much of a fucking coward to face this sober.

"I need to go," I mutter to my dad, picking up my jacket from the back of the chair.

Jessa

Why does everyone wear black at these things? Riley would have hated it. He would have wanted a celebration and lots of color. He would have wanted pizza and steak at the wake, not cheese platters and quiches. He wouldn't have wanted classical music and hymns. He would have wanted something uplifting, something funny, maybe even some ironic Celine Dion.

I tried to argue this, but how could I win against my mother's zoned-out zombie face and my father's closed door? My dad barked the orders and here we stand, staring at the flag-draped coffin surrounded by grotesque-smelling displays of white calla lilies. How can Riley be in there? I think as I study the coffin. I still can't understand. I keep expecting to see him walking through the crowd, keep expecting to hear his voice, his laugh. Every knock on the door—and there have been many over the last few days—I keep expecting to be him.

My mother is standing beside me. She's wearing dark glasses, but I know behind them her eyes are foggy and dull. She isn't crying. For the first time in five days she's quiet, and that scares me more than the hysterical crying. How many Valium has she taken?

On my other side my dad stands rigid in full Dress Blues, the constellation of stars on his chest blindingly bright. He must have been up all night polishing them. His head is held high and his expression is as rigid as his back is straight, yet when I look closer, I see the cracks starting to appear in the carefully constructed facade: the quickness with which he swallows, the quiver of his chin, and a trembling bottom lip. He's barely holding it together and the realization surprises me, because it means that I'm the only one out of all of us who isn't falling apart, and I wonder why that is, *how* that is, and then I feel another wave of guilt wash over me.

I haven't cried at all since that first morning. I keep wondering if maybe there's something wrong with me. I can't even make myself cry. I've lain on my bed for hours forcing myself to think of Riley, dredging up memories from way back—of us as kids, of Riley teaching me to swim, of Riley and me hiding in a closet to evade the wrath of our father, of Riley spending two hours trying to pull out a splinter of glass from my foot when I was about nine, of Riley letting me tag along to watch him and Kit skateboard, even though it drastically reduced their level of cool. I've spent whole afternoons holding Jo's hand, watching her cry, and I've felt nothing, just a strange detachment as though I'm inhabiting the body of a stranger with no connection to the people around me.

Even now as I stand staring at the stars and stripes draped over Riley's coffin, I feel nothing except a weird emptiness and echoing bewilderment.

Jo is standing beside my mother. Her mother and sisters are with her, comforting her as she cries.

Finally, I lift my head and scan the dozen marines who are off to one side, holding their guns at the ready for the final salute. He's there. My heart slams into my mouth, and I think for a moment that I'm going to collapse, because the ground starts shaking beneath my feet. I wasn't sure if he would be here. Kit's dad told me he was home, that he was going to be here, but he hasn't answered any of my phone calls, so I wasn't sure I believed it. But seeing him now, eyes fixed resolutely ahead, his chin held high and his back ramrod straight, I finally feel a surge of heat rocket up my throat and tears start to burn the back of my eyes.

I fight both the urge to call his name and my instinct, which is to run to him. Instead, as the chaplain drones on about noble sacrifice and greater good, I stare at Kit, willing him to look my way. But he doesn't. He keeps staring resolutely straight ahead. His jaw tenses, though.

I know he can feel me watching him. So why won't he look at me? Why has he been ignoring my calls? What's going on?

Kit's dad told me he was struggling to deal with what had happened, but what the hell does he think *I'm* doing? Having an easy time of it? I've lost my brother.

I'm torn between wanting to run over there and throw myself into his arms, to sob and cry and rage against him, and wanting to race over there and punch him and hit him and scream at him that I hate him. Because how can he do this to me? How can he ignore me like this? How can he not know how much I need him right now? I hate him so much. And I love him so much. And I know he's hurting. But so am I.

Riley's commanding officer takes the podium and starts to speak, but I don't hear any of it. I can't concentrate on anything. My breathing is so loud in my ears it mutes everything else, and I can't tear my eyes off Kit.

Finally the time comes to toss earth onto the coffin, though. It's the part I've been dreading most. Jo and I go together, our arms gripped tightly around each other. The soil dribbles through my fingers, and the sound it makes as it hits the top of the coffin—that hollow pitter-patter—makes me flinch. It's followed by a dozen ear-splitting cracks as the marine guard sends a volley up into the sky. I look over and see Kit pulling the trigger on his rifle once, twice, three times, his expression set in stone. Jo lets out a terrible sob as the sound of the volley fades. I can barely hold her up, and someone comes forward to help me.

When I turn around, I see my father standing at the head of the grave, his face carefully arranged into a blank expression as he stares down at the coffin now half-obliterated by clods of dirt. Tears brighten his eyes, and his hands are clenched at his sides. I feel an urge to go to him, to bury myself in his chest and have him hold me, to hold him, but I can't seem to make my feet move, and I'm not sure how he'd respond if I did go to him.

My mother is standing in front of the row of white plastic chairs holding the folded flag from the coffin as though she's been handed a joke. She looks completely lost, unsure what to do, until Didi walks over to her and puts her arm around her to lead her away.

Someone is talking to me. I glance at them and recognize the someone as Todd. He's saying something to me, but I can't make out the words properly so I just say "thank you"—my stock reply whenever anyone speaks to me these days—and turn away. I need to find Kit. I need to talk to him.

The service is over. Everyone has started disbanding, scattering between the rows of square gravestones like ants, heading toward the line of black limousines waiting at the entrance to the cemetery. I scan the crowd two times, my eyes frantically flying to the men in uniform, checking them each off in turn, before finally accepting that Kit has gone.

Kit

could feel Jessa's eyes on me the whole time, could sense her trying to get me to turn and look at her. And what did I do? I ignored her. I kept staring straight ahead, focusing on the cool steel of my gun locked against my shoulder, the reassuringly heavy resistance of the trigger beneath my finger, focusing on anything but Jessa, anything but the coffin, anything but the images crowding at the edge of my vision trying to get my attention almost as insistently as Jessa.

At one point I did throw a quick glance her way. When she and Jo were standing at the graveside, I saw her catch Jo as she stumbled. I wanted to go to her then, to both of them, and beg forgiveness. I almost dropped my rifle to the ground and ran to her. I had to fight to stay where I was, force myself to keep staring into the middle distance with a blank face.

And even now, with the service coming to an end, I don't see how I can go over there and talk to her. How the hell do I walk past her mother, knowing that her son is dead because of me? How do I walk past her father, knowing how much he's always hated me, how much he must wish it were me that was dead and not Riley? He must have read the report by now. He must know that it was my fault, that I was negligent, that I broke the rules, and because of that Riley is gone.

Has he told Jessa? I almost hope he has, because I know I can't tell her. What could I possibly say? She asked me to take care of him. She made me promise. And I failed her.

As soon as the chaplain stops talking, as soon as we fire off three volleys in a farewell salute and the funeral guests start to wander back toward the limousines that are waiting, I shoot a glance in Jessa's direction, and my heart takes a beating when I see her talking to none other than Todd. I spin around and start heading away from the mourners, away from the grave, away from Jessa. All I can think of is putting some distance between me and everyone else.

I veer like a drunk toward a large oak tree and duck behind it, pressing my forehead to the bark, sucking in air as though it's going out of fashion and grabbing at the tree to stay upright. Out of nowhere a sob bursts up my throat, taking me by surprise. I punch the tree, savoring the jolt of pain that vibrates up my arm, the flames that shoot through my hand.

I punch the tree again and again in a fury, and by now I'm sobbing so hard that my nose is running and everything's a blur, but it feels good. It feels like release. And maybe if I keep punching, the pain in my fist will eventually engulf me completely and cancel out the pain raging inside. But suddenly, just as I jerk my arm back to throw another punch, someone catches me around the waist and hauls me backward. I try to fight them, kick them off, but I'm half-exhausted with all the punching and they're holding me too tight.

"Son, it's okay," my dad whispers. His arms are a vise, and

at the sound of his voice I instantly stop fighting and collapse against him. He holds me up and I just cry. I cry onto his shoulder just like when I was a kid and he came to tell me my mom had died.

When all the funeral guests have left and the limousines have driven off, my dad and I walk back toward the grave. Ushers are stacking the chairs, dismantling the podium and carrying it away, and picking up the litter. The flowers surround the graveside like white-dressed mourners. They look wrong—the kind of flower you'd see at a grandmother's funeral.

Riley always said he wanted a huge party if he died. And maybe that's why it doesn't feel as if he's really dead, as if this funeral or even this grave is his. But then I read his name spelled out in a floral display (he would have laughed at that), and it hits me all over again with the force of a tornado: He's dead.

My dad and I stand side by side. Two men with shovels are hovering at the edge of the grave, and I see my dad gesture at them to give us a minute.

"What do I do?" I ask after a minute of silence, staring down at Riley's coffin. I look at my dad, feeling tears still streaming down my face. What I mean to ask is, how do I get through this? I know I've done it before, with my mom, but that was different. I wasn't to blame. Then I had cancer to rage against. Now I have only myself to blame, and I don't know how to handle it. I look at my dad.

"You need to say good-bye properly," he says. "He was your best friend, Kit."

I frown and look away.

"I know you're angry and you're hurting and you just want to run away and find some way of burying the pain—believe me, I know. Why'd you think I was drunk for six years after your mother died?" He shakes his head. "Don't make the same mistake as me, Kit. Jessa's hurting. So is her family. You need to be there for her, for Jo. I wasn't there for you and your sister. I failed your mother." He squeezes my shoulder. "Don't fail Riley."

My eyes burn as though I've had acid thrown in them.

"I don't know how I can face her," I say so quietly I wonder if he heard me. "I don't know what to say."

"You'll figure it out," my dad says, putting his hand on my shoulder.

I drop my dad home and then drive to Jessa's house. Cars are double-parked the whole way up the street, so I leave the truck around the corner, parking in exactly the same place I used to drop Jessa after our make-out sessions. They seem so long ago now—like they happened decades and not mere weeks ago.

The front door of her house is shut, but through the window I can see crowds of people gathered in the living room holding paper plates of food. I take a deep breath, forcing myself to remember my dad's words. He's right. I can't walk away. I owe it to Riley. I owe it to Jessa. I owe it to Riley and Jo's unborn child to be there for it. I need to tell Jessa to her face exactly what happened. I need to beg her forgiveness. And then maybe, if she can forgive me, we can find a way through this together.

Before I make it to the door, though, it swings open and someone walks out. I stop dead in my tracks. Jessa's dad is marching toward me, his face stony yet his eyes blazing. He stops in front of me, barring my way, and the first thing I think is, *He knows. He's read the report.*

"Colonel," I say, saluting out of habit, and because I don't know what else to do or say. The last time we saw each other I was yelling at him about what a shitty father he was. Fuck. I start having second thoughts about coming. What was I thinking?

"I told you the last time you showed your face to get off my property and not come back."

"I'm just here to pay my respects," I say quietly, keeping my eyes on the ground.

"I need you to leave," he says. "And to stay the hell away from my daughter."

I look up at him sharply.

"The last thing she needs is you in her life. She's just lost her brother."

I grit my teeth. Isn't that exactly why she needs me?

"I read the report," he says next. "Abandoning your post?"

I stare at my shoes, trying to breathe calmly, though my head is starting to whirl and the crackling of flames is filling my ears. He knows. Of course he knows.

"I'm writing you up for insubordination and dereliction of duty," he says. "I should have done so a long time ago."

I stay quiet, letting his words hit me square in the face. It's nothing less than I deserve.

"Because of you, my son is dead," he spits. "Are you going to go in there and explain that to Jessa? That the reason her brother is dead is because of you?"

I don't answer, but I do look up at him.

He makes a face, a sneer of disgust lifting his top lip. "I didn't think so. The best thing you can do right now is walk away and stay away. For good, this time."

He glares at me for several more seconds before finally shaking his head and walking back inside, his shoulders slumping.

I watch him walk inside and shut the door behind him. Unable to move, I watch him through the window winding his way through the crowd.

Briefly, just briefly, I catch sight of Jessa standing with her back to me, her blond hair a lighthouse beam amid a sea of black. The sight of her is enough to snatch the last of my breath away. I clutch my side, forcing myself to back away, because he's right. I'm no good for her. I'm no good for anyone.

Jessa

Through the window I catch a flash of blue. Someone—a friend of my father's—is talking to me, but I walk away mid-sentence, leaving them standing there, and cross to the window to get a better look. My heart thumps hard in my chest as I see that it's Kit. He's come! But then, with a sinking feeling, I see him turning and walking away back toward the street and all the parked cars.

I push past crowds of people standing in the doorway talking in hushed whispers and rush into the hallway.

"Are you okay?"

I spin around. Didi is standing in front of me.

"What do you need?" she asks me.

Didi is about the only person other than Kit's dad who I've been able to cope with being around since Riley died. She doesn't beat about the bush or cry in front of me. She doesn't pat my hand and speak in meaningless platitudes about how it will all be okay and that time will heal all.

"I just saw Kit," I tell her breathlessly.

Didi looks around the hallway.

"No. Outside," I clarify.

Didi takes hold of my hands. "Go," she says. "You need to talk to him."

I shake my head. "I can't just go," I say, thinking of my mom, who's currently sitting in the living room out of her head on Valium surrounded by women offering her glasses of water, tissues, and pigs in blankets.

"You guys need to talk," Didi says. She's borne the brunt of my five days of grief compounded with anguish over Kit's silence. Her theory is that he's suffering from PTSD, not, she claims, that that fully excuses him from being an asshole.

When she sees me hesitating, she pushes me toward the door and thrusts some keys into my hand. "Go," she says again. "Take my car. I'll cover for you."

Kit's truck is parked in his driveway. My heart is beating so fast it feels as if it might explode out of my chest as I walk up the path to the front door. When I pull out the keys, I hesitate for a minute, wondering if I'm doing the right thing. What if he doesn't want to see me? I mean, I know already that he doesn't want to see me. If he did, he would have answered my calls. He would have hung around after the funeral. He would have come to the wake.

Well, screw him, I decide. It isn't all about him. It isn't just about what he wants. I want to talk to him. I *need* to talk to him.

It's anger that propels me through the door, fury that has started to bubble through my veins. I run up the stairs and storm straight into the bedroom, words already bursting on my tongue. But he's not there. His jacket is hanging over the back of the chair, though, and his gloves and hat are laid out neatly on the dresser. I contemplate the room, the half-folded camping mat on the floor—he's not even sleeping in the bed—but before I can make sense of it, a noise makes me jerk around.

Kit is standing in the doorway. He's yanking off his tie, and when he sees me, he freezes like that, his arm caught halfway, so it looks as though he's trying to strangle himself. His arm drops slowly to his side.

The first thing I notice is that he has dark shadows under his eyes and hollows beneath his cheekbones. The word "shell-shocked" comes to mind, those stories of First World War soldiers who came back from the trenches with their nerves shot to pieces. The second thing I notice is that his hands are bloodied, the knuckles bruised and swollen as if he just tried to punch his way out of a steel cage. My stomach heaves at the sight. I have to stop my legs from moving toward him, because seeing him, being this close to him, seeing him hurt and in pain, is making all the defenses I've put up crumble to dust.

It takes Kit a few seconds to recover from the surprise of seeing me standing in his room. He falters, letting his guard down for just a moment, and in that moment I see something flare across his face—a look of total devastation—and it instantly dissolves my anger and makes me stumble toward him.

He turns his back on me before I reach him and crosses to the dresser. I stop short and stare at his back, my throat closing shut.

"Kit," I say, putting my hands on his arms, "please, talk to me, tell me what's going on."

His back muscles lock and his head remains bowed. I turn him slowly around to face me.

"Kit," I say, taking his face in my hands, trying to make him look at me.

He won't. He stays resolutely staring at the ground. But I feel the subtle shift in his body. I can read him. He's too familiar to me. His breathing has become shallow and the pulse beats rapidly in his neck; his shoulders slump.

I stroke Kit's cheek and he closes his eyes, a look of anguish passing across his face that I want to wipe away. I want to make it better. I reach up on tiptoe and kiss him. He's unresponsive at first, but I press myself against him, and after a few seconds I feel his resistance start to fade. Slowly he starts to kiss me back, and I wrap my arms around his neck to stop him from pulling away. His arms finally come around my waist and he draws me tight, pulling me close, and a sob catches in my throat because finally I don't feel like I'm free-falling into a bottomless abyss anymore. I feel like I've been caught.

I open my mouth, and our kiss suddenly becomes frantic, desperate. The familiar taste of him, the intoxicating smell of him, the burning heat of his lips—I can't get enough—and as he laces his fingers through my hair and forces his tongue into my mouth, I realize that we're both trying to claw our way back into the light, trying to find some kind of redemption, or some way of overcoming the pain.

Kit's hands start ripping at my dress and my own fingers start tearing at his shirt, and all I can hear is the rasp of our breathing, the frantic beating of my pulse like a drum in my ears. All the pain fades, all the memories disappear, the world becomes a faint blur at the edges of my consciousness. All there is is the here and now and Kit and the fire in my body. It's a feeling I don't ever want to stop, that I focus on with all my might, because on the other side is only grief and darkness.

We fumble with each other's clothes. I forget the shirt and

tear at his belt, and he gives up trying to undo my dress and instead just lifts the skirt and pulls my underwear roughly aside. Without a word exchanged, both of us breathing hard, Kit lifts me onto the dresser, shoving all the things on top of it to the side. I wrap my legs around his waist, desperate to draw him inside me, my hands tugging at him, and in the next moment he pushes into me.

I let out a cry that's half anguish and half ecstasy. Kit drives into me with a grunt, and I grip his shoulders and throw my head back. He kisses my neck, bites me, sucks hard enough that I cry out again. He pulls me to him, his hands gripping my thighs, holding me in place, forcing a pace that's taking me quickly to the edge. I'm happily free-falling again, tumbling down into an abyss, but one that feels like oblivion, one where pain doesn't exist.

I open my eyes and see Kit has his eyes screwed shut. I whisper his name and they flash open and we stare at each other, both of us panting, sweating, trembling, and I see, even through the desire dulling his eyes, how haunted he looks beneath it, how he's not fully with me but someplace else, and with a jolt I'm brought right back to the moment as the memories start to flood in. I close my eyes and turn my head away from him, not willing to be drawn back there just yet, wanting to hold on to the feeling of Kit inside me, wanting to recapture the possibility of oblivion, wanting, above all, to forget.

Kit

She turns her head away, squeezing her eyes shut, and the action jars me. She can't even look at me. Driven by something I don't have words for, I lift her off the dresser, turn her around so she has her back to me, and then push inside her again. This way she doesn't have to see my face.

She gasps loudly, a sound I know well, bending forward and bracing herself against the top of the dresser. It spurs me on, and so I put my hands on her back and drive into her harder—harder than I've ever done before—not wanting to hurt her but because I can't stop myself, and because she seems to need it like this as much as I do, and I'm lost in her, totally fucking lost in her, can't get enough of the feel of being inside her after so long. For the first time in five days my brain empties; the screams and cries stop echoing, my muscles stop trembling, the pain eases.

Jessa lets out another cry. Her muscles contract tight around me and I know she's about to come. I push deeper and deeper, owning her, wanting to find my own escape, and then she does come, loud and hard. I can feel my own orgasm building, but suddenly, just before the release, I realize what the fuck I'm doing. I'm not even wearing a condom. Breathing unevenly, I pull out, stumbling backward.

Jesus Christ, what am I thinking? This is Riley's sister. It's the day of his funeral and I'm fucking his sister. What the hell would he say? What would her father say? I haven't even told her the truth yet. Disgusted with myself, I turn around, dark spots bursting at the edges of my vision, the room starting to tilt.

I hear Jessa say something but I shake my head. I can't look at her. I'm too ashamed, and my vision is blurring anyway.

"Kit," she says again.

I turn. She's standing, flushed, against the dresser, her hair and dress awry, one hand clutched to her side, looking so beautiful and so fragile that another wave of self-loathing washes over me.

"What?" she asks. "What is it?"

I can't find the words. All I can do is shake my head. Jessa takes a step toward me, the look on her face so devastated and confused that I hold up a hand to stop her and close my eyes automatically so I don't have to witness it, because then I'd have to confront the fact that I'm the one that put it there.

"You should leave," I manage to say.

I can feel her standing there in front of me, not moving, so I risk opening my eyes. "Get out," I say again.

The smell of acrid smoke fills my nostrils, the roar of flames starts to build. I press my hands to my ears to block it out.

"Just go!" I yell, turning around.

My chest is crushed as though I'm lying beneath rubble. I can't breathe.

I barely hear the door slam over the sound of screams in my head.

From: Jessa Kingsley <jessajkingsley@rocketmail.com>
To: Kit Ryan <kit.ryan@vmail.com>
Date: September 7
Subject: Please

Kit, please answer my e-mails.

From: Jessa Kingsley <jessajkingsley@rocketmail.com>
To: Kit Ryan <kit.ryan@vmail.com>
Date: September 11
Subject: Why?

Your dad told me you've shipped out. You left without saying good-bye. How could you do that?

I don't know what happened between us. I don't understand anything that's happened. I don't understand why Riley is dead. I don't understand how one day I can wake up and everything is okay in the world and the next day I wake up and nothing is okay. Nothing will ever be okay again. That's how it feels. And I don't know how I'm supposed to get through this without you but you won't even talk to me. What's going on?

Please e-mail me back. I love you.

From: Jessa Kingsley <jessajkingsley@rocketmail.com>
To: Kit Ryan <kit.ryan@vmail.com>
Date: September 13
Subject: Come back to me.

Your dad called me and told me everything. Kit, how could you ever think I'd blame you for what happened? I can't imagine what you're going through. I hate it that you couldn't talk to me. Please talk to me now.

It's not your fault he died, Kit. It is NOT YOUR FAULT. You have to stop blaming yourself. Riley wouldn't want you to. I don't want you to. Please. I need you. I miss you. Please come back to me. I love you.

Jx

From: Jessa Kingsley <jessajkingsley@rocketmail.com>
To: Kit Ryan <kit.ryan@vmail.com>
Date: September 30
Subject: Stardust

Someone posted this on Instagram and it made me think of you. Of us.

Everyone who terrifies you is sixty-five percent water.
And everyone you love is made of stardust, and I know sometimes
you cannot even breathe deeply, and
the night sky is no home, and
you have cried yourself to sleep enough times
that you are down to your last two percent, but

nothing is infinite,
not even loss.

You are made of the sea and the stars, and one day
you are going to find yourself again.

F. Butler

From: Jessa Kingsley <jessajkingsley@rocketmail.com>
To: Kit Ryan <kit.ryan@vmail.com>
Date: October 8
Subject: hello?

Are you there?
I miss you.

From: Jessa Kingsley <jessajkingsley@rocketmail.com>
To: Kit Ryan <kit.ryan@vmail.com>
Date: October 31
Subject: Hi

Why are you doing this?

From: Jessa Kingsley <jessajkingsley@rocketmail.com>
To: Kit Ryan <kit.ryan@vmail.com>
Date: December 5
Subject: are you there?

I feel like I'm talking into the void. Are you even getting these?

It's been 100 days since Riley died. People keep telling me that it will get better with time, but I don't believe it. Did I tell you that Didi keeps sending me care packages and books about coping with grief? I can't bring myself to read them because reading them would be like accepting he's gone for good—do you know what I mean?

Every morning I wake up and check my e-mails and I still keep expecting to see ones from Riley and from you in my inbox. When will I stop hoping? Your dad says he hasn't heard from you in weeks. Are you okay? Even if you don't want to e-mail me, please e-mail him.

He's so worried about you. He says they offered you counseling and that they've moved you to a desk job. Guam. I couldn't believe they sent you there until your dad told me you requested it.

I want to speak to you so badly. I miss you, Kit. You remember those trips out to the desert? When you pointed out the North Star to me? I look for it every night. I remember you telling me how the North Star is the star you use to navigate and find your way home. I keep hoping that one day you'll use it and find your way back, because that's how it feels—like you're lost and I'm waiting for you to find your way back. I'll keep waiting, Kit.

I love you,
Jessa x

From: Jessa Kingsley <jessajkingsley@rocketmail.com>
To: Kit Ryan <kit.ryan@vmail.com>
Date: January 19
Subject: hey

Dear Kit,

How are you? I'm sorry I haven't e-mailed for a while. The holidays were hard. I ended up in the hospital for a few days. The doctors said it was depression and gave me a prescription for some meds. I didn't fill the prescription. I keep thinking of my mom. She walks around like a zombie all the time. She doesn't eat. She doesn't talk. I think I'd rather feel everything than be like that. Just, sometimes it gets too much. I guess you know what I mean.

Anyway, I'm better now. I went with Jo to one of her prenatal scans. Kit, she's having a boy! It was so amazing seeing the little heart beating and seeing him kicking. I've attached a picture for you. You might have to blur your eyes a little. That's the head on the right. He's sucking his thumb. Jo's doing okay. She has good days and bad like me. My dad is the biggest surprise. It's like he's a totally new person. He's no longer having any episodes. He even apologized to me for his behavior—for kicking me out. We go on these walks together most mornings, sort of a ritual now, and I know it's his way of trying to rebuild bridges with me. I just wish he'd had the chance with Riley.

He's set up a trust in the baby's name and arranged for Riley's pension to go to Jo and the baby—he pulled some strings, so even though they never got married they're going to treat it as if they were. She gets all health care covered, so I think that's made everything suddenly much easier.

The other news is I've started classes at USD. I enrolled last week. I figured I needed something to focus on and my dad said I couldn't just stay in bed all day every day. I'm taking Psych 101, English lit, and a few other things.

Please write. I love you. I miss you.
Jessa x

From: Kit Ryan <kit.ryan@vmail.com>
To: Jessa Kingsley <jessajkingsley@rocketmail.com>
Date: January 19
Subject: Re: hey

Dear Jessa,

I've started this letter so many times and I've never been able to finish it. So here goes again . . .

I'm sorry. I'm sorry that Riley is dead. I'm sorry for ignoring your e-mails and for not being there for you. I'm sorry I've hurt you. There isn't a day that goes by that I don't wish it had been me that died and not Riley. If I could go back in time and change everything I would.

I'm sorry I left without a word. There's no excuse for my behavior but please know that it had nothing to do with you. I was a mess. I haven't been able to talk to anyone for months. And I felt too guilty and didn't know how to tell you the truth about what happened. I couldn't bear the thought of you knowing.

I got all your e-mails but I didn't read them until last week. I couldn't face it and I guess that makes me the biggest coward you'll ever meet. I'm sorry. I'm sorry I never replied. You needed me and I wasn't there for you. I don't even know how to ask your forgiveness because I don't deserve it. I'm just glad you're doing better.

I'm better too. I've started seeing a therapist—twice a week— you'd like her. She reminds me of Didi.

I never thought I'd be the kind of guy who needed therapy, but they made it a condition of me keeping my job. She's helped me a lot with getting the panic attacks under control. Working in a room the size of a janitor's closet helps too—there aren't too many surprises, only the occasional rogue paper clip. I asked for the posting. I have to thank your dad, ironically. The demotion worked out. Kind of funny that I totally get where your father was coming from all those years. Looks like I'll be spending the remainder of my marine career behind a desk, but I'm okay with that.

I don't know what else to say, Jessa. My therapist says I should just write down whatever comes into my head.

So here goes. Here's what's in my head . . .

I miss you.

I love you. Even though I long ago gave up the right to any sort of claim over you, I can't stop loving you. I won't ever stop. You're in my blood. You're the only thing that got me through this, Jessa. Because even during the bad times, the worst times, the times I'd wake up in a cold sweat, my heart thumping, the times I'd think the only way out was by killing myself and just having it all go away, I'd think of you and it would pull me back out of whatever dark place I'd fallen into.

You're my light, Jessa. My north star. You asked me once to come back to you and I told you I always would. I'm working on it. It might take me a little while, and I know I have no right to ask you to wait for me after everything I've done, but I'm going to anyway because the truth is I don't know how to live without you. I've tried and I can't do it.

So please, I'm asking you to wait for me. I'm going to come back to you. I promise. And I'm going to make things right. I'll do whatever it takes. I'll never stop trying for the rest of my life to make things right between us.

I love you. Always.

Kit.

P.S. Thanks for the photos of the baby.
P.P.S. USD huh? What happened to USC and acting?

I sit back in my chair taking a long, deep breath, staring at the words on the screen, my heart beating in time with the cursor. My hands are shaking slightly. Down the corridor I hear a door slam and I jump. Sweat snakes down my back. Fuck. My

eyes blur as I reread the e-mail. What the hell am I thinking?
Before I can stop myself, I hit delete.

From: Jessa Kingsley <jessajkingsley@rocketmail.com>
To: Kit Ryan <kit.ryan@vmail.com>
Date: February 17
Subject: news

Dear Kit,

I wanted to write and let you know that Jo had the baby. He was
born two days ago, weighing in at a healthy 9 pounds. Jo's named
him Riley Kit Kingsley.

I was at the birth. It was amazing, Kit, the most incredible thing
I've ever experienced. I was so scared that he would look like Riley
and that I wouldn't be able to look at him or hold him because of it.
And he does and it's so wonderful. He looks exactly like Riley. The
same eyes, the exact same expression—you know how Riley used
to look when he was pissed at something? (Jo says it's gas, but I
swear he's inherited Riley's personality.)

It's the most amazing thing, Kit. It's like he's given us all a new
start. Even my dad is totally in love with him. You should have seen
him hold him for the first time. He cried. My mom is even smiling
again and is almost back to normal.

And that's why I'm writing really. It's not just to tell you about
Riley, but also to tell you that this is the last e-mail I'm sending you. I
can't keep writing into the void.

I don't know how you're doing—your dad says he doesn't hear
from you either. I wish I could see you, speak to you face-to-face, but
I have no idea when or even if you're ever coming home.

I know you must be hurting and I wish there was something I could do to make it better. But I'm hurting too, Kit. He was my brother. And I didn't just lose him. I lost you, too. Part of the grief process is letting go. I've finally let go of Riley and am moving on. And now I need to let go of you, too.

I'll always hold you in my heart and think about you but this is the only way. Thank you for all the beautiful memories.

Kit

stare at the computer screen, my heart beating in my throat, nausea bubbling in my stomach. The hiss of static fills my ears, and my eyesight starts to blur. For a moment it feels as if I might be having another panic attack, but after forcing myself to breathe and count to ten, the sound starts to fade and my eyesight returns to normal.

The words on the screen unblur and I read them again, swallowing hard when I take in the news about the baby's name and then gripping the arms of my chair when I reread the last paragraph.

Finally I tear my eyes away and stare at the wall. What did I expect? I shake my head, snorting air through my nose. What the hell did I expect? That she was going to wait for me to get my shit together? That after treating her so badly, after ignoring her for so long, she was going to wait for me and accept me back into her life with open arms?

It's been almost six months. Six months of silence. I've only got myself to blame.

I look back at the computer. If I was any sort of man at all,

I'd e-mail her right now and tell her how sorry I am, I'd beg her forgiveness, I'd tell her that I understood and wish her well, but I can't. Because as I already know—as has already been discovered—I'm no sort of man at all.

I stumble to my feet, pushing my chair to the side, and am about to turn off the computer by pulling the plug when I change my mind. I sit back down and, with a shaking hand, the static starting to buzz in my ears again, I hit delete on the e-mail and then on the dozen other e-mails from Jessa that are clogging up my inbox.

Jessa's right. It's time for a new beginning. The best thing I can do is let her go, stop thinking about her, move on. I left it too late. I'm one big fuck-up.

After I've deleted all the e-mails, I glance at the clock. It's almost five. I grab my stuff and walk out the door, heading in a daze back to my room on the other side of the base. Once there I quickly get dressed, pulling on my jeans and a T-shirt, and head straight back out again.

I make a beeline for the nearest bar. It's a sleazy faux-Irish pub with floors so tacky with spilled beer my shoes stick to it as though they're trying to stop me getting to the bar. There's a pool table in one corner and a dozen or more booths ringing the room—all empty for the moment—though this being Guam and there being nothing else to do on the island, it won't be long before the place is packed with marines coming off duty.

I sit down on a stool at the bar and signal to the bartender. He ambles over and asks what he can get me. I stare bewildered at what's on offer: beer, spirits, soft drinks. I don't know what to ask for. I just know that tonight I want to drink myself into oblivion.

"Whatever is going to get me drunk quickest," I answer.

The bartender's eyebrows shoot up. He flips the dish towel he's carrying over his shoulder, turns to grab a glass, and fills it with some amber liquid from a bottle before setting it down in front of me.

"Woman trouble?" he asks.

I pick up the glass, eyeing the contents. A voice in my head is yelling at me to put it down, turn around, and walk away now, before it's too late. I think of my dad and his drunken rages—his purple face, his slurred words, the time I found him passed out in a pool of his own vomit on the sofa—but then I shove the memory away. Who's here to see me get drunk anyway? What does it matter if I drink myself into a coma? Or pass out in a lake of my own vomit? Who's going to care?

I down the contents of the glass in one go. It burns my throat and makes my eyes water, and when I slam the glass back down, I feel a rush as the alcohol immediately lights a fire in my stomach.

"Another," I say, wiping the back of my hand across my mouth.

The bartender sighs but then, seeing the tattoo on my arm just visible beneath the bottom of my sleeve, decides not to argue. I'm guessing he's seen more than his fair share of angry servicemen and knows the best bet is just to give them what they want.

He pours me another drink, and I down that one too and then a third. My head starts to spin a little. My limbs loosen up. The hard knot in my stomach starts to relax. When the door slams behind me, I don't even jump. I laugh under my breath. Wow. I can't believe it's taken me six months to realize that getting drunk is the answer.

I pull out my phone and start scrolling through the photo album. My fingers are clumsy and slow, but I feel a startling mental clarity, and when I get to the photos of Jessa—the ones she sent me of herself topless and the ones I took of her in her underwear—I know exactly what I have to do. I haven't looked at them in six months—couldn't bring myself to before now—and now I find myself unable to look away. Even though my breathing has stalled and it feels as if someone's stabbing a skewer between my ribs, I can't stop looking.

Her smile. That's what strikes me first. It's hard to believe she was smiling like that because of me. *For* me. Has she smiled like that since, I wonder? The pictures become blurry, and I realize it's because I'm crying. Angrily I hit delete. *Delete. Delete. Delete.*

Stumbling off my stool, I signal the bartender to get me another drink. He eyes me nervously, looking at the phone in my hand as if it's a gun or a bomb.

"She's gone," I say to him. "I deleted her."

A look of pity crosses his face before he nods and picks up my glass. I start laughing. And then I down the fourth double shot. The room lurches sideways. I collapse onto the stool and rest my head on the bar with a sigh.

I'm not sure how long I stay sitting like that, drifting in a welcome fog, but suddenly I feel someone put their hand on my shoulder. I jerk upright, half falling off the stool, grateful to the bar for catching me. My eyelids are heavy as lead. Someone's standing in front of me, but it takes a while for my eyes to focus.

"Dad?" I say, thinking I must be hallucinating.

My legs give way. My dad catches me as I stumble. The bar stool tumbles sideways and hits the ground.

"Dad?" I say again, and through the fog in my head I can hear that my voice is broken. It sounds like I'm crying.

"I'm here, son," my dad answers.

Jessa

"Your parents are going away for the weekend, I hear."

I glance sideways at Todd. He's opening the micro-wave door, trying to look nonchalant, but I know what he's implying and my pulse elevates.

"Yeah," I mumble, busying myself with unloading the dish-washer. "It's their anniversary. I think my dad's trying to make up for being a total asshole for the last eight years. It's all part of the recovery process."

"Yeah? That's great," says Todd. "I was thinking maybe I could . . . um . . ." He clears his throat. "Maybe I could stay over." He shoots a nervous look my way.

I pretend not to notice while trying to figure out what to say. It's been two months. I guess I can't keep putting him off. And it's not like I don't like him. Todd's been good for me. He's been there for me. And so what if I don't feel the same way about him that I felt about Kit? So what if I don't get the same level of butterflies? Maybe that's a good thing. Maybe that's what hap-pens when you grow up. And at least Todd would never have the capacity to hurt me like Kit did.

Todd takes the bottle from the microwave and tests the temperature of the milk against the inside of his wrist. I smile at him and kiss him on the lips as I take the bottle from his hand.

"Okay," I say. "Yeah, sure."

His eyes go wide. He has so much more of the kid about him than Kit ever did, but I guess he's three years younger.

"Seriously?" he asks. "You're sure?"

I nod and he grins. My stomach sinks a little, and I try to ignore it.

Todd puts his arms around my waist and pulls me nearer so he can kiss me. I let him, trying to summon some enthusiasm. When Todd first asked me out I said no. We met again at college; we're taking some of the same classes and started off as friends. Then one day he invited me to the movies and I went, not expecting it to be a date, but it ended up being one all the same. I think I saw him as a way to get over Kit, because even though I had e-mailed Kit and told him we were over, I still couldn't stop thinking about him. I thought Todd might help me forget about him. So far, no luck, though maybe after the weekend that will change. Todd's good-looking; he's sweet; he's smart. He's not as funny as Kit and the chemistry isn't as electric, but there's the added bonus that my parents love him. And now I'm an only child, I feel the pressure of wanting to please them even more than I did before. It's part of the reason I enrolled at USD.

Just then baby Riley starts crying. I pull out of Todd's arms and walk into the living room where Riley is sitting in his bouncy chair playing with a rattle that Didi bought him. Picking him up and settling down on the sofa with him, I marvel at how much a baby can totally and utterly turn your world upside down. Before Riley, I honestly didn't know how I'd ever learn to smile again. I didn't think I'd ever be happy. And now I'm the happiest I've been since it all happened.

I look after Riley whenever I can, and my mom and dad babysit while Jo's at college. Everyone's happy with how it's worked out. Riley grabs the bottle out of my hands. For a three-month-old he's remarkably clear about his needs, and just like his dad he goes after what he wants with a directness that makes us all laugh and recall the way Riley pursued Jo.

After his bottle, Riley does his usual routine and spits up on my shoulder when I'm burping him.

"I'm going to take him upstairs to change him and put him down for a nap," I tell Todd, who's sitting at the table in the dining room working on a term paper.

Just as I get to the stairs, the doorbell buzzes.

"Let's get that, shall we?" I murmur, shifting Riley onto my clean shoulder. I answer the door, and my heart skips a beat at the sight of Kit standing on the doorstep.

For several seconds I can't speak. My whole body goes rigid with shock. I can't even breathe. He's leaner, older look-ing, tanned and healthy looking—that's all I notice. That and the fact he's wearing the same pair of jeans he wore the night we first made love. My heart has wedged into my throat like a chicken bone, and a storm of emotions whips up in my stom-ach, making me feel instantly sick. I'm torn between wanting to throw myself at him, hurl myself into his arms, and wanting to slam the door in his face.

"You cut your hair," he says to me.

I stare at him. That's all he has to say? That's the first thing he's going to say to me after nearly nine months of silence and dozens of unanswered e-mails?

Eventually I nod because I don't know what else to do.

"You look like Mia Farrow in *Rosemary's Baby*," he adds.

I can feel my face getting warm as he stares at me, and I look away. I cut my hair short on a whim, shortly after I started dating Todd. I couldn't stand the way he'd brush it behind my ear, because every time he did I'd be reminded of Kit doing the same thing, and now that Kit's standing in front of me that's all I can think of and I'm suddenly regretting cutting my hair.

In my arms Riley suddenly gurgles. I see Kit's eyes fall on him, the bright glare of tears before he hastily blinks them away. Those eyes—the blue of a summer's day—how could I have forgotten just how blue they are? "Can I . . . ?" he asks, swallowing hard.

I turn Riley to face him and see the wave of emotion wash over Kit's face as he meets his godson for the first time. He reaches out a hand, tentatively, and rests it on Riley's head, stroking the dark thatch of hair before tucking him softly under the chin. I watch Kit's face transform, just as everyone's does when they see Riley for the first time, at the shock of seeing this mini version of Riley and the wonder of it.

As momentous as this moment might be, though, I'm just not ready for it, so I swap Riley into my other arm and take a step backward, suddenly aware that I have baby vomit on my clothes.

"What are you doing here?" I ask, finally finding my voice.

"I'm back on leave," Kit answers.

"I can see that."

"And I wanted to see you."

I press my lips together. My stomach keeps rolling over. Whether it's the sight of him after so long, or the shock, or the fact that I've just remembered Todd is in the house, I don't know. But anger has started to flow through my veins. He can't just show up like this. What is he expecting?

"Why?" I ask. My voice has a sharp edge to it, and I see him flinch a little. He studies his feet for a moment before looking up at me again.

"Because I need to talk to you."

I shake my head, almost laughing. "*Now* you need to talk to me?" I ask. "It's a little late, Kit."

He frowns and bows his head, and for a moment I'm thrown back to that last day—the day of the funeral when he refused to look at me after we had sex. Does he remember that? The memory hits me as hard as a punch to the gut—it's something I've worked hard to forget. I tried to erase it just like I erased the pictures of him on my phone. But then Kit looks up and I see, in that brief moment of eye contact, all his regrets, all his pain, all he's suffered written clear as chalk on a board. I see how hard it's been for him to get to this point, the awful journey he's been on, and how much it's taken for him to come here today to face me. Even so, I quickly squash my sympathy.

"It's too late," I say again.

"I thought you might say that," Kit says, nodding. "But I needed to try anyway." He takes a deep breath. "I'm staying at my dad's. If you change your mind—" He stops abruptly, and I see he's staring over my shoulder.

I whip around. Todd's standing behind me. He's wearing the formal expression I often see him wear around my father. He curls his fingers around my neck in a way that always makes me tense and stiffen my back, but doubly so now. Shit. I don't want to rub anything in Kit's face, but I guess, like everything else, it's too late for that.

"You okay, babe?" Todd asks me.

I wince but force myself to smile. "I'm fine," I say. "Kit was just leaving."

I turn back to look at Kit, feeling my cheeks burning, barely able to look at him. But Kit's expression is blank, his eyes arctic cold. He's staring between us with his lips pressed together, and his focus seems to rest on Todd's hand gripping the back of my neck. After a moment he glances at me and gives me a look that feels like a knife being slashed across my heart, then he nods and starts to walk away.

Flustered, I shake off Todd's hand and walk back inside the house, kicking the door shut behind me with my heel. My heart is beating so fast and I'm shaking so hard that Riley starts to fuss in my arms, obviously picking up on my mood.

"What did he want?" Todd asks me with an unmistakably irritated tone.

"I don't know," I say.

Just then the doorbell goes again. I look at Todd, seeing the annoyance flare in his eyes. Oh God. Todd opens the door before I can get to it. Over his shoulder I see Kit standing on the doorstep. He looks out of breath, his cheeks are flushed. He frowns at the sight of Todd and tries to peer past him.

"What do you want?" Todd asks, edging sideways to block his view.

"I want to talk to Jessa," Kit answers.

"She doesn't want to talk to you," Todd says.

"Yeah?" Kit asks tersely. He glances over Todd's shoulder at me. "Do you love him?" he asks me, nodding his head at Todd.

The directness of the question stuns me. My mouth falls open. What the . . . ?

"Do you love him?" he demands again.

"Kit, it's none of your business," I stammer, feeling the weight of Todd's gaze on me.

"Fine," he says. "It's none of my business. I have no right to ask you—I get that—but you need to speak to me. If you send me away, I'm just going to keep coming back until you do."

I look at Todd. He's glaring at me. I look at Kit. His jaw is pulsing.

"Fine," I say angrily, seeing that otherwise there's going to be a scene. "I'll talk to you."

A look of disappointment crosses Todd's face, but he buries it quickly. I hand him Riley with a shrug of apology. Once he's gone upstairs, I step out onto the front porch, pulling the door shut behind me. I have a feeling Todd's going to want to eavesdrop, and I have no idea what Kit wants to say, but I'm sure it's not going to be something I want Todd to hear. I'm not sure *I* want to hear it. I've moved on. I've made a new life for myself. Kit can't just waltz back in because he's finally managed to deal with his issues.

I cross my arms over my chest, partly because my heart is rattling around like a rogue ball bearing inside me, and partly because I'm scared of what I might do if I don't control my hands.

"What do you want?" I hiss.

"I want you," he answers.

I reel backward.

"Fuck," he murmurs, looking away and running his hands through his hair. "This is not how I planned to do this. I didn't mean to say that."

"You mean you actually had a plan for this?" I ask.

"Yeah, can't you tell?" he answers wryly.

I try not to smile. Goddamn him. I refuse to smile.

"The plan was to come here and say sorry and beg your forgiveness. That's all. I didn't come here to be an asshole. I didn't come here to try to get you back. I know it's too late for that. But then I saw him," he continues, frowning. "That guy Todd." He looks at me now with an expression of disbelief, shaking his head. "And fuck it . . . I can't just walk away. I can't do it. I tried. I got as far as my bike."

I stare at him, unsure what the hell he's trying to say.

He takes a deep breath. "Oh man, I'm screwing this up." He shakes his head. "Let me do this like I planned." He takes another deep breath, as though gathering his thoughts, and holds my gaze. "Okay," he begins. "I'm so sorry, Jessa. I'm sorry for everything. I can't tell you how much I regret everything I did. I wrote to you so many times and then I'd hit delete, because how do you tell the girl you love that you killed her brother?"

His words hit me like shrapnel. I draw in a staggeringly painful breath.

"How do you make up for not being there for her when she needed you most? I can't. All I can tell you is I was a total fuckup. It's not an excuse, but for a really long time I was a total mess, and it's taken me all this time to sort myself out."

I close my eyes. He doesn't know how long I've waited to hear these words.

"That's all I planned to say to you. I was going to say it and then walk away. That's what I had planned out in my head. Because I knew I had—*have*—no right to expect anything, or forgiveness, after everything I've done."

I don't say anything. I can't. My brain is still struggling to process the fact he's here, let alone the words he's just said.

"But then I see you," he says, "and I realize that I was an idiot to think it would ever be that easy." He stops and frowns hard for a moment down at his feet before looking up suddenly.

"Do you love him?" he asks, startling me all over again. "If you honestly love him, I'll walk away. I won't ever bother you again," he says.

I'm so furious that I could spit. How dare he? It's too god-damn late for any of this. "Yes," I say. "Yes, I love him."

Kit's face crumples with disbelief, his lips parting, but then he steadies himself and straightens up.

I'm breathing hard, trying not to cry. I can feel my face burning. Why did I just say that? I don't love Todd—I just want to hurt Kit. I want to hurt him the way he hurt me. I want him to feel for just a moment a fraction of the pain he's caused me. I know it's not fair, I know he's had his own fair share of suffering to deal with too, but now it's too late to take it back. I remember him saying to me once that he didn't ever want there to be any kind of untruth between us, that he wanted to know everything I was thinking and feeling, but how can I put any of what I feel into words? How can I tell him the truth when I'm not even sure what that is any more?

Kit looks away over his shoulder, chewing his lip as though pondering his next move. Is he going to leave? My stomach tenses. Finally he looks back at me. "I don't believe you," he says. He takes a step toward me, flustering me with his near-ness, with his smell, which shouldn't be so damn familiar after so much time and which shouldn't still affect me the way it does.

"I think you still love me," he says, "even though you don't want to."

I glare at him, fury battling my instincts.

"Because that kind of love, Jessa," Kit continues, "doesn't just disappear. It doesn't just fade. I still love you. I'll always love you. And I think you feel the same way about me. And hell, I know I don't deserve it. I know all I deserve is your hatred. But if there's a chance, a single chance that you might still love me, then I'm not going to throw it away. Because I've been through hell and you're the only reason I'm still standing." He pauses. "So tell me the truth. Do you love him?"

I don't answer.

"Does he know you like I do? Does he know exactly how you like your eggs in the morning—just a little bit runny?" he asks. "Does he know that you're allergic to roses? Does he know that when your nostrils flare like that it's because you're trying to stop from crying and that when you say 'yeah, sure' it usually means 'no'?" He takes a step nearer. "Does he make you see stars?" he asks in a low voice. "Does he call you his *north* star? Because that's what you are to me. You're the reason I made it home."

I squeeze my eyes shut.

"Does he know exactly where to kiss you?" Kit murmurs and startles me by brushing his hand just beneath my ear. "Just here?"

My eyes flash open as I suppress a shudder.

"Does he know exactly how to touch you?" he asks, his gaze falling to my mouth. "Does he tell you that you're all he thinks about? Does he tell you that he lives for you? That he breathes for you? That he dreams of you every damn moment, awake and asleep? Does he tell you any of that?" He pauses to look at me and I try to keep a blank face. "No, I didn't think so," he says quietly.

I narrow my eyes at him, taking a small step backward to put some distance between us, because his nearness is muddling me almost as much as his words.

"He might not say or do any of those things, Kit, but he does keep his promises. He wouldn't walk away and not come back."

"I did come back," Kit says under his breath.

I shrug. For a few moments we stand there watching each other. My fingers hurt from gripping my sides so much. I'm trying not to cry, but with each breath it feels as if the sob is going to come tearing out of me. "It's too late," I finally say.

"Okay," Kit says after a beat. I watch him struggle to compose his face. "I'd better be going then," he says. "I'm sorry."

And after all those words, with me watching him half in disbelief and half in horror, words rising mute up my throat and bursting silent on my tongue, I watch him walk away. Does he not see? I want to scream and call him back. I was just testing him. I don't want him to leave. I want him to stay—to fight for me, to prove to me that he really means it, that he isn't ever going to walk away again. But he's failed the test.

"That's right," I whisper as he walks toward his bike. "Walk away. That's what you're good at."

Kit

I'm standing in exactly the same place I stood almost a year ago on the day of Jessa's birthday party. This is where I came when I was trying to decide whether to go after her or walk away. I stood here staring at the waves slamming into the pier, trying to weigh up the pros and cons. It wasn't possible to stay away from her then. And now? I think. If I'd stayed away then, would things be different now? Would Riley still be alive? It's those kinds of thoughts I have to stop myself from thinking or else I end up following them down rabbit holes and getting lost for hours, sometimes spinning out completely and having a full-on panic attack.

Part of my therapy was learning how to cut the thoughts off as soon as they arise. There's no point in thinking *what if*. What is *is*, and there's no changing it. The only thing to do is move forward.

Does the same philosophy apply to this situation, I wonder? Should I just accept it, cut Jessa off and move on? For the last three months, ever since my dad found me in that bar in Guam, I've been working so hard to edge back from the precipice, the whole time keeping Jessa in my sights like a lighthouse in the dark. My dad was the life ring that stopped me from sinking. Without the two of them I don't think I'd be here today. I'd probably be passed out drunk somewhere, maybe dead.

Though I try to push it away, the memory of Jessa's face when she opened the door flashes into my mind. I know I saw for just a split second after the initial shock had passed and before she rearranged her face into blankness something resembling joy. I didn't imagine it. I know she was happy to see me.

She was thinner than I remember, and grief seems to have rubbed away the last traces of girlhood. Her face was more defined, her eyes bigger, though maybe it was just the short hair making them stand out more. But the biggest difference was the lack of spark in her eyes, as though she'd shrunk back in on herself. I shake my head, trying to jar the memory loose, but it doesn't go anywhere. It won't be going anywhere for a very long time. Man, she was even more beautiful than I remembered. And Riley . . . the thought that passed through my mind when I saw Jessa standing there holding the baby was that *that could have been us*. That could have been Jessa holding *our* baby. Stupid dream. That's never going to happen now.

My teeth clench hard enough to crack as Todd's face superimposes on Jessa's. In my darkest times I'd sometimes imagine Jessa with another guy, but he was always faceless and nameless. Seeing Todd walk up behind her like that made my blood run cold. What was that with his fucking hand on her neck? I thought I might rip his arm clean off when I saw him do that. And calling her *babe*? I take a deep breath, reminding myself I have no right to get angry. She waited for me for months, and I didn't even have the decency to e-mail her. Why am I surprised she's found someone else and moved on?

But did it have to be Todd? Is she having sex with him? I slam my fist into my hand and lean over the pier railing, breathing deeply, trying to banish the images that start flooding through my head. Don't go there, I warn myself, but even so I can't stop myself from picturing Todd undressing her, kissing her, taking her to bed. Does she like it? Does she want him the same way she wanted me? Do they make love or just have sex?

I don't believe she loves him. Or is that just me not wanting to believe it? Did I imagine the look in her eye when I brushed my hand against her neck? Did I imagine the quiver in her voice when she told me it was too late? Did I imagine the slight flush in her cheeks? Isn't that a telltale sign she's lying?

"Hey."

I spring upright and glance over my shoulder. A girl is standing there. She's about Jessa's age, with long brown hair, dark eyes, and a copper tan that in twenty years is going to make her look like an old leather bag. She's wearing Lycra shorts and a sports bra that don't leave anything to the imagination.

"You're Jessa's ex, right?" she asks, out of breath. She's clearly stopped mid-run.

"Um, yeah," I say. She looks familiar but I can't place her. "Ex. Right." The word sticks in my throat like an ax blade. It's the first time I've admitted it out loud.

She smiles widely, showing off perfect teeth the color of polar ice caps. "I'm Serena? Remember me?" And when she sees my frown, she adds, "From prom?" Every sentence sounds like a question.

"Oh yeah," I say, suddenly recognizing her as the girl who was being pawed in the stairwell. "How you doing?" I ask halfheartedly. I'm not in the mood for small talk.

COME BACK TO ME

"I'm great," she says, wiping sweat from her brow. "How 'bout you?"

I laugh under my breath and look away. "Yeah. You know . . ."

"What are you doing?" she asks.

What does it look like I'm doing? I feel like asking. "Just hanging out," I say.

"You're a marine, aren't you?" she asks.

"Yeah," I say, before remembering that's not true. "Well, not anymore," I clarify. "My contract just ended." After four years I'm now out, just like I promised Jessa I would be. Out, with no idea what I'm going to do next.

"Wow," Serena says, crossing her arms over her chest in a way that shows off her cleavage to better advantage. "So what are you going to do now?" she asks, and I look at her sideways because it seems the question might have a secondary meaning. I'm right, it does. She's licking her lips and staring at mine.

"I don't actually know," I say, choosing to ignore the suggestion.

"You want to go get a coffee?" she asks.

"Um . . . ," I say, thrown by her directness.

"Or maybe something else?" she asks, seeing my hesitation.

It's clear from the way she's staring at me exactly what the something else is. I muse with not a little incredulity at the timing. After a year of no women, of not even looking at another woman, and within half an hour of Jessa telling me it's over, I'm being offered sex, what looks like no-strings sex. But I hesitate.

She's now playing with her hair, twiddling it between her thumb and forefinger, still looking at me with a small smile playing on her lips. From the tilt of her chin and her posture, one hand resting on her hip, it's obvious she thinks that there's no way I'm going to say no, and for a few seconds I do think about it. I think about what it would be like. How it would feel. How it might help me forget for five minutes everything that's going on in my head. It's tempting. It's been so long since I've been with anyone and I miss closeness. I miss affection. It might even help me get over Jessa. Isn't that what's recommended? Doesn't it help you move on—screwing someone else?

Serena raises an eyebrow as though wondering what's taking me so long to decide, and just like that I come to my senses. What am I thinking? The thought of going there turns me cold. The only person I want to be close to, lose myself in, is Jessa.

"Nah, I'm good," I tell her.

She looks startled for a second before recovering and tossing her hair over her shoulder like an uptight stallion before a race.

"Whatever," she says, before jogging off, her ponytail swinging angrily.

I laugh under my breath and turn back to contemplating the waves.

A couple of hours later when I get home, my dad's where he can normally be found, doing the thing he can normally be found doing. He's in the kitchen making coffee.

"What happened?" he asks.

I wonder if he's been here for the whole day, pacing the kitchen, waiting for me. He looks like he's drunk about fifty cups of coffee in that time. The bags under his eyes have bags, and I know he's worried that I might relapse. I think his own alcoholic past has made him nervous. But I'm not an addict. At least, not in the usual sense of the word. The only thing

I'm addicted to is Jessa, and that drug is well and truly off the menu, unobtainable, so how can I possibly relapse?

"I told her," I say.

"You told her sorry?" my dad asks, unable to disguise the nervousness in his voice.

"Yeah," I say, and then, shooting him a sheepish look, add, "and maybe a little bit more than that."

My dad arches an eyebrow. "What'd she say?" he asks.

I shrug. "She said it's too late. She's moved on." Putting the words out there makes it seem more final.

"What are you going to do?" my dad asks, pouring out the coffee.

"I'm going to sign up for another four years."

There's a long silence. My dad has frozen with the kettle in his hand mid-pour. I don't say anything. I've spent the last four hours down at the beach trying to get my head together and figure out the future, and this is what I've decided to do.

"I thought you were out," my dad finally says.

"Guess not," I answer.

My dad's mouth pulls down at the edges. I know he was looking forward to having me home for a while. "You sure?" he says. "You're not just reacting?"

"Nope," I say. "Well, okay, maybe. But I don't want to stay around here. I can't. Too many memories. Everywhere I go." I don't add that I can't stand the thought of running into Jessa and Todd.

My dad frowns. "What about LA?" he asks.

I look away, out the window, feeling the sting. "That was our dream," I say quietly. "Mine and Jessa's. I don't want to do it on my own."

"But four more years?" my dad asks, giving me a look.

"Yeah," I say. "I can make corporal again, maybe sergeant in a year or two."

"You want to go back into a war zone? You think you're ready?"

I turn back to him. "Yeah. I think I am."

My dad holds my gaze for a long beat, and I have to fight not to look away. Is he right? Am I just reacting? The thing is, I can't see another way. It's what I decided down at the beach. The Marine Corps is all I know. Those dreams I had of opening a café, of moving to LA, seem stupid now, naive. Maybe with Jessa I could have done it, but now I don't have the motivation. There's no one to do it for.

My dad sighs heavily and then hands me a mug of coffee. I take it.

"Thanks, Dad," I say. "For everything. For getting me through the last few months. I couldn't have done it without you."

My dad gives me a rueful smile and slaps me on the shoulder. "Well, I couldn't have gotten sober without you and your sister, so I figure I owed you."

We drink our coffee in silence for a while, and when I finish I put my mug down.

"I'm going out for a bit," I say to my dad.

"Where are you going?" my dad asks.

"To the recruitment office. Get my papers signed before I change my mind."

Jessa

"Have you thought about what you want to do for your birthday?"

"Huh?" I turn to look at my mom.

We're folding laundry together—babies seem to create a crazy amount of mess, and my mom likes to help Jo out as much as possible so she can concentrate on her studies.

"Your birthday—it's next week. Have you thought about what you want to do?"

"Oh, no," I answer vaguely. Truthfully I've been trying to avoid thinking about it because my birthday also happens to be the anniversary of the day Kit and I first got together. Thinking back to that night—of our first kiss behind the bushes, the road trip out into the desert, of lying out under the stars— only makes me sad . . . though not thinking about it seems to make me sadder. Once again I try to push the memory of this morning out of my mind, though I fail. I can't stop remembering Kit's face when he told me he wanted me, and then again when I told him it was too late. I don't think I'll ever be able to forget his expression.

"What's up?" my mom asks, folding one of Riley's blankets. "You seem a million miles away."

"Nothing," I say. I'm still getting used to these conversations with my mom. It's only since Riley was born that she's snapped out of her stupor and stopped taking the Valium. She's started to be more engaged with life again, and with me. I can't put it all down to the baby. My dad's resolution to be a better father and husband seems to have something to do with it too.

"Is Todd going to take you somewhere nice?"

"I don't know," I say, busying myself with a pile of bibs.

"Are things okay with you two?" my mom asks.

I think about not saying anything, but she'll probably find out anyway from Kit's dad. "Kit came by this morning," I tell her.

My mom stops folding and stares at me. "He's back?"

I know my mom is desperate to talk to him, to reassure him she doesn't in any way blame him for what happened. She still thinks of Kit as her second son.

I nod. "Yeah, he's back."

"What did he say?" she asks, the laundry totally forgotten.

I take a deep breath. "That he loved me. That he wanted to be with me. All this stuff about how sorry he is and how much he wants to make it up to me." I laugh and shake my head.

My mom doesn't say anything, and when I glance at her out of the corner of my eye, I see her eyebrows are almost meeting her hairline. "And?" she asks. "What did you tell him?"

I shrug and snap out a sheet. "I told him it was too late. I mean," I rattle on, "of course I told him no." I start folding with swift, precise movements. "I can't believe he thinks he can just waltz back into my life like nothing's happened and expect everything to be the same. It isn't. I've moved on. I'm with Todd now."

I stare down at the sheet in my hands. It looks like it's been folded by a toddler with one hand tied behind his back. I shake it out in frustration and start again. For the last five hours all I've been able to think about is Kit, about our conversation. I've been replaying it over and over, each time getting more and more frustrated and angry. My head is in as much disarray as the sheet.

"Do you like him?"

I look at my mother sharply. "Kit?" I ask, confused. These girly chats are new ground for us, and I'm not entirely comfortable talking to her about boys. Maybe that's a holdover from having to date Kit in secret.

"No. Todd."

"Yes," I say, a little too fast. "Of course I like him."

"I mean *really* like him?" my mom asks.

"Yeah," I say. Then add, "I think."

"You think? You shouldn't have to think about it, Jessa."

I drop the sheet back into the basket. That thing is never going to get folded. "I don't know what to do," I admit, and as soon as I say it, it feels like a little bit of the weight has lifted off my shoulders. I look at my mom. There's too much confusion in my head. I can't think straight.

"Yes, you do," my mom says.

I can't help the frown. "Kit?" I say. "You think I should break up with Todd and get back together with Kit?"

My mom gives me an *it's obvious* kind of look, and I shake my head firmly. "I'm not going to do that. No way."

"Do you see yourself marrying Todd?" she asks.

Marriage? What? What is she talking about? "No! I'm only eighteen! Are you crazy?"

"Did you see yourself marrying Kit?"

I draw in a breath and think about lying, but then I close my mouth and nod. Because I did. I used to dream all those things—weddings, babies, rocking chairs on the porch—not that I ever admitted it to him or anyone else.

My mom smiles smugly. "There's your answer, then. You only live once, Jessa."

I snatch one of Riley's onesies from her hands as she reaches for it from the basket. She's struck a chord. Kit's words from long ago come back to me: *Life's short, you only get one shot. Make it count.*

"It's not that simple," I say, shaking my head to try and dislodge the memory of Kit.

"Yes, it is," my mom answers. "Your father didn't marry the right person, Jessa. He should never have married me. He loved someone else."

The casual way she's just thrown that into the conversation blindsides me, renders me totally speechless for several seconds. I watch her as she continues to fold, a faintly sad smile on her lips.

"But . . ." I shake my head, trying to clear the confusion. "What?"

"I was his rebound," my mom says. "The same as Todd is for you. He married me because he wanted to hurt her, and by the time I found out I was second best, the consolation prize, it was too late. I was pregnant with Riley."

She keeps folding clothes as though what she's just told me isn't any kind of big deal, isn't one of the most heartbreaking things I've ever heard. It can't be true. "No," I say. "Mom . . ." My own heart is breaking for her. How could my dad do that? How could she live with him this whole time knowing that he loved someone else?

"It's true," my mom says, and then looking up and seeing my expression she adds, "It's okay. I was an idiot." She smiles rue- fully. "I was young. I knew something wasn't right, but I ignored my instinct and went ahead and married him anyway. I was madly in love with him. And it wasn't his fault he was still in love with someone else."

"It was his fault," I say, suddenly outraged. I was just manag- ing to forgive my father for being an asshole to Kit and Riley, and now this. "He shouldn't have married you, not if he was still in love with someone else."

She gives me a pointed look and I squirm. Shit. Am I just as bad as my dad? Am I being totally unfair to Todd? I hadn't thought so until now. But it's not like I plan on marrying Todd . . . so then, why do I feel so bad? I squeeze the thoughts out of my head. I'm getting distracted.

"Why did you stay with him?" I ask.

"Because of you two children. Once you have kids, everything changes. And I knew that leaving him, taking you two with me, would have destroyed him."

"But I don't understand," I say to my mom. "What happened? Who was Dad in love with?"

My mom glances at her watch. "It's a long story and Riley's going to be awake in a moment. Jo's going to be here in half an hour and I want him fed by then."

"Okay," I say, flustered, my head spinning.

"And you have someplace to be, don't you?" my mom asks as she takes the basket of laundry and heads for the door.

"Where?" I ask.

She pauses in the doorway and looks back at me. "Isn't there someone you need to see?" She gives me another pointed look and, just like that, as if she's turned on a light in my brain, everything becomes clear to me. I know exactly what I need to do.

"Thanks, Mom," I say, rushing past her.

Just as I reach the door, I turn and do something I haven't done in a long time—I race back and throw my arms around her and hug her. For a moment she falters; I hear the breath catch in her throat. Even though the laundry basket is wedged between us creating a barrier, it feels as if a lot of other invisible barriers have just been broken down, and when I rush off again, breathless and in a mildly euphoric state of panic, I feel so light and free that I burst out laughing as I run up the stairs, and my dad, coming out of his study with his car keys in his hand, stands stock still in the hallway and watches me, his mouth falling open.

"Slow down!" he calls out as I trip on the top step in my haste to get to my bedroom and find my phone.

I look over my shoulder. He's smiling up at me. I grin back at him.

"Can't!" I say. "I'm late for something."

Kit

All these rows of white stones—like rows of teeth growing out of the earth—give me the creeps. I feel like I need to tiptoe, or at the very least apologize to the people I'm walking over.

As I weave between the gravestones, I try not to think of the last time I was here. I barely remember much of it anyway, thankfully. The only thing I recall clearly is trying to kill a tree with my fists. I broke several bones in my hands, and now they ache like hell whenever it rains and make me associate cold weather with death.

I come to Riley's grave and take a deep, jarring breath as I read his name carved into the stone. I sit down cross-legged in front of it, and for a while all I do is stare at the dates, finding it hard to believe that so much time has passed, feeling frustrated at all he's missed, angry at how short his life was, that he never really got to live it. I look at the fresh bunches of flowers, wondering who left them—Jessa? Jo? His mom?

"I miss you, man," I finally say.

I wasn't sure what I was planning on doing when I got

here, whether I'd just say a few words in my head or nothing at all, but once I open my mouth, it all comes rushing out. "I'm sorry," I say, tears burning my eyes. It feels like the floodgates are opening after being cemented shut for the last nine months, and suddenly I start to cry. "I fucked up," I sob. "In so many ways. I wasn't there for Jo and I hurt Jessa. You told me you'd beat the crap out of me if I ever hurt her, and I have." I pause to swallow away the rock-shaped lump in my throat. "I wish you were around to beat the crap out of me. But I guess on the upside, at least I get to keep my balls." I laugh through my nose, snorting snot. "That's what everyone's always telling me to do—try to focus on the positives in my life. That's one, I guess. I still have my balls. I don't have too many other positives to focus on right now." I shake my head and wince. "What am I doing? Here I am complaining about that and you're dead. Sorry."

I'm sitting in front of a grave talking to thin air. I must look like a madman. But I don't care. This is what I need to do, I realize. I've needed to do this for a while, and it feels cathartic to finally get everything out into the open at last, out of my head. And maybe there is nothing here, nothing more than bones turning to dust, but it feels like Riley is here with me, some part of him at least, and that he can hear me. And if there's the slightest chance that he can, that he's listening right now, then I want him to know the truth of everything.

"I'm sorry it was you and not me," I say. "I'm sorry I've been a shit friend. I'm sorry you never got to meet your son." At this point the tears start to fall freely. "Dude, he's so perfect. I wish you could see him. I'm going to be the best godfather ever," I say, choking on the words. "I'm going to be there for him, I swear it, Riley. I'll take care of him and Jo. I promise you I won't let anything bad ever happen to them." Can he hear me? I so want him to hear me. To believe me. "Your dad's taking care of them too. Crazy, huh? You had to go and die before he stopped being an asshole. Kind of sucks. But it's true. I know, are you spinning in your grave at the news? Jessa told me he's helping Jo out. He's set up a trust in the baby's name. Cool, huh?"

For a few minutes I just sit there not saying anything, letting the silence of the place seep into me. For the first time in nine months, my mind feels unclogged, clear, and the tension in my body is ebbing away. I look around at the graves. Being around dead people is actually kind of peaceful. I wish I'd done this sooner.

"In other news," I finally say, breaking the silence, "Jessa broke up with me. I totally deserved it," I add quickly. I try to imagine what Riley would say if he were here. God, I miss him. I miss being able to talk to him about stuff like this. I miss the banter and the jokes and the laughter. "She's got a new boyfriend—remember that guy Todd? She's dating a guy called *Todd*. Jesus." I rip up a clump of grass. "Man. I really fucked up. Your dad must love him, though, because unlike me, Todd actually gets to enter the house." I laugh to myself for a moment before I remember once again the look on Jessa's face when she told me it was too late. The laughter fades away. I bow my head. "I still love her, Riley," I say.

Oh man. Riley is probably rolling his eyes somewhere on the other side, telling me to get my shit together and stop crying like a baby. "So that's my news," I say, finally looking up. "What's happening with you? What's it like on the other side?"

I'm met by silence. I get up, feeling a thousand years old but a thousand times lighter, too. I tap the top of the gravestone. "I love you, bro," I say. Then add, "You see my mom, say hi to her for me."

I check my watch. It's twenty minutes before the recruiter's office shuts. I need to get a move on.

Jessa

I don't have a key anymore to Kit's place, so I pound on the door, my mouth dry and my heart beating so fast I think it might burst. What am I going to say to him? Am I doing the right thing? My gut answers for me. My stomach is doing backward flips and loop the loops. I'm so excited I feel like I might throw up right there on the doorstep. Kit's truck is in the driveway, and the familiar sight of it sends a ripple through me. I look at my phone. I've tried calling him, but his phone is switched off.

After what feels like a lifetime, the door finally opens, but it's not Kit standing there, it's his dad, and the words that had gathered on the tip of my tongue instantly dissolve.

"Oh, hi," I say, recovering. "Is Kit here?"

Ben shakes his head. "No. He's gone out."

"Where?" I ask. "I need to see him."

"He's gone to the recruiter's office."

"What?"

"He's re-enlisting."

"No," I hear myself say.

"He felt it was the only thing to do."

Ben's expression isn't accusatory—he's far too compassionate for that, but that's the way I take it anyway. I know Kit. I know he's doing this because of me. Damn, I think to myself, my head starting to swim—I'm too late. How can I be too late?

"If you hurry, you might just catch him," Ben says, glancing at his watch and grimacing.

I look up sharply. Catch him? Is there still a chance? He nods at me, and that's all I need to take off running.

"Good luck!" I hear him yell after me as I slam the car door.

The recruiting office is on the other side of town. The whole way there I'm in a crazed panic. Transplant teams carrying donor organs are probably less frantic than I am right now. I try not to think about what I'll do if he's already signed on the dotted line, and start praying. I haven't prayed since Riley died, but I pray now, fervently, my foot on the floor, weaving in and out of traffic on the freeway like I'm in *Fast & Furious*, thanking God that Kit taught me to drive and asking him to intervene on my behalf and stop Kit from signing any papers.

I screech to a halt in the only free parking space (divine intervention?) and race across the lot, leaping over a low wall and sprinting toward the door with the MARINE CORPS RECRUITING OFFICE sign over it. Out of breath, I make it to the door and throw myself against it. It doesn't budge and I rebound off it. It's only then that I notice the closed sign right in front of me. I check my watch. It's two minutes after five. I rest my head against the tinted glass and try to peer through to see if anyone is in there. The office is dark, though. All I can make out are some posters on the walls and two desks, papers neatly squared away on both. Are Kit's signed papers there?

Feeling faint, I turn around and stand there for a few seconds, completely dazed and unsure of what to do. I'm too late. I'm too late! I kick my foot hard against a nearby potted plant and let out a cry. Why did he have to do this? Goddamn him. I burst into tears, and my foot starts to throb. My head is still clogged with thoughts, most of them confused. Was I really going to stop him?

I take a deep breath and rub my eyes, forcing myself to get it together. I step away from the door, noticing the CCTV camera pointed at me. I've cried enough over Kit—I refuse to cry anymore. Maybe this is just the way it's meant to be. Maybe it's all for the best.

My phone chooses this moment to start ringing. I pull it out and glance at the display. It's Todd. Oh God, I'm late. We were supposed to meet at five. I totally forgot. My finger hovers over the button. I'm not sure I can handle talking to him right now. He's going to want to know where I am.

I stare at my reflection in the glass door. It's like looking at a ghost—a dull, gray, miserable-looking ghost. The phone keeps ringing. Maybe I should just say nothing. Todd need never know. We can just carry on like we were.

I turn away from the ghost in the door and press the green button. "Hey, Todd," I say, forcing a smile.

Kit

Turning away from Riley's grave, I freeze mid-step. Jessa's dad is standing just a few feet away, watching me. He's holding a bunch of flowers in his hand. Out of uniform he doesn't cut quite such an intimidating figure, and I notice that he looks much, much older than when I saw him last. His hair's now completely gray. He's softer too. His shoulders are still broad and he's still a well-built man, but he seems somehow turned inward, his posture no longer ramrod straight but slightly slumped. His eyes, etched with grief lines, no longer have that fierce sniper intensity to them.

"Oh . . . I'm sorry," I stammer. "I was just . . . I'm just leaving." Fuck. How long has he been standing there? Did he hear everything I just said? Oh man. I walk past him, fast, not daring to meet his eye.

"No. It's okay," he says as I pass him. "You don't have to leave."

I stop and turn to stare at him, unsure if he's joking or not, but he just nods at me wearily before taking a step toward the grave. He drops to his haunches stiffly, as though he's bone tired, and starts straightening out the old flowers and arranging the new ones. It's him that's bringing the flowers. The realization surprises me. Does he come here a lot, then? By the looks of all the flowers, I'm guessing he does.

"Do you come here often?" I ask. As soon as the words are out of my mouth, I cringe. Way to go, Kit. Make it sound like you're trying to pick him up, why don't you?

He nods at me. "Almost every day."

Wow. Okay. I take that in. My dad used to visit my mom's grave every day too. I stopped after six weeks because I couldn't face it anymore, couldn't handle staring at a mound of grass imagining her body decaying beneath me.

"Hasn't got any easier, has it?" I say.

He looks up at me. "Not yet it hasn't."

"It does eventually," I say quietly. "One day you wake up and discover that it hurts just a little bit less. And then maybe after a year or two it does start to fade." I stop abruptly. I don't know why I'm telling him this.

Kingsley nods at me, and I see his brow creasing into a familiar frown. He stands up slowly, as though he has the weight of a planet resting on his shoulders.

"I'm sorry," he says, looking me directly in the eye.

"Excuse me?" I say, thinking I must have misheard.

He clears his throat. "I owe you an apology," he says. "I've been doing a lot of thinking these last few months, speaking to a lot of people—counselors, shrinks, whatever you want to call them—doing a lot of soul-searching. I come here and talk to Riley a lot too. I find it helps the most, actually, talking to him."

Crap. I shuffle nervously. Does he know that that's what I was doing too? In a mild state of panic I think desperately back, trying to remember everything I said. Did he hear me call him an asshole?

"I wasn't fair to you," he says now. "On the day of the funeral. You were there to pay your respects. I shouldn't have turned you away like that."

I'm too stunned to say anything. Colonel Kingsley is apologizing? To me?

"I was angry," he says with a faint shrug of his shoulders. "I needed someone to blame."

"Yeah," I say quietly. "I know that feeling."

His eyes narrow, and I see a trace of the old sniper in him. "It wasn't your fault," he says. "The only people to blame were the people who strapped explosives to themselves and blew themselves up. *They* killed my son, not you."

I've heard this a thousand times from a dozen different people, most of them paid to say it, but hearing Riley's father say the words is like the prison door swinging open.

"I swapped post with him, though," I say, the words rushing out of me so fast it sounds like a sob.

"We've all done that. We've all broken the rules. I was wrong to punish you. You'd been through enough."

I stare at him, not quite believing. He's a colonel. He cited me for disobedience. I was demoted because I broke those rules, moved to a desk job in Guam. And now he's admitting it was no big thing?

"So," he says, "you seen the baby yet?"

I nod, speechless, my head whirring too hard and too fast to keep up with the change in the conversation's direction or to formulate words.

"Looks like Riley, don't you think?" he says with a grin that lights up his face.

"He does," I say, unable to stop smiling as well.

"And Jessa?" he asks, giving me a sideways glance before focusing his attention somewhere on the middle distance.

"Um," I stammer, my heart starting to race. Is it a trick question?

"Have you seen her?" he asks. "I'm assuming so."

I can't lie. "Uh. Yes, sir," I say.

A grin tugs at his mouth. "She tell you to get lost?"

I laugh under my breath. "She might have."

He grins wider. "That's my girl."

Yeah, I should have guessed he still wouldn't be happy about me going anywhere near his daughter.

"Damn it, though," he says, shaking his head. "Not sure what she sees in that kid Todd. Starting to wonder about her taste in men."

My head flies up. He doesn't like Todd? The knowledge enters my bloodstream like a drug, making me far happier than it probably should. I try to hide my smile, because really, what does it matter that he doesn't like Todd? He doesn't like me, either.

"Listen, I've got a story for you, Ryan."

I look at him sideways. What the fuck is going on? This man has hated me for years, and now here we are at the graveside of his son, shooting the breeze, telling stories like we're old buddies? Has he lost it or something? Has he taken one too many Zoloft?

"I've never shared this with anyone, except of course with Riley on one of our many one-sided conversations." He tips his head at the grave. "They're pretty cathartic, aren't they?" he says, giving me a pointed look.

Oh shit. He heard. I wince and look away, automatically scanning the cemetery for the nearest exit point. Where's this conversation heading? Is this whole friendly routine just a way of drawing me in like a fish on a line before he clobbers me on the head with a rock?

"I was once in love," he begins, grabbing my attention back instantly. "I was about your age. This girl—" He pauses and takes a deep breath in before letting it out in a long exhalation. "She was the most beautiful woman I've ever seen. She took my breath away. All I wanted to do was make her happy." He glances at me. "I would have walked over hot coals for her."

I do a double take. Those were exactly the words I used to him about Jessa. Does he remember? Is that why he's throwing them back at me?

"She was the love of my life, and I lost her. It was during the Balkan conflict. There were things I saw in that war that will stay with me forever." He glances across at me. "I think you know what I'm talking about. Things you can't put a name to, things you can't talk about to other people, least of all your family."

I give him a small nod. I do know what he's talking about, but it's still weird for me to discover we have anything in common at all, let alone that we share something like this.

"For a while I couldn't stand to be around people," he goes on. "I stopped writing to her. I couldn't put words down on paper, couldn't make sense of what was in my head."

I fall silent, holding my breath. He could be describing me. The strangeness of his confession, how exactly his story mirrors my own, is spinning me out.

"I said a few things I'll always regret and pushed her away, until the point came where she broke up with me. She sent me a letter, told me it was over. Damn near broke my heart. For a year she was all I could think about. I didn't look at another woman, couldn't think about another woman. But I didn't call her either, didn't write. My pride was too wounded. And I was too messed up." He pauses to look at me. "Sound familiar?"

I don't nod, but I don't shake my head either.

"But when I get back home I have it all planned out. I'm going to make things right with her. I'm determined to find a way to get her back. I'll do whatever it takes. And so I go over to her house and what do I find? She's dating someone else. And not just anyone. My best friend."

I let out the breath I've been holding. It all makes sense now. The photograph of him and my dad on the wall in the garage. The comment my dad made about my mom and Jessa's dad. The pieces fall into place with the kind of staggering alignment I can only imagine blind people experience when they get their eyesight back.

"Yeah, that's right," Kingsley smirks. "Your father was one charming son of a bitch. I'll give him that. He moved in there the moment he saw she was free. He'd always had his eye on her, and your mother, like I said, was beautiful, like a movie star, turned heads wherever she went."

He smiles to himself sadly, and my gut writhes as though a nest of snakes just woke up. Holy shit. This is too much information too fast. My mom dated Jessa's dad? And they loved each other? But . . . he's such an asshole. What the hell did she see in him? Then I remember Jessa telling me her dad didn't always use to be this way. I recall the picture of my dad and him when they were about my age, how much fun they looked like they were having. Maybe he wasn't always such an asshole then. It's like discovering there is an end to the universe; truly mind-melting.

"I was so goddamn mad at him," he continues, not seeming to notice my shock, "I didn't even bother to fight for her. And you know, if I'd buried my stupid pride and told her how much I loved her, she would have broken up with him and come back to me. Because what we had"—he looks at me, his eyes so bright and clear they remind me of Jessa's—"was something you don't find every day. It was real. But I didn't fight for her. I walked away. And I raged about it for a few weeks and drank myself stupid until my father took me aside one day and told me to man the hell up and to go after what I wanted. He told me I was letting another man take what should be mine, and that the best things in life are things you have to fight for. That's what makes life worthwhile, he said. So I did. I went around to your mother's house and I told her that I wanted to marry her, that if she became my wife I'd spend the rest of my life trying to make her happy, and you know what? I know she wanted to say yes. Because she loved me. Don't get me wrong—I know she loved your father. But not like the way she loved me. We were different. We were that one in a million."

I'm struggling to comprehend everything he's saying, and I'm angry, too, because he's suggesting that my mom loved him more than she loved my dad and I don't want that to be true. "So why didn't she say yes, then? If she loved you so much?" I ask.

"Because she was pregnant with you."

The fog dissolves. I finally get it; I understand why he's hated me all these years, why he hates my father. I'm what kept them apart.

"So do you see what I'm saying to you?" he asks, interrupting the thoughts that are flying around my head like debris after an explosion.

COME BACK TO ME

"No," I say.

"My God, you *are* stupid. What the hell does she see in you?"

I think that's supposed to be rhetorical, so I stay quiet.

"My daughter loves you," he says in the face of my silence. "I admit I wasn't exactly thrilled when I found out you two were dating, but I can't stand here and let Jessa screw up her life. She loves you," he says again. "And if I'm not mistaken, I heard you telling Riley that you still love her."

"It's too late," I mumble, echoing Jessa's words.

He huffs loudly. "Did you not hear a word I just told you?" He shakes his head at me, exasperated. "You were wrong about one thing, you know. About me not knowing my daughter. I've been watching her these last nine months. She's been mourning not just Riley but you, too." He takes a step toward me and lowers his voice. "I saw the girl she was blossoming into when you were around. She's lost that bloom, Kit, that light in her eyes. I want you to give it back to her. God knows, I helped put it out too and I'm trying now to make it up to her. She's all I've got left."

He swallows, and I watch him struggle to get his emotions under control; his eyes brighten with tears. "And if you don't," he says to me, "you'll spend the rest of your life regretting what could have been, wishing you'd had the guts to fight that little bit harder. Believe me."

"I've tried," I say, trying to get my head around the fact he's no longer warning me off Jessa but telling me to fight for her. "She's not interested."

"Are you a goddamn marine or not?" he suddenly roars.

My back straightens automatically and my heels click together before I remember that I'm not anymore. "No, sir," I answer. "Not anymore."

He does a surprised double take at the news but then dismissively shrugs the comment off. "Once a marine, always a marine," he tells me. "And marines never goddamn quit." He takes a step toward me and pokes me in the chest with his index finger. "You get back in the ring."

"Yes, sir," I shout back.

He nods at me, seemingly satisfied, and I breathe out, feeling dizzy all of a sudden. What the hell did I just agree to? Then I see that he's right. Of course he's right. What the hell was I thinking? I'm a stupid idiot. He's right. I pat my pockets, searching for my keys, my phone. I need to go. I need to find her. I spin around and head for the exit.

"Oh, and Kit?"

I turn back. Kingsley's standing with his hands on his hips, looking vaguely triumphant and a lot more like the Colonel Kingsley of old.

"I have a room full of trophies back at the house—remind me to show them to you sometime," he says.

Hah. "Got it," I shout, grinning before breaking into a jog.

Jessa

Once I finish the call with Todd, I switch off my phone and throw it onto the passenger seat, and for a few minutes just sit behind the wheel of my car staring into space. I feel hollow and empty, like a buoy floating on open ocean, alone and untethered.

The one thing I learned after Riley's death was that I could either sink or learn to swim again, but now I realize there's also a third option—floating. Life might be easier if I don't try to fight it and instead just let it pull me along. Floating was what I did before Kit, and it's also what I've been doing with Todd. It seems like the easiest option. It certainly doesn't take much effort.

I start the car and pull out of the lot. I don't have a destination in mind, I just feel the need to drive, and unconsciously, when I hit the freeway, I take the route east, heading in the same direction Kit took that first night when we went stargazing out in the desert. I wonder what subconscious thought is pulling me in that direction and wonder if it's really the best idea to churn up more memories when I'm trying to forget him, but because I've decided just to go with the flow of things, I keep driving.

About two miles out of town, though, I see a sign for the cemetery where Riley is buried, and on a sudden whim I throw the car across three lanes and take the exit, ignoring the blast of horns from the cars I cut off.

I drive slowly into the parking lot. I've only been to visit a couple of times since the funeral. When I think of Riley, I don't like to think of him dead, lying in a coffin beneath the ground. I like to think of him alive, so when I want to feel close to him, I go to the places where he used to hang out: the beach, the pier, the basketball court. I spend time with baby Riley.

Climbing out of the car, I think about Kit, wondering if I'll see him before he leaves. Maybe it's all for the best if I don't ever see him again. What good could possibly come of it?

I'm walking with my head down, so I don't notice the person standing in the way until I bump into them.

"Sorry," I mumble, and try to walk around them, but they step sideways and block my path. I look up, and all the breath leaves my body in a rush, leaving me swaying on my feet. Kit's standing right in front of me as though my subconscious has conjured him out of thin air. I have to blink a few times to make sure I'm not hallucinating.

"Hi," he says, looking as shocked as I am.

"Hi," I stammer.

"I—" he says, at the same time as I say, "What are you—?"

We both stop. I notice Kit looks anxious, out of breath, like he has someplace to be.

"I was just visiting the grave," he says. "Riley."

I nod. I can't seem to look at him. My cheeks are on fire.

"I . . . I went around to your dad's," I say. "He said you'd gone to the recruiting office."

"Yeah," Kit says.

I stare down at the ground, tears smarting my eyes. I don't want him to see me crying, though, so I force myself to blink them away. "Right. Okay," I say. Shit. I don't know what to say to him.

"Jessa?"

I look up. "I don't love him." The words just fly out of my mouth before I can stop them. I ram my mouth shut.

"What?" Kit asks.

"Todd." Again I ram my mouth shut. Why am I telling him this?

A smile seems to twitch for a moment at the edge of Kit's mouth, but he shakes his head and it disappears. "Okay. But listen . . ."

"I love you." Nope. Can't seem to stop myself.

Kit looks as stunned as I feel. "What?"

Suddenly I realize something, something momentous, something that makes me want to hit myself because I've been so blind and so stupid. How did I not see until now?

"It doesn't matter," I say in a rush, "if you've re-enlisted for another four years. I'll wait. I don't care. I want to be with you. With *you*. No one else."

Kit blinks at me, raising his eyebrows. "You'd wait for me for four years?"

I nod. "Yes. Four. Forty. Whatever. I want to be with you, Kit." There, I've said it, and it feels like I've just sprouted wings and am lifting up into the air, light as a bird.

"No," Kit says.

"Yes," I answer angrily, falling straight back to earth. "This isn't your decision."

A grin splits his face. "No, I mean you don't need to wait," he says, stepping toward me. "I didn't re-enlist. I'm a free agent."

He didn't re-enlist? The news hits me with the force of an electric shock. Before I can say anything, he continues. "I came here and I had the weirdest conversation with . . . well, never mind." He shakes his head and pinches the bridge of his nose. "The long and short of it is that I was just leaving to come and find you."

"You were?"

"Yes," he says, reaching for my hand.

"Why?" I ask, as my throat tightens. The feel of his hand in mine, his touch, has started some kind of chain reaction through my body. Little tremors start to travel up my arms and down my spine.

"To tell you to ditch Todd and come back to me."

I draw in a breath as he pulls me closer so I'm standing almost chest to chest with him. His free hand strokes my hair behind my ear. "Because you're my girl," he whispers. "You're mine, Jessa. And I'm yours. And I'm an idiot for walking away, but I swear to God I'll never walk away again."

I look up into his eyes, noticing that the haunted look I saw at the funeral has vanished, that lost look I saw the last time we made love is nowhere to be seen. He's looking at me the same way he used to look at me before Riley died.

"You promise?" I ask, still not sure if I can believe it.

His jaw tenses. He takes my face in his hands and fixes his eyes on mine. "With my whole heart," he says fiercely. "I'm back. And I'm not going anywhere ever again."

And then he kisses me. My body responds automatically. Even though nine months have passed, it may as well be nine seconds, the connection between us is so instant. Nothing has changed. I melt against him. It's as if I've been frozen for nine months and now I'm waking up, his lips, his hands, his touch all forcing the heat back into my body, setting me alight from the inside out.

I kiss him back as though I'm trying desperately to find my way back into the light and he's holding the torch. I had forgotten how it felt to be in his arms—the memory could never do it justice—and now I press against him, wanting to remember.

We're breathless, both of us shaking and crying when we pull apart. There's a burning ache inside of me, one I haven't felt in so long, one I never felt with Todd.

As if he's read my mind, Kit asks, "What about Todd?"

"I broke up with him. Twenty minutes ago. I told him I was still in love with you."

Kit smiles and takes my face in his hands to kiss me again. I will never get tired of his lips. "God, I've missed you," he whispers.

"I can tell," I answer with a sly smile, because he's pressed against me and suddenly there's only one thing I want to do. I glance over his shoulder and see his bike.

"Take me for a ride?" I murmur.

"Where do you want to go?" he asks.

"Home," I say, and he knows without having to ask that I mean his house, *our* room, *our* bed.

He takes my hand and pulls me toward his bike, striding purposefully, and I know with a thrill that races through me that this is going to be one fast ride.

Mila Gray

"Wait," I say, digging in my heels, my stomach falling out of me. "Isn't that my dad's car?" I ask, pointing at the BMW at the edge of the lot.

"Yeah," Kit says with a small smile.

I give him a confused look, but he shrugs it off and tosses me a helmet.

"Come on, let's go," he says. "We've got a lot of catching up to do."

I grin at him because I know exactly what kind of catching up he means, and it isn't going to be the conversational kind.

"And then," he says, helping me do up the strap before lifting me onto the back of the bike, "then we have a whole life to plan. I was thinking a road trip and then a move to LA. What about you?"

He kicks up the stand and revs the engine. I wrap my arms around his waist.

"I don't care where we go. Just so long as we go there together."

Epilogue

The wedding is taking place on a cliff above the beach. The weather is glorious. Days like this always take me back to that first summer with Kit when we were a secret and everything was touched with a golden, magical kind of light.

I look across at him now, and my heart gives a quick kick at the sight of him in his suit. If anything he's only gotten sexier over the years, and though he always jokes that one day I'm going to run off with one of my leading men, there's no possible way anyone could ever come close to making me feel the way Kit does. With just a glance he has the power to make me come completely undone.

Aware of me staring at him, he looks my way and gives me a smile, his eyes slipping down my dress. I know exactly what he's thinking and have to look away to hide my blush.

He links his fingers through mine and leans over to whisper in my ear. "Have I told you how beautiful you look?" he asks.

I shake my head while laughing under my breath. "Shhhh," I whisper, focusing my attention back on the bride and groom.

Jo looks stunning in her white dress, so much so that I have to wipe away a tear. Her groom is gazing at her with an expression of such unadulterated love that it makes something catch painfully in my chest, and I have to swallow away the lump in my throat as I watch them exchanging vows. Though I wish it was my brother up there marrying Jo, I'm thrilled that she's found someone to take care of her. He's a good guy. And he adores her. The fact that he adores little Riley, too, makes me even happier.

I watch the little monkey who's standing between them holding a cushion with the rings on it. He looks so like Riley that it's hard to tear my eyes off him. He turns just then and, grinning a gap-toothed grin, waves at my mom and dad, who are sitting beside us. My dad is beaming as if this is the proudest day of his life, and I notice he and my mom are holding hands, my mom wiping away tears.

Kit's dad is officiating at the ceremony, and I watch his blue eyes light up with happiness as he pronounces them man and wife.

"That's going to be us next," Kit murmurs in my ear, sending a shiver up my spine.

I feel a flutter in my belly at the thought, a quickening inside me that feels like a butterfly stretching its wings for the first time. I can't wait for it to be our turn, but the wedding we have planned is going to have to wait. Next month I'm away on location in Hawaii filming, and I have two other projects lined up for next year. Things are really starting to take off. It's already getting to the stage where I'm having to wear a hat and dark glasses when I go out in public—something I'll never get used to. The paparazzi even followed Kit and me here to the wedding and are waiting outside for a money shot.

After the wedding, as everyone gathers to drink champagne

and the bride and groom are having their photos taken, Kit takes my hand and leads me over to my parents.

"What are you doing?" I ask him.

"I think we should tell them, don't you?" Kit answers.

"What? Now?" I ask, hit by a flurry of nerves.

"It's okay," Kit says, grinning at me over his shoulder. "I'm wearing a bulletproof vest."

I know he's kidding. There's no need anymore for one of those. These days Kit and my dad get on pretty well. Since he retired, my dad has mellowed even more. He and my mom come and visit us in LA quite often, bringing little Riley, who loves hanging out at Kit's restaurant (which he named Riley's). His favorite part is following the waitresses around and watching the bartenders mix drinks, which is slightly worrying seeing how he's not yet six.

My dad hugs me and kisses me on the cheek. "That was beautiful, don't you think?" he asks, gesturing at the flower-decked arch where the ceremony took place.

I nod. My mom squeezes my arm. I know today is equal parts wonderful and difficult for her, as it is for all of us.

Kit and my dad shake hands.

"How's the business?" my dad asks Kit straightaway. He's taken a keen interest in Kit's restaurant ever since he started winning awards and being featured in the papers.

"Great," Kit answers. "We're going to be opening a sister restaurant in New York next year."

"That's fantastic," my mother says, giving Kit's arm a squeeze.

Just then Jo and her new husband Marc walk over arm in arm, little Riley swinging off Marc's hand. He lets go and jumps straight into Kit's arms, and watching them, I feel a swell of emotion. Kit's going to make the most amazing father. If Riley could see this right now, I know he'd be smiling. As though he knows just what I'm thinking, Kit puts his arm around my waist and draws me close.

"Dad!" he shouts over the heads of the crowd, getting his father's attention.

His dad is locked in close conversation with Jo's mom, and they both look up. I notice Jo's mom is blushing, and the two of them look like teenagers who've been caught doing something they shouldn't. Oh my God. Am I imagining it? Is there something going on between them? That would be so wonderful, I think to myself. If anyone deserves a second shot at love, it's Kit's dad.

They walk toward us, and I watch speechless as Kit's dad and my dad exchange a few words of lighthearted banter. I will never get used to seeing those two talking and getting along.

When everyone's gathered around, Kit clears his voice. I stare at the ground and take a deep breath, grateful for Kit's arm, which is an anchor around my waist.

"Everyone, we have some news," he announces.

"At damn last," my dad interrupts.

"John," my mom reprimands with a smile.

Kit looks at me and again I get that butterfly flutter, a feeling of something unfurling and blossoming inside me. His eyes burn into mine, and I suddenly flash back to the first time we made love. The expression he wears now is exactly the same as then, and I know just as I did then that he's all I'll ever need.

"We're getting married," Kit announces with a grin.

Everyone immediately lets out excited squeals, and Kit has to struggle to be heard over the top of all the laughter and clapping.

I glance nervously at my parents, unsure of their reaction, memories of how my dad reacted to Jo and Riley's news racing through my mind. But he takes a step toward me and pulls me instantly into a hug.

"Congratulations," he says in a voice choked up with emotion.

I squeeze him back hard, and then my mom, too, who is all kinds of excited and already trying to talk to me about wedding dresses and flower arrangements.

We're swept up in a celebratory round of embraces, and it isn't until about forty minutes later that Kit and I get a moment alone together again. He pulls me under the flower-decked arch. Below us the waves are crashing onto the beach. The sun is sinking low in the sky, painting golden shadows across Kit's face.

"So Jessa Kingsley, soon to be Ryan, think you can handle spending the rest of your life with me?" he asks.

"I think so," I say teasingly, biting back a smile.

"I love you so much," he says now, putting his arms around me and pulling me against his chest. I feel his lips in my hair. He strokes it behind one ear (it's long again now) and drops a kiss on my neck.

I shudder against him.

"Are you mine?" he murmurs.

"Always," I answer as his lips find mine.

Acknowledgments

This book would not have been written had it not been for Venetia Gosling, the editor who signed my very first book, *Hunting Lila*, and many more since then. I feel so very lucky to have found such an amazing mentor and champion.

Thanks too to Amanda, my agent, to whom I will always be eternally grateful for her advice, support, and enthusiasm.

Becky Wicks, fellow author and friend, whose daily missives lift my spirits and who, as my very first reader, gave me the encouragement to keep going.

J, for everything, but most of all for your love.

My girlfriends, who are the funniest, smartest, most wonderful bunch of women. I'm so blessed to have you in my life: Jessica, Rachel, Meg, Helene, Nic, Vic, Sara, Lauren, and Asa.

All the bloggers and fans who tweet, e-mail, blog, and encourage me to keep writing on the days I feel like just eating ice cream and throwing my laptop in the pool.

Catherine Richards, Eloise Wood, and Juliet Van Oss at Pan Macmillan for all their help and support.

Finn Butler, who wrote the glorious poem about stardust

that Jessa sends to Kit, for giving me kind permission to use it in my book. For more beautiful words check out her website: http://greatestreality.tumblr.com/.

The team at Simon & Schuster US: my lovely editor, Nicole Ellul, and the fabulous Patrick Price, Mara Anastas, Lauren Forte, Katherine Devendorf, Brian Luster and Jeannie Ng (thanks for the Americanising . . . or rather, Americanizing), Karina Granda and Tom Daly for the design, and Kelsey Dickson for the publicity.